*For Lisa Marie and Cherry,
who inspired me, encouraged me,
put up with my insanity,
and still love me anyway.*

"I'm not for sale."

"Good," he said hoarsely. "Then there's no mistaking this." Between the space of one breath and the next, Phin sank to his knees in front of her, his eyes brilliantly dark, glittering like ancient gold in a face suddenly taut with the heat Naomi knew drew him like a moth to flame.

That's what she was.

Fire.

"Phin," she warned him, "you're going to get burned."

"God, I hope so," he said roughly, and kissed her.

He kissed her like a man drowning, in desperate need of air. He feasted on the full, lush curve of her lips as if starved.

She wanted him. Wanted this.

Wanted more.

By Karina Cooper

LURE OF THE WICKED
BLOOD OF THE WICKED

Coming Soon

ALL THINGS WICKED

KARINA COOPER

LURE
OF THE
WICKED

A DARK MISSION NOVEL

AVON
An Imprint of HarperCollinsPublishers

AVON BOOKS
An Imprint of HarperCollins*Publishers*
10 East 53rd Street
New York, New York 10022–5299

Copyright © 2011 by Karina Cooper
Excerpt from *All Things Wicked* copyright © 2012 by Karina Cooper
ISBN 978-0-06-204690-1
www.avonromance.com

First Avon Books mass market printing: July 2011

Avon Trademark Reg. U.S. Pat. Off. and in Other Countries, Marca Registrada, Hecho en U.S.A.
HarperCollins® is a registered trademark of HarperCollins Publishers.

Printed in the U.S.A.

10 9 8 7 6 5 4 3 2 1

CHAPTER ONE

Πaomi West was a damn good missionary. Her Mission file lauded her as one of the best witch hunters in New Seattle.

Nice to know that the Holy Order of St. Dominic had faith in her. At the very least, her fellow Mission operatives thought she was hot shit.

If they only knew what crawled under her skin and sent her heart pounding hysterically within the cage of her ribs, they'd yank her off the streets faster than a bullet to the head.

The voice in her ear faded and she tucked a finger against the tiny comm speaker. Alan Eckhart's voice sharpened into crystal clarity as he continued to outline the operation specs. The team briefing after the Mission briefing. Blah, blah, fucking blah.

Naomi's muscles vibrated, taut with strain as she listened to the team lead drone while studying the panoramic view from the top floor of her lavish hotel suite.

She touched the surface of the floor-to-ceiling windows, her fingers silhouetted to shadow by October's dying sun. It turned the thick smog blanketing the lower levels to burnished fire, seeped into the rat-infested shit-hole that was New Seattle's barely civilized foundation, and vanished in the ever-present miasma. Most of the metropolis was too far below her to see, but Naomi didn't have to see it to recall the acrid stink of rotting garbage.

Anxiety, thick and vicious, curled in her throat as she turned away.

"Look, I don't care what the Mission says," she said into the tiny mic inset into her ear. "I am not going to be stuck up here forever. This is bullshit."

"A week, tops." Eckhart's voice aimed for soothing.

It scraped over Naomi's raw nerves like a serrated knife. "If I'm lucky," she muttered.

"You don't have to be lucky, Nai, you're good."

Good, nothing. She was trapped. Stripped of her piercings, scrubbed and buffed, wrapped in designer clothing, and locked behind the walls of a gilded fucking cage.

"I'm better than good," she told him flatly. Not ego. Fact.

"Exactly. Which is why you were chosen."

Give me a fucking break. "Aside from the security check coming in, I'm not seeing much by way of surveillance. I told you, *anyone* could do this job."

Eckhart chuckled. Or choked, she wasn't sure.

"Of course there isn't major surveillance, Nai. It's a spa," he replied dryly. In the background, she heard the familiar white noise of the mid-low Mission offices. Where she should be right now.

Where she desperately wanted to be. She took a deep breath, held it for a long moment before easing it out on a carefully modulated sigh. "I still don't see why Parker couldn't get someone else to play dress-up."

"No one with your credentials." It came out a sigh. No matter how many times they'd had this argument, she wasn't going to eat it any easier. She grimaced, opening her mouth, but he cut her off. Wheedling, for fuck's sake. "Come on, Naomi. It's not exactly a maximum security prison."

It might as well have been. She turned, saw sumptuous furnishings and bold color, and closed her eyes against the insistent pressure in her head.

It was as if she'd gone back in time. Only she wasn't a child. And her name hadn't been Naomi Ishikawa for almost twenty-five years.

Except now it *was* again. Because the Mission said so. She flinched. "Shitfuck."

"You're so pretty when you go blue." Eckhart sighed again. "All right, give me the rundown on the place."

Naomi's fist clenched over the hard metal of the comm. "The city to grounds elevator takes eight minutes to get to the top. Surveillance is minimal and discreet, but hard to hide with all the glass. One camera at the lobby doors, one camera in the main elevator inside the resort, and that's it. The lobby's full of money and empty of people. Eckhart, I need those goddamn blueprints."

The man whistled a distinctive three-note tune.

"Jonas is still working on it. Says the blueprints are locked up tight."

"Why?"

"Dunno, but smells like money or politics to me. Probably both."

"Great," she snarled. She shoved her free hand through the glossy strands of her black hair, took the three steps to the divan, and turned. "What you're saying is that the Church doesn't have a legitimate in, which is why they whored me up and sent me up here." It lashed out, a vicious whip of anger too sharp even to her own ears. She jammed a thumb and forefinger into her eye sockets, squeezed them shut until the pressure ate away at the light searing the inside of her skull.

Politics. Goddamn politics.

"What I'm saying is—" Eckhart began sharply, only to cut himself off. She knew why. It was another old argument, one that they circled like wary dogs. He lowered his voice; his version of soothing. "Look, not everything can be handled with a gun and an attitude."

Except Naomi *knew* he was wrong. Almost anything could be handled by just that, and right now, she was missing one half of the fucking equation.

Naomi paced to the window again, already knowing what she'd see as the setting sun sank toward the smudged horizon. A shimmering pool of polluted air ate at the dark spaces long since gathered between the towering skyscrapers. It hid the filth, the desperation, the shoulder-to-shoulder chaos that lived—no, that *existed* miles below her.

She was anonymous down there. Unknown, a damn good witch hunter in a team of them.

But up here, she was just a tool of the Church who had run the show since the earthquake had eaten the old city. Fifty years of guidance, of planning, had raised New Seattle from the ashes of the old ruins. Fifty years of powerful Church support had installed the Mission to a place of prominence; each operative was trained from childhood to protect humanity from the murderous practitioners of the witchcraft that had killed hundreds of thousands of innocent people in one devastating sweep.

Naomi had been a missionary for over twenty years, and she still didn't play the political game. That was why she was just an agent, and not a team lead. Or a desk jockey, like the director.

She was an operative.

A killer.

And Naomi liked it better when she could pull out her gun—which she didn't fucking *have*—and get to work the way she worked best.

"Whatever," she said tautly as she whipped around and stalked back to the fancy sofa, "can we just get to the part where you get me a gun?"

He whistled again. The three-note tune that said he was working it out. That it was complicated. "Nai," he said slowly, "what's going on?"

"It's a rich-bitch haven—"

"No," he cut in. The sound of voices faded in the background. His voice lowered. "I don't mean right this second, I know you hate topside. I mean, what's going on with *you*? You were in jail when we went looking for you."

She snorted. Trading one jail cell for another didn't

warrant any kind of gratitude. Pitted cement walls or sleek wallpapered hallways, it was all the same to her.

Naomi dropped her hand, stared at the sectioned, gilt-framed mirror hanging over the polished snowy marble fireplace and didn't recognize the naked face staring back at her. Lavish mouth, high cheekbones sharp enough to cut, straight black hair without a trace of the electric blue streaks she'd worn until yesterday. No piercings.

God, she missed her piercings.

Aside from the crusted scab slashing diagonally over her nose, she looked rich. Pampered. Soft.

She looked like her mother.

It was enough to send her pacing again. Windows to sofa, sliding bedroom door, and back to the sofa.

Damn the Mission. Damn the new Mission director who'd decided that locking her up behind the polished doors of New Seattle's premier resort and spa was the only answer to a problem they'd all decided was going to be hers.

And damn the panic riding her so hard, it hummed like an electrical current inside her chest.

Abruptly Naomi sank to the arm of the sofa. "Alan," she said wearily, "why the fuck am I here? Joe Carson isn't a witch, he's a missionary. Why do I have to execute him?"

"Joe Carson isn't your average missionary, Nai. You remember that mess with Smith? Imagine if he'd survived long enough to go rogue."

Ice pooled at the base of her spine.

It had been only three months. Three goddamn

months since the missionary she'd first known as a boy in a godforsaken orphanage had turned on them.

Turned on her.

Missionary Silas Smith and his witch lover had gone up in smoke, caught in an inferno set by a coven of witches deep in the ruins of Old Seattle. There hadn't been anything more than rubble and charred, unrecognizable flesh by the time the Mission had gotten through the chaos.

The new Mission director had some serious questions to answer, and another rogue agent on her turf wasn't going to help her do it.

Naomi pressed her fingers to the front of her designer jeans, to the spot low on her abdomen where the seal of St. Andrew lay dormant. Protective.

An early warning signal that arced with blue flame when witchcraft was used on her, calling on the holy energies of St. Andrew to combat whatever malicious intent a witch's magic would cause. Which came in handy when she was on a mission to kill *witches*.

There were no witches here to kill.

She rose again, strode past the decorative awning that separated the bedroom from the parlor, and surveyed the too-large bed with its lavender and gold silk bedspread. Her nose wrinkled. "The sooner I do this, the sooner I'm out, right?"

Relief tinged his voice as he replied, "Right."

"And little Miss Parker isn't planning some sort of bullshit extended operation?"

"*Director Adams* knows how much you don't like this op, Nai," Eckhart said, correcting her with a sigh.

"You made that extremely clear. Just get the job done, and you're out."

"Okay, lay it on me."

"Joe Carson is a murderer."

"So am I."

He hesitated, just a fraction of a second. It was enough. Her mouth twisted in edged, cutting humor. "It's different," he finally said. "Carson's wanted for the murder of two Church officials and four civilians, and he's a suspect in the disappearance of Mission evidence."

She frowned. "Wait a damn minute, this wasn't in the briefing. Mission evidence? Was our vault compromised?"

"No, thank God, not ours. We don't keep anything really dangerous there, anyway," he said. "The director's headquarters got hit sometime last week and they only just found the breach. Be glad you weren't there yesterday. Adams damn near froze the place out."

"Nothing pulling the stick out won't fix," Naomi muttered. She rolled her eyes when he cleared his throat in pointed reprimand.

She didn't have to like Director Parker Adams, but she did have to work with her. *For* her.

"Sorry," she added. "What was taken?"

"Let's see. Some old newspaper clippings and a pot full of odds and ends. Prequake junk, as far as we could tell."

"Helpful. I still think instead of hunting him, we should just bring him in for processing."

"Not our call."

"But if his team had done *their* job—"

"Again, Nai, his local missionaries tried. As soon as the flag landed on his file, he vanished."

And they couldn't process what they couldn't find.

Naomi grimaced. No one knew what processing really meant, but the rumors persisted. Everything from chemical lobotomy to brainwashing; torture disguised as cleansing to simple disposal.

Dangerous, heretical rumors. The Church didn't like rumors. Or questions it couldn't answer.

"This has been going on awhile. A missionary doesn't just wake up one day and decide to murder six people."

"Doesn't matter. Get your attitude together and do what needs to be done. They're watching you, Nai."

"Fuck off."

"I'm serious." Eckhart hesitated. "Naomi, you've been flagged by the Church for surveillance."

Flagged. Like Joe Carson.

Anger wrapped itself into a tangle, a knot of fury and sudden fear. Naomi blew out a hard, laughing breath. "Well, that's great. Guess I'll run off and murder for them some more."

"Jesus, Nai, don't say that. That's the kind of stuff you're always getting in trouble for. The only thing saving your ass right now is your success record. You're a damn good missionary, but you've been pushing it and you know it."

Translated, if she didn't toe the line this time, she'd be out on her ass, no matter how fucking good she was at what she did.

Same old song and dance. "Whatever," she said not bothering to try for sincere. She turned away from the pile of luggage that stored a fortune in exclusive clothing and stalked back out of the bedroom. "What I meant was, I should go tend to this mission that the Holy Order of St. Dominic has found to be necessary and just."

Eckhart paused. She could practically hear him grinding his teeth. "Naomi. You're cracking at the seams. Get it together, or you're going to get us *all* flagged."

"I'll be in touch as soon as I've got something worthwhile to report."

"Naomi—"

"Understand this." Naomi tucked her index finger against the tiny black mic at her ear, pushed it in closer so that he couldn't possibly miss a single note. "One way or another, I'm going to put a bullet in this shit-fucker's brain. When I get out of here, I'm going to get my piercings back and get laid." She smiled at his snort. "You are welcome to come along for either."

"You need help, West."

"Yeah. Get me a Beretta."

"I'll see what we can arrange," he said, and didn't waste his time saying good-bye.

As the line clicked off in her ear, she gave in to the fury licking at her every breath. She tossed the palm-sized unit savagely across the room. It rebounded off the brocade settee, thudded to the carpet.

It didn't make her feel better.

Watched. She was being watched by her own fucking team.

Flagged.

Fine.

Smoothing her hair back over her shoulders, she

yanked her crumbling concentration firmly back into focus. It didn't matter what Carson was. Missionary, witch, or other.

The Church said kill.

She'd get right on it.

She took one step toward the bedroom and froze as the oiled metal doors of the suite elevator hissed open behind her. Sudden, visceral awareness lifted every hair on the back of her neck.

Nerves prickled; a circle of fire searing through the tattooed seal low on her belly. *Witchcraft.*

Instinct took control of her body, launched her to the side as pain and power converged inside her skull. Sheer adrenaline ate away at the last vestiges of confusion, and she hit the ground rolling.

She collided with a polished end table, saw boots and a sage green uniform in the corner of her eye, and swore as a lamp crashed to the floor by her head. Pain made her slow, sticky under the hammering of magic and the protective burn of the Mission tattoo. The edges of her vision wavered in black and excruciating red.

"What the fuck," she gritted out as she struggled to get to her feet. Her knees wobbled, shredded by the witchcraft drilling through her skull.

"Jesus, she wasn't kidding." A masculine voice, gritty. Focused. "You're tougher than I thought."

Sucking in air, her lips peeled back from her teeth and she came up swinging.

His curse fractured as her fist found his ribs; she cursed hard enough for both of them as her knuckles collided with bone. He bent double with the impact and she stepped in, grabbed his wrist, and slammed him vi-

ciously against the back wall. Naomi locked her forearm against his throat, panting with the effort.

A painting swayed, crashed to the ground in the
sudden silence of his constricted airway. The pain re-
ceded.

He was old, she realized. Older than she'd thought,
underneath stocky muscle and hands made of calluses.
The fingers he locked around her arm in desperation
were work-scarred, nails clipped to the quick. His hair
was cut in severe military lines, liberally peppered with
gray. A full bar mustache covered his upper lip, but it
couldn't hide the scar puckering the skin just by the side
of his mouth. His bulbous nose and bushy gray eyebrows should have conspired to give him a harmless,
kindly demeanor.

The wild glint in his deep blue eyes betrayed the
truth.

Even as one part of her brain cataloged his description, the rest of her battled back the too-fast surge of
her own heartbeat. Too much adrenaline. Too damn
fast. Pins and needles prickled at her face.

Not now. Scraping her attention together, she bared
her teeth and gritted out, "Who are you?"

"Fuck y—" He choked as she flexed her shoulder,
driving the edge of her forearm harder against his
throat.

The fragile bones in his neck grated together as he
turned purple. She thrust her face into his. "You have
about thirty seconds before— Shit!"

Harder, stronger than she expected, the witch seized
her sweater and shoved. Seams stretched, popped.
Her feet tangled in the one he locked behind hers. She

flailed, hit the floor on her ass. He stepped in immediately, cocked a leg, and rammed one booted foot into her ribs. Again. She rolled with the momentum as pain screamed through her chest, but she couldn't see past the colors swimming through her head. Vibrant reds and bruised purples.

A rough hand closed over the back of her neck, shook hard, and sent her sprawling. Pain rocketed through her body as she collided into the settee. Ass over skull, her knees buckled over the low cushions and sent her flailing over the back of it.

The back of her head slammed into one unyielding corner of the small end table beside it and the scene flickered, a synaptic overload of pain and magic.

Naomi shook her head hard; her chest squeezed, labored to inhale the oxygen that wasn't making it to her brain. She tensed, teeth clenched as she forced her muscles to move. He didn't come at her again. When the onslaught of magic ceased, it ended so completely that it left her reeling.

She clung to the back of the elegant couch, gasping for breath as her lungs constricted. Hysteria. It wrapped around her chest and made it too damned hard to breathe.

Her peripheral vision flickered. Naomi launched herself out of the way, hit the table again, and clutched it for support as the room whirled.

Nothing came at her.

Forcing air into her struggling lungs, she dragged herself to her feet as the suite elevator doors closed. Leaving her with the impression of sharp blue eyes and the lingering snap of killing magic.

"Son of a *bitch*," she snarled, and lunged for the control button. Her palm slapped down too damn late. She sucked in a breath, held it. Let it out. Another. Calm.

Controlled.

Fuck. Naomi kicked the steel doors until the suite echoed with it. Her toes throbbed in protest.

She watched the light buttons as the elevator descended with the powerful witch inside. Seventeen. Sixteen. Fifteen. . .

Should she try to outrun it and take the stairs? Hell, he could get off at any floor before he reached ground level. She'd never catch him.

By the time the elevator made it all the way back to her suite on the top floor, she'd scuffed the hell out of her knee-high leather boots and knew her assailant would be long gone.

The doors slid open with an expensive *whoosh*. She limped into the elegantly mirrored box and barely kept herself from putting her fist through the reflective glass.

No gun, no bullets. She'd thought this bullshit operation was going to be as witch-free as Sunday Mass, but the lingering prickle around the skin of her abdomen proved her wrong.

Dead fucking wrong.

The woman who shot out of the residential elevator and into his arms rang every bell in Phinneas Clarke's head, and then some.

Most were alarms.

Trouble. Capital T kind of trouble, with long, long legs and a taut, trim body that fit against him like a custom suit. Plastered to the wall by her surprised momentum, the back of his head rebounded from the wall-papered panel and knocked a peal of thunder through his skull as he found his hands suddenly full of warm wool and soft curve.

She buckled, slid against the front of his body until his brain shorted out, and caught herself against his chest. One knee jammed between his legs—mercifully shy of wrecking Phin's vulnerable flesh—and her fingers twisted into the lapels of his suit jacket, providing an awkward angle of support.

Warm, denim-clad curves filled his palms, and he realized he'd caught her by the definitely taut muscles of her ass. For a long moment only the whispered lilt of the created spring behind them filled the shocked silence.

His lips twitched.

Naomi Ishikawa. According to the dossier he'd compiled from her people, his newest guest was an heiress who couldn't stay out of the kind of trouble that got rich girls put on a very short list.

Phin could see what her handlers meant.

Her hair was sleek and black, reminiscent of the Japanese heritage that defined her cheekbones and shaped the almond tilt of her eyes. She was fine-boned, slender, but tensile; clearly a woman who enjoyed a good workout. The easy strength he felt in her slim body was proof enough of that.

The rest of her was pure American supermodel, right down to the wildly long legs that tucked her at just about his eye level.

His gaze centered on her flushed face, and the raw-looking scab slashed diagonally across the bridge of her fine, straight nose. Miss Ishikawa looked as if she'd stepped into the ring with a prizefighter and lost.

The elevator doors eased shut beside them. Her eyes narrowed. "Are you all right?"

He wasn't sure. Were his fingers still curved around her rear? Did having a beautiful woman plastered against his chest count as all right?

He shook his head. Hard.

"Shit," she said, a husky snort. Sharp eyes searched his face as one warm, long-fingered hand slid around the back of his neck. "What's your name?"

"Phin," he managed, and shifted. Just enough. "And I don't mean to be rude, but could you remove your knee?"

The hand at the back of his neck stilled. Desperately he tried not to smile as she looked down at his chest. At the locked press of her hips against his and the sleek, denim-clad leg she'd braced between his knees in the confusion.

He hoped to God she couldn't feel his pulse against the curve of her thigh.

Her gaze flicked back up to his. Crinkled just enough to let him know she did. "Sorry," she said lightly. "Tell you what. You move your hands from my ass and I'll move my leg from your—"

"Got it," he said hastily before the heat uncurling through his veins could get any hotter than the pressure at his crotch. Carefully he pulled his all-too-eager hands away from her body. She eased from the tangle of balance and limbs, and as the warm weight of her withdrew, Phin was absurdly grateful that he could breathe again without inhaling the raw, clean scent of her skin.

"Sorry about that," she said, readjusting the loose neck of her sweater. She frowned down at the fraying threads at the collar. "I should come with a warning."

And how.

He straightened, prodding gingerly at the back of his bruised skull. "I can think of worse ways to make your acquaintance, Miss Ishikawa."

Her shoulders stiffened, subtly enough that he would have missed it if he wasn't watching her. Her gaze slammed to his in sudden, razor-edged acuity. In that split second, Phin felt as if those strange blue-purple eyes had taken him in, cataloged every inch from his expensive shoes and newly rumpled suit to his brown, curly hair, and shelved him neatly under a label he wasn't sure would be flattering.

Then her mouth curved up; an easy, blinding smile.

Phin's gut clenched, liquid quick awareness that bit deeper than it should have.

"Naomi," she corrected.

"Naomi, then." He offered a hand. "Phinneas Clarke. Welcome to Timeless. Normally we strive not to maim our guests."

Her gaze flicked to his hand. When she took it, her grip was firm, her skin cool and somewhat damp. Phin managed not to look down in surprise when his thumb brushed over the rough indication of her abraded knuckles.

Trouble. Definitely trouble.

"No harm done." She extracted her hand a shade sooner than manners strictly dictated polite. He didn't miss the way she dragged her palm against the fabric of her sweater. "Did you see anyone else go by?"

"Not until you trampled me."

"Damn." Her gaze skimmed the interior atrium courtyard behind him, dimly lit by the lampposts scattered under the cultivated trees. "Is your head okay?"

Her eyes were shadowed, too hard to read. He couldn't tell what she was thinking. Not that he was sure he'd have any better luck in full daylight, either.

Intriguing.

He smiled, crooked with apology. "I've had worse. It's definitely one way to make introductions."

She tipped her face to the early night sky, ten floors above them and trapped behind the wide skylight. "You were headed into the elevator," she observed, tucking stray tendrils of black over her ear. "Don't let me keep you."

It had been a long time since Phin had felt so thoroughly dismissed. Challenge rose like a banner in his chest. "Actually I was on my way up to see you."

One fine black eyebrow arched. "Me?"

"To introduce myself."

The sound she made was noncommittal.

His gaze dropped to her mouth, and Phin couldn't help but realize how easy it'd be to taste that overly lush curve of her lip. She was tall enough in her boots that he'd only have to tilt his head a fraction to close the distance.

And earn himself a mean right hook, if the condition of her knuckles was any indication. No, thank you. He liked his features exactly where they were.

She watched him, sliding her fingers into the front pockets of her hip-hugging jeans.

"And now that I've successfully made an impression," he added, his voice roughened, "I'll let you get back to whatever it was you were doing. This really can't get any more awkward."

The look she slanted him glinted. A darker kind of humor. Something that bit. "I bet you say that to all the girls."

"Just the ones who throw themselves at me."

Her laughter surprised him, rich and throaty. There was an edge to it, a brush of smoke. Just wicked enough to remind him of the warmth of her skin against his hands, the texture of her soft wool sweater, and the curves beneath. Just feminine enough to make him remember it'd been too long since he'd met with anyone for an evening out. Or in. Phin pursed his lips and whistled soundlessly. He made a point to keep his hands off the guests. They weren't here to be hit on, and that kind of fraternization was bad for business no matter how prettily it came packaged.

But Miss Ishikawa was going to make him work for it.

"I was exploring," she said, shrugging one shoulder. "Point me toward the nearest exits, won't you? Briefly," she added.

"Your wish is my command. The lobby is behind me, through the park."

"Park?"

"Well, it's not as big as the old parks, but you're welcome to explore it at your leisure." He raised a finger toward the wide double doors at the end of the courtyard. "The ground floor maintains the pools and a fully equipped gym. There are personal trainers for your convenience, if you require assistance." Then he pointed to the elevator doors behind her. "Seventeen residential suites. Each on their own floor."

Naomi glanced over her shoulder at the elevator. "Is that the only way in?"

"Stairs lead to each floor, but they're for staff use and emergencies only. Your people got you the top floor," he continued with a smile. "Best view."

"Anything else?"

Phin jerked a thumb to his right, where a green exit sign glowed in the distance. "That's the services center. There are ten floors, ranging from dining to socializing to relaxation and beauty, all yours from that elevator. Did you receive your program?"

"Program?"

"Your people scheduled your services in advance," he explained, and couldn't help curiosity from leaking into his voice as her mouth twisted. "If you don't like the choices—"

"I'm sure whatever they are will be fine and dandy," she said, her expression so indifferent that he wondered if he'd misread the signs.

"The program should be in your suite." He'd make a note to check with housekeeping. "This atrium connects all three towers." As if she'd read his mind, her gaze flicked to the third set of doors. Answering her unspoken question, he added, "That's the family quarters. As much as I'd love to show you my parlor—"

"Got it, slick," she said, her lips twitching. "I'll keep that in mind."

"And that's it." It was the shortest, most precise tour he'd ever given.

Not that she cared, he realized wryly. The smile she

flashed him was distracted. "Great," she said, dismissal once again clear in her tone. "Thanks."

"Of course." He stepped out of her path, easing down the few steps separating the surrounding walkway from the central garden. "Welcome to Timeless, Naomi."

The next few weeks were going to be woefully long with this particular heiress around. Phin let out his breath in a silent sigh of relief as she turned away. "Good night, then," she said. "I'm sure we'll meet again soon."

"Do you need anything right away?"

Naomi flung a hand to the side without turning. "No. You're an interesting man, Phinneas Clarke."

He grinned at her back. "Phin, and if that's not a compliment, I'd like to take it as one."

Her shoulders lifted. "Take it however you—" she began, then froze as a muffled, ragged scream echoed through the courtyard.

CHAPTER TWO

She didn't wait to see what the so-polished Phin Clarke would do. She didn't even consider what an equally polished heiress should do. As the first cry reverberated through the dimly lit courtyard, Naomi whirled and sprinted toward the pool hall.

Somewhat to his credit, Phin was barely a second behind her.

He'd labeled this the pool hall. She didn't know what to expect as she barreled through a second set of doors. Water, obviously, maybe a splashing swimmer in distress. She didn't like to swim, but she steeled herself to dive into whatever body of water she had to.

The screams shifted into panicked screeching that echoed eerily in the vast space. A quick glance took in a truly massive pool area. Two full-sized swimming pools and eight different bathing pools filled every available floor space, each rimmed with gold-veined white marble. Some bubbled, some boasted waterfalls, some steamed in welcoming heat. Along the walls inlaid with what looked like imported bamboo, doors vanished into mysterious interiors.

She homed in on a mid-twenties blond in a bright pink bikini hammering on one of the doors, screaming incoherently.

Naomi ran across the stylish slate flooring, the water-slick stone precarious as hell in her heeled boots. Phin broke off behind her, slammed a hand on an intercom she hadn't seen by the door. She didn't stop to check what he said. She slipped twice, managed to right herself before she tumbled ass over elbows into treated water.

With a sick feeling of dread building in her stomach and adrenaline boiling through her blood, Naomi caught herself on the door frame of the sauna beside the hysterical girl and pushed her out of the way. She slammed her hands around her eyes as she pressed her face to the hot pane of glass set into the door.

Beside her, the blond grabbed fistfuls of her wet hair in rigid, petrified fingers. "Oh, God, hurry," she pleaded. "She's not moving!"

Steam rolled thick and white through the sealed room, too dense to see a damn thing. Dread unfurled into cold certainty. "How long has she been in there?" Naomi asked.

"I don't know!"

Naomi grabbed the door handle, jerked on it with all

of her might. It didn't budge. "Where are the locks?" she demanded.

"It's mechanical." Phin's voice was grim behind her. "Maintenance is on the way."

Naomi pushed away from the door, checked the gauges placed discreetly around a shiny gold panel. They vibrated in the red.

The blond threw herself at the door. "Grandma!"

"Cally!" Phin's voice boomed across the pool, echoed in distinct, modulated authority. Calm, even despite the volume. Despite his pallor. "Barbara, I want you to go with Cally."

"But—"

"We'll get your grandmother out, all right? You need to go over there where it's safe." He took the blond by the arm, turned her forcefully, gently, toward the small crowd of guests and staff gathering at the end of the room. "It'll be okay, just go with Cally."

A trim redhead in the Timeless green uniform hurried to collect her, wrapping an arm around the blond's shoulders. "Come with me," she said in low, soothing tones. "Everything's going to be fine."

Naomi didn't know if that meant help had been called. It didn't matter. Another few minutes and anyone in that locked-up sauna would be ready for a side serving of butter.

What the fuck was going on in this spa?

"Give me your jacket," Naomi ordered swiftly.

"What—"

"Give me your goddamn jacket!"

Phin stripped off his tailored coat. She took it, shook it out, and wrapped it tightly around her right arm.

This was going to hurt like a bitch.

Shouldering him aside, ignoring his startled protest, she pressed her back against the door and turned her face away.

Pain was the least of her problems.

In one brutal slam of her padded elbow, the window-pane fractured. Air hissed wildly. A crack split all the way past her ear, sent aching shockwaves clear to her shoulder.

It wasn't enough.

Steam whistled from the sudden vent, blisteringly hot. Holding her breath, the trapped steam sizzling by her cheek, she brought her arm up and slammed her elbow harder into the glass. Fractures split, segmented up the pane.

Another crash, and pressure shattered the rest. Shards exploded outward in a glittering storm, tinkled to the treated floor like diamonds. The crowd jumped, screamed.

Naomi ignored them, coughing as she batted at the air in front of her face. With a fierce surge of adrenaline hammering through her blood, she grabbed an edge of the window.

Phin caught her arm. "Naomi, don't—"

She flicked him a glance, noted the hard edge to his mouth. Shaking her head once, she rolled her shoulder, disengaging as easily as if he'd never touched her, and leveraged herself up and through the narrow break. One spiky heel caught on the windowpane, wrenched her ankle, and she pitched to the floor on a stream of choked curses.

She couldn't breathe. Hot, thick air slammed into

her like a fist. She was drowning in a hot blanket of steam, like breathing in lava. Coughing, she forced herself to her hands and knees and croaked, "Hello?"

Muffled voices trailed through the broken window, died in the stifling heat. She strained to hear through it, but only a faint, muffled rattle of pressure and machine filled the choking silence.

Fuck. Not good.

"If you can hear me, help is on the way!" She crawled forward, squinting in the roiling steam. It filled her lungs, strangled her as it soaked through her clothes in seconds flat. All but blind, she cursed as her foot snagged and sent her sprawling. Swore again as her hands found hot skin and wet spandex. Damp, stringy hair.

Relief flickered. "I found her!" she shouted.

But was she alive?

The light over the sealed door guttered. Electricity crackled, sparked a blue-white arc over the door and exploded in a shower of sparks.

The locks slammed open.

With a shudder of displaced pressure, the door swung wide and sweet, blessed cool air rolled in on Phin's heels, battering her sweaty skin. Soaked to the bone with steam and sweat, Naomi sucked in the fresh oxygen as she struggled to maneuver the old woman to a sitting position. Her dead weight strained Naomi's balance.

"Shit—"

"Easy." Phin slid his arms under Naomi's, heedless of the wet tracks her saturated sweater left on his designer shirt. His features set into harsh lines. "Let her go," he ordered quietly. "I've got her."

"She's not breathing." Naomi ignored his direction,

rearranging her grip and curving her arms around the woman's knees. "Grab her shoulders, keep her steady."

"I can—"

"Just do it," she snapped. His mouth closed, lips sealing into a thin, taut line, but he didn't argue. Together they navigated through the door and out into the fresh, cool, richly oxygenated air.

"Here," she gasped, sucking in as much air as she could. "Hurry."

They knelt to set the sweat-soaked woman on the tile, and Naomi ignored Phin beside her, tuned out hysterical sobbing from somewhere in the small crowd, and bent over the woman's head.

She was so thin. Fragile as hell in her one-piece bathing suit, her gaunt limbs sticking out of the obscene splash of color and too damn still. Her skin was cherry red. Naomi prodded at her thin throat. It took too long, but she found it.

A pulse.

Thank God.

The routine came as familiar as breathing. Naomi checked her throat, cleared it, and folded her hands over the woman's chest. Four pumps, sharp, short bursts of pressure, and she covered the woman's mouth with her own. She breathed hard, fighting back the spots flickering in her peripheral vision as her lungs protested.

Another breath. A third.

Four more pumps against her chest. "Come on," she gritted out. "Three, four—come on!"

Before her second round of breath, the old woman gagged, coughing violently.

Phin wrapped an arm around the woman's back,

pulling her up to sit. She hacked and choked, gasped something unrecognizable, and over her head, Phin's eyes locked on Naomi.

Stark, raw gratitude lingered there. Approval.

Much more appraisal than she needed.

Naomi sat back on her heels, scraping back her stringy hair, and deliberately looked away. She didn't need his gratitude.

And she sure as hell didn't want to answer the questions she saw behind that silent, raw acknowledgment.

She backed away, striving for indifference. For casual relief. Just a run-of-the-mill heiress doing her good deed for the day. Flushed and sticky with sweat, she stripped off her sweater, balled it into a sodden mass between her hands, and watched Phin take control with easy, deliberate authority.

Even with sweat drying on his face, with his pale gray dress shirt stained, wilted, and damp, they listened to him. As a gurney arrived and they carried the woman out on a stretcher, the small crowd nodded as Phin promised to investigate the accident. He assured them gravely that they would take every precaution and check every automated system in the resort. His expression was concerned. Everything about him was steady.

Blah, blah, and fucking blah. Naomi ignored the wide set of his shoulders and watched the crowd instead.

Four guests. Seven staff, some wearing the dusky green uniform that the witch had worn, and others in crisp black and white.

Were any of them in league with Joe Carson? With the unknown witch?

Or was this just the accident it looked like?

She pictured the shower of sparks above the door and licked at her lower lip thoughtfully. Her head pounded, a wicked echo of exertion and the knot aching at the back of her head. She'd give someone's left nut for pain-killers.

Instead she inhaled the pungent odor of hot chlorine and drying sweat and watched the group trickle out. There'd be talk tomorrow. Gossip.

Questions.

She rubbed the back of her neck and narrowed her eyes at the two women who remained behind, industriously cleaning up the mess of towels and broken glass. They wore identical light green dresses designed to accommodate the kind of work she imagined hotel staff had to do. Clean, laundry, fold shit. She didn't know.

They looked upset. Worried. They looked at their boss often, as if gauging their own reaction to his. Waiting for him to reassure them, maybe.

He directed the dispersing crowd back to the double doors and Naomi watched them as they filed out, eerily silent in the wake of the nearly fatal accident. None looked like accessories to murder. But then accessories rarely did.

She stood cautiously, locking her unsteady knees before they dumped her right back onto her ass. Although she wasn't cold in her clinging, wet camisole, goose bumps rippled over the bare skin of her arms.

Death by steam. Not a pleasant way to go.

She cleared her throat. "Has anyone called emergency services?"

Phin scraped a hand through his hair, forcing his

damp curls to stand on end. "No." The structured planes of his face were taut. Troubled. Inquisitive as he studied her.

She turned away. "I'll call—"

"No," he repeated. "They've taken her to the clinic. We have an excellent doctor and staff in house. She's in the best hands possible. She'll be fine."

Naomi jerked her gaze back to his. Read steely resolve as it locked into place. Her eyebrows jerked upward. "Are you serious?"

"Yes. Our facility is state-of-the-art."

"That woman almost died," she pointed out. Low, even tones. "She needs an emergency room."

"She's being taken care of." He actually meant it. Dumbfounded, she stared at him until he looked away, gaze sliding over her shoulder to fix on the open door with its yawning, broken window. "This was an unfortunate accident—"

"Fuck *you*," she breathed. Spots flared like mini novas in front of her eyes, keeping time with the aching pulse in her skull. Suddenly shaking with rage, Naomi's hands balled into fists at her side as Phin's gaze slammed back to hers.

Narrowed. "I beg your pardon?" he said quietly.

Her lip curled. "You're going to risk that woman's safety because you can't afford the bad press?"

He flinched, but one hand slashed through the air. "My hands are tied. Alexandra is an extremely private person."

"I don't care if—"

"She *chooses*," he cut in with the same quiet, deliberate, *maddening* tone that made her want to deck him square in his too-pretty face, "and in fact insists on maintaining a level of privacy that does not include visits by emergency services."

"That's completely—"

"—what we're contractually obligated to do," he said, his tone as unyielding as the cloudy rose slate beneath his feet. "Now, you should have the clinic check out your arm."

"My arm is fine," she bit out. "That woman—"

"It's your choice, Miss Ishikawa."

Point made. She clicked her teeth together before she said something she was positive rich girls didn't say in the company of polished men like Phinneas Clarke.

His expression remained hooded. Untouchable. "Since you refuse medical care, housekeeping will bring you a cold pack before it bruises. If you'll excuse me." He walked away without another word.

She swallowed every word welling up in her throat, beat down the fury and disgust.

Son of a bitch. She just knew his mind was already going over whatever glib platitudes he intended to foist on everyone.

The man had a silver spoon jammed so far down his throat, it was no wonder his words came out with the same polished gleam. Phin Clarke was smooth.

But how smooth?

The witch in her suite. The old woman in the sauna. Did he know more than he let on?

No. The raw fear in his eyes as he'd maneuvered the unconscious woman out of the death trap of a sauna hadn't been faked.

Had it?

Shit.

And then there was the uniformed witch in her suite.

"Fuck!" she snarled, ignoring the startled glances from the two women who cleaned up the remains of the glass she'd shattered.

Was Timeless harboring witches?

Wouldn't that just make her goddamn day.

CHAPTER THREE

Naomi turned, shaking her head, and hesitated as a door across the hall eased slowly closed.

Her gaze flicked to the staff as caution slipped into the exhausted vacuum of leached adrenaline. One maid, a teenager, diligently swept glass into a dustbin. The other, a dark-skinned woman with closely cropped brown hair, hummed something off-key as she vanished into the empty sauna with another broom in hand.

There was nobody else to enter the locker room clearly marked for women. She hadn't seen anyone else enter or stay.

Instinct spiked a warning, and she ran for the swinging door as the teenager with the shard-filled dustpan stepped into her path.

"Move!" Naomi bit out. Too late.

Glass scattered in a fine arc as they collided. As if in some awkwardly maneuvered dance, Naomi wrenched her around, caught the flying dustbin in one hand, and tossed it heedlessly back at the flailing maid. Plastic hit stone; the maid managed an inquisitive "Mmph!"

Naomi didn't stop to check on either. She sprinted between the colorfully tiled pools, pushed open the door, and dodged its rebound as it slammed back at her on well-oiled hinges.

Checking behind it was habit, and she stalked into the luxurious locker room ready for anything. A fight, an attack, anything, god damn it.

She caught a glimpse of her own narrowed eyes in the wide bank of mirrors, frowned at the color riding high on her cheeks, and ignored the silvered surface as a rasp of movement echoed from the adjoining room.

Darting through the access frame, she barely managed to process the warning flicker. Cursing, she dropped to the floor as a glint of gold sailed over her head, just where her skull had been seconds ago. Metal rang like a bell, gonged once as a decorative urn bounced off the wall. It clattered to the stone floor, rolled lazily before it tapped the edge of an elegantly gilded shower stall.

The echoes died away into silence sharp as a knife.

Her pulse skittered; pounded with the sudden anticipation of danger.

Hell, yes. Almost better than sex.

This was what a mission should be.

Naomi shoved to her feet, stepped over the slowly spinning vase. "Come out, come out," she taunted. Her voice bounced from tiled wall to wall, thrown back at her in flat echoes. The room wasn't huge, but floor-to-ceiling panels segregated the shower stalls, leaving too many places to hide.

Mirrors adorned the wall behind her, reflected back the shades of dusky green and lavender that seemed to be the spa's signature colors.

Nothing moved around her.

If she searched the room, she'd run the risk of leaving the exit clear. But was there another exit somewhere else?

Her empty fingers twitched, desperate for the solid weight of her gun.

Cautiously she crossed the floor. Her shoes clicked loudly, echoes dogging every step as she checked every extravagant shower stall, every corner. She stepped over the pile of flowers, noting how quickly the rose-colored slate sucked at the water.

She was close. The vase hadn't been dumped out that long ago. Where the fuck had the bastard gone?

By the time she'd made a full circuit, anger spiked a sharp burn through her chest. There was nobody here. No footsteps, no breathing, *shit*, not even a whisper of sound under the constant hum of the spa's electrical grid. There were no other exits.

Just in case, she reached up and tested the decorative vents inset into each wall.

Locked fast.

What the *hell* had she missed?

She whirled, strode through the single exit, and made a full circuit of the front dressing room. Finding nothing but rows of lockers, shelves, and mirrors, she pushed through the door and pinned her gaze on the two maids still cleaning up.

The younger one slanted her a wary glance.

"Did anybody come through here?" Naomi demanded. "Within the past five minutes."

"No, ma'am," the older woman replied. "Just maintenance." She jerked a thumb toward the brightly lit, still leaking sauna. Masculine voices echoed from the interior.

Naomi locked her teeth before she gave in to the urge to scream. "Thank you," she managed.

"Are you all right?"

No. She was not all right. She was so far from all right that the first idiot to cross Naomi's path was going to get decked. She plastered on a smile that made her jaw ache. "Fine. Sorry about the mess."

They both said something pacifying, but Naomi didn't care. She turned and left, long legs eating up the ground as she studied the large, open hall.

Ten different pools, one major exit.

Two attacks in one day. Maybe the same one, maybe not. One witch. One ghost in the form of a rogue agent.

Jesus fucking Christ.

What else could go wrong?

In the privacy of the family wing, Phin could allow his mask to drop. His hands shook as he scraped them through his hair. Nausea clenched in a stomach roiling with belated terror, so he paced, stalking room to room in the pretty, elegantly decorated suite as he went over and over the scene in his mind.

What had caused the doors to malfunction? The doors were only locked after hours as a safety precaution. Never *ever* during the hours that guests used the spa area. Why had the steam regulators gone haywire? The monthly maintenance had been done three weeks ago.

Oh, God. Why hadn't either of his mothers contacted him yet? Both had hurried to the clinic at his call, and he hadn't heard anything for too long. Was Alexandra all right?

The elevator door slid open just as he reached for his comm, and Phin whirled. The look on Lillian's face caused hope and fear and nervous energy to collide somewhere on his tongue, leaving him splaying his hands in wordless demand.

Lillian Clarke's green-gold eyes were tired, but her reassuring smile loosened the tight ball of anxiety in Phin's chest even before she answered his unspoken question. "Alexandra will be all right," she said firmly. "She's exhausted, but resting well."

Phin's shoulders slumped as he half slid into a large wingback chair. "Jesus Christ," he breathed.

"I believe we can drink to that."

He could only nod.

A tall, elegant woman, Lillian kept her hair gray-free, bright as gold on a summer day. She kept it rolled into a neat, chic twist at the back of her head, and didn't fuss with anything but plain, undecorated pins. Effortlessly polished, her aging features were strongly defined, aristocratic, and just a shade too square.

Now her handsome face was set in calm, encouraging lines as she poured a layer of russet liquid into two crystal glasses. "Here," she said as she pushed one into his hand.

His fingers closed on it out of habit, but he frowned as he glanced at the elevator. "Isn't Mother coming?"

"She's going to stay with Alexandra for a while." Lillian perched on the arm of the chair, her gray, neatly tailored suit as unruffled as if she'd just stepped away from her desk. Phin sipped at the brandy in his glass.

It warmed a path from tongue to stomach, and loosened another anxious knot.

He glanced at the framed photo of his two mothers on the end table beside him. In stark contrast to Lillian's svelte sophistication, Gemma Clarke's nut brown curls, round cheeks, and warm, dark eyes couldn't help but give an impression of cheerful, bohemian housewife.

It was one of many differences that he adored about them both. He'd spent his life intercepting the small, secret glances like the one they shared in the photograph, and Phin felt a sweet, familiar squeeze in his chest.

His parents were his world. They'd built Timeless, founded it when the city was just coming to terms with two decades of reconstruction. Passed it on to him as he became a man. Nothing had shaken him so badly as the almost fatal accident to one of their guests.

"I'm going over and over it," he admitted suddenly, fingers clenching on the glass. "I pulled up the logs first thing."

Lillian smoothed back his hair with a steady hand. "Tell me what happened, my love."

He sighed, shaking his head. "I don't know. We heard Barbara screaming—"

"We?"

"The newest guest, Naomi Ishikawa. She was with me." Phin took another bracing swallow of brandy and replayed the scene again. The Asian beauty with the cool smile had broken through the sauna window, as easily as if she'd known exactly what to do. *How* to do it.

It was so vivid in his mind's eye that he flinched. The impact must have hurt. More than she'd let on.

"With you, you say?"

He met his mother's measured gaze and couldn't help his sudden smile. "I'd only just introduced myself, Mother." And how. "Since I was unavailable when she checked in, I was giving her an abbreviated tour." His smile faded. "When Barbara started screaming about her grandmother, Miss Ishikawa took off like a shot. I don't know . . ." He sighed. "The sauna door was locked tight and the gauges already in the red."

She rose, transferring her half-empty glass to the end table beside her, and rubbed the back of her neck with stiff fingers. "Have you informed maintenance?"

"They've already been called." He stood, tired body protesting, and stretched. "But I'll be going back down now that I know Alexandra's okay. Will you be all right? Should I stay?"

"You are entirely too big to be sleeping in our bed, Phinneas."

Her dry humor quirked an answering grin from his lips. "If you need anything—"

"You are one floor beneath us, I know." Lillian's smile warmed. "You're a good boy."

"I had excellent parents." He bent to brush her perfectly powdered cheek with a kiss, inhaled the comforting scent of rose and the almond oil balm Gemma made for her wife's arthritis; so familiar that adoration welled like a warm, soothing tide. Eased his frustration to something he could control. "Give Mother my love."

"I will. Try to get some rest."

The answer he gave was as noncommittal as he could make it, and he knew Lillian's gaze sharpened on his back as he called the elevator and stepped inside.

It couldn't be helped. Not only did Phin have to locate the cause of the malfunction, but he had to figure out how to explain it to a woman who was very possibly the most powerfully connected client Timeless had ever hosted.

Alexandra Applegate was so much more than Lillian's dearest friend. She also happened to be the grandmother to the Order's current bishop and the Church's most dedicated patron. Ties that helped keep the officials off his back.

Mostly.

Despite the fact that the Church didn't agree with the concept of two women raising a child in the civilized eye of the city, it was in part due to Alexandra's strong commitments that they left Timeless alone. Mostly alone.

The right set of taxes helped.

He rubbed his forehead as the elevator eased to a stop. The doors slid open, and he stepped out into one of the many discreet halls marked for staff use. Within seconds, the comm unit clipped to his belt hummed.

"Phin Clarke," he said by way of greeting.

"Mr. Clarke, it's security." Eric Barker's voice was tinny over the line, but serious. "I'm running back the feeds as we speak. We have another problem, though."

Phin raised his eyes to the ceiling. "Of course we do. What is it?"

"A new package was set to be delivered tomorrow, but transport canceled."

He slowed to a stop. "Please tell me that you've had one too many and are pulling my leg."

Barker had worked for him long enough to know when he was being serious. "If I were drinking on the job, sir," he replied evenly, "I would invite you. I'm sorry. It's true, we've lost one of our checkpoints."

"Which?"

"The second."

Damn. Phin checked his watch. "It's too late to arrange something else. That's the longest part of the whole route."

"The backup transport will be notified, but it could take a while. He has to be located, first."

"Have you tried the Pussycat Perch?"

There was a beat. "Which level, sir?"

"Mid-lows. More lows than mid," Phin added wryly. "Peter enjoys the crush in the lower city dives."

Keys clicked in the background as Phin waited. Then, with some relief, Eric told him, "I'm sending some folks now. Sir, should we be rushing the transport?"

"At this point?" Phin rubbed his face. "We don't have a choice."

"Can we do that?"

His tone was wry as Phin replied, "We *are* the operation, Mr. Barker. We can do anything."

"Yes, sir. I'll send notices through the channels to expect an earlier delivery than normal."

Damn. Triple damn. This sort of late-notice rush could end up scaring half his contacts underground, but it couldn't be helped now. "Gather Maia and her family," he said. "I also want Diego's family on this load, and if there's room, put Mary Beth in there."

"That's—"

"Pushing it, I know." Christ. What choice did they have? With the attention Timeless was about to receive, they'd need to get as many of his protected refugees out to safety as possible. "Mary Beth has been separated from her father for three months. I want them together, Mr. Barker."

"What about Diego? His family is only half gathered."

"Who do we have?"

"Looks like we've got his aunt and niece in laundry, and his nephew's working the grounds. We're missing Diego's mother and brother, and . . ." The man trailed off.

Phin ground the heel of his hand into his forehead. "Tell me."

"No one's seen his brother since the missionaries went sniffing around Diego's old apartment."

"Damn it!" He fisted his hand, lowered it before he did something stupid. Like slam it into the wall in front of him. "We have no more time to waste. Gather who we have and send them. Diego will . . ." What? Come to terms with the fact that the Church had just hunted down and probably killed his brother?

Not likely. Phin closed his eyes. "Get on it, Mr. Barker."

"Yes, sir."

Phin disconnected the comm, reattaching it to his belt with practiced familiarity as he studied one of many wallpapered panels that made up Timeless's maze of hallways. Behind it, hidden beneath the brilliant mechanics of a tiny, invisibly placed switch, one of a handful of concealed corridors tunneled through the resort walls.

If all had gone well, thirteen hours from now would have seen a small knot of people ferried through those tunnels.

Smuggled like illegal goods. Or slaves.

They might as well have been, as far as the Church was concerned.

Instead, in about ten minutes, eleven people were going to be guided through the nest of hidden corridors that was Timeless's dirty little secret. If the Church— if *anyone* beyond his carefully cultivated little nest of contacts ever found out about his illegal underground railroad, Timeless would be screwed.

And so would his family.

They all knew the risk. It was worth it.

Except when they lost one. Jesus. Diego had been smuggled out almost six weeks ago, the Church hard on his heels, and Phin had personally promised to deliver his family to him.

Every loss bit deep.

Sighing, Phin turned and strode for the discreet door that would place him in the main quad again. First he had to work with maintenance to fix the sauna, figure out what the hell had gone wrong with it. He needed something, anything to tell his guests.

To tell the Church.

He pushed into the courtyard and paused to let his eyes adjust to the dim atmosphere of the garden illumination. As it always did, the whispered rush of the running water slipped over him like a soothing blanket.

The carefully nurtured park, small as it was, made him smile.

Shadowed by the old-fashioned lamps, towering trees reached for the skylight far above, spreading slowly shedding limbs in every direction. Red, gold, and wilting brown crowned oaks sharing quarters with naked cherry trees, green firs, and leaf-bare maples. A hunkering, twisted weeping willow greedily drank the saturated earth around the cultivated pond.

The courtyard had won awards from the city government. It had sheltered lovers in the shady niches of its twisting paths and provided a small boy ample opportunity to work out excess energy raking its interminably shedding leaves. It was as much home as the buildings around it.

It pissed Phin off to think that a careless slip of technology would put that at risk. He set his jaw, then froze when a shadow moved beneath the hanging willow branches.

Black hair. Long, slender legs.

He hesitated, swallowing a sudden frisson of nerves as Naomi Ishikawa's slender body skimmed through a patch of light. She crouched at the edge of the artificial pond, dipping her fingers into the clear water. Her jeans faded into the gloom, but he didn't need light to see the taut muscle of her thighs as she balanced neatly on her heeled boots.

Phin found himself turning, stepping off the landing and along the paving stones winding through the miniature forest. Her head tilted as if she heard him coming. But she didn't turn around.

"Don't you have media reports to spin?" Her voice

was as cool as the water caressing her fingertips, and Phin raised his gaze to the skylight before he gave in to the sudden surge of terse words clogging his throat.

She'd saved a woman he loved dearly. He owed her more than petulance.

"I'm sorry if you think that I was out of line," he said instead. The water whispered, babbling softly through the foliage. Through her fingers.

Naomi chuckled. The husky sound jerked his gaze to the line of her back, shoulders bare and pale in the dimness beneath the willow tree. They moved, once. A kind of shrug. "I could almost take that as an apology, Mr. Clarke."

"Phin."

She rose with a fluidity that stuck his tongue to the roof of his mouth, turned to face him with nothing of her earlier anger in her features. Her eyes were cool, banked, hard as hell to read. "Is that woman all right, then? I'd assume you wouldn't be here if she wasn't."

"She's fine. Resting, now. Miss Ishi—"

"Naomi." Too fast. Her lips quirked as if she knew it; a half-tilted, mind-altering curve. "Just Naomi."

Tension ratcheted through his body. "Naomi," he repeated. "Thank you. If you hadn't been there . . ." He didn't know how to finish the thought that hovered so close. Wordless fear gathered into a tight ball in his throat, and his voice trailed to silence.

She shook her head. "No gratitude required." Easing past him on the narrow path, she flicked her wet fingers as easily as if she were flicking his appreciation away. Droplets scattered into the dark.

Without thinking it through, without even realizing

he'd meant to, his hand snaked out. Caught her arm before she could ghost past him.

Her body stilled. Her head tilted, blue-violet eyes settling on his hand as if surprised. Thoughtful.

Too damn nonchalant.

He wanted her disturbed. Phin wasn't sure where it came from, or why. Maybe it was the anger he nursed about Diego's brother. Maybe it was the pent-up adrenaline of the night.

Maybe it was her.

He didn't stop to consider the implications or consequences. His fingers tightened. "Naomi."

"News flash, slick. I'm not one of your paid women," she said, her husky voice low and even. Her gaze flicked to his. Burned. "You can't manhandle me, and I don't suggest you try."

The barb landed squarely through the fine layers of his control. Irritation should have undercut the sexual haze coloring his brain, but to his surprise, her prickliness resonated like a challenge thrown at his feet. His gaze sharpened.

Hers pushed. Provoked.

Screw it. "Offhand," Phin replied softly, "I can think of half a dozen ways to manhandle you."

He didn't wait for the dare. Didn't wait to see if she'd deny the offer he hadn't spoken aloud. The knowledge of his intent slid into her eyes, curled in behind their shadowed depths an instant before he let go of her arm to slide his fingers along her jaw.

She turned slowly. Degree by breathless degree.

Somewhere, deep in the part of his brain not beating its chest in masculine claim, he decided that he really liked her boots. They added a full four inches of heel that topped her off at exactly his height. It didn't take any effort to tilt his head, just a fraction, and slide his lips over hers.

Naomi didn't fight him. He half expected her to take a swing, was ready to duck if she did. He gave her room to do it, his fingers loose at her chin, gentle. Just a touch.

And she stayed.

Shocked still in the shadows, she let him kiss her. Slowly. Deliberately. Rubbing his lips against hers, Phin did nothing to deepen it, to invade her space any more than he already had. But as her mouth parted, as his upper lip caught against the insanely sweet fullness of her lower, a muffled sound caught somewhere in her chest. Hitched her breath.

Wanton. Feminine. Music to his ears.

He wasn't the only one treading on thin ice.

Her fingers slid over the open collar of his shirt and fisted. Phin angled his head more fully and took her mouth in a new kiss, a wicked, thorough tasting that left nothing to chance. Nothing to imagination. Lips and tongue, he swept into her mouth, into damp, welcoming heat to claim the attraction he knew simmered just under her so-cool facade.

She met him, stroked his tongue with her own on another sound, one that rocked straight to his gut, right to the hard erection she might as well have grabbed, he was so aroused. Her response wrapped around him like a noose, pulled tight until he went nearly blind with wanting.

He didn't close the distance between their bodies,

didn't dare risk the shock, the sheer torture of what the feel of her curves would do to him. He feasted at her mouth and knew, *knew* this single kiss was going to replay in his dreams for a long damn time.

It would have to do. He didn't dare take it any further than this.

Naomi Ishikawa was a lot more fragile than she let on. He knew it, the split second she opened her mouth to him. The way her breath caught in her chest and her eyes drifted shut under his practiced, teasing exploration.

When he disengaged his lips from hers, moved his head back far enough that he could look into her slowly opening eyes, it thrilled him down to his toes to see her shock. A hazy wash of arousal.

Phin let go of her face, slid his palms along her bare arms, and reveled as she shuddered under his touch. Curling his fingers around her wrists, he gently tugged her hands away from the wrinkled disarray of his collar.

Her tongue flicked out, slid a slow, wet line over the center divot of her bottom lip. It knocked an answering pulse of heat through his blood.

"Oh . . . kay," Naomi murmured. Awareness slowly filtered back into her eyes. Returned the shadows, the wariness. It warred with the arousal coloring her cheeks.

Phin's smile widened. "I just wanted to make it clear," he said, finally giving in to the temptation that had gnawed at him since the moment he met her. He touched his thumb to her bottom lip.

Felt it firm, move as she murmured, "Make what clear?"

"That I don't have to pay for my women."

He expected anger, maybe indignation. Naomi surprised him. Laughter rose like a visible warmth behind her exotic features, and Phin suddenly hoped to be surprised by her again.

Frequently.

"Good night, Phin," she said, amusement thick in her voice as she stepped deliberately out of reach.

Dismissed again. Phin's smile was wry as he watched her turn, his eyes on the sleek, denim-clad ass sauntering away. Even at an easy lope, she walked with purpose. With surety.

And, he noticed as she leaped over the three steps that joined the quad floor to the landing, without the refined sort of grace he expected from a finishing school—trained heiress.

Easing out a hard, laughing breath, he curled a finger into the suddenly too-warm fold of his collar and couldn't help but feel in over his head as he turned resolutely for the pool hall. Near-death malfunctions, drop-dead gorgeous heiresses, and the threat of breaking his own cardinal rules.

Life just couldn't get any more out of the ordinary.

Until she turned, her key card held jauntily between index and middle fingers. "By the way," she called out, "you should check your security cameras. Betcha a dollar they'll reveal what went wrong."

Phin studied her, one eyebrow arching up slowly. "Are you asking me if we have security cameras, Naomi, or are you hoping we don't?"

Her head tilted. "That depends. If I were to, say, indulge in some *very* inappropriate behavior with a certain slick operator in some of these halls, would we—"

Her grin widened into a slow, sultry line. "That is, would this hypothetical man and I be seen everywhere we tried go?"

Lust shot straight to his groin. So did all the remaining blood in his brain. "Not," he managed, "everywhere." Close enough, but he knew a blind spot or two.

Or three or four or— *Jesus God, help me now.*

Her eyes flashed, pure sensual violet as the elevator doors slid open behind her. "Just wondering," she said lightly.

Phin rubbed his face with both hands as the shiny elevator doors closed on her smile.

CHAPTER FOUR

Failure. God damn it, he didn't *do* failure.

Joe Carson watched the old woman sleeping in her narrow clinic bed and cursed silently. He'd been so sure of Alexandra Applegate as the perfect bait. She wasn't just rich, after all, she was special. Important.

Sure, it'd been a risk. A calculated one. She could have died in that sauna—the risk wouldn't have been worth it if he didn't make it *real*—but he knew they had the means to make sure she didn't. All the damned witches had to do was bring out the fountain.

No harm, no foul. The Church got what it wanted.

But overhearing that snot-nosed brat explain about the woman's ludicrous privacy contract was enough to make him want to kill something. Bare-fucking-handed.

Why hadn't he known that? Fuck. God take them all, he hated this sacrilegious tomb and its goddamned aberrant clientele.

But he couldn't do anything about it yet. Patience. It was the stakeout to end all stakeouts. He could do patience.

He had to. He'd had the perfect vantage point, the perfect box seat to watch the opera unfold, but no.

The missionary had to ruin it.

That should have driven him insane. It should have worried him. Instead he'd barely escaped her sharp eye and quick mind, and even now he smiled from the cramped hole he hid in.

Naomi West would make it fun. Much more fun than he'd thought when he'd first taken on this operation. It wasn't her fault she'd stuck her foot in it, after all. Like him, she was just doing her job.

But now he had to plan a little more carefully. A little more cautiously. It wasn't like shooting oily fish in a barrel anymore.

The Church had dealt its hand. Joe wondered if it knew that it was playing itself at the table.

He imagined that his fellow missionary was well and truly pissed at losing him. It'd been damn close. Only the vase he'd thrown at her had given him the time to get away, but she was tough stuff. Mission-suit Teflon.

And if she ever got her hands on him . . . He didn't laugh, but it was close. Swallowing back a bubble of eagerness, he didn't so much as shift a muscle. Strain already ripped through his cramping limbs, but he could hold it until the Second Coming if he had to. Tenacity. That's what made him a damn good missionary.

And based on what he knew about Naomi West, that's what made her almost as good as he was.

Almost.

Joe let out a silent sigh. Of relief. Of anticipation.

Of appreciation.

Timeless made it so damn easy. He relished Naomi's unspoken challenge. Finally. A woman worth her weight in bullets.

He tipped his head, studying the round figure of the woman perched in the chair beside the bed. She read a book too battered to see the name of, thick-rimmed glasses on her nose. The golden lamp haloed her brown hair, and anger streaked through him again. Pooled like bile in his skull.

It should have worked. That lock should have held on for a full three minutes longer, a timer set to force the bishop's favored grandmother into cardiac arrest, at least. Emergency services could never get to Timeless in time to save her life.

The Timeless witches would have had no choice but to reveal their secrets then.

Instead she'd been dragged out. In shock and a little worse for wear, but nothing a good night's sleep and some herbal gunk couldn't fix.

Damn it.

Maybe it was the sudden pressure change in the sauna, or something he hadn't factored. He certainly hadn't counted on his fellow missionary. Why?

He set his jaw, locking his knees tightly in place at his chest, and bided his time. Like a spider, he thought. A hungry, brilliant, venomous spider.

Surrounded by fat, clumsy, little flies.

CHAPTER FIVE

She'd spent most of the night pacing.

When dawn crept into the rain-slick windows of the too large suite, Naomi finally collapsed into a fitful, uneasy sleep. She woke to more gray rain and a thin, wintry light splashing weakly against the glass. The desk unit attached to her nightstand chirped brightly.

Blearily she picked up the hand receiver. "Hello?"

"Good morning, Miss Ishikawa," said a pleasant female voice on the line. "This is your morning program courtesy call."

Her what? Naomi elbowed herself up, shoving back her hair from one eye. "Say that again?"

"Your services start at eight," explained the patient—*fuck*—bright voice. "If you prefer to eat first, breakfast is served at the dining floor. Shall I reschedule your services for later?"

Jesus Christ. "No," she muttered, and hung up the receiver on whatever chipper rainbows the voice expected to stream at her next.

Plan. She needed a plan. Wait, no, shower, coffee, and then plan.

It took effort to drag herself into the shower. Sleeping well, Naomi had learned a long time ago, was something that happened to other people.

The first five minutes of skin-searing spray stripped the stupor from her brain. The last five was all she needed to scrub her hair and body with the first bar of soap that came to hand. Her mind slowly eased into gear, and by the time she dragged the fluffy, sinfully soft towels over her wet skin, she could think without feeling as if she climbed through a fog.

"All right," she said. Her own voice jarred in the peaceful morning quiet. "Rogue missionary hiding in spa. Check." She didn't bother with makeup. "A witch hiding in spa. Double-check." Naomi brushed out her hair, dragging the thick bristles through it until it shone with health.

"Why?" she asked the steamed mirror. "What do either have to gain?"

Carson was a missionary. Missionaries hunted witches. Was it possible Carson was tracking the mysterious witch who'd attacked her?

No. That didn't explain Operation Black Tie. Whatever Carson was after—witch or no witch—the Holy Order wanted him dead.

So then why had the witch with the bushy mustache

attacked her? To make her afraid? Warn her? Assault could have been a good tactic with anyone else, but she wasn't anyone else.

Naomi didn't do scared.

You're tougher than I thought.

His words. To test her, then. Had he expected her to roll over and die? She rubbed her forehead, grimacing at the dull ache at the back of her head. Two adversaries, then. Until she could figure out who was what and where, she'd have to watch her back. Hard.

"So, why the old woman?"

Good question. Naked, absently fingering the tattoo low on her abdomen, Naomi gathered the only thing she could find that wasn't silk, cashmere, or worth more than she was.

She wasn't sure how appropriate a mesh sports tank and the skintight running pants she'd found were, but the damn place was a spa. She didn't think she'd need anything fancier.

She checked the clock on the mantel and sighed. By seven-fifty, she was in the elevator and staring at the digital readout on the schedule surreptitiously left on the front table.

The rest of the team was sure to have a good laugh over this one. They probably shit themselves as they signed her up for these so-called services.

What was Naomi West doing today?

Things that would make her *pretty*.

Things that would make her scream inside the masked confines of her refined façade.

Naomi didn't do scared, but she did anger. She did it well. "You shitfu—"

The elevator doors slid open, and Naomi clamped her mouth into a determined smile as a short, incredibly curvaceous woman turned to greet her.

Her tamed curls shone in the light, almost the exact shade of Phin's, and her demonstrative eyes were as dark as chocolate. Naomi immediately recognized where he'd gotten his dimples as mirror twins appeared at the sides of her wide mouth.

So that much of his lethal charm was genetic. *Fantastic.*

A pale purple tailored skirt suit belted the beautifully hourglass cinch of her waist, outlining the kind of curves Naomi had always admired. Her hair was pinned in a way that made her curls look like an effortless crown.

She was lovely. In a round, polished dumpling sort of way. Even the lines spreading from the corners of her eyes added to the inherent . . . *Hell*, Naomi didn't know. Appeal. Comfort.

She was real, somehow, more real than the plastic setup Naomi had expected from the polished Phin's genetic line.

She actually looked like a mother.

Phin's mother.

She swallowed, suddenly feeling every inch of her long, gangly five feet and towering ten inches.

"Miss Ishikawa, good morning." Welcome simmered in her pleasant contralto. Warmth practically beamed from her round, matronly features as she held her hands out. "I'm Gemma Clarke. Naomi, thank you, we owe you such gratitude."

Unable to get away from this one without causing more trouble than Phin was worth, Naomi let the woman take her hands. Gemma's palm was warm, dry, her grip stronger than expected as it enfolded her fingers.

Working hands. Despite herself, a sliver of respect uncurled from Naomi's lingering annoyance. "Don't mention it," she said. "I just happened to be nearby." *Chasing a witch.*

Kissing the woman's son in the dark corners of the strange garden.

But where had Gemma Clarke been?

Naomi's smile masked the sudden surge of adrenaline skating across her nerves. This was the part she hated the most.

Mysteries weren't her thing, either.

It made no sense for Gemma to sabotage her own spa. She'd lose money. She'd lose face and clients.

Would she have more to gain by killing the old woman? Naomi resolved to find out.

"Nonsense," Gemma was saying brightly, unaware of Naomi's closeted scrutiny. "Without you, who knows what might have happened?" She gestured to the readout in Naomi's other hand. "Is that your schedule, dear?"

Another slice of irritation. She gritted her teeth, managed to say with at least a shred of urbane interest, "It is."

Gemma's eyes lit up as her dark curls bent over the screen. Lavender wafted under Naomi's nose, and her mouth twisted.

Most prisons smelled like sweat and bleach. Lavender probably qualified as a step up.

"Oh, lovely. You've been set up with Joel for a massage at one. Let me tell you, the man has hands that should be dipped in solid gold." Casually Gemma linked her arm through Naomi's and guided her toward the second elevator. "You want the fifth floor for the rest, of course."

Feeling like a bit of flotsam caught in a hurricane, Naomi allowed herself to be bustled across the courtyard and into the elevator while Gemma babbled cheerfully. She covered a lot of ground in a few short minutes, from the amazing properties of the minerals inset into each special room in the above floors, to the staff she'd combed the world to find.

Her head spinning, she was caught entirely off guard when the shorter woman reached up and seized her chin in strong, short fingers. "My dear, what on earth happened to your face?"

"A glass bottle." The words slid out of her mouth before the rest of her caught up. Naomi edged her grin upward, forcing herself to sound as relaxed as she didn't feel. "Seriously, it's nothing."

Brown eyes sharpened. Appraised. "Can I ask you a personal question?" In that slow, steady, steely tone, Naomi recognized Phin.

He certainly was his mother's son.

Naomi's smile twisted at one corner. "Can I stop you?"

"Did someone in your family hurt you?"

A bubble of laughter rose in her throat. Naomi hastily swallowed it back. "No. Really, it was an accident."

Mostly in that she hadn't been quick enough to get out of the way. The bar had been smoky, the music loud, and it had taken one jackass, two of his buddies, and a beer bottle to put her down.

They'd all ended up in jail. She'd ended up in Timeless.

Same thing.

Gemma patted her hand. "All right. We'll put something on it so it doesn't scar. Come along."

As if on cue, the doors slid open, and anything Naomi wanted to say, intended to say, died on her tongue.

Jacuzzis. Smaller, more personal tubs. Beautifully embroidered silk screens that provided privacy without losing the social atmosphere, and rooms set at intervals around the whole of the main foyer all combined to create a vast floor that seemed both welcoming and exotic at once. Plants spilled out of every available nook, softening the inherent austerity of porcelain and more slate tile.

Metal and sturdy wood had been placed in precise, clean lines of seating, screens, furnishings, and troughs filled with some kind of steaming, green water. All of it looked like implements of elegant torture.

Lavender tickled her nose again, but mixed with steamy currents of fragrances she couldn't place. A sharper aroma pierced through everything else, something that smelled like tea but burned like whiskey in her lungs.

Naomi drew up short, knowing her brows were knitting together and unable to wrench them apart. "Wow" was the safest thing she could manage through the sudden, violent swearing in her head.

Gemma's smile was a beam of pride and satisfaction. "I'm so glad you like it. I love this floor." She approached a massive white desk, rows and rows of shelves laid out behind it. Each held a series of folded pastel lavender and pale green towels, thick and fluffy.

Reluctantly Naomi followed.

Behind the desk, an older woman with shoulder-length gray hair gathered a collection of towels from one shelf. "Mrs. Clarke, good morning," she said crisply. "Miss Ishikawa, I hope you slept well."

Too overwhelmed by the sheer volume of *beautification* locked in a single room, Naomi could only nod vaguely.

Did they keep a running tab on everybody? Pass out pamphlets of each guest to the staff? She felt suddenly, wildly trapped. An ant caught under a magnifying glass.

She rubbed at the back of her head. Deliberately dragged her fingers over the lump that still ached there until pain knocked back against her skull.

Pain helped.

"Agatha, how are you?" Gemma's greeting sounded like a mother, like a caring employer, but she moved like a general. Every motion practiced, every gesture crisp, she extracted a lavender robe from the collection of fabric and shook it out.

"Very well," Agatha replied. "The day guests will be arriving within the hour."

"Excellent. Dear, put this on." Before she could refuse, Naomi found herself ushered toward a small room near the desk, the door shut firmly behind her. "And take all undergarments off," Gemma added through the panel.

Fuck. This was it. Naomi glanced wildly around the

small changing room as if another exit might be hiding in a hamper. The schedule had started with a manicure and a pedicure.

Nails. Polish. Buffing.

She'd done it just a few days ago, doing it again was redundant, but harmless enough. She had to meet the guests somehow.

When she stepped outside again, Naomi wordlessly passed her athletic clothes to the waiting Agatha. The woman put them in a locker and handed her a key, ticked something off on her clipboard, and gestured over her shoulder. "If you wait one moment, I'll escort you—"

Naomi hooked the key to the robe belt. "I've got it."

If she waited around for an escort, she'd wander right into the elevator and forget to come back.

Naomi followed the attendant's gesture, rounded the edge of the desk, and hoped to hell the knee-length robe stayed belted securely. She was pretty sure the knot would hold, but she didn't usually make it a habit to go around in public with just a thick bit of terry cloth between her naked body and the rest of the world.

Modesty wasn't one of her character traits. The problem was the goddamned setting.

Soft music filtered from discreetly hidden speakers, the air smelled fresh, with just a hint of soothing lavender. The heated, dark green slate tile warmed her bare feet as she padded through the wide, almost empty room. Only a few cheerful staff members moved around what Naomi figured were stations, readying supplies and talking softly among themselves.

Naomi scrutinized them all, but none of them looked to be big enough, cagey enough, to be the witch who'd ambushed her. No handlebar mustaches. No scars.

She could only be so lucky.

She skirted the edge of a shallow pool tiled in vivid shades of blue and green, and narrowed her eyes at a porcelain tub filled with steaming water. The source of the sharpest fragrance emanated from whatever it was that turned the hot water green.

She found Gemma waiting by a chair that looked as if its only purpose was to lure unwitting guests to pliant, vulnerable sleep. Naomi's frown didn't ease. "What am I smelling?"

"St. John's wort," the woman replied easily. "When poured over the skin, it soothes anxiety and burns. Taken in a tea, it'll ease cramping. Sit, there's a love."

Despite the flow of explanations, Naomi rubbed the back of her neck, frown deepening. "Mrs. Clarke—"

"Gemma, dear," she corrected sweetly. "Have a seat. This won't take long."

Naomi ran her palms down the plush material of the robe. Her fingers set the locker key swinging, and she frowned down at her bare shins.

She had great legs. She just preferred to show them off in a skintight miniskirt in the middle of a dance club than here.

"Come on, I don't bite."

But here she was. *Plan*, she reminded herself, and sat. She met Gemma's rich dark eyes as the woman cupped her chin with a strong hand and tipped her head up to the light.

Sympathy flickered there.

Naomi's fingers curled into the robe. "You know, it's really fine."

"It's already forming scar tissue, is what it is." Gemma clucked her tongue as she withdrew a small, unmarked jar from somewhere behind Naomi's head. "You really should have gotten this clipped."

She really should have done a lot of things. *Duck* ranked among the first. Her mouth tightened. "Look, I don't need—"

"Close your eyes." Ignoring her completely, Gemma slathered something cold and wet onto the dense ridge of crusted scab. As the fumes hit her eyes, Naomi flinched and squeezed them shut.

She smelled peppermint. Something thicker, almost denser in flavor. Lavender, of course. She'd been smelling lavender since she got off the damned front elevator.

The small, imperceptible ache at her nose eased into languid, fluid warmth.

Surprise tilted her head. With her eyes screwed shut, she lifted searching fingers to her nose and found it damp. Her fingertips immediately tingled. "What is this?"

Warm hands enfolded hers. "Don't touch it," Gemma warned. "It's got a bit of numbing to it, which is why the vapors will knock your socks off at first. Give me a good solid ten count and you should be good to go."

"Numbing? Will my face go dead?"

"Not unless you use the whole pot and then some. And for heaven's sake, don't ever drink it. My son did that once, on a dare."

Naomi swallowed a laugh. "How'd he do?"

"It took months for him to smell peppermint again

without turning green." She heard the sound of glass and metal, punctuated by the click of Gemma's shoes on the tile. "All right, take a look around."

First one eye, cracked slightly in muted apprehension. When it didn't sizzle out of her eye socket, Naomi opened the other and focused on Gemma's round, smiling face hovering over hers.

She shifted. Wrinkled her nose, her forehead.

Not even a twinge.

Now if she could get more of that stuff for the back of her head, she'd be great.

"Well?"

Naomi grinned, oddly relieved. "Perfect."

"Wonderful!" Gemma clapped her hands with infectiously cheerful exuberance. "Sit back, my dear, you'll have Lacey today for your nail care. She's amazing, a true gem."

Already half out of the plush chair, Naomi let the woman guide her back into the depths of the smothering cushions, her heart sinking with her body. "Great, I can't wait."

Four hours later, her false enthusiasm flagged completely.

Her nails were trimmed, shaped, polished, and buffed to a sparkling shine. She'd drawn the line at pink polish. Her face had been scrubbed, peeled, abraded, slathered in some sort of vegetable concoction, scrubbed again.

Her body was shiny and pink from the rough, skin-shedding process the matron of torture had called a body scrub, and if she smelled honey ever again, she was going to throw up. Spending thirty minutes drenched in it was enough for a lifetime.

It was all she could do to smile through the anxiety battering at her exposed skin. If it seemed more like baring her teeth than happiness, no one told her.

Throughout the process, Naomi noted a small handful of residential guests and a steady flow of one-day visitors. There was a man who had introduced himself as Michael Rook, long sticklike legs slightly bandied beneath his robe. Greta Hollister, a sweetly shy blond who didn't say much, and the redheaded British pop star the others called Jordana.

She didn't factor in the steady stream of day guests whose faces and names started to run together after the first hour.

As she soaked her stripped, burning legs in a shallow, heated pool, Naomi watched them come and go. They trooped in as singles or pairs, some in groups of three. The men and women mingled, each wearing robes like hers. For more personal services or privacy, they were escorted into separate private rooms.

The cynical part of her brain speculated on what other kind of *personal services* Timeless offered on the side.

The staff worked like multiple limbs from the same brain. No guest was allowed to wander unnoticed, each person effortlessly passed from station to station, specialist to specialist. It was so graceful, so unassuming that Naomi recognized the slightly shell-shocked look most of the guests wore.

Maybe they called it relaxing. Naomi called it checking out.

It took effort not to sneer.

"So, you're the heiress we've been hearing so much

about." Water splashed up around Naomi's thighs as Jordana plunked herself on the heated tile beside her and slid her perfectly toned, stripped pink legs into the water.

Naomi arranged her features into a smile. "Naomi." She didn't offer a hand.

Neither did the redhead with the absolutely magnificent display of cleavage between the lapels of her mint green robe. She smiled easily enough, arranging her robe to reveal the maximum amount of leg possible. "This place is something else, isn't it?"

Hell wasn't the word Naomi should offer. "That it is," she said instead. Mild enough. "Do you come here a lot?"

"No, it's my first time." She tipped her head toward Naomi, dropping her voice. "Although between you and me? If it puts me in Phin Clarke's circle, I'll be here every chance I get."

It took even more effort not to laugh out loud. Naomi wasn't going to claim that she knew him any better than the pop tart sizing him up, but something told Naomi that he wouldn't touch the redheaded barracuda with a harpoon.

She ignored the slow, lazy curl in her belly, the awareness of something hot and entirely unwelcome at the mention of his name. Phin wasn't her business.

Except in the suspected-accessory-to-harboring-a-fugitive sort of way.

Right.

"I mean," Jordana was saying, straightening her perfect legs and raising just the tips of her fire-engine red toenails out of the rippling, heated surface. "Really, I mean, have you seen him? Oh. My. God. The man has, like, shoulders you wouldn't believe."

"Wouldn't I?" Naomi murmured. Her gaze drifted past the singer toward the steady stream of people, of conversation. Snippets assaulted her from every direction.

Stocks. Travel plans. Family. Feed channels and the future. So normal.

Assuming *normal* meant the kinds of plans that involved private jets and personally funded tuition at universities that didn't accept applications from people like her.

Her jaw shifted.

"And really, it was so terrible." Jordana sighed sadly. It jerked Naomi's attention back to her, to the gossipy glint in her hazel eyes.

"Oh?" What had she missed?

Clearly pleased to have a coconspirator, Jordana scooted her amply rounded ass across the tile. "Didn't you *hear*?" she demanded gleefully. "After the accident, Phinny ordered every maintenance tech to show up and get to the bottom of the mess. It was, like, three in the morning."

Had he slept at all?

Naomi forced herself to remember that she didn't care. "Did they find the problem?"

Jordana frowned, puzzlement shaping the cosmetically enhanced angle of her eyes. "Problem?"

"With the door?"

"Oh!" Her expression cleared. "Who knows? You'll have to ask them."

"Oh, of course." The urge to grab the shallow redhead by the scruff of her neck and plunge her face-first into the shallow water made Naomi's fingers flex with greed.

Spoiled, selfish little—

"And then I heard that after she got out of the clinic, Alexandra Applegate left at dawn."

—fly on the goddamn wall. Naomi straightened. "What?"

"Alexandra Applegate. Don't you know who that— Oh." The singer nodded, as if reaching some conclusion. "You're not from here, right?"

"Right," Naomi murmured, but her mind was spinning. Alexandra Applegate. *Hell.* Of course that was who the old woman was.

Why hadn't the Mission warned her the bishop's own fucking grandmother was here? Why the fuck hadn't she recognized her?

Except she'd never met the woman, and pictures just didn't match up to lobster red skin, stringy white hair, and blue lips.

"Whatever." Jordana rolled her eyes, flicking wet fingers across the pool. "She probably went home and sobbed into her million-dollar wardrobe. I heard that she was ready to shut this whole place down, which would piss me off. I mean, I just met Phinny."

Naomi didn't have the patience for this shit. "Shame," she said dryly. "Well, nice chatting with you." She pulled her legs from the warm water, awkwardly getting to her feet on the marble ledge.

"Sure!" Jordana waved her newly polished nails. "Hey, maybe later we can go shopping together. I'd love to show you my favorite stores. There's this salon, I bet it'd do wonders for your hair."

More clothes. Another haircut. More money. Naomi's smile stretched her cheeks into aching points as she retreated.

Behind her, the flamboyant woman's failure of a whisper sighed out a long, verbal shrug. "I don't care how much money she has. Did you see her *face*?"

Enough time, and Jordana's would have matched it.

At the desk, she retrieved her clothes from the efficient Agatha, smiled stiffly through a reminder that her massage appointment would begin precisely at one, and barely managed to get to the elevator before she couldn't take it anymore.

She needed out. Somewhere, anywhere. She was smoothed and buffed and polished and depilated.

She looked like a goddamn marble statue. Like some rich, pampered— *Shit*. Like every other goddamned perfect woman in that fucking beauty spa.

Fuck her team's sense of humor. Fuck the so-called relaxation she was scheduled to sit through, and shit-fuck to the man named Joel with the magic hands.

The last thing she needed—*wanted*—was to be alone inside her own head.

CHAPTER SIX

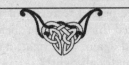

Two of the suites have checked out." Lillian's voice in Phin's ear registered stalwart resignation as he made his way through the halls. "Alexandra and her retinue, of course, with her regrets."

"I imagine she went home to be tended by her own doctors," Phin murmured, bypassing two of the staff's personal athletic trainers with an easy smile and nod.

Nothing to see here.

He shifted the comm to his other ear as Lillian continued, "And the sweet doctor from New England."

Damn. He'd been hoping for a good word from the man whose words carried a lot of weight on his side of the coast. Pausing in the hallway, Phin pinched the bridge of his nose. "How did he seem when he left?"

"Quiet. He expressed no displeasure, praised the

staff's precision and care. However, he checked out a full four days early. I think we can extrapolate from there." In the background, he could hear the muted *click* and *tap* of her keyboard. He could easily picture her in the small, beautifully furnished office tucked just beside his, posture ramrod-straight and hair elegantly upswept off her shoulders.

Like a picture-perfect secretary of ages past.

Phin squeezed his eyes shut behind his fingers. "Okay," he said again. "All right, it's not a complete loss. Was Alexandra all right?"

"Your mother took excellent care of her, like she always does."

"Is she okay?"

Lillian sighed, briefly. "Tired, but she's out and about now. What about the accused witches you ferried out last night?"

"Seen out safely, thank God. Joel and the team returned home by midnight with nothing out of the ordinary to report."

"The backup driver was found, then," Lillian surmised in her simple, factual way "Excellent. Now, what about the sauna?"

Phin turned, checked down both ends of the hallway before allowing himself to slump back against the wall. He could still hear the grim technician's report, echoing like a death knell in his head. "Sabotage seems the likeliest cause."

The sound of keys stilled. "Excuse me?"

"The technicians ran a full diagnostic. They were up all night."

"Which means," surmised his mother, who knew

him all too well, "that you were, too. I trust you've managed a nap?"

Phin grimaced. "I'm fine. The sauna, however, is not. We've put up a barricade to make sure no one else goes in, but I suspect guests will be avoiding all of the hot rooms for a while."

"Tell me about this sabotage."

"The short version? Someone crossed the wiring to short-circuit the lock for the disinfectant mode." His head echoed like a hollow drum as he let it drop to the wall. "It didn't hold under the humid conditions, which was the only thing that probably saved Alexandra's life. Another few minutes—"

Lillian hummed a low note of dismissal. "Another few minutes wouldn't have been the end of it, but that's neither here nor there. The important thing here is finding this saboteur."

He dropped his hand from his eyes, staring blankly at the bank of glass windows that separated the main gym from the surrounding workout rooms. "That's the catch, isn't it? Firstly, who would want to do something like this?"

"An enemy?"

"Whose?" Phin murmured. "It would need someone with the know-how." A sudden flash of turquoise caught his attention, and he tilted his head. He straightened from the wall supporting his weary weight when the vivid color beckoned again.

"Have you crossed the technicians? Maintenance?" Lillian hesitated. "What of the temporaries you brought in through the basement?"

"Mmm." Footsteps soundless on the carpet, Phin

slowly meandered toward the glass bay. "All of our technicians have been with us for over a year. If it was one of them, which I doubt, it had to be a crime in the making for a very long time. And why now? Alexandra is a frequent guest."

"And the others?"

Phin frowned. His fingertips settled over the cool windowpane, his gaze homing in on Naomi Ishikawa. She was hard to miss.

Impossible to ignore.

"I don't think so," he said, distracted by the way her cropped turquoise top hugged her chest like a second skin. It left her back bare from neck to shoulder blades, let him see the smooth flex and ripple of taut, toned muscle as she worked over a body-sized punching bag.

"Why?"

"Take my word for it. Mother, I'll call you back." Without waiting for her reply, Phin disconnected the unit.

He couldn't look away. There was something addictive about Naomi, something inherently fascinating. The way her taped fists slammed into the rough material of the swinging bag, the way she moved like a dancer one minute and a lethal fury of limbs the next. Her ponytail bounced and swayed with every jab, every hook and cross.

Phin grinned as she spun on the ball of one foot and slammed the smooth, bare expanse of her shin into the bag. The impact cracked like a gunshot.

The woman worked over a bag like she'd caught it insulting her mother. It was one hell of an exercise regime.

Phin unfolded the digital screen on his comm unit and tapped in a quick series of commands. Within seconds, Naomi's designated schedule filled the readout. His smile widened.

She'd turned down Joel for a bone-rattling beatdown.

Either she was a sucker for punishment, or she was—
Something else entirely.

Like a saboteur? Phin's smile faded as he snapped the unit closed. Impossible. She'd been with him when the screaming started.

But before? She'd said she was exploring.

He shook his head. Paranoia wasn't a flavor that suited his palate, and a check on the internal security feed would verify her whereabouts easily enough. Hers and all the other guests'. If all of them proved to have time-stamped alibis, he'd have to start looking at staff.

Another thunderous crack ripped through the gym, its impact muffled by the glass. She danced back, shaking out one reddened, tape-wrapped foot, and smoothly shifted her weight.

Fascinating.

Tucking the comm into his inner jacket pocket, he turned and circled the bay of windows. She was so engrossed in murdering the innocent workout bag that she didn't see him approach. Didn't hear his initial, subtle cough.

Shoulders moving, liquid control, she drove fast, sharp fists into the bag. Her trim waist slid in fluid lines he assumed meant that she dodged imaginary punches from her imaginary assailant. Thigh muscles flexing, she propelled one knee into the bag. They stretched and flexed again as two more hard, jarring knee thrusts followed it.

She was hell on mostly bare feet.

Swinging wildly, the ends of her ponytail lashed at her sweaty shoulders like black silk. It clung to her skin. To silver glinting at the base of her neck.

Phin's mouth went suddenly dry.

A barbell; two small, delicate beads. They gleamed like stars centered at the gentle flare where her neck met her shoulders, winked wickedly, maddeningly.

A piercing. A hidden, secret jewel he never would have expected. Not from the stunning heiress with the Japanese name. Not from any woman he'd ever known.

Lust curled like a live wire in his gut, tightened an already attentive erection to a violent, painful squeeze. Phin must have made some move, some raw, strangled sound, because she turned.

Her cheeks glowed pink with exertion, eyes bright. Breathing hard, she took much longer than Phin liked before she dropped her guarded hands and eased her stance into something less vigilant.

Only somewhat less threatening.

But he couldn't see the damn barbell anymore. Scraping the melted fragments of his mind back together, Phin followed the direction of her eyes. Helpfully he picked up the green water bottle she'd left on a bench beside him.

"Having a good workout?" Phin handed it over, bottom first.

She filled her mouth with the cool liquid, drank greedily, her throat working as he watched. He wanted to run his tongue down every inch of that sweaty curve where her shoulder met her neck. *Jesus.* Trouble.

"Yeah," she finally said. Wiping at her mouth with the back of her arm, she added huskily, "Nice equipment."

"Thanks." He managed calm, even as a slow flush climbed up his neck. She wasn't talking about him. At least he didn't think so. She meant the gym equipment, not the dangerously sensitive pulse knocking around in his crotch.

But not thinking about it wasn't working. Not while she stood there. Watched him.

Hell, breathed.

The top, he decided, didn't do her figure any justice. Made for sports, it pressed her breasts nearly flat, banded her tightly in a way he knew was necessary for the kind of workout she liked.

But it was hardly fair.

His gaze trailed over that taut, turquoise curve, slid over the sweaty gleam of her neck. Her reddened cheeks. It centered on her nose, and the slash across it that looked somehow less aggressively uneven. Smoother.

Familiar.

A corner of his mouth kicked up. "You've met my mother."

"What?" When he gestured to his nose in mirrored indication, Naomi winced. She raised her fingers, but didn't touch the slash. "She put something on it. It feels better."

Yes, that was Gemma all over. Unable to help herself. Phin's smile widened. "It looks better, too. You're supposed to be finishing up a massage right now, aren't you?"

Her eyes narrowed. "So the schedule tells me." Naomi turned, seized the still-swinging bag with both hands.

Smooth. Too smooth. Phin hoped she didn't catch his small, rough sound of amusement. Of hunger. "Do you have something against massage?"

"Is that going to be a problem?" The cool pitch of her too-casual voice warned him off.

That glinting silver jewelry at the back of her neck made him want to beat on his chest and throw her over his shoulder. He rubbed at his forehead, black edges of humor creeping in through a haze of lust. "Not at all."

"You're not going to run back to my people and tell them?"

He met her appraisal directly and matched the sharp ends of her mockery with a forthright, easy smile. "You're the one staying here, Naomi, not them. It's your money and your call."

Her lower lip worked, pulling to the side in a way that made Phin wonder if she had a habit of biting the inside of her lip. Telling. She had a lot of tells, he realized.

A lot of signals.

All designed to drive him crazy.

"Hmm." It wasn't a thank-you, but he'd take it. Watching him, wary, she raised the underside of her taped forearm to her mouth and caught at the layers with her teeth.

The flash of white, of damp pink as her lip caught on the edge of pale tape, was sexier than a sweat-soaked, punch-happy, troublemaking heiress had any right to be.

"Here," he said gruffly, closing the distance between

them with a few short strides. He wrapped his fingers around her sweaty wrist, gently angling her arm around so he could find the edges of the tape.

It put him too close to her. Too close to the adrenaline-fueled fragrance of her damp skin, to the smell of the soap she'd used in her hair, like spring rain and lavender.

Too close to her upturned eyes staring into his.

The sticky tape caught at his fingertips, resisted. Tore. As he unwound it, layer by layer, something in her stance changed. Shifted. He looked up, met her eyes as she stepped closer, fully into his space. Bare, taped feet to his polished shoes. Sleek, muscled thigh to his slacks.

Chest to chest.

Eye to eye.

Phin's fingers tightened on her wrist. It was all he could do to force back the awareness, a wild temptation that unfurled in him like a banner. A silent, echoing cry. "Naomi—"

Her eyes lit. "Shut up, Mr. Clarke."

He did. The instant she leaned forward and fused her mouth to his, he had nothing left to say. Control be damned. Barely leashed desire detonated in his head, shredded every trace of common sense as heat spiraled from her lips to his. Her free hand fisted in his collar, captured him close as her mouth opened, beckoned.

Aggressive. Demanding. She was all that and something a thousand times more primal as her tongue swept into his mouth; the velvet stroke of her tongue slid against his and he surged forward, slammed her back against the rough bag.

Phin wasn't going to stand there and let her think she had him. Even if she did.

Even if he knew he'd already lost.

The impact rocked them closer together, threatened to knock them over until she braced her legs against the floor and pushed back against the swaying bag.

He stepped into the welcoming vee of her legs, trapped her against his chest, his hips, the hard edge of his erection. Perfect, spiraling focus, a point of pleasure so intense he could only revel in the mind-shattering heat of her body, the soft curves compounded by elastic muscle.

Just the feel of her, the scent of her damp skin, was enough.

Enough to scream a warning. To wave red flags in his mind's eye. "Jesus," he managed, his voice strained as she tore her mouth from his. Naomi's laughter drifted like smoke over his jaw, his neck. Her hips tilted, ground against him, and Phin groaned as he seized her waist.

Too hot. Too fast.

He hadn't wanted to push her.

Taut with the effort, his hands strained against every impulse to haul her closer. To pull her into his skin and burn them both up to ash. She had to slow down, *he* had to slow down before she stroked him right into an explosive orgasm he wasn't prepared for.

But Naomi wasn't letting him play nice.

The sharp edge of her teeth bit a line of fire into the skin of his neck. He gasped, pleasure and pain combined into a wild surge of need. "Naomi—"

"No," she murmured. She lifted her head, pulled her fingers through his hair to meet his gaze with a glittering need of her own. She twisted, throwing a leg over his thigh. His hips jerked of their own accord, and he gritted his teeth. Locked every muscle.

Just the press of her body. Jesus, just the demand, her laughter. Unable to help himself, he slid his palms up the sleek heat of her flat belly. Her ribs. He found the edge of her cropped tank top, worked underneath to encircle one constrained breast.

She filled his hand perfectly. Her nipple peaked hard into his palm, and he groaned. Her breath hissed out from between her teeth.

Phin found his hands full of ice and fire, of silk and steel. All the conundrums he didn't know how to tame, not right now.

Maybe not ever.

She curved into his body like he was the last thing she'd ever need, and the heady combination of hazy violet eyes and the beckoning pulse of her body against him was too much.

Too damn fast.

He dragged her hips upward, pushed her higher against the bag. The slick material of her athletic shorts glided like water over him. The juncture of her legs slid over the hard length of his pulsing, desperately hard cock, and she rode him, legs wrapped hard around his waist. Rode him as if their clothes didn't exist, as if she could drag herself over him and feed on the shudders of sensation between them both.

It was torture. It was hell.

It was pure heaven.

Naomi gasped, her cheeks flushed, back arching. Her fingers knotted in the mesh netting that kept the athletic bag supported, kept her supported against it. Gone with lust, with the crazy intoxication of her scent, her sounds, Jesus, her own sexual madness, Phin angled her body, dragged her over him again.

And again.

Her body trembled. Tightened under his hands. She threw her head back, eyes clenched shut. Pink swept across her chest, across her shoulders, her throat. He felt her desperate release build in the tension surging beneath her skin.

Curling one hand around the back of her neck, his fingers brushing against the hot metal beads she hid so well, Phin jerked her away from the bag. He pressed her face to his shoulder and gritted his teeth as her wild, muffled cry washed over him, as she went rigid against him. Around him, locked hip to hip.

He was, he reflected as he braced himself against the rough bag behind her, a complete masochist.

For a long moment there was only the sound of her breathing. Of his muted heartbeat thundering against his ribs. It matched hers, beat for beat. Slam for slam.

She stirred.

Naomi's legs uncurled from around his waist. Pliant, fluid, she eased her taped feet back to the floor and pushed her damp hair from her face. She smiled languidly, as satisfied as a cat surrounded by defenseless canaries.

"Well," she said, casual as the wind. "That was nice."

"Oh, no." Phin caught her arm when she shifted, held it when he could read her intent to escape as easily as if she'd announced it.

She glanced at his hand, measuring it. Her gaze turned curious, amused, as it flicked back to his. "What?"

"It's not going to end here."

Amusement faded. Her lashes narrowed, a thick line of edged black. "Oh?"

"Yeah." Phin let her go, slowly, and stepped back from the maddening feel of her body before he pushed it one limit too far and made a mess of himself.

Naomi stretched languorously, those sleek muscles moving like silk under her skin. Her arms locked over her head, her back arched in sinuous challenge. "What makes you think I'm interested in anything else?"

With need, the temptation of her battering at his unfulfilled body, Phin wasn't going to play her game. Not now.

Later. After he'd taken care of the erection practically begging for attention under his shorts. He flashed a smile he knew would annoy her. Easy, knowing.

The kind of smile that said, *I've seen you come and loved every second of it.*

Her smile faltered. Her lips parted on a small, almost imperceptible breath.

One point for him.

Laughter split through the gym, the isolated contest of wills, and shredded the small pocket of silence around them. Naomi stiffened, her gaze jerking suddenly over his shoulder. Phin glanced behind him to watch a handful of day-trippers enter the far entrance. Each carried towels and complimentary water bottles.

They chattered and teased one another. None of them spared more than a glance toward Naomi and

Phin. Phin grinned at the sudden wary tension that ratcheted her body.

He leaned forward, handed her the water bottle she'd dropped around the same time she'd kissed him stupid. "Guess we'll have to be more careful next time," he murmured in her ear.

Naomi drove an elbow into his chest. "Next time, my ass," she hissed.

She sidestepped him, shoulders rigid as he laughed softly at her back. "You can run, Naomi."

She didn't acknowledge the threat.

Phin didn't pretend it was anything else but.

CHAPTER SEVEN

Ten minutes of ice-cold water was more punishment than any man should suffer for a woman. Shivering, Phin turned off the shower and thought it wasn't *nearly* as terrible as what he was doing to himself.

Lusting after a guest? Check.

Lusting after a guest he suspected had more baggage than she let on? Check.

Acting on it anyway? That was the kicker.

But there was something about Naomi that pulled on every nerve, every sense he possessed. He wanted to like her. He wanted to help her.

And, he admitted in silent aggravation, he wanted to peel her out of that facade of cool, calculated amusement that she wore like a goddamn mask.

He wanted her eyes dark and clouded with passion, not wariness. Her mouth gasping his name.

"Whoa," Phin muttered, and ground a fist into his eyes until he couldn't count the pulse in his crotch anymore. A cold shower wasn't going to help if he just kept at it.

Deliberately he slid the shower stall open and reached for a towel as he thought about the day's notes. He'd made it as far as the repairs scheduled for the sauna tomorrow when the comm unit he'd tossed carelessly to the counter vibrated itself onto the floor with a clatter.

Hurriedly, wrapping the towel around his dripping waist, he scrambled to collect it before the caller hung up.

"Wait a minute." He fumbled with the earpiece, swore, and gave up when it slipped through his slick fingers. He pressed the speaker to his wet ear instead. "Phin Clarke. How can I help you?"

"Firstly"—Gemma's voice all but vibrated the line with amusement—"you're nowhere to be found mid-afternoon. Now, either you've managed to entangle yourself with someone quite pretty for the moment—"

He winced. "No."

"—or you're hiding," she finished on a chuckle. "As the lovely Jordana has just now entered the dining floor, I'm going to lean toward the latter."

Phin shifted the comm to his other ear, snagging a hand towel from its neat rack to blot at his dripping hair. "Jordana would eat me alive, Mother, and you know it." He sighed, knowing it for the long-suffering sound it was. "Neither. I was tired from being up all night with the technicians, so I took a quick shower to wake up."

"You poor dear," Gemma crooned, suddenly nothing but contrite. "Are you doing all right now?"

Feeling only a little twinge of guilt, he said simply, "Foggy around the edges, but fine, Mother, don't worry about me. Is there a *secondly* in there somewhere?"

"What? Oh! Yes, there is."

A beat. Phin grinned, quickly raking a comb through his hair. "And it would be?"

"Family meeting."

The comb slid through his fingers and clattered to the counter. Phin grabbed at it, missed, and sent it spiraling into the sink. Biting back a sound of irritation, he focused on the comm instead. "When? Where?"

"Soon as you can make it to your mother's office, dear."

Phin grimaced. "I'll be there in ten minutes."

Gemma hummed a farewell, disconnecting the call before Phin could shake the water off the small screen.

He dressed quickly, left his suite tidy and dry behind him. Within the ten minutes he'd promised, he made it to the floors tucked underneath the public levels and entered Lillian's office.

Two sets of speculative eyes greeted his arrival.

Lillian perched one hip on the rich rosewood desk, her suit tailored to chic simplicity. The muted plum color brought out a diamond shine in her golden hair, made her eyes look luminous gold and green. Beside her, Gemma sat in the matching chair, one hand threaded loosely with Lillian's, palm to palm.

Lillian's eyebrow arched in regal Hollywood flair. "Exactly on time."

Phin shut the door behind him, ruefully spread his hands. "What did I do now?"

"Nothing." Gemma grinned, revealing the dimples she'd passed on to him. "I think."

"Gemma."

The woman smothered her amusement at Lillian's murmured warning, clearing her throat. "Right, well, let's get right to it."

"Have a seat, my love," Lillian added, inclining her perfectly coiffed head toward one of the two chairs arrayed before the desk.

Feeling a little like a boy called before the dean, Phin sat. "All right." He sighed. "But this had better have everything to do with the accident, and not the ongoing discussion of my love life."

"Or lack—" Gemma clamped her mouth under Lillian's warning squeeze. He didn't miss the flex of his mother's fingers, the shift of her beautiful eyes. "It does," she said instead.

"I filled your mother in," Lillian explained, her tone crisp. Professional.

Down to business, after all. Phin straightened. "The sauna accident looks targeted, but it makes no sense." He rubbed at his jaw idly. "It's no accident, that's clear. The good news here is that the technicians can get it fixed within three days, if the parts are available."

The women exchanged a glance, worry and relief tangled.

"What?" He frowned. "What's going on?"

"Maybe nothing," Gemma said, only to smile wanly as Lillian stated, "Your mother has a concern."

"Oh, no." Phin pinched the bridge of his nose between two fingers. "No, no, I don't want to hear that."

"Maybe it's nothing," Gemma repeated, rising. Her bow-shaped mouth intent, she put her hands on her hips and frowned fiercely at them both, lines drawn between her dark eyebrows. "It seems so random, so out of the blue. I can't believe it was just about poor Alexandra."

Lillian adjusted the sleeve of her jacket. Sharp, tight movements. Frustration. He knew the signs, knew each woman as well as he knew himself.

Both were worried, antsy.

Phin rubbed at the edge of his nose, but it didn't soothe the ache forming behind his forehead. What did they all have to go on? Nothing. One nearly fatal accident.

Damn it.

"What about Naomi Ishikawa?"

Phin jerked his head toward Lillian. His eyes narrowed. "What about her?"

"Who is she, really?" She tapped her long, unpainted nails on the desk in a sharp staccato. "What do we know about her?"

"Lily, you don't think—"

Phin cut them both off, rising to his feet with a surge of sudden, angry energy. "Naomi has nothing to do with any of this."

Lillian frowned, a deep furrow of her carefully penciled-in eyebrows. "No," she said, shaking her head. "I don't know what your involvement with that woman is—"

"I'm not—"

"—but you can't afford to look at this with anything else but impartiality," she finished in neat, clipped tones, overriding him as easily as if he'd never spoken.

He bit back an angry retort. Mouth tight with the effort, he turned and studied the gilt-patterned wallpaper that lent the office a warm, old-fashioned touch. He knew he looked sulky, like a kid caught with candy in his pocket before dinner, but if he unfolded his arms now, they'd know he knew it.

And he wasn't ready to explain why he thought Naomi was in the clear.

Why he *wanted* her to be.

A warm, gentle hand slid over his shoulder. Down his back. "Phin," Gemma said softly. "Baby. We mean well."

"For you," Lillian said firmly, "and for Timeless. We have too much at stake here, Phin, you know that."

"I know." He took another deep breath, a solid inhale. Let it out slowly. He turned, wrapped both arms around Gemma's shoulders, and rested his chin on top of her curls. He met Lillian's gaze across the room.

It killed him to see her eyes soften so much. Warmed him to see them brim with the love he'd spent his life immersed in.

Despite his worry, he smiled. "I know, Mother, and I'm sorry. Naomi Ishikawa," he continued quickly before she could say anything, "is a woman desperately in need of some relaxation time, but I don't think she's wired enough to pull something like the sauna stunt."

"Actually, I agree." Gemma laced her fingers around his forearms, her hair tickling his chin as she shook her head. "She isn't the patient sort, and whatever that was, it needed patience. I suspect that Miss Ishikawa is much more inclined toward something face-to-face. Her nose," she added dryly, "makes that clear."

"Not to mention," Phin pointed out, "she came from her suite before all of it happened, and she hadn't checked in early enough to do any wiring herself."

Mouth pursing in thought, Lillian stared past them for a long, silent moment.

"Lily?"

"I can't shake the feeling that something is very off about her," Lillian said flatly. She braced her weight on one hand, fingers flattened on the desk. It was as close to a slump as he'd ever seen her get. "I don't trust her, not completely."

"I don't, either," Phin said in quiet agreement. It bothered him to say it, to acknowledge it. "But it wasn't her."

"I like her." Gemma tipped her head up just enough to smile up at Phin, squeezing his arms affectionately. "She's hurt, and I don't think she's entirely whole, but I like her."

Suddenly feeling like a particularly interesting butterfly pinned to a wall, Phin grimaced. "Can we get back to the part where this isn't about me?"

"Oh, stop." Gemma laughed, swatting at his cheek.

"But he's right," Lillian added. She smoothed long fingers over her chignon, tucking in tendrils that didn't need tucking. Nerves.

Phin sobered. "Mother, what can we do?"

"I've had the staff informed to keep watch for anything out of the ordinary," she replied. Her elegant mouth twisted. "At my request, security has begun a thorough study of the in-house feeds."

"What about the secret halls?" Phin straightened, frowning. "Joel knows about them, as does the extraction team, but we've been careful."

"Nobody else knows about the secret halls," Gemma assured him. "The blueprints were destroyed shortly after the building was finished."

"As far as we know," Lillian murmured. But the tension slowly eased out of her. Inch by inch. "Mr. Barker is thorough and has proved to be more than discreet."

Phin nodded. "Does he have help?"

"Yes, however, none of the temporary staff is involved." Lillian smiled halfheartedly. "I know you mean well by these people you're rescuing, Phin, but this is too delicate a situation to allow them to meddle in."

He winced. "They wouldn't meddle," he began, and subsided when Gemma's fingers tightened at his wrists. He dropped his chin to her hair again. Rubbed it gently back and forth.

She smelled like the lavender she used to scent the soaps for the spa. It calmed him enough to say mildly, "Okay, that's fine. No temporary help. We've already cut down to a bare crew of them anyway, and we can't rush the refugees any faster than we have to. Any undue suspicion now will alert the gate guards and bring the Church on our heads worse than it may be already."

"All right." Lillian rubbed the back of her neck with stiff fingers. "I am so proud of what you do, Phin, we both are. I want you to know that."

Warmth bloomed in his chest. Adoration, gratitude. Love.

And suspicion. The set of her expression warned him there was more. "But," he prompted.

"No buts," Gemma interjected. She stepped out from his embrace, shaking her head. "Just that. We're proud of you. There are entire families who wouldn't be where they are without your help. You've given them hope, found them homes out where everyone was so sure there'd be none."

"People are industrious," Phin replied simply. "The accused we help are willing to work hard. They'll make it."

"And they do," Gemma said earnestly. "I just know they're out there happy and well."

Jaw working, Lillian fell silent.

Phin crossed the room, ignored her perfect polish to wrap his arms around her shoulders. "I love you, too."

"Oh, Phin." Lillian's hands splayed over his back, rubbed gently. "Just be careful," she said into his chest. "Gemma isn't the only mother with a concern."

Gemma threw her arms around them both, and Phin shifted to let her into the circle. Holding the most important women in the world, he breathed in their mingled scents and perfume, wrapped himself in the warmth of their love, and wished to hell he was the only one up at night.

Worrying was what this family did best.

Pressing a kiss to each warm cheek, Phin promised, "I'll be careful, and I'll keep an ear to the ground." He looked down at them both, met hazel eyes and sweet brown. "Promise me that neither of you will do anything rash."

"Of course," Lillian said, amusement like a spark of

gold in her suddenly crinkled gaze. "Have I ever done anything rash?"

"Never." Phin gave them both a final squeeze, stepped away. "I'll get to work on the underground now. If you need me, I'm in comm reach."

Gemma smiled ruefully. "You always are. In the meantime, keep a close eye on Naomi, all right?"

Lillian's smile went crooked. "Is that for our safety or his interests?"

"Mother," Phin groaned, and waved both hands in surrender. "Fine, I'll stay close by her."

"Like it'd kill him." Gemma chuckled as he turned away.

Phin left them, good-natured aggravation melting into too many logistics, too many problems, and a rapidly sinking sensation that time was slipping away. He had a cargo of people to move out too soon after the last, and he'd have to do it without raising eyebrows.

Behind him, the women watched the door click shut. For a long moment, neither spoke.

Then Gemma shifted back into Lillian's embrace. "Nothing rash," she said, lacing her fingers loosely at her wife's hip. "Besides defying your glitterati family and eloping with a mid-city whor—"

Lillian seized Gemma's mouth in her fingers, pinching her lips closed with a frown as unbending as steel. "Don't you dare, Gemma Clarke," she said fiercely. "Those were their words, never mine. Never, ever yours."

Gemma's lips moved. Curved upward as she pressed a kiss to Lillian's fingertips. "I love you," she murmured. "I wouldn't change anything for the world."

"Neither would I, Gem." Lillian allowed herself to sink against Gemma's supporting embrace, into the soft curves of the body she was so fortunate to hold every night. To admire every morning. "Two aging women. What will the world do with us?"

"Screw the world," Gemma said smartly, and Lillian laughed. "Everything will be fine, love." Smoothing one hand over Lillian's long, slender back, Gemma nuzzled her hair. "We're safe here. Phin is strong and capable—"

"He takes after his mother."

"Both of them." Gemma captured the other woman's chin in her fingers, tilted Lillian's face up, and smiled with everything that was so classically Gemma. Adoration. Warmth. Love.

The light of the world.

"Timeless will stand long after we're gone, Lily." Gemma touched her mouth to hers, a kiss as sweet and gentle as summer sunshine. Lillian's skin warmed. Her heart swelled.

It almost drowned the worries feasting at her soul. Almost.

"Will Timeless matter?" Lillian reached up, threaded her fingers tightly with Gemma's. "When you're gone, will it matter?"

"I don't know." Her grip tight in Lillian's, Gemma's smile widened. "But I'm in no hurry to find out."

"Thank God. I don't know what we'd do without you, anyway."

CHAPTER EIGHT

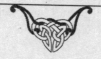

Bzzzt!

Blood faded to moonlight, dreams to wide-eyed consciousness as the comm unit buzzed a warning in her slack hand. Naomi braced herself on one arm, already fumbling with the earpiece before her brain kicked in.

"What?" she growled, her voice thick and heavy with sleep. "What the hell time is it?"

There was a pause. A muffled cough. "It's only ten."

"Fuck." She dropped face-first back into the pillow, inhaled lavender and detergent, and threw herself off the mattress. She landed on her feet, barely, but she had to catch herself on the nightstand. It rattled, its lone lamp teetering dangerously. "Fuck! What? Do you want?"

"Grumpy."

"Jonas," Naomi snapped, catching the porcelain lamp with one splayed hand. "I will kill you. Do you hear me? I will break your skull like a—" She frowned. "Where's Eckhart?"

"Hunting down leads."

"For me?"

"No, unrelated. Different case entirely. Or it's a lie to visit some chick," he added with brief, clipped amusement. Over a comm line, Jonas Stone's voice was impossible to mistake. Nobody else pulled as clear a tenor.

Or as lighthearted a check-in.

She rubbed the sleep grit from her eyes, rough gouges that did nothing to pull the remnants of nightmares from her mind. "Great," she muttered, knowing she sounded bitchy and unable to care. "Why are you calling me?"

"Why are you sleeping?"

Because she was a goddamn coward. Naomi's mouth curled. "Because I spent all day being *pretty*."

"Uh." The line hummed with a short, charged silence. "What?"

"Never mind." Naomi turned, studying the dimly lit room through slitted, burning eyes. "I came up here to change and must have passed out. I was tired."

"Hey?" A cautious question. Gentle. "Are you all right in there?"

Damn.

Of all the people at the Mission, of the missionaries who spent more time going than coming, Jonas Stone saw more than he needed to. Knew more than he should have.

It pissed her the hell off. She'd always felt as if he . . . *handled* her. He was the one confined to crutches for life, and he handled her.

"I'm fine," she said, assurance clipped. "I was just tired. Now that you've gotten me up, I can get back to work."

"How about a report, then?"

Naomi fought the urge to drop her face into the nearest pillow and stay there. A week sounded good. "Fine," she muttered, and told him about Alexandra Applegate.

Amid the clatter of Jonas's quick typing, he whistled. "Wasn't expecting that."

"Care to explain why no one told me the bishop's grandmother was in here?" she growled. "Pertinent fucking information, don't you think?"

"I'm sorry, that was my fault." The remorse in his voice effectively stomped on her roiling temper. She grimaced. "But I swear to God, Nai, I didn't know she was there. I can't get to the guest files."

"Why?"

Jonas sighed. "The whole block is on its own closed loop. Nothing in, nothing out. Timeless doesn't even tap into the city feeds."

"Fuck, really?" She jammed a thumb into her left eye and rubbed until the ache in her head faded to a dull roar. "This operation is the shittiest . . ." She paused. A glint of light pierced the bedroom window, the faintest flicker. "Hang on."

"What's going on?"

"Shut it." Naomi approached the window quietly, well aware that she was a few hundred feet above anything that could see her through reflective glass. Still, she sidled in at an angle, her shoulders pressed back against the wall as she bent to scan the ground seventeen stories below.

She squinted. "The city elevator is moving."

Computer keys tapped rapidly over the line. "Which one?"

"Main line. It's the showy one that links the place to the city streets." She leaned close to the glass and hissed out a curse.

"What?"

"I can't see worth shit up here. Jonas, damn it, tell me someone packed me some binoculars."

"I'll do you one better." Pride licked through the comm. "Check the patchwork purse."

"What?"

"Your bags, Nai. Look for a multicolored purse in your luggage."

"The rainbow one," she said, and grimaced when he hummed assent.

Naomi backtracked quickly, stumbling over clothes and discarded shoes she hadn't gotten around to putting away yet. Neither had anyone else. Aside from one overly competent witch, Timeless took privacy seriously.

She skidded on something silky, slipped and caught herself on one hand and both knees. She grunted.

"What was that?"

"Nothing." She searched through piles of useless shit for the big, chunky purse that she'd sworn she wasn't taking anywhere. The thing practically glowed, bright patches of gleaming, metallic material. Easy to find in the dark, too.

Naomi swiped it up from its nest of carelessly discarded luggage, yanked open the snap, and searched the inside.

Wallet of some kind, silk scarves, sunglasses— Jesus, how many sunglasses did one woman need? And underneath it all, a small, solid case. "What, this?"

Amusement colored his tone as he replied, "Given I'm not with you, Naomi, I'm going to assume you know what binoculars are."

Naomi snapped the case open and frowned. "They're tiny."

"They're interchangeable between light and night vision," he retorted, "and they're reticule-sized."

"They're *what*-sized?"

"Hell on toast, woman, just try them."

She hurried back to the window. Praying she wasn't too late, Naomi lifted the binoculars to her eyes. The world slammed into sudden, razor-sharp clarity. "No shit!"

"Great, aren't they?"

Naomi couldn't help but grin fiercely as she picked out every last detail on the ground beneath her. Visual cues flashed; stark green contours that shifted around each identifiable object as she changed targets. Text scrolled past the bottom of her vision, each shape and focal point neatly cataloged within the lenses.

"Its processing is fairly limited, but the onboard chip'll recognize most basic shapes," Jonas explained smugly. "Who loves you, babe?"

"Everyone." His snort echoed in Naomi's earpiece as she trained the lenses on the ground. The elevator doors slid open, easing wide as the locking panels lifted.

"What are you seeing?"

Her grin faded. A skinny figure clambered out of the elevator, two heavy bags over his shoulders.

"Naomi?"

"The boy that runs the elevator," she said slowly. "Nice kid. He's carrying bags."

Jonas clicked his tongue. "Sounds like a late-night guest."

"Looks like it." Naomi watched, adjusting the piece in her ear with one finger. "Listen, this op is a hell of a lot more complicated than we thought."

"Why? What happened?"

Anger sizzled over her skin as she muttered, "Witches."

On the ground, another figure left the elevator. A woman, Naomi realized, with a scarf around her head and sunglasses as large as her face perched on her nose, even in the dark. She swept down the walk, and Naomi grimaced as she recognized the attitude that swept right beside her.

A guest, all right. One of the so important elite.

"Wait a second," Jonas was saying in her ear. "Witches? Are you serious?"

"Yeah." The word edged out of her chest, a disgusted sigh. "Someone was waiting for me when I got here. Sneaked in behind me and laid in with magic before I'd even settled."

"Carson?"

"Nope. Different guy," Naomi said, raising the binoculars again, "He should have killed me."

"Man, don't say that."

"Mmm." Naomi's eyes narrowed as she tracked the

woman's attendants. Four more men stepped out of the elevator, three of them carrying two or more bags.

And they thought Naomi had baggage.

"So you got him?" Jonas prodded.

"No," she replied. "I had him dead to rights and he pretty much went balls out. By the time I got off the floor, he'd made a clean getaway."

He sucked in a breath.

Her smile clipped, Naomi redirected the binoculars to the end of the path, aiming them toward the wide doors that welcomed guests to the lobby. The light spilling out of the building formed a corona of neon radiance, but she picked out the silhouette of someone waiting. A concierge, maybe. Another woman.

"How do you zoom in on this thing?" she asked, ignoring the strangled sound of Jonas's impatience. "I need to see who's at the door."

"Holy crow, Naomi," he said tightly. "There's a witch in there and you let him get away?"

She hesitated. "For now," she admitted. "He caught me off guard, but he won't stay hidden for long. Zoom?"

"There's a toggle on the top. Seriously," he urged quietly. "No shitting me, here. Are you okay?"

"Yeah." Under her searching forefinger, a bit of metal shifted. The device thrummed soundlessly, and in the space of a heartbeat, the concierge's face filled the lenses. Naomi committed her to memory. Blond, tall, elegantly suited, and smiling.

She rolled her shoulder, but it didn't ease the pinch of tension in her neck. "The seal did its thing, but he got in close enough to almost lay me out. It's just a knot on the back of my head. Sloppy as hell. So, did Eckhart tell you about my gun?"

Jonas's teeth clicked together; all too familiar a sound on the end of her comm feed. "Naomi—"

She jerked her head, glaring at the comm she'd left on the bed. "I'm *still* a missionary, Stone," she said tersely.

Over the earpiece, he took a breath. Then, sighing, he gave in. "Yeah, Alan told me. I'll see what we can do. We can't get in there, so you'll have to get out to retrieve it."

"I can get you in."

"Nope. We've got our orders."

"Shitfuck," she muttered. Politics. "Fine, I'll manage something." Below, as the woman stepped into the light pouring from the open door, she watched the concierge greet her warmly, take both her hands, and kiss the air beside each cheek.

She hated that fucking affectation. It was the first thing she'd ever learned from a mother too petrified a dirty child would smear her makeup.

"You're so ladylike," Jonas drawled. "Have you made any other progress?"

"No." She wasn't going to go into detail about the ghost in the locker room. Not until she had details to give. Distracted, she watched as neon green lines traced each figure below. Like a constantly shifting computer screen, visual patterns flared and vanished from her sight. Lowering the device shut off the processor.

She raised the binoculars again and blinked at the terminology suddenly flashing in the lower right of her vision. "Couldn't you come up with a better term than *life form*?"

"It seemed only right."

"Christ, you're a nerd. Jonas, why the hell am I— *Shit*." Amusement leached out of her as a fist of sudden adrenaline spiked through her chest. "Where did he go?"

"Who?"

"Three porters." Naomi straightened, bracing one hand on the glass as she swung the binoculars back along the lit walkway. "Three, god damn it, where's the fourth?"

"Naomi? What are you talking about?"

A flicker of movement at the northeast corner of the rocky courtyard had her swearing as a door she'd never noticed before eased shut, sealing in a thin seam of light. "This place," she gritted out between clenched teeth. "I hate this fucking place. There's hidden doors built into the goddamn wall."

"Did the guest use one?"

"No." She swung the binoculars back to the woman and her entourage of Timeless staff. "She probably didn't even notice one of the help disappear. I'm going to go locate this sneaky bastard and see what he knows."

"Sure," Jonas said. "Be careful."

Seventeen floors below, the woman removed her sunglasses, sliding them into her purse as she turned the full force of a megawatt smile on the concierge.

"Get me those blueprints before— Oh, God." Naomi's voice cracked.

Green light caught on the woman's white scarf, flared, and Naomi snatched the binoculars away. Threw them as if she could erase the face lovingly shaped by the light of the resort lobby.

"Naomi?" Jonas's voice, tense in her ear. "Naomi, what's going on? What's happening?"

"I—" Her lungs seized. Wrenched.

"Naomi!"

Shit. Shit, she couldn't breathe. "I'll be in touch for the gun," she managed. She dropped the line, cut him off mid-question as she struggled to pull oxygen into her chest. She raised one shaking hand to the glass.

The lobby's golden glow turned into a streamlined seam of light as the doors slid closed on the last of Abigail Ishikawa's entourage.

The comm vibrated on the mattress behind her. She ignored it. Jerked the earpiece from her ear and tossed it to the bedspread beside it. Shaking, every muscle taut, Naomi sank to the floor under the window and struggled to inhale. She hugged her knees tightly to her chest.

She was here. Abigail Ishikawa, in the flesh. Twenty-four years of nothing but locked-down memories, and now her mother had come to Timeless. To her.

But not for her.

Never *for* her.

And God only knew what name the woman used now.

City lights streamed through the glass, a faded glow that picked out the pretty, rumpled covers over the bed. The mess of clothes and accessories on the floor at the foot of it.

But she didn't see any of that. Not here, as her eyes burned with fury, with the memories she'd never wanted to keep.

A crackling fire, cheerfully blazing from within a polished mahogany mantel. No pictures lined the gleaming wood. She'd always remembered that. No happy childhood photos. No signs that any of them had ever existed.

The orange glow filled every inch of the cozy, book-lined study. Katsu Ishikawa wasn't a reading man, but the books lent him an air of intelligent sophistication. He enjoyed feeling the age of the text around him, knowing they held words to civilizations long since buried.

To a five-year-old, he was the smartest man in the world. The only person who truly loved her. Who understood her.

The only parent of two who had wanted her.

And the woman who had never wanted her had just stepped into the lobby of New Seattle's premier resort and spa.

Naomi jammed a fist in her mouth as she fought back the rising tide of panic. She sucked in air through her nose, pried open her eyes to stare at the dark bedroom that was nothing like that penthouse so long ago.

It didn't matter.

She blew out a breath. Took in another. Longer. Stronger.

It didn't fucking matter. In. Out.

Her skin prickled, tingling pinpricks that danced over her face and hands. She breathed, struggling for it, fighting for it.

Naomi slammed her head back against the wall. It shuddered. The glass rattled. "No," she gritted out. Pain radiated from the bruise there, swamped the synapses trying so hard to fry her into hysteria. She clenched her teeth, fisted her fingers.

She inhaled, held it, and launched herself to her feet. She didn't have time to be broken. The room swam around her, walls taut and hemming her in as she struggled to maintain her balance. Her fingertips tingled, the skin of her face prickling as if a swarm of bees converged on her skin, but she dashed her forearm over her eyes and stalked to the elevator.

Focus.

The man who had vanished had been about five feet and six inches. Hundred and seventy pounds, she guessed, forcing her brain to engage. Her nails bit into her palms as she stared at the indifferent panel of the elevator door. Maybe one hundred and sixty.

Pain fragmented through her chest. She ignored it.

The sneak had been a porter, or at least someone familiar enough to go unnoticed by the rest of the staff. Carson? No, too short.

The witch? He seemed similar enough. Did he have the run of the place?

Could it be all of this fucking prison's people were in on this mess?

In on Carson's plot, or witches?

Were they the same problem? Had Naomi stumbled on a nest of covert witches? A new coven?

Damn it.

She swallowed back an aftershock of anxiety, locking her jaw around the rapid pulse of panic simmering under her skin.

A minute. She needed just a minute, and then she'd call the elevator. The last thing she needed was some other sympathetic guest asking after her well-being. Gossiping about her.

Worse, she didn't need rumors getting back to Phin.

His face appeared entirely too easily in her mind; eyes dark as chocolate, sweet as sin. The memory of Phin's smile dragged over her raw nerves like a physical caress, and Naomi jammed her fists against her eyes until they burned.

She'd been stupid to tease him like that. To cross that boundary and let the easy confidence he wore so well eat away at her control until she'd fallen to abstract pieces in sheer pleasure.

She'd been stupid, but she wasn't wrong. The family sure as hell wouldn't risk their own affluent business harboring witches, or assassinating Alexandra Applegate under their own roof. The man liked his designer suits too damn much.

The plain silver door slid open on a hiss of released compression. Blearily, working on automatic, she reached for the guest card tucked into the waistband of her rumpled pants.

Then remembered she hadn't punched the call button.

A circle of blue light seared the skin of her abdomen.

"Jesus—" She whirled to the side, danced back from the stocky man who launched himself out of the elevator at her. His fingers closed on her skin, grasped wildly as she wrenched away.

He didn't need contact to make it hurt.

Naomi's smile was all teeth. "Fancy meeting you here."

He thrust out a callused hand, and she focused on the faint brown lines etched into his palm. Magic seared the air. Invisible, it skipped over her skin like a thousand tiny stingers, and the seal blazed in answer, beating away the intrusion. Blue light poured from the mesh fabric of her pants.

The tattoo burned like a bitch when it repelled witch-craft. Too much pain.

Teeth bared, he stalked toward her, forcing her to stagger back toward the bedroom. Less room. She wanted him cornered. "Who the hell are you?" she demanded.

The witch didn't give her time to put distance between them. He closed on her. Ate up the carpeted floor beneath his workman boots and left her backpedaling too fast for balance. She tried to dodge, tried to think through whatever magic that fucking tattoo of his wove.

He lunged at her; she wrenched back. Too slow. One broad palm slammed into her stomach and she buckled.

Her head. The seal. Her back as she collided into the sharp edge of sliding door between sitting room and bedroom. Her vision went supernova through the pain infecting the inside of her brain.

She gritted her teeth as one large hand fisted in the front of her athletic tank. "Witch hunters," he growled, yanking her away from the supporting panel. His eyes filled her vision, snapping blue. He walked her backward, into the bedroom. "The only thing keeping you alive right now is the fucking tattoo you all wear."

She bared her teeth. "That's what you think."

"Won't matter for long."

He punched like a goddamn tank.

Naomi spun with the momentum of fist to face, pain exploding across her nose. The scab split, cracking like so much brittle meat, and blood splattered across the elegant dupioni comforter as she crashed into the mattress and rebounded.

The pressure of his magic eased, ebbed for a split second. She hit the floor, rolled away, and leaped to her feet before he could catch her again. Blue light flickered against the dim interior. Reflected in the witch's bottomless blue eyes.

"What do you want?" she demanded. Buy time. She needed to get him away from the absorbent carpet.

Blood was a pain in the ass to hide.

He flung out a hand, and the angry buzz of oncoming magic filled her head again. "Doesn't matter what I want," he replied tersely. "The boss says you're toast."

"Boss?"

His fingers splayed, and for a split second, Naomi swore that the faint brown lines of his odd tattoo blistered red.

She squinted through the pressure squeezing her head. "Who sent you?"

"Who sent *you?*"

Fuck. Her heels slid on the pile of scattered clothing. Naomi caught herself against the bathroom doorjamb and blinked the stinging slide of sweat from her eyes. Blood glided over her upper lip, hot and metallic.

"Oh-kay," she said, mouth curling into a razored smile. "Fine." She wasn't going to play this game any longer than she had to.

On the scale of things, he wasn't the strongest witch she'd ever faced.

"You want me, you son of a bitch, come and get me."

He bull-rushed her. The stupid ones always did.

CHAPTER NINE

"Excuse me, Mr. Clarke?"

Phin looked up from the computer monitor he stared at, gaze focusing slowly on Cally Simmons. She leaned in through his open office door. Quickly he rearranged bemused inquiry into a welcoming smile and surreptitiously checked his tie to make sure he hadn't dropped any of his hastily inhaled tea on it.

He'd been up even before most of the kitchen staff. Breakfast had been every man for himself.

Cally's smile tipped crookedly as she stepped inside. "Is now a good time?"

"Of course," he replied. "Come on, have a seat. How are you?"

Besides tired, which he noted in the bruised color beneath her dark green eyes. Was she sleeping? Not well, by all the signs.

"Fine, thanks," she said, sinking into a chair. "I just wondered if I could . . . talk to you for a second."

That sounded ominous. He straightened, devoting the whole of his attention to the worried shape of her features. "What can I do for you?"

"I don't want to make any trouble," she began, and he smiled reassuringly.

"Nothing you say will make it past this office, okay?"

She pushed back her bangs from her eyes. "It's just that I really appreciate what you're doing for me, and I'm not trying to be a hassle. Agatha said not to bother you with this."

"Did she, now?" Phin leaned back in his chair, rapidly assessing the woman. She met his gaze with a forthright sincerity that impressed him.

She was a hard worker. Bright, fairly confident, and easy to work with. He'd never caught her making excuses. He liked her. And he trusted her, as far as temporaries went.

Admittedly, given he had exactly four of them left on his roster, that trust didn't extend too far.

He rubbed at his jaw. "What is it, Cally?"

She hesitated. "You know Mark?"

"Offhand, I know three," Phin replied with a wry smile designed to put her at ease. "Which floor?"

"Maintenance."

"Mark Vaughn, yes."

Cally clasped her hands, tucking them between her knees. "He's gone, sir."

"What do you mean?"

"He never showed up for his shift," she explained. "I only know because I was upstairs in the dining floor when Agatha came to talk to a few of the others about it. I heard her say that he's never late."

Phin didn't know the older man well, but he knew enough to agree with the assessment. Mark Vaughn was a new hire, but he hadn't missed so much as a minute of work since signing on three weeks ago. He'd had a stellar application, no triggers on his background check. Not much for talking, but he was a good man for fixing just about anything.

Agatha had recommended him after he'd fixed her apartment water heater. And now he was missing? Phin resisted the urge to pinch the bridge of his nose.

"Mr. Clarke, I know this isn't normal, but . . ." Cally's teeth flashed as she sank them into her bottom lip. Again, in a move he recognized as telling concern, she pushed at the fringe of red hair hanging over her eyes.

She was nervous.

Phin reached out to touch the desk in front of her, as carefully as if he were offering a hand to a spooked stray. "Cally," he said gently. "It's all right. Whatever is on your mind, you can tell me."

Her smile flipped crooked. "It's probably nothing, but I thought I should tell you that I've felt a little uneasy lately."

"Uneasy?"

"A kind of hunch," she explained slowly. "All I know is that when I heard Mark was gone, I wanted to come tell you right away."

A hunch. *A concern.* Damn. "I really appreciate it," he said, deliberately keeping his tone gentle. "I'll check with his home address. More importantly for now, are you all right?"

"I wish I knew." Her hands twisted at her chest. "I feel like something is waiting, you know? Watching."

He frowned. "Watching you?"

"No," she said, making a face. "No, I mean, not me specifically, but just . . . watching."

Phin tapped a finger on the desk. "There are cameras all around," he pointed out, but the look she levied him suggested that she didn't appreciate his appraisal of her intelligence. He smiled ruefully. "Not that, then?"

"No." Cally shrugged. "I know things look bad for you—for us," she amended, "but I wanted to let you know that I'm . . . pretty sure that sauna wasn't an accident. I think Mr. Barker was right about there being an intruder. And," she added quickly, "if I can help? In any way?"

"Can you see through walls?" he asked, not entirely joking as he ran both hands through his hair.

She blinked. Fast. "Would that be helpful?"

"No, probably not." He smiled in calculated reassurance, making sure that none of his worry leaked through to bolster her own. Cally was tired; it was obvious that she'd spent more than her fair share worrying about it. "Let me handle this and you just keep your head down, okay? In a few days you'll be headed out."

Cally straightened, her eyes widening. "Out? I thought I was here for at least another three weeks."

"We're going to have to move faster than we thought," Phin replied. "Any extra scrutiny is going to be a problem for everyone."

"Do you think they'll send people?" Her hands

clenched. "Church officials?" Her voice dropped. "Missionaries?"

"Not if I can help it," he said grimly.

"It's a dangerous thing you do, you know that."

As she watched him, her gaze steady and clear, he shook his head. "The alternative isn't anything I want to be part of."

Cally's smile crinkled her eyes. "You're a good sort."

Maybe. He rose to his feet, circled the desk to enfold her work-rough hand in his. "Thank you. You're doing great, Cally, just hold out a few days longer."

She chuckled, her green eyes a dark slash of wry amusement. "Sir, I can honestly say this isn't the strangest job I've ever had to take on. Don't worry about me. I'll let you know if this unease turns into anything tangible."

"Tangible?" He hesitated. "Like . . . a vision?"

"You'll sleep better if you think so," she replied with a crooked smile.

"That's . . ." Phin thought about it. "Either encouraging or incredibly nerve-wracking."

"I'm good. Don't worry." She got up, flattening both hands on top of her head to stretch the kinks from her back. "But I think I need to get some food before I begin work at the dining floor. Do you need anything else? Can I bring you anything?"

"Just get some rest," he replied firmly. "You've done more than enough."

Cally grinned. "Does that mean a raise?"

"And maybe a pony," he replied in the same light tone. Her laughter eased some of the tension from his neck as she flashed him a thumbs-up.

Phin watched her exit his office, bracing his hands on the surface of the desk. After a moment's thought, his smile fading, he reached for the comm and keyed in the security office's frequency.

"Security, Mr. Clarke, how can I help you?" Eric Barker's voice sounded as tired as Cally's elfin features had looked.

Wincing in sympathy, Phin deliberately smoothed his tone. Crisp, professional. "I'm calling to check in on the results of the investigation."

"Yes, sir. All guests are accounted for. We've begun the process to verify the scheduled hours and where-abouts of Timeless staff, but—"

"You suspect an intruder," he cut in smoothly. "Yes, I heard."

Embarrassed silence filled the feed. Then, "Yes, sir."

Phin sighed. "Who else have you told?"

"Just the team." Eric paused awkwardly. "I must have slipped a sweep. I'm sorry, Mr. Clarke, I'll be more careful about where I speak in the future."

"Thank you. In the meantime, I need you to do something for me."

"Say the word."

"Right now, I need you to contact Mark Vaughn's home line." Phin's fingers danced over the keyboard inset into the polished wood desk. He rattled off the number.

"Got it," the security officer replied. "What am I looking for?"

"His whereabouts. He didn't show up for his shift today, and I'd like to make sure he's all right. And," Phin added as he studied the personnel photo of the gray-haired maintenance man, "find out why he isn't here."

"I'll be in touch soon."

"I'll be waiting." Phin disconnected the line and stared up at the stucco ceiling.

It wasn't that he mistrusted Eric. Or any of his staff. Until now, Phin would have said without a doubt that he trusted them all. Each had gone through a meticulous hiring process, a background study, interviews. Timeless promised discretion. He needed discreet staff, and that's what he had.

Except for the temporaries. But their access was limited. They worked at the spa with assumed identities that Timeless provided, and then they were ferried out of the city to one of a handful of homesteads scattered throughout the country.

What would any of them have to gain by murdering a guest?

Except this guest was the bishop's own grandmother.

Phin scraped his hair back from his forehead. As the idea filtered through his tired brain, he closed his eyes. Groaned out loud.

A temporary had the means. The in. The safety.

And, damn it all, the motive.

But which? Cally?

Impossible. Phin was a man who trusted his instinct, and everything in him told him Cally Simmons was exactly what she appeared to be: a witch desperately afraid for her safety. A good woman.

Marco Gonzalez? Greg Swenson? Both men had worked for him for two weeks. He didn't know if they were witches, but the interviews his staff had conducted assured him they weren't killers, rapists, or thieves. They each worked hard—one in pool maintenance and one in the kitchen—and he'd never heard so much as a whisper of unease about either.

They did what he suspected witches and accused witches did best: kept their heads down and stayed out of the line of fire.

Liz? One of the best temporary masseuses he'd ever had the pleasure to give safe haven to. Joel adored her. Mostly, Phin thought wryly, Joel adored that he could foist his more difficult clients onto her.

That left Hep. No last name given. An olive-skinned boy who had been so scared when he'd first arrived that he'd slept in the laundry room for fear of being found by the missionaries who had taken his family.

Phin squeezed his eyes shut. The kid was all of twelve. Maybe thirteen. If he'd tried to murder the bishop's grandmother, Phin was certain it wouldn't be through some elaborate sabotage scheme.

His instincts were rarely wrong. And yet. . .

And yet. A temporary had the strongest motive.

The comm buzzed in his hand. He jerked, scowled as his heart skipped a surprised beat, and stabbed the connect button. "Talk to me."

"It's Barker, sir," came the clipped greeting. "Mark Vaughn isn't home, or at least isn't picking up the comm line. Shall I send someone?"

"Yes. I want him found." Phin disconnected after Barker's assurances. A knot curled hard in his stomach, he dialed Lillian's number into the comm.

She answered almost immediately. "Yes?"

"Mother, I had a thought."

Though he made an effort to sound casual, Lillian's tone sharpened. "What's wrong, Phinneas? Are you all right?"

That was his mother. Wired in.

He pulled one hand over his face and stared blankly at the neat stack of storage boxes tucked against the wall. Read the precise, blocked labels on each. "I'm fine," he said. "Mark Vaughn didn't show up to work today, and either he's the one, or I think one of the temporaries could have been our saboteur."

A pause. "What makes you think so?"

"The only lead I have on Vaughn is that he's gone. Which is why I'm thinking it's more likely one of the temporaries." The words lumped in his throat, each one a knot of betrayal. Worry. He cleared it hard. "They have the motive, Mother." Phin sighed. "What better way to get back at the Church than murder the bishop's family?"

"That's a great deal of speculation, my love."

"But it's the only explanation that fits. They're all—" He caught himself, frowned. "They're all *temporary*. I can't shake it off."

"Well, we'll start investigating their whereabouts," Lillian assured him, her voice as crisp as if they were speaking about laundering the sheets. As if she hadn't warned him about this very thing. "I assume you have a plan to locate Mr. Vaughn?"

"Yes, Barker's sending someone to his place now."

"Lovely. Which do you think did it?"

"And that's the kicker. I can't see any of them pulling this off."

Lillian clucked her tongue thoughtfully. "Then," she said slowly, "what about the ones recently let go?"

The idea was so obvious, so crystal clear, that Phin sank back to his chair and let his forehead thunk against the desk. "Any of them could have done it," he groaned. "Any of them. They knew they were leaving. And then I *helped them escape*. What the hell was I thinking?"

"Easy, my love," she said softly. "You don't know that any of this is true. While we investigate, Timeless will continue as it always has. In the meantime, I'd like you to do me a favor."

He straightened, wary. "What?"

"Don't," Lillian warned, a sudden dash of amusement clear on the line, "take that tone with me, son. I do remember where you sleep."

Phin snorted.

"I was going over the logs last night," Lillian continued. "Naomi Ishikawa appears to be avoiding her schedule."

"Yes, I know." Phin glanced at his watch, saw it was just past noon. "I was going to ask you about that."

"Do you know why?"

"No," Phin admitted. "Not really. But I can tell you she enjoys the gym." And how. The memory of her body against his still branded his skin, his brain. A sweet, steady reminder of what he hadn't taken advantage of. Yet.

"So you've seen her today?"

"Not today." Phin frowned. "Why?"

Lillian hesitated. "Just . . . a suspicion."

"Mother—"

"Do me a favor," she cut in mildly, "and cross-reference her schedule with Abigail Montgomery's."

"She's here, then?" Phin winced. "When did Her Royal Highness arrive?"

"Don't call her that. She arrived last night, a full fourteen hours ahead of schedule. And in style," Lillian added dryly. "As always."

"Great. What are we calling her this time?"

"She's still married to James Montgomery, at least for the moment," Lillian replied with a sigh. "Mrs. Montgomery will do."

"Noted. What am I cross-referencing for?"

Her voice brightened. "Good morning, Mr. Rook. I'll explain later," she said into the comm. "For now, just check that they aren't scheduled in the same services, and let's try to limit their social interaction, shall we?"

"All right." He sat back at the computer, fingers tapping slowly into the keyboard. "I'll be in touch."

"Thank you, my love. Oh, and keep Miss Ishikawa away from the dining areas." She disconnected before Phin could ask any of the questions that leaped to his tongue. Her voice cut off mid-greeting to another guest, another welcome. Another cheerful conversation.

Lillian enjoyed making herself available during mealtimes, talking with the guests, directing events subtly from within the group. A personal touch. She had an eye for people, which meant she had reasons for asking him to keep the two women separated.

He just wished he knew what the hell was going on. Anywhere, for that matter.

"And," he murmured as he checked both women's

schedules, "they're good." Not that it'd matter. Aside from a morning's worth of pampering, Naomi had avoided her services like the plague. Yoga, relaxation, massage, she hadn't shown up for any of it.

What the hell did she do all day?

Staring at the monitor, he tapped his fingers on the edge of the inset keyboard in absentminded echo of his mother's fidgeting habit.

Keep her away from the dining floor. Abigail loved her social time. Phin was absolutely convinced she came here because of the captive audience, so that meant she intended on reigning over them all again. Her Royal Highness, the much-divorced queen of the wealthy city scene.

Keep Naomi away from Abigail.

Why?

Collecting his jacket from the coat rack, Phin shut and locked the door behind him. He kept his thumb pressed to the small scanner until the distinctive sound of tumblers sliding into place assured him it was as secure as it was going to get.

He caught himself whistling as he headed for the elevator.

It had taken way too long to clean the suite bathroom, but it would pass muster if anyone came looking. Timeless didn't leave chemicals just hanging out where any of their elite clients could stumble over them.

Water and frothy shower gel could clean only so much.

Naomi had spent the night cursing the stupid son of a bitch who'd allowed her to slam his head against the shining porcelain toilet. He'd bled out on the tile floor.

Nastier invectives rolled off her tongue when a search of his body revealed only a duplicate of her security card. No ID, nothing other than a Timeless uniform and that fucking card.

She'd wrestled him and the bloody towels into the armoire and cranked the internal temperature of the room to as cold as it would go, but the corpse wouldn't keep long. She'd have to find Carson before the dead witch started to smell.

Four hours later, what promised to be a foul temper had blossomed into a headache that no amount of Gemma's numbing cream could cure.

The place was a godforsaken maze. Scouring just two floors left Naomi frustrated, tired, and worse, empty-handed. The place was huge, larger than any single building had any right to be, with hallways that branched off in every direction and stairwells that her key card wouldn't grant her access to.

Using her comm, she mapped every hallway she could find and didn't have any excuses when a blue-eyed man in a dishwasher's apron escorted her back to the public corridors.

On the plus side, she'd seen signs of security where she'd figured there was none. Maybe that meant Phin had more sense than she gave him credit for. Now if she could just get her hands on that security feed.

In the elevator again, she touched the next floor button, glancing up at the camera lens nestled into the corner as the lift glided into motion.

How could she ask?

Better yet, could she patch Jonas into the closed system? Maybe he could find something they didn't know how to look for. With a hell of a lot less questions.

The elevator doors slid open, that near-soundless hiss of air and oiled mechanics. Naomi stepped off the elevator, and it was as if she'd crossed some sort of sound divide. Suddenly engulfed in utter quiet, she couldn't help her automatic effort to keep her shoes from clicking on the tile. It was as hushed as a tomb.

As stifling as the sauna, with none of the steam.

The layout mirrored the beauty spa one floor above. Open area, doors set into the walls, but there were no windows here. No pools. It was darker, more enclosed. Sand and sculpted rock took the place of plants, and the gleaming floor was midnight black marble veined with brilliant violet and gold.

The surrounding doors were shut, solid panels of dark wood inlaid with a strange collection of minerals, stones, shells, and metal.

It smelled different here. Thick, heavy, like incense. Musky, spicy instead of floral. Smothering. Warm, but not humid.

A handful of people spread out on the black floor, towels under their heads or digital books in hand. They looked content. Relaxed. Heat pushed up through the soles of her boots, warmed her feet even in heels.

Feeling overdressed in her dark wash denim and sky blue silk blouse, Naomi frowned and backtracked quickly before someone tried to stuff her into another robe.

Small hands braced her as she nearly backed into a brunette wearing the spa's typical green. "Excuse me, sorry," the short woman whispered quietly, raising a finger to her lips as Naomi whirled. "My name is Liz, are you here for a massage appointment?"

Flicking her gaze to the people on the tile, Naomi barely managed to keep her lip from curling. "No," she murmured. "Wrong floor, sorry."

"No problem." Liz gestured over her shoulder. "If you ever want to visit, simply turn left upon entry to store your clothes, okay?"

"Yeah, thanks."

Hell would freeze before she locked herself in this soundless tomb. Naomi turned, reached for the elevator button, and tensed when the doors slid open without her help. She fought back an uncurling tendril of anxiety.

She had every right to be here.

Naomi Ishikawa did, anyway.

Inside the elevator, Phin leaned against the railing, effortlessly casual in his crisp gray slacks and forest green button-down shirt. He'd worn a tie this time, something patterned in abstract shades of olive, gold, and bronze.

It brought out the sudden wary gleam of his dark eyes. The flash of awareness as Naomi's cool smile froze to brittle crystal.

"Just who I wanted to see. Shall we?" The tone of Phin's voice carried a warning. The gesture he made to the quiet floor behind her went ignored.

Naomi's palm slammed into the frame, blocking the sensor and sending ripples of shock from wrist to shoulder. She ignored that, too. Her mouth dried to bitter cotton as the woman beside Phin glanced her way, blue eyes raking over Naomi in silent, preoccupied inquiry.

She was beautiful.

Still beautiful, even after all the years she fought off with surgery and restoratives. Her chin-length, wavy hair was as icy blond as Naomi remembered, not a thread of gray to ruin a carefully cultivated appearance of agelessness and impossible youth. Her eyes were expertly lined, deliberately lashed, and her makeup flawless.

But Naomi could pick out the tiny surgery scars by her ears. The nearly invisible lines marring the perfection of her eyes and bracketing the mouth that was almost as full as her own.

When she said nothing, Naomi read indifference, complete lack of recognition, and subsequent dismissal a single nanosecond before an empty, insincere smile shaped her mother's cosmetically plumped lips. "We are going down," she said clearly, and turned her lovely, timeless gaze back to Phin. "The rudeness of some people just—"

Phin moved. As if released from a spell, he surged out of the elevator, wrapped one hand around Naomi's upper arm as he said breezily, "Excuse me, Mrs. Montgomery."

Naomi's crack of bitter laughter broke on a curse as he spun her away from the elevator, whirling her hard against his chest. Around the hand he slid against the back of her head, pushing her face into his shoulder, he muttered, "Be quiet."

She smelled warm soap and male as she sucked in a breath to say something, anything. As she struggled to pluck coherent words from the soundless litany of fury drilling through her ears.

The doors closed on Abigail's puzzled frown.

Adrenaline surged through Naomi's veins. It rocketed from the sudden vise in her chest through her blood, pounding in her skull. Her body shook; rage, bitter laughter—*fuck*, disappointment—fueling her as she shoved at Phin's chest. "Let me go," she spat.

Features set in hard lines, determined edges, Phin glanced over her head. Naomi didn't give a damn about the curious eyes probably aimed their way. She hoped they fell out of their goddamn skulls.

Before she could say as much, he seized her wrists and jerked her toward one of the doors. Her boots scraped on bare tile as she staggered over the rim of the heated floor.

Carried by an anger she couldn't think through, she launched herself at his back.

And somehow, he knew.

He spun, jaw hard, and yanked sharply enough on her wrists that she buckled, plucked from her trajectory and cursing. Voices gasped in unison, digital readers hit the marble floor, but he didn't stop. Hauling her bodily into his arms, lean muscles like iron bands, Phin carried her inside a small room bathed in gold light.

He ignored the hum of voices behind him, and firmly, gently shut the door.

Seething, Naomi wrenched out of his grasp. She choked on everything she couldn't say, slamming her foot into the bolted massage table in the center of the room, and caught her breath as pain fractured through to her brain. She kicked it again, harder. The frame splintered audibly; the candles flickered.

"Go ahead," Phin offered mildly. She spun back, panting, her fists clenched at her sides. He looked cool and unruffled, not a hair out of place, with his hands in his pockets and the metallic threads of his tie reflecting back the candlelight.

Unruffled, except for his glittering eyes, golden points of flame.

"Keep at it, if you want." Angling one shoulder against the door, Phin added, "The room's soundproof. They all are. Clients come here for peace and quiet, so do what you need to do. Yell and scream, if you like."

"Don't you dare," Naomi bit out. Every word snapped from her chest like a coiled spring wound too tight. Ground too sharp. "Don't you fucking patronize me."

"I'm not." His gaze steady, he nodded at the massage table behind her. "Go for it. Kick it until you break something." He paused, then offered quietly, "Or you can tell me what's wrong."

Wrong. What was wrong with Naomi West?

She wanted to laugh, but she knew if she did now, it'd come out a raw sound too close to a sob for her to risk the effort.

To risk his pity.

What the fuck *wasn't* wrong?

Her fingers clenched tightly enough to send pain ratcheting through her arms. She gritted her teeth until her jaw threatened to lock. Until she could breathe through the fury and pain and, god damn it, memory that scorched. Blackened to the bone.

Phin sighed. "I'm not going to pry, Naomi. It's your life."

Her laugh cracked loose. "What do you know?"

For a long, silent moment, Phin studied her. Measured her. There was nothing on his face that Naomi could cling to, nothing in his eyes that she could extract and fling back like a weapon. He gave her nothing, damn it, nothing to hang her anger on.

Just steady, patient regard.

To her horror, tears burned behind her eyes. She stiffened, swallowing back the knot in her throat in desperate, furious resolve. She wasn't going to cry.

That wasn't a victory her mother would ever claim again.

"Fine." Phin straightened. "Lie down."

She shook her head. "What?"

He deftly removed the cuff link at one sleeve. Tossed it into a small crystal bowl, *clink*.

Her mouth went dry.

His fingers agile, he unhooked the other with quick, neat precision. It rattled into place with the other one, metal and glass. "Lie down," he repeated slowly. "On the table, with your shirt off."

"Not even if you—"

"Look," Phin cut in, his tone as calm and conversational as if they only discussed the chances of rain on an autumn day. "You're wound so tight, I can practically see reality bending around you." Briskly he rolled up the cuff of one sleeve, bared a lean, muscled forearm sprinkled with golden brown hair.

Her eyes locked on his hands. Long fingers. Wide palms. Her brain stalled.

As he rolled up the other sleeve, he jerked his chin to the table. "So strip off the shirt, and lie down, okay? I've never met somebody more in need of a massage."

Her body jerked. Surprise. Bottled anger. But to her shock, Naomi found herself reaching for the tied hem of her blouse. The silk rustled between her fingers.

For a brief, jagged instant, Phin's eyes met hers as the hem cleared her face. His gaze skimmed over the set of her mouth, her shoulders.

The scarlet lace that cupped her breasts.

All at once, her rage shimmered into something else just as searing. Turned over into an arousal so deep, so tight, it slipped like wine through her blood, made her slow to react as Phin's voice reached across the strained silence.

"And the bra," he rasped. Rough. As taut as the impressive erection Naomi clearly saw straining against his slacks. Clearing his throat, he nodded to the table when she shrugged out of the lacy bra. "Facedown."

Skin shivering, every nerve awake and trembling, Naomi dropped the silk and lace to the floor. She climbed onto the table, settled into place, her breath tight and sharp with anticipation. With wired, leashed impatience.

The cushion was soft against her forehead, thick and lush against the sensitized flesh of her breasts. It cradled her face, blocked her view of everything but the floor beneath her head. She watched the candlelight flicker, dance, and jump with every move Phin made. She heard a drawer open, heard liquid slide as he rubbed something that smelled sharply spicy between his palms.

When they touched her, Naomi thought she'd climb out of her skin with wanting.

He had strong hands, wide, fearless palms that traced her spine, hot skin to skin. His thumbs edged into corded muscle stretched tautly across her back, eliciting a gasp, a groan from her throat.

She couldn't see where Phin stood. Couldn't hear him, couldn't feel anything but the slow, torturous slide of his hands on her back. His strong fingers dug deeply into muscles that all but screamed under pressure; he found every kink, every knot, every goddamned trigger in her neck and shoulders.

And he worked in silence. In eternal, excruciating quiet.

She didn't know how long she held out, but Naomi couldn't keep back a moan of relief, of mingled pain and need as his magical, oil-slick fingers found the taut muscles in her neck. Her toes curled as he thumbed the side of her throat.

Her eyes flew open as he traced the barbell she'd stubbornly left in place at the back of her neck.

"You know," he murmured, and she gasped to feel the heat of his breath fan over her ear, "the first time I saw this, it just about killed me."

Shuddering, she managed, "Why?"

"It's telling, isn't it?" Phin caught the back of her head, smoothed her hair out of the way to dig his fingertips into the vulnerable ache behind her ears. She sighed. "As far as anyone else knows, you're a nice girl. Nice clothes. Nice smile."

Her incredulous laugh caught on a low, husky moan. He tore it from her chest, coaxed it from her lips with every inch of muscle he subjugated under his clever hands. Her skin hummed, burned deliciously from the oil.

From Phin's touch.

"And then one day, you wear your hair up, and—" Naomi tensed as his lips brushed the nape of her neck. As his tongue slid over the small, silver piercing and the flesh trapped between each bead.

Heat scorched like lightning to her belly. Flooded her system with a wave of breath-shortening electrical shocks. "Oh, God," she groaned. "Phin—"

"No." He flattened his hands on her back, held her when she would have rolled over. Her fingers curled into the table edge, fisted into the plush coverlet. "I'm not done."

"Damn it," she gritted out, and sighed out another thick, rough sound of pleasure as his lips touched her shoulder. "Phin. Jesus, *Phin*."

His laughter ghosted across her slick back. Raised every fine hair with a shudder. "What will you give me?"

"What?" Naomi tried to struggle, tried to command her body to get it together, to get off the damn table, but he dug his thumbs into that hollowed edge by her vertebrae again. Dragged his fingers all the way down to her waist. To the muscles below, tight and sore with her frustration-fueled workouts. "Oh," she whispered. "Do that again."

He did, drawing another groan, another gasping sigh from her lips.

"A date."

"Whatever," Naomi murmured. "Fine."

"Tonight."

Eyes half closed, her arms limp by her sides, she barely managed to move her head as he hit that sweet, mind-altering slide of muscle at her shoulder blades. "No clothes for it," she sighed. "Spa."

She could hear the grin in his voice as he said, "Meet me at the front desk at four."

Alarm bells began to clang in her head. Muted. Flat. "Wait, what?"

"And, Naomi?" One oil-slick hand edged into her hair. Cupped the back of her head, held her still as Phin bent to take the shell of her ear between the sharp edge of his teeth. He bit down, soft. Deliberate.

Lust rocketed straight to her soul. She gasped.

"Wear your hair up."

By the time she remembered how to breathe, Phin was gone, the door shutting silently behind him. Her skin all but crawled with awareness, with a current of tactile electricity. One part was the oil. It tingled, warmed her skin.

The rest was *all* him.

She rolled over on the table to stare at the color-ful seascape mosaic inlaid into the ceiling, but Naomi didn't see anything but Phin. His face, edged with the same need that clawed at her. His eyes, banked hard with the same lust. He wanted her.

But he hadn't taken her. Not here.

He had plans. "All right, slick," she murmured, her heartbeat echoing the need pulsing between her legs. Through her veins. She'd play his game.

Slowly, deliciously shivering, she spread her palms over her breasts. Cradled each sensitized mound of flesh and nerves and imagined what it would be like to have Phin's fingers there. His mouth on the hard, tight buds of her nipples.

She'd play, but she wouldn't play it fair.

CHAPTER TEN

He found Lillian at the front desk, poring over the electronic guest book. "At what point," Phin demanded quietly, "were you going to tell me that Abigail Montgomery and Naomi Ishikawa are related?"

His mother's eyes narrowed. Flicked up to him. "So it's true?"

"I'm asking you."

"And I was hoping you could tell me," she admitted with a small, tired frown.

Phin braced one hip against the desk. Around him, the soothing melody of harps and flutes did nothing to ease the tension ratcheting through him. One part worry, concern. One part blind lust.

All of it Naomi.

He raked his fingers through his hair. "I saw them side by side—"

"Phin!"

"She caught me by surprise," he admitted dryly. "If there's one thing I'm learning, it's that Naomi is going to be exactly where you don't want her."

"Oh, no." Lillian's expert makeup couldn't hide the circles under her eyes, or the flinch that set lines around her mouth. "What happened?"

He reached over, smoothed back a tendril of golden hair over her ear. "Naomi looks a little like her," he admitted. "And Abigail set her off badly just by being there, but—"

How did he explain it? How did he wrap his head around the fact that the two women seemed to have such different reactions to each other?

Anger, fury in one. And pain. Phin knew that Naomi would be so much more livid if she'd known how much he saw in that raw, unguarded moment. When her violet eyes had filled with so much rage. So much hurt.

"Mrs. Montgomery didn't seem to recognize her," he finally said. "Nothing. Not a flicker."

"That poor child." Lillian rubbed at her forehead. "I can't imagine what she must be feeling. Maybe Gemma—"

"Don't," he cautioned swiftly. "Don't bring it up, don't let on. Whatever is going on there, whatever relationship those two have—or don't have—it's obvious that Naomi doesn't want anyone to know."

For a long, harp-accompanied moment, Lillian studied her son's gaze. The set of his face, which he knew was tense. He couldn't help it. Even his smile felt stiff as he shook his head. "Just trust me on this one."

"I do, my love." But she cupped his chin in her palm, lifting his face to the light. Her hazel eyes were no less sharp, for all her fatigue. "You're in trouble, aren't you?"

God, yes. "Of course not, Mother. I'm just making you aware that your potential problem is most definitely a reality." And falling hard and fast for a woman whose entire makeup seemed to consist of complications.

She arched a single, shaped eyebrow. "And?"

Phin's smile went crooked. "And," he added, spreading his palms on the counter space, "admiring how pretty your suit is today."

"Flattery, my son," Lillian said crisply, "will get you nowhere." But her eyes sparkled as she released his chin. "Will you be at dinner?"

At her elbow, the desk unit flashed a blue signal.

Phin edged away. "No, I've got plans."

That eyebrow nearly reached her hairline. "What sort of plans?"

The lights flashed again. Tucking his hands into his pockets, he hedged, "I'm eating out tonight."

Lillian picked up the earpiece, mouthed, *Stay put,* in silent demand, then added, "Concierge, how may I—"

Nothing changed in her tone. Nothing in her posture or her face, but he knew his mother. A barely perceptible shift drew Phin to a complete stop. He frowned, leaned over the desk to place his ear beside his mother's on the line.

"—unbelievable amount of gall to tell me that everything is fine when I know it isn't. So you better start looking for any messages that Katie left, because I *know* she left something!" An English voice, sharp with annoyance.

To her credit, Lillian waited patiently for the woman to take a breath. "Jordana," she said soothingly, "this is Lillian Clarke speaking. Please, calm down and tell me exactly what the problem is."

"Haven't you been listening?"

Phin exchanged worried glances with his mother.

"I said," Jordana continued hotly, "that my assistant is gone. She left, probably to go do something or fix something or whatever it is she does when I'm busy, but Katie doesn't just *vanish*. She always leaves me messages so you better talk to the last girl polishing her nails at that fucking desk and find it."

Lillian tapped at the monitor inset into the concierge desk, scanning through logs quickly. "I'm sorry, there are no messages for you." A sinking pit sucked out the bottom of Phin's stomach as he read the screen over his mother's shoulder. "And as far as we're aware, Katie is still in the building."

"No, she isn't." Jordana blew out a hard breath, fuzzing the line. "She isn't answering her comm, and— Oh, no," she gasped. "Oh, God, I was so drunk last night. We had a fight."

Phin's eyebrow slid up his forehead, an unconscious mirror of Lillian's quiet inquiry.

"Is there any way she could have just, you know, left? Without checking out?"

"Take a deep breath," Lillian coached gently. "I'll have our security team go over the feeds, all right? Where are you?"

"The dining hall, having a good, stiff drink." She lowered her voice. "If that bitch just walked out on me . . ." Her voice cracked.

"Let's just concentrate on finding her for you," Lillian replied, meeting Phin's eyes with mirrored concern and uncertainty. "Has she ever left you for long?"

Phin was already shaking his head as Jordana said icily, "Katie knows who signs her paychecks, Mrs. Clarke."

"Of course," Lillian murmured, gaze grave as it settled on him. "I'll get our security on this right away. We'll find your assistant, Jordana."

"She'd better be dead," the pop star spat, "or I'll kill her myself."

"Let's avoid either," Lillian said smoothly into the mic. "In the meantime, my staff is at your disposal. I am so sorry for the inconvenience, Jordana, rest assured we will investigate this matter fully."

Phin withdrew from the conversation, but the cold knot still wrapped tight in his stomach gnawed at him. Quietly he unclipped his comm from his belt and cracked it open. Within moments, Barker answered the ring.

"Security."

"Mr. Barker, I need Katie Landers's last whereabouts located in the feeds." Phin kept his voice low. "She's about five feet four inches, with light brown hair and thick rimmed glasses."

"The singer's guest, right?"

"Yes."

"I'll feed the data into the recognition software," Barker replied immediately. "Is there a problem?"

Aside from the worry gathering like an anchor in his

gut? He turned away from Lillian's quiet phone calls and pinched the bridge of his nose between two fingers. "I hope not."

"Right, well, I've got a handful of entries in the scanner logs." Keys clattered over the line as the security lead worked. "She last used her pass to reach the ground floor."

"When?"

A pause. Phin stared blankly at the fountain as it splattered musically against marble. "Two hours ago, sir."

"And before that?"

Over the line, Barker blew out a breath. "The scanner recorded her card at the dining hall first thing this morning. Then she left for the beauty floor, and then— Huh. That's odd."

Phin frowned. "What?"

"She went from the beauty floor to her suite without— No, there has to be something wrong with the scanner. Toby'd mentioned he thought it was getting loose or something."

"What?" Phin repeated, tension edging every line of his body. Behind him, Lillian hung up the desk unit.

"Well, sir, the logs have her leaving her suite, but there's no record of her entering it. I'll have the techs look at the scanner."

"Do that. What about Vaughn?" he asked, already too damn tired to hear the answer.

"I sent Toby down to the address listed on file. It was empty. His possessions were still there, though."

Phin swallowed a curse as it surged in his throat. "Clues?"

Barker made a small sound of annoyance. "Toby found gambling tickets from a mid-city place called the Last Way Out. Dated last night."

"Oh, for God's sake."

"We'll stay on it, sir. In the meantime, we'll locate the assistant. I'll be in touch."

Phin clipped the comm back to his belt. He turned as Lillian set the desk receiver into its charging unit.

She sighed. "When it rains, it most certainly pours."

"No kidding," Phin replied grimly. He rubbed his face, scraped his fingers over his scalp as a steady throb blossomed to a full-blown headache. "Fuck."

"Phin," Lillian reprimanded. "What did you learn?" He outlined it briefly, and shook his head as she asked, "Is it possible the scanner really is broken?"

"We'll find out."

"So what do we do?"

"Round-the-clock security." He rocked back on his heels, suddenly dead tired. The jangle of harps only seemed discordant to his aching brain. "What about Katie?"

"It's possible she really did leave," his mother said. "And also possible that she's still in the building somewhere. Security will do its job; Phin, you go take Miss Ishikawa to dinner." Lillian's smile deepened into a too-knowing curve as his glance slid sharply to her. "I was not," she added, "born yesterday."

He shook his head. "I can't go now. What if something else happens?"

"Then we will deal with it as we always have," Lillian replied. Her chin came up; long, thin hands laid flat on the desk as she leaned over it. "Take your date and go."

He swayed. Torn, Phin knew his mother was right. Short of filling the corridors with hunting dogs he didn't have, he couldn't do anything that his mothers couldn't do themselves.

But if something happened—

"Phinneas Clarke." Lillian's tone sharpened. "Do remember that your mother and I successfully managed this business long before you were old enough to *say* discreet, much less be it."

A sudden burst of warmth made him smile. Feeling all at once sheepish and overwhelmingly concerned, Phin leaned over to press his lips to her offered cheek. "Fine, but we'll be back after dinner. No excuses."

"That is your choice." Her smile mirrored the tenderness in her gaze as she reached over and straightened his tie. "Do go put on something more suitable. You have oil on your sleeve."

Damn it. Heat seared his face, burned all the way to his ears as he checked both arms. His smile was much less casual than he intended as he found the shiny blot of massage oil that darkened the green fabric at his forearm.

Knowing anything he said wouldn't matter, Phin cleared his throat, nodded, and turned back to the garden doors.

"And, Phin?"

He glanced back. Lillian watched him from behind the desk, one hand settled regally on its surface. The other curled over her trim hip, stern echo of the caution in her voice as she added, "Please be careful."

"I will. I'm going to call Swann's and see about finagling their waiting list."

"I mean—" Lillian caught herself, put one hand to her neat bodice and shook her head. "Never mind. Have a good time, darling."

He hesitated. But when he would have said something, anything, she waved him away, already once more engrossed in the computer screen by the time he managed to swallow the lump of love, of unease in his throat.

With a resigned sigh, he left through the lobby doors, crossed the garden proper, and made his way to the small, inconspicuous hall that led to the family wing. He'd shower, change, and make the calls he needed to make.

He'd start, Phin thought grimly as he fingered the slick stain on his sleeve, with calling in extra security.

"I've got good news and I've got bad news."

Naomi smoothed clear, liquid gloss over her mouth without looking in the mirror, her glance flicking instead to the comm on the marble countertop. "Great. What?"

Eckhart's voice was as pleasant as ever. If Jonas had told him about her little episode, she couldn't read it in his easy inflection. "Miles is set up to deliver your weapon whenever you're ready."

She brightened. "Great! I'll send a message just as soon as I know where I'll be able to meet him."

"He'll be on call." His voice twitched into annoyance as he added, "And we've hit another snag getting the blueprints."

Unable to dredge up the energy to be annoyed, Naomi moved her shoulders in a halfhearted shrug. "Oh, well. I've mapped out the dining floor, the lounge, the beauty suite"—she repressed a shudder—"and the, I don't know, I think they call it the quiet room."

"Mapped out?"

"The place is a fucking maze. More staff corridors and offshoots than hell."

"I don't think," Eckhart replied dryly, "that hell has staff corridors. Still, it's good to know you're in over your head."

She wished she could have argued with him, but the sheer fact was just that. She was. Naomi grimaced, smoothing the sleek gray dress over her hips. "I told you this was stupid."

"Maybe." Eckhart sighed. "Have you run into anyone suspicious?"

It was on the tip of her tongue to give him Abigail Montgomery's name. She realized it before Eckhart had even finished speaking. Bringing the full inquiry of the Church down on the woman's selfish, empty head would make Naomi laugh like nothing else; sheer shits and giggles.

But that would end with the Church's eye turning right back to her. Flagged.

Processed.

"Naomi?"

"Just the dead guy in the wardrobe," she said, sighing. "The guests all seem fairly normal, at least the ones I've seen. Lots of people come in for day passes, but they don't have the same run of the building."

"What about the ones you haven't seen?"

"There's a couple recluses, but gossip suggests they don't leave their suites for hell *or* high water. I have to get my hands on the guest list."

Eckhart's frown matted into a grumble. "Christ, we're only a quarter through the official staff records over here."

"That many?"

"It's a spa with more staff corridors than hell," Eckhart reminded her. "What do you think?"

"I think that parallel just keeps drawing itself," she said wryly.

"What about that witch?"

"And we're back to the dead guy in my wardrobe," Naomi said with a twisted smile. "Did you get the photo I sent?"

"Yeah. No ID as yet. Any chance you took some samples?"

"I did." She glanced at the armoire. "While I was using expensive bath gel to clean the blood up."

"Nice. Give them to Miles, it'll give us a better lead," Eckhart said.

"Okay." Frowning, she snatched the ugly patchwork purse from the floor and added, "I'm headed out. As soon as you get your hands on those blueprints, I want them."

"If they exist," he said. "I'll tell Miles to be ready." He paused, and for a brief second she heard a low, almost imperceptible three-note whistle. "So, who are you going out with?"

Naomi bit back a smile. "I'm just getting out while I can."

"Uh-huh." He didn't sound assured. "Just try not to break him."

"Hey—"

"And don't forget the blood."

"Fuck you, Eckhart." Naomi disconnected the comm, dropped the unit into the rainbow-vomit purse, and went in search of the white pea coat she'd seen somewhere in her luggage.

Of all the outfits the Mission had set her up with, none of them screamed *date with the spectacularly sexy Phin Clarke.* Hell, if she had her way, she'd have strapped herself into something made out of buckles and synth leather, replaced all her piercings, and hauled him out to the Pussycat Perch or the Shell Casing for a night of grueling, sweaty, skin-to-skin dancing.

Watched him take his turn feeling like a fish on a hook.

Instead she was wrapped from shoulder to knee in gray designer silk and sporting crimson stiletto boots that likely passed for the rich-bitch version of fuck-me fashion. It would have to do.

Naomi shrugged into the coat, pulled the purse over her shoulder, and tried not to grimace at the horrifying rainbow leather. It was the only purse big enough to conceal a gun and a handful of bloody swabs.

She didn't think she'd manage to get away with a holster in the dress.

She rubbed her hands together, glanced briefly into the mirror hanging over the mantel, and, wordless, offered an extended middle finger to the neat, put-together reflection before leaving the suite.

Naomi made it as far as the garden before nerves curled into a tight little ball of uncertainty in her chest.

What the hell was she thinking?

This wasn't her world. Phin wasn't her type. Here she was, Naomi West, missionary, headed out to the topside nightlife as if she belonged, looking every inch as if she belonged—

She hesitated at the lobby door.

But she didn't belong. Not here, not with him, not out there. It was all an act. Fine. She needed out, she needed her gun. She needed to get the blood samples to Miles.

She *wanted* to bend the oh-so-smooth Phin Clarke into knots. Break him into delicious pieces, so that when she left this godforsaken prison with its ignorant, sheltered inmates, Naomi could say she had one bright, interesting moment that didn't involve bullets and blood.

Gritting her teeth, she shoved open the double doors, made it two steps in before her skin prickled in sharp awareness. Wrenching her gaze from the fountain, she met the palpable, speculative wall of three pairs of eyes. Staring at her.

Phin's twinkled. Challenge.

Another game? Raising her chin, Naomi's pace lengthened, her heels echoing as she crossed the marble floor. "Phin, Mrs. Clarke," she offered by way of greeting.

"Good afternoon, dear," Gemma said as she straightened. Beside her, standing by the computer monitor, a striking woman with wheat gold hair smiled at her. Calm. Serene.

And more than a little appraising.

Although Naomi recognized the tall silhouette, she'd eat her purse if the woman was any kind of concierge.

"Naomi." Phin's hand slipped to her lower back as he gestured to them both. "You've met my mother, haven't you?"

"Of course," she began, only to frown when the older woman's smile deepened.

"Now I'd like to introduce you to my mother, Lillian Clarke. Mother, Naomi Ishikawa."

Naomi's eyes narrowed. Flicked from Lillian's strong features to Gemma's chocolate dark eyes, shining with merriment. To Phin, who watched her with the same easy smile that shaped Lillian's mouth. "By marriage?"

He shook his head. "Nope."

Naomi's fingers twitched. "You think you're so clever," she murmured, and patted his cheek. His eyes flickered—surprise or something else, she couldn't tell—and she stepped out of his reach, offering a hand to the striking blond. "It's nice to meet you, Mrs. Clarke."

Nice to meet the woman who had air-kissed Abigail Montgomery the night before. Nice to look into her clear, green-gold regard and smile as if she hadn't a care in the world.

As if she weren't wondering just how much this second mother knew. About her. About the body she'd shoved into the polished armoire.

About the things she'd done with her son.

Planned to do still.

The woman's eyes gleamed. "Lillian, won't you?" Her grip was gentle, her fingers long and fingernails devoid of polish. A single gold ring glittered on her ring finger, matched twin to the woven band on Gemma's.

"Lillian," Naomi repeated dutifully. She brightened her smile to skin-searing wattage, turning it on Phin. He blinked. "I am ready when you are."

To kick your ass from here to the lower city streets, she added silently. Her jaw felt stiff, smile too tight.

"Have fun," Gemma said gaily. "Do deliver my best to Franco, won't you?"

"Of course, Mother." His hand firmly back at Naomi's hip, he bent to press a kiss to the woman's cheek. Gave the other woman, his other mother, the same farewell.

"Be careful." Lillian touched his chin, shot her a small, narrow smile. "Both of you."

Naomi let him guide her away from the desk. Firmly held her tongue as he beat her to the double doors and propped them open for her.

Only part of it was anger.

The man looked good enough to eat. His suit was something smooth and tailored, some designer who specialized in crisp lines. Simple. It was a dark, smoky gray, offset beautifully by the black button-down shirt beneath it. He didn't bother with a tie, leaving the collar open to frame the lines of his neck. The barest hint of muscle below it.

He'd brushed his hair back, held it in place with some kind of fine pomade, and Naomi couldn't help but notice how it showcased the angled lines of his cheekbones. His smooth-shaven jaw.

Silver cuff links, different from the ones he'd removed earlier, winked as he gestured across the garden to a small, discreet door.

Naomi gritted her teeth. "What the hell was that?"

"My parents," he replied mildly. He didn't let her stop, kept a firm hand at the curve of her lower back as he guided her into the corridor.

Naomi shrugged out of his grasp, easily keeping pace with his long stride. "Don't give me that bullshit. That was a setup."

This time his eyes glinted when they turned to her. Flicked to the spiky knot of her upswept hair. His slow, easy smile made her want to climb inside his skin and lick him bloody. "You wore your hair up."

"Don't change the subject," she retorted, but his obvious appreciation triggered a low, liquid slide of awareness. Of anticipation. "You purposefully didn't tell me about your parents."

"It's not my fault you don't pay attention." Phin paused at a thick wooden door, one hand braced on the panel. "I don't hide my life from people."

"Cleverly shed blame." Naomi looked up at him, at the smooth lines of his indulgent expression, and admitted to herself that she couldn't decide between licking him and punching him.

Maybe she could punch him square in the mouth. And then lick it better.

"What's the problem, Naomi?" He raised his eyebrows, smiled right into the face of her irritation, and touched her lower lip with the tip of his index finger. "Are you mad because you didn't know or mad because they wanted to meet you?"

"Neither," she snapped. "I—"

She what? Why was she mad? Because she felt set up? Because she didn't want to know that Phin had two mothers?

When she didn't even have *one*?

She shoved at the tendrils of hair framing her face, shaking her head hard. "Never mind, can we just go?"

"Your wish," he murmured, and swept open the door.

It led to another corridor. Another simply decorated,

nicely painted hall. Without another word, he led her past several intersections, past doors that led somewhere Naomi couldn't see.

They walked through a wider foyer, its brass elevator free-standing in the middle of the round, open room. Columns decorated the walls, beautiful vases and lush potted plants offering vibrant color to the pale cream shelves inset into the walls.

"I live here," Phin explained as he caught her craning her neck to see what lay beyond the elevator frame. "This is the family wing. Across the compound is the staff wing."

"Your staff lives here?"

"Some," he replied, and swept open another door, another simple lock. "Here we go." Naomi stepped into the chilled, dark recesses of a parking garage.

She raised her eyebrows. "Who knew?" She should have. Why hadn't Mission intel mentioned a parking garage? Of course there would be other ways to get to the resort. Deliveries wouldn't come through the elevator.

Damn it. She wanted blueprints almost as badly as she wanted her gun.

"Your chariot awaits." He pointed toward a sleek silver luxury car with its engine idly humming. It was almost as long as a limousine.

Almost as redundant and self-indulgent.

Heiress, she reminded herself tightly, and stepped off the landing. Phin followed her closely, chuckled when a man in a neat black uniform stepped out of the car to open her door for her.

"Thank you," she said stiffly, sliding into the roomy, extravagant interior. Cream-colored leather, real leather unless Naomi's tingling fingertips were wrong, enfolded her weight, smooth as butter. She could stretch out her legs, take up an entire seat, and still there'd be room for five more in the excessive space.

"Thank you, Martin." Phin slid in beside her, unbuttoning his coat with one deft hand. "Champagne?"

"Are you serious?" *Heiress*, her Mission brain warned again. "Not before dinner," she covered quickly. "It goes to my head."

"I'm glad to hear it."

She frowned, bracing both hands against the seat as the car slid into motion. "That champagne goes to my head?"

"That anything does," he said lightly. "Still." He reached over, slid open a compartment to reveal two crystal glasses and a bottle of what Naomi could only assume was expensive champagne. "It's here if you want some."

She was half tempted. Mostly because it was something for her hands, her mouth to do that wasn't pushing Phin down on the butter-soft seat and exploring his concealed chest, his stomach, his—

She flicked a glance at the opaque window panel that separated the driver from the back. Jumped when Phin's low, knowing laugh slid into the collar of her coat and wrapped like a vise around her ribs.

"I didn't bring the massage oil," he said, stretching out his legs across the clean, pale floor of the car. His shiny, polished shoes nudged her red boots. Just a touch. "But I can probably find something just as good."

CHAPTER ELEVEN

His hands filled her imagination. The warmth of his palms. His deft fingers kneading, stroking, feeling her body. Heat swirled low and tight. Naomi straightened. "You wish," she retorted lightly.

"You're tense again."

Outside the tinted glass, rain splattered, turned the muted lights of nighttime traffic and the glow of the city in shimmering rivulets. It hummed. Different from the steady, unending thrum of the mid-low levels beneath them, but just as alive.

Hungry.

Her eyes flared. "I'm wondering what I'm going to have to pay for this night."

"Pay?" Phin smiled. He studied her, from the tips of her crimson boots to her smooth, bare legs crossed under the hem of the silk dress. To her mouth. "I thought you said *I* had to pay for my women." The glow in his eyes should have scorched everything it touched.

A corner of her glossy mouth quirked. "I'm not your woman."

"Am I paying for you?"

"I'm not for sale." Naomi wanted to climb inside those eyes and cover her naked body in sweet, dark chocolate. Only vaguely aware of this little contest of verbal words, she slid her tongue over her bottom lip, easing the tip over that missing center ring. His eyes flamed to wicked, hungry life as he watched her lick the gloss away.

"Good," he said hoarsely. "Then there's no mistaking this." And then he wasn't across the car anymore. He wasn't in the opposite seat. Between the space of one breath and the next, Phin sank to his knees in front of her, his eyes brilliantly dark, glittering like ancient gold in a face suddenly taut with the heat Naomi knew drew him like a moth to flame.

That's what she was. Fire. And she couldn't help the sleek, intimate tug of arousal between her legs, the uncurling warmth that spread through her limbs like liquid silver as he speared his fingers into the loose wave of her gathered hair and tilted her face between his palms.

"Phin," she warned him, her eyes on his, "you're so going to get burned."

"God, I hope so," he said roughly, and kissed her.

He kissed her like a man drowning, in desperate need of air. He feasted on the full, lush curve of her lips as if he starved. He wasn't rough, he didn't force her, but, God, he didn't have to.

She wanted him. Wanted this.

Wanted more.

The luxury vehicle purred around them like a sleek cat as he swept his tongue into her mouth. It slid between her lips the way she wanted another part of him to mimic, deep, claiming. Assaulting every sense. She tasted the smooth rasp of his tongue, the minty, wet heat of his mouth, smelled his musky aftershave and drew it deep into her lungs. Wanted *more*.

Impatient, her breath catching, she pushed at his jacket. At the too expensive material that he shrugged out of, leaving it crumpled to the floor.

A low sound of approval rasped from his throat, jerked when she struggled with the buttons of his shirt.

Phin tore his mouth from hers, let her take in deep, shaking breaths of air as he pushed her hands away and slid his fingers around her hips. "Damn it," he muttered, wrenching her off the seat and into his lap. Her knees hit the floor, sharp points of rasped pain. He grunted, hissed out a breath as her thighs bracketed his waist.

As the center of her body settled over him like it knew exactly what it wanted. What she wanted.

"Not," he managed, "the way I'd imagined this."

He pulled off her coat, tossed it over his shoulder without care for the snowy white fabric. His fingers mapped her ribs, her breasts. Plunged into the neckline of the gray dress and found the same scarlet lace that she'd known he wanted to touch in the massage room.

She'd worn it just for him tonight.

"Your fault for assuming," Naomi replied raggedly, even as her head fell back. A groan escaped her. His clever fingers rolled her nipples, teased them to tight peaks of nerves, and she closed her eyes in pure, leashed ecstasy. "So good."

"Unbelievable." His chuckle strained from him, broke when he slid one hand under the hem of her skirt and found her bare leg. She choked on a gasp, sucked in a breath as his fingers slid across the sleek warmth of her inner thigh. "I intended to take this slower."

"Fuck slower," she murmured, and jumped when his palm centered over her. It pressed hard against her clit, lace and all. She moaned, her skin going up in flames. "A-actually, no, never mind. Fuck me, Phin. Just me. Right now."

His eyes blazing, every muscle tensed, leashed, he laid her back on the seat. Spread her legs, his hands rough and shaking. Without warning, his fingers curled around her red lace thong, pulled it aside. Naomi grasped at the hem of her dress as he freed his erection from his slacks.

This. This was what she craved from Phin Clarke. This part of him, raw and wanting.

Jaw hard, he bent over her, pressed his mouth to the wild pulse at her throat. "I'm sorry," she thought he muttered, and then couldn't think at all as he slid inside her with one powerful thrust.

She braced her arms above her head, slammed them into the seat to keep from colliding with it as she moaned, jagged and unrefined. He caught her mouth with his, captured her wordless encouragement as he withdrew from her desperate, yearning body and slid deeper, slick and hard and hot. It spun wild heat into nuclear fission, filled her with so much sensation, so much *him*.

Her legs tightened around his waist as Naomi's climax shattered, too fast and intense. It rolled over her, a wave of sensation so forceful it bordered on pain. Phin drank her wild cries, pumped his hips, desperate to feel every clench of her muscles, every velvet squeeze of her orgasm. Stroked her with his own body until he stiffened, toned muscles rippling in his back as he came hard, trembling with the effort to keep himself upright.

She was laughing before their mingled sweat started to cool.

Gasping for air, Phin lifted his face from her neck, his eyes hazed. Rueful. "That," he said slowly, "was not the way this evening was supposed to start."

Naomi's laughter flowed through her body. Made him flinch, hiss in shock and sensation as it wrapped around his still deeply seated cock and squeezed.

"Don't do that," he managed, and smoothed one hand over her hip. "You're going to kill me."

Naomi shifted, her heart slowing its rapid beat. She took in a deep breath, struggled to keep it from trembling. "I don't plan on it," she said, and hoped her tone sounded as light as the fervent prayer wasn't. "I've just started with you."

Phin smiled. Slow, knowing, it reached from his mouth to his eyes, made them gleam with a promise Naomi didn't know how to read as he said, "It gets better."

She elbowed herself up, mind spinning in a thousand directions, and flinched as the driver tapped discreetly on the dark panel of glass between the seats.

Phin offered her a plain white handkerchief. "We're

here," he said as the car began to slow. The bastard looked smug, satisfied.

Used.

A touch of smug satisfaction curled in Naomi's chest, too. She'd made him move sooner than he'd wanted. Made him act when he wanted to wait.

Made him come harder, faster than he'd planned. A delicious shiver curled through her. That's exactly how this was going to be.

Her rules.

Her choice to walk away.

She met his eyes, held his heated gaze as she slowly dragged the handkerchief over the still-pulsing cleft between her legs. Her muscles jerked under the rasp of soft cloth.

Knew he noticed when his nostrils flared, cords gathering in his neck as he tensed. "You're beautiful," he said, voice low and intense.

Too intense.

Because it was the easiest response, she laughed, crumpling the cloth in one fist and throwing it at him. "You're impossible." He caught it out of the air, folding it delicately between his fingers.

When he brought it to his nose, inhaled deeply, Naomi's smile faded. She knew what he smelled; she could smell the mingled fragrance of them both, her musk and his, just on the air between them. A slow, coiling spring tightened in her belly, between her legs, and she forced herself to remain seated. To clamp her traitorous knees together and button her coat.

She fixed her hair. Loosely upswept and tousled was such an easy fashion to mimic. "So where are we?"

Naomi strove for carefree, for casual curiosity. For easy indifference.

"You'll see. Naomi, are you protected?"

She didn't laugh. She wanted to, but his expression was so serious as he tucked in his shirt. Smothering her smile, Naomi nodded. All missionaries were. It was part of the yearly physical. But he didn't need to know that much. "I'm safe," she said lightly.

The look he gave her burned. "Not the word I'd ever apply to you, sweetheart."

A shiver ghosted over her skin. So intense.

So . . . *sweet*. Shit.

The door opened, Phin's uniformed driver standing on the other side. She saw night and rain-hazed lights behind him. Something made of glass.

Topside security.

Grimacing, she ignored the driver's proffered hand, smoothed down her dress as she stepped into the bitter cold. Her knees only wobbled a little.

Her chest wobbled a hell of a lot as Phin unfolded from the car behind her. The man wasn't like any agent in the Mission. She knew there was muscle under that so-expensive suit, but he hadn't earned it fighting for his life in the lower levels of New Seattle. She doubted he'd ever been past the security checks on the city's highway.

He'd be useless in a fight. Useless in the streets below where the sun didn't reach.

So why the hell did her throat go tight and achy when he said stupidly sweet stuff? When he touched that spot low on her back?

Phin took a black umbrella from the impassive driver,

smiled at the man as if he hadn't just been screwing his date in the backseat of the man's car.

If the driver knew— *No*, Naomi thought, shaking her head with a grim little smile. Martin knew. Phin probably paid him too well to so much as bat an eyelash.

Phin snapped open the umbrella, raised it over her head as he gestured to the storefront at the end of the small walkway. "We'll be stopping here for a little while, then on to dinner. Are you ready?"

"I have no idea," Naomi said dryly. "I don't know where we are." It was somewhere in the heart of the downtown district, somewhere topside where business and the elite rubbed elbows with each other. She could see that in the neat, precise blocks, in the carefully planted trees placed in exact lines down each street.

In the cameras on every corner and slow, low-flying patrols of the sec-comps. About as safe as a low-security prison.

Not very safe, and still a prison.

The Cathedral of St. Dominic would be five minutes away by vehicle. The Mission had an office up here, but Naomi wasn't sure exactly where. She didn't come up here if she didn't have to.

Phin's fingers curved around her hip. "It won't kill you."

A grim slash of amusement had her shutting her mouth on the words that would only encourage him to ask questions. Questions she wasn't prepared to field.

After all, as a missionary, she'd gotten really good at finding things capable of killing her. She'd also gotten better at killing them first.

He led her up the walkway, to the glass door that didn't have a sign or logo. Nothing to indicate what it was, where she was. Frowning, she tipped her face up, peered past the edge of the dripping umbrella. "What are we doing here, Phin?"

"Getting ready." His casual lack of information earned him a look she knew wasn't friendly, but he chuckled, dipped his head to trace her lower lip with slow, lingering caress of his tongue.

Her blood warmed, sizzling away the cold that tried so hard to curl into her coat.

"Trust me."

"I really don't," she said, wry, brutal honesty, and he touched her cheek. His fingertips were cold, but gentle.

His eyes held hers steadily. "I know."

When the door swung open, mechanically operated from somewhere inside, he guided her into the warm interior. Naomi frowned impatiently while he shook out the umbrella. The foyer was simple, decorated in stark, modern lines. She didn't know anything about fashion, not this kind, but she guessed it was supposed to be plain, edgy.

Without anything on the walls, it just looked empty to her.

"Andy?" Phin's voice echoed down the hall.

"Come on in!"

The voice that floated back was smooth, polished, and decidedly not a voice that belonged to an Andy. Naomi's eyebrows rose as he gestured.

"After you."

The world that Naomi stepped into unfolded as unexpectedly as the woman who reigned over it.

The studio practically screamed stark modern edge, decorated in clear-cut lines of black and white. Everything was one or the other, every piece of furniture, every mannequin, everything down to the black-framed mirrors, the white carpet, the white veins in black marble. The lights set into the ceiling were harsh and unforgiving, as austere as the decoration that surrounded her.

But it wasn't the decoration that had her gasping in surprise. The real color blossomed from every corner, every wall-to-wall display of evening gowns, day suits, luxurious lingerie, every conceivable item for every part of a woman's day.

Knowing her jaw was hanging open, unable to stop herself from staring, Naomi spun in a slow, overwhelmed circle.

"What kind of goddess have you brought me, Phin?"

A short, slim platinum blond crossed the open, white-carpeted floor. Her herringbone suit was bright, blaring red, the pants cut too long in the leg and designed to fall neatly over her wickedly pointed black stiletto heels. She wore no blouse under the structured, fitted jacket, only a black lace bra showing just enough ample cleavage to catch the eye.

Her diamond white hair had been razored straight at her chin, her bangs a long, unforgiving line swinging just over her wide, blue eyes. She was arresting, strong-featured, with cheekbones high enough to give her face an unforgettable edge, but it wasn't her too-wide smile that set Naomi's hackles up.

It was the easy, familiar way she looped her arm through Phin's.

And the easy, too familiar way he kissed her cheek.

"Andromeda Nikolai," he said, turning to place the short girl directly in Naomi's reach. Her fingers itched. "This is Naomi Ishikawa. Naomi, an old friend, Andy."

A little blood would make her face look less severe, Naomi decided as she took the woman's offered hand. Andy tugged her down to kiss the air beside each cheek.

It took effort not to crush the slender fingers in her grasp. "Nice to meet you," she murmured.

"Any friend of Phin's has absolutely questionable taste," the woman named Andy said cheerfully. "But I'm pleased to meet you, Miss Ishikawa. I understand you're in need of a gown."

Naomi straightened. "Am I?"

"Isn't she?" Andy turned, found Phin where he'd wandered to a rack of sumptuous emerald green silk. "Phin, you didn't tell her?"

"No." Naomi put a hand on her hip. "He didn't tell her. What's going on?"

When Phin only pulled a gown from the rack, something draping and shimmery, Andy shook her head. She turned back to Naomi, blue eyes dryly amused, and said, "I guess that's that. Now, I've got your measurements—" Naomi's face must have betrayed her sudden, fierce resentment, because the diminutive woman laughed. "I have an eye, don't worry. Phin didn't measure you in your sleep."

"I don't sleep around him," Naomi muttered, and then palmed her face with one hand when Andy's smile turned wickedly amused. "That's not what I meant."

"But it will be!" she singsonged gaily. She caught Naomi's arm in one hand, a digital readout with the other. "I have an idea of what I'd like to see you try on, but I'd like to know what your personal taste is."

Naomi felt like a dog towed along on a leash as she followed the woman to a small, brightly lit sitting room. "Something not gray?"

"Oh, no." Andy's energy infected everything around her. Against her will, Naomi found herself liking this strange, platinum-haired whirlwind. Even just a little. "Nothing simple or plain for you. Phin?"

"Already miles ahead." Phin's voice drifted out from between racks of clothes. Naomi found herself placed in a fitting room, the slatted door shut firmly on her half-formed protest.

Staring at the glossy black wood, Naomi could only throw up her hands.

Why not? She usually liked picking out clothes. Granted, her clothing didn't usually cost the same as a new fucking car, but hey, she was Naomi Ishikawa. This was par for the goddamned course.

And a great opportunity to get what she really needed. Quickly she dug through the rainbow bag and located her comm. It was the work of moments to send out a message.

If getting a gun back in her hands meant sitting through yet another clothes fitting, she'd do it with a smile and like it all the way.

A tap on the door had her throwing her comm back in the purse. "Yes?" She swung open the panel, came face to taffeta with a frothy concoction of midnight blue.

"Try this," Andy began, and then thrust the gown into her hands with an impatient sound. "You need to be quicker, goddess. Here." Before Naomi could stop her, the woman stepped into the dressing room. Andy had quick hands, impossible nerve, and she found herself stripped to her underwear before she could do more than roll her eyes.

"Wow." Andy put her hands on her hips, studied her from the tips of her clear-polished toenails to the crown of her tousled hair. The red lace contrasted with her pale skin, a shade darker than Andy's own suit. "You're stunning."

"I'm—" Her mouth pursed as Naomi tried to find the perfect word.

"Overwhelmed?" The woman pulled the dress from her hands, found the zipper Naomi hadn't noticed, and tugged it off the silk padded hanger. "Confused? A little ticked off?" Her grin wicked, Andy spun her finger in the air. "Yes, you are certainly dating Phinneas Clarke."

"Naked," Naomi corrected firmly. "I'm naked, is what I was going to say."

"Partially naked," Andy said, and held the dress open for Naomi to step into. "Beautifully in disarray. If I had my camera—"

"I'd jam it down your throat."

Andy's sharp peal of laughter was all Naomi heard as she struggled into the gown. "I like her, Phin!"

"Mine," she heard from beyond the fitting room.

Naomi blew out a breath, then winced when she caught a glimpse of herself in the three-paneled mirror. The material hugged her figure, its sleek lines a stark contrast to the pouf of sheer material gathered at the shoulder. The same material lined the square back, trailed down to her hips and flowed in a smooth wave to the floor.

Luxurious. Decadent.

Mine, he'd said. She blinked at the mirror.

"Oh, God." Andy looked horrified. "No, off, now."

Naomi complied, a flicker of amusement edging out irritation. "Is this one of yours?"

"It's all mine, honey, and—hey, Phin? No pouf."

"I'd stay away from taffeta in general."

Naomi jerked her eyes to the mirror and caught Phin lounging in the black lacquer door frame. Color framed him in a sea of material, but it was his slow, smiling appraisal that sent flutters through Naomi's stomach.

Ridiculous, since he was talking about a dress.

Straightening her shoulders, she stepped entirely out of the gown Andy held for her and turned slowly, spinning in a deliberate display of naked limbs, the taut, flat muscle of her belly.

"I didn't know you knew dresses." Her tone was husky. Suggestive. Mocking, Naomi knew and didn't moderate it. She glanced at Andy and asked with as much sincerity as she could, just to piss him off, "Is he gay?"

Andy laughed her ass off. "No," she managed. "God, no. The man just has immaculate taste. Especially about what looks killer on a woman's body."

His eyes skimmed over her face. Her mouth. Touched her curves, as physical as the remembered the feel of his hands on her.

Red lace and warmed skin.

Naomi raised her chin and knew exactly how futile this was as she pressed a hand to the lace-covered tattoo at her abdomen. She knew how this would end.

Blood and bullets.

His gaze turned to fire. To wanting.

And then he nodded at Andy. Crisp. "Absolutely no taffeta. She'll look like a parade queen." With that, he was gone, leaving behind a selection of gowns hanging from the slats on the door.

Andy tossed the midnight blue gown to the floor. "Next!"

CHAPTER TWELVE

Naomi Ishikawa was all woman.

Phin hadn't doubted it, not for a second. As she tried on dress after dress, he watched the rigid line of her back slowly ease. Watched wary irritation melt into something warmer, something much more relaxed. Much more amused.

Fun. Naomi was having fun.

The thought made him want to insert himself into that easy niche of feminine laughter and kiss her until her breath fragmented in her chest.

As something dangerous fragmented in his.

He rubbed at his sternum idly, surveying the picked-over remnants of Andy's design studio. Something else. He was missing something, something perfect.

He heard the click of her wicked heels before her voice, quiet. Judging. "You like her."

The top of Andy's ice blond hair barely came to his shoulder. He glanced down at her, at her wide, shrewd blue eyes. He couldn't lie, not to her. She knew him better than that. "Yeah."

Her mouth twisted. "You sure know how to pick them."

Shared memory sparked between them both, mingled laughter and an indulgence so brief, it barely registered as a footnote in her ambitious career.

Or so Phin figured.

Still, he turned, tucked a finger under chin. "Hey," he said. "What is it?"

"Oh, you know," she said lightly, and braced a hand on his shoulder to bring him down to her level. Her lips were warm, brief on his cheek. "Remembering good times. I'm tapped out, did you find anything else?"

"I liked the red." Phin let her change the subject, but he kept her hand tucked in his. His best friend.

He hoped it was enough.

She grimaced. "Too obvious." A beat, and then her mouth flipped up into a catlike smile. "But one of my best."

Phin chuckled, turning again to study the starkly contrasting viewing studio. "The black velvet—"

"Ugh, no." She waved that away, effortlessly freeing her hand with the gesture. "It practically flattened her chest. She looked like a twelve-year-old boy in a skirt."

"Impossible," Phin argued. "Besides, did you see what it did for her—" He stopped. Frowned. "What is that purple thing there?"

Andy followed his gaze, her smile widening as she saw what caught his attention. She hurried across the floor, dug through the clothes hanging together until she could find the start of the material trailing from the bottom of the rack.

"I had," she crowed triumphantly, "completely forgotten about this. This is it, Phin." Fabric shimmered through her arms like violet moonlight, as fragile as spun silk. It caught the harsh light from the ceiling, reflected it back in shades that made him think of the heart of a thunderstorm, a purple sheet of lightning.

He whistled. "Go stop her from trying anything else on."

"Naomi?" Andy pitched her voice to carry. "This is it!"

Phin heard Naomi's muffled question, heard Andy's excited nonanswer, and grinned. He checked the wide face of his watch, reassured they'd have plenty of time before the reservations anybody else would have had to wait months to make, and barely kept from climbing into that damn fitting room himself.

The knowledge that she had spent most of the past two hours wearing nothing but red lace and his scent had steadily redirected the flow of blood from his brain and into his pants.

Tonight was going to be exquisite agony, and he'd already had her once.

He stared into the ordered chaos of Andy's studio and wondered if everything was all right in Timeless. Not for the first time, he checked the comm clipped to his belt, saw no message, and was only partially relieved. They'd call if there was a problem.

He just couldn't shake the certainty that there was.

Behind him, Andy cleared her throat. He turned, expectant, and saw only her. Smiling in knowing sympathy. "We're going to go ahead and fix her hair and makeup. You go fix yourself a drink."

"Is it perfect?"

"You'll see," she said, and vanished back into the elegant fitting room station.

Phin obeyed, but only because the urge to peer over the top of the paneled wall was too strong to completely ignore. Rueful, he crossed the studio, stepped into the large, equally as stark office, and helped himself to Andy's carefully stocked bar.

He drank the expensive imported whiskey slowly. It'd take them time to prepare—growing up among women taught him time was a given—so he made himself comfortable behind Andy's black metal desk and cracked open his comm unit.

At the very least, he could get some work done. It kept him from drinking too fast, and his brain from what was going on in the dressing room.

Only half of the smooth whiskey remained when Andy cleared her throat from the door. Phin set down the glass, rose, and hesitated when she said simply, "Stay there." She vanished again. Shadows mingled, feminine voices murmured.

He felt as if the air had been punched out of his lungs as Naomi took her place.

Her hair had been swept off her neck, coiled into sleek curls and pinned in place with diamonds that winked like stars in a tapestry of night. Her makeup was subtle, luminescent. It swept her eyes into more dramatic lines, polished her mouth to a lush, tempting gleam.

Her expression was cool, indifferent, but he knew her better than that. Beneath the material that cupped her body like a lover's hands, her muscles were rigid with tension. And Jesus, she didn't need to worry.

"You—" Phin swallowed hard. "You're stunning."

The gown's lines hugged her body, its corset strapped tightly under her bust and beaded with gold in diagonal patterns. It pushed her breasts high, shaped her cleavage to something he didn't think he'd be able to resist staring at all night. Her shoulders remained bare, porcelain smooth, while more of that soft, shimmery material draped over her arms in faux sleeves.

And her legs. God in heaven, Phin was going to die a happy man. The slit in the side of the draped gown stopped a hairbreadth from the band of red lace he hoped she still wore beneath. It was signature Andromeda, intensely sexy and completely unapologetic.

But Naomi wore it like it was made for her. Just for her, and her long, long legs.

"Phin?" She tilted her head, the column of her slender throat moving as she swallowed. "Hello?"

"Wait a minute." Phin circled the desk. Very slowly crossed the office to stand just out of reach. It only got worse—better, Christ, *worse*—the closer he got. She looked like a goddess, like some kind of moonlit creature of the night, and he—

"I expect," Andy said severely from behind her, "that she will arrive to Swann's in the same condition that she is now."

Naomi shifted, a flush of color sweeping over the tops

of her lovely breasts, over her shoulders and cheeks. Her eyes filled with laughter, knowing and wicked, as they met his. "Yeah," she said softly. "Same condition."

She turned, and his eyes flicked to the strappy stiletto heels on her feet. They were barely noticeable, a glint of gold crossed over her ankles. He wanted them over his shoulders. *Now.*

"Uh, yeah," he managed hoarsely. He cleared his throat, met Andy's narrowed eyes and tried again. "Absolutely, perfect condition. Andy, you're a genius."

"No," she corrected, and tucked her arm in Naomi's. "I'm an artist. *She* is the perfect canvas." When she offered her other arm to him, Phin took it. He matched Naomi's smile with his own as Andy led them both to the door. "Have fun, behave"—this with a stern look at Phin, who had the grace to smile sheepishly—"and for the love of all that is holy, Naomi, try the dessert. I don't care what, you just must have something and think of me."

"I'll do that."

Despite her polished shine, Naomi looked glazed enough that Phin took pity on her. He touched her shoulder, felt the electrical twinge all the way to his chest when his fingers encountered bare skin. The faintest edge of a faded scar. "Why don't you go to the car," he said. "I'll be right there."

To his surprise, she didn't argue. She turned, holding the rainbow purse that didn't match the gown in one hand and a sleek gold handbag in the other, and bent to receive Andy's air kiss. "Thank you," she said, a glint in her eyes. "It was great meeting you, Andy."

"I expect you to tell everyone that you're wearing an

original Andromeda," the designer said brightly. "I'll have work until the next earthquake."

Naomi turned, sliding him a thoughtful look over her bare shoulder, and proceeded down the steps. Martin hurried to meet her, holding an umbrella over her head. His expression was rapt. Awed.

Kicked in the gut, and Phin knew the feeling.

"Thank you, Andy." He bent to kiss her cheek. "You know I owe you."

"Boy, do you," she said indulgently, and caught his arm when he straightened. "What do you know about her, Phin?"

Her eyes were serious, her tone lowered enough that he frowned. "There's a lot I don't know," he admitted. "But I can tell you this: She's funny, and smart. She's gorgeous—"

"Clearly," Andy interjected wryly.

"I mean on the inside, too." Phin looked up, saw her step out of the way of a man in a dark overcoat walking by. He said something to her, something flattering, because she smoothed a hand over her gown and smiled.

Naomi's gaze flicked to Phin, but he couldn't read it in the dark.

Andy's fingers tightened on his arm, brought his attention back to her. Worried. "Do me a favor," she said quietly. "Just do this and we'll call it even, okay?"

Covering his fingers with hers, Phin promised, "Anything."

"Ask her about her tattoo." When his eyebrows rose, Andy smiled, a resigned curve without humor, and patted his hand over hers. "Enjoy your evening, honey. She can keep the dress."

Before he could ask anything else, she pushed him toward the waiting car. Toward Naomi's silhouetted profile, waiting now inside the warm interior.

"Same condition," Andy reminded his back, and Phin sighed. Her laughter followed him all the way to the street.

Naomi watched him carefully when he slid inside the opened door, banking a sudden, vivid smile as he tucked himself on the opposite seat. He slid as far into the other corner as he possibly could.

The gown revealed too damn much of her long, smooth legs, crossed at the knee. And no visible tattoo.

"It's going to be a long drive, isn't it?" Laughter deepened her voice, that smoky edge that wrapped like a hand around an erection that didn't need any more help. He jerked. "Would it help if I—"

"Don't," Phin said tightly, locking his hands around the seat, "breathe. Or we're going to end up exactly where we were when we arrived."

"Oh." Naomi uncrossed her legs, crossed them again in slow, wicked challenge. "Well, okay, then."

Phin reached for the champagne.

Miles would have to tail them to Swann's.

She glanced out the window, eyes tracking the muted shades of light and motion filtered out by the dark glass. He was out there somewhere, she knew he'd have to be.

If not, she was going to hunt him down in this purple dress and kick his ass. She wanted her gun.

Her skin tingled, as physical as a caress, and she knew Phin was watching her. Again. Still. A part of her reveled in it, knowing he found her irresistible in this wretched, cloud-spun dress, and a part of her knew he only *saw* the dress. The rich girl.

The heiress.

Still, it was one night. Dinner, a dress, Phin's hands and mouth on her, what would it cost her? Tomorrow she'd start pushing Carson. Harrying him. She'd find out where he hid, how, and take away his ground. She didn't have time to wait for blueprints anymore.

Tomorrow she'd have bullets to give him.

Just for tonight, she could be Naomi Ishikawa.

Her gaze slid back to him, to the set of his jaw, his glittering eyes, across the dark interior. "So. Swann's."

His mouth quirked. "Andy has a big mouth."

"Lover?" Naomi kept her voice casual, but she saw his smile deepen, saw him nod in the shadows.

"For a little while."

"What happened?"

Phin placed his empty glass back into the sideboard. "She wanted a career more than she wanted a partner." He glanced at her.

Or, she realized with a sudden wash of humor, her cleavage. Shifting, she hooked a finger into the tight edge of the corset. Pulling on it didn't give her any more room to breathe. The damn thing was boned with steel. "You don't seem very broken up about it."

When his glance flicked back to her face, amusement settled over his features like a shroud. "It was almost eight years ago, Naomi. We were both young. I was focused on Timeless, and she wanted her design studio." A beat. "I turned thirty-two earlier this month. I lost my virginity when I was seventeen, and no, it wasn't with Andy. My first kiss was at a birthday party for a schoolmate. I was ten, she was eleven. Would you like to know how many people I've slept with?"

Her chin lifted. "Only if you'd like your rosy view of me tarnished beyond repair." Saccharine sweetness dripped from every word.

His eyes narrowed. Through a veil of relaxed, pleasant good humor, his gaze glittered dangerously. "Really."

The car slowed. Naomi meant to hold that gaze, to show him that she could sit in a luxury car, wear a designer dress, and lose nothing of the woman he didn't know she was, but light shattered over the tinted windows. It exploded like fireworks, drawing a sudden frown, swift tension as her gaze jerked to the window.

"Welcome to Swann's," Phin said dryly.

"Reporters?" Naomi didn't like the look of it. Too many people. Photos. Her face in the news. Worse, on Phin's arm. "I don't like reporters."

"They barely qualify as that." Phin shifted, reached behind him to tap on the glass between the seats. It eased down, Martin's capped head tilting as he guided the car through a line of similar luxury vehicles.

Naomi scowled. Busy night for the rich and infamous, wasn't it?

"I have phoned ahead, sir," Martin was saying in neat, precise tones. "They are prepared around the back."

"Thank you." The window eased up as Phin turned back with a smile. He straightened his jacket. "That should take care of that."

"Phin, I don't—"

He shook his head, one hand raised. "Relax. It's a

date, Naomi, I'm not asking you to marry me. I might ask you to show me that scrap of red lace again," he added with a boyish smile that pulled at something sharp and bittersweet, "but it's not really the same thing."

No, it wasn't. And she could handle showing him the ice blue lingerie Andy had sneaked into the room when he wasn't looking. Only about a thousand times sexier than red lace. Naomi's own smile didn't do anything to ease the ache forming in her chest.

Nerves. That was all. She smoothed the skirt of her gown as the lights faded away and the car eased to a gentle stop.

The front door slammed. Then Martin's shadow by her window.

Phin got out first, leaving her to gather the sweeping hem of Andromeda's gown. When he reached back, his hand splayed and steady, Naomi let him help her out of the car.

Let him pull her just slightly too close. For too long.

The cold autumn air ghosted over her skin like icy nails, but his arm was warm around her back. His eyes hot and approving as they met hers.

His smile undid every good manner she didn't have.

Ignoring Martin, ignoring the muted frenzy of lights and voices just up the block and around the corner, Naomi tilted her head, closed the distance between them with a low, impatient sound. Hungry.

His arm tightened, his body tensed, but his mouth— Oh, his mouth. It took her kiss, her brand, and turned it back on her. Made her forget the cold night air as his lips moved over hers, soft and damp. Sticky sweet with her own lip gloss.

Fresh and male and so very much Phin.

Her breath caught. Her nipples beaded in the slow, molten reaction of her blood and his flavor. Unable to stop, to separate, she slid her fingers into his hair, cupped the back of his head and pulled him closer.

His mouth to hers. Her breasts pressed hard and hungry to his chest. His thigh inserted between hers, so close to the sensitized flesh framed in decadent lace and silk.

His erection, thick and insistent against her abdomen.

She broke off with a muted laugh, a chuckle caught on the edge of something wilder, one hand braced against his chest. "Okay, slick." She managed casual, but it came out breathy. More needy than she wanted.

His eyes were shadowed in the darker privacy of the secondary street, but his smile widened in pure male satisfaction. Sliding one hand under her elbow, he eased her away from the car, put his lips to her ear, and murmured, "You taste like candy."

It was such a simple comment, a matter-of-fact observation. She did taste like candy, like something sugary and sweet. It was the lip gloss Andy had put in her bag. She knew that.

But his breath ghosted over her ear like a warm caress. His lips brushed her sensitive skin, his fingers tight at her elbow, and that simple observation slid like a pure aphrodisiac to the damp, pulsing heat between her legs.

Dessert? She wasn't sure she'd make it through dinner.

Her knees rubbery, Naomi straightened her shoulders and stepped out of reach. To save herself.

The man was potent.

He nodded at the impassive driver busily watching nothing in the opposite direction. "Martin, I'll call when we're ready for pickup."

Around the corner, lights exploded in a frenzy of flash bulbs. It peppered the side street wall, sent shadows dancing across the rain-slick brick. Naomi glanced at the street entrance, saw a figure turn the corner.

She recognized the tweed fedora tilted at a jaunty angle.

Finally.

"Of course," Martin said, and tipped his hat with a ghost of a smile shaping his thin lips. "Enjoy your dinner, sir. Ma'am."

Now she just had to figure out how to get Miles inside, or get the gun from him on the outside.

"Naomi?" Phin offered his arm, even as the polished glass door slid open beside them. A man in a crisp white shirt, black jacket and slacks waited with a wide, welcoming smile.

She glanced back over her shoulder once. The car pulled away, briefly highlighting Miles's hunched shoulders and sodden raincoat in its headlights.

He wasn't close enough. She couldn't tip him off now.

"Sure," she said, too brightly, and looped her arm through Phin's. More lights, more voices raised in a cacophony of shouts and names she didn't recognize.

Brick chipped into uneven edges over her head. Shards scattered, rained to the ground, to the opposite wall. A fleck skimmed over her forearm, and adrenaline slammed into her system as a thin red line blossomed in its wake.

Miles's voice echoed from wall to wall. "Get down!"

Without looking, without even thinking, she tightened her grip on Phin's arm. She wrenched him around, kicked the hem of her gown away from her delicately heeled foot, and swept Phin's legs out from under him with the same fluid movement. He hit the pavement before surprise had time to form in his eyes, on his face.

Naomi was a breath behind, pinning him.

Sparks flew from the wall over their heads, shards of brick scattered like shrapnel. All concern, ignorant of the danger, the maitre d' hurried out of the warm safety of the restaurant.

He flinched when a tiny chip of brick sliced open his cheek.

"Get back inside!" Naomi shouted, but the idiot raised his fingers to his face.

She didn't hear the rapport of gunfire. Couldn't separate it from the roar of a crowd half a block away, but the man went down like a broken doll as crimson bloomed like a gory flower over his chest. The glass around him puckered. Shattered.

Too late.

Naomi was already moving. Rolling away from Phin, she snatched the hem of the gown in her hands and leaped to her feet. "Miles!"

The missionary plastered himself against the opposite wall. "Sniper!" he shouted, and threw the small black case he carried with effortless strength. It slammed into her chest, knocked the wind out of her, but she caught it safely.

Finally. For fuck's sake, a gun!

He caught the rainbow purse she hurled back at

him. "Clarke is priority one," he ordered. "Get him to safety." Miles took off, back toward the lights. He'd circle the building, she knew, leaving her to get Phin out of the area. Knowing she stood in the bright pool of light from the restaurant, as obvious a target as if she'd doused herself in neon and painted a target on her back, Naomi ripped the case open.

"Naomi!" Phin knelt over the unconscious man he couldn't help if a bullet found his skull first. His jacket was torn at the elbow, smeared with mud and moss.

Andromeda's beautiful dress would never look the same, even if she could have gotten the grime out.

"Leave him," she ordered, steeling herself from caring. From worrying about the fragile silk and lustrous color. Her skin, his life, was more important, damn it. "Phin, get out of the light!"

Her fingers closed over the grip. A Beretta—not her favorite gun on the go, but oh, the relief. For a single fraction of a second, Naomi let herself heft the gun in hand. She felt its solid, cold weight in her palm. The trigger at her index finger.

An extension of her arm.

Another rapid hail of bullets scattered the glass at her feet. She danced back, jumped away from the interior lights. This time, there were no screams of excitement, of attention, to hide the sound. Gunfire crackled like a muffled clap of thunder, like sound sucked into a padded room. Muffled, but not silent.

"Damn it, Phin, get over here."

"But—"

She sprinted across the pool of light, fisted a hand in his collar, and jerked him to his feet. He staggered, rolled into her. One fragile heel snapped loose from her delicate shoe as Naomi braced his weight, as she tried to keep Phin from falling back into a perfect target.

His expression was shocked, grim, his eyes somewhat glazed as he caught at her arms with bloody, angry fingers. "What is going on?"

She pushed him, gun in one hand, hard enough to break his hold. "It's— *Fuck*!" She spun with the weight of it, with the velocity of a bullet tearing a furrow over her shoulder. Too close to the artery. Too damn close to her fucking throat.

Exactly where Phin at been a half second before she'd pushed him out of her face.

She caught herself on the wall, rebounded as pain tore strips of gold and red out of her vision. "Run!" she gritted out through clenched teeth. *Move.* She just had to go, and keep going until they were safe.

No time to bleed.

Gritting her teeth, she jerked Phin off the sidewalk. Shoved him toward the flashing lights and chaos of the reporters and arrivals. She didn't give him any time to speak, to ask questions.

Knowing he was white with shock, shaking with the same fear and the wild adrenaline that coursed through her own system, Naomi fisted a hand in his jacket and pushed him ahead of her. Up the street.

Priority number one.

She deliberately placed herself between him and the sniper who wasn't too good with his aim. Or, she thought as pain burned a throbbing line all the way to her trigger finger, exactly good enough.

Sparks flared on the wall behind them, more brick

shrapnel. She didn't know if they hit her, couldn't feel a damn thing but adrenaline and the bullet crease the bastard had already given her, but it gave her the strength to shove Phin around the corner. She pushed him into the chaotic knot of people sealed behind hip-high grating and Swann's uniformed security.

Phin slammed to a halt. Before she could argue, he tore the gun from her grasp, jammed it into the back of his pants, and wrapped fingers like vises around her arm. "Stay close." He jerked her hard against his chest as the first of the mob turned to look at them. "Smile," he ordered tightly, and draped his arm over her shoulder.

Right over the bloody, burning crease. She nearly buckled under the pain.

It barely registered when he seized her arm and wrapped it around his waist. He gripped it there, supported her weight as it flagged.

"Smile," he repeated urgently.

She did. Somehow, through lips that felt icy and too tight with strain, she smiled.

"Hey, it's Phin Clarke! Who's the new lady?"

"Pretty girl, Mr. Clarke, has she had too much to drink?"

"Hey, Phin, man, let's see you kiss her!"

"Is this one the one?"

Phin said nothing, simply guided them deeper into the crowd of hungry journalists, past the photographers who spun like startled deer, caught between Phin's presence behind the security line and whatever wealthy person Naomi couldn't see at the front entry.

Swann's security hastened to unbuckle the gate,

swing it wide to let them through. He cupped her arm tightly, kept it hard against his ribs as he navigated toward the front gate. They passed the stream of cars stopping one by one to discharge famous, rich, ignorant passengers.

"Keep smiling," he ordered from the corner of his mouth. The photographers, sharks to blood, obviously hesitated. Almost as one, they swung like pendulum from their retreating backs to Swann's welcome carpet.

By the time they stepped out of the lights, the crowd a dull roar behind them, Naomi could breathe without seeing spots in front of her eyes. "Stop," she said. "Stop, we need—"

"We need to get you back to Timeless." Phin pulled out his comm, dialed swiftly. "Martin, we're one block left of the restaurant. Make it fast. Call ahead, let my parents know we're coming."

He didn't look at her as he clipped the unit back to his belt. Not really. Instead, his sleeve drenched with her blood, he shrugged out of his coat and draped it over her cold, shivering shoulders.

His expression was a hard, impenetrable mask in the dark.

"Stay out of the light," she said, cradling her arm. "Stay back in the shadow. You'll be a harder target."

"We're going to discuss how you know this." His voice mirrored the unyielding planes of his face, as hard as the fingers he kept wrapped around her uninjured arm. "Soon."

Naomi's smile razored a line in the dark. "No," she murmured, pain making it tremble. She sucked in a hard, clearing breath. "We really won't."

She didn't know what he paid the man, but Martin knew urgency when he heard it. The car came tearing up the street, slowed to a halt just in front of them. Phin opened the door and put her inside it as if she were a small child needing help with the buckles.

He was gentle. He didn't have to be, but Naomi felt his care with the way he handled her, watched the shape of his mouth twist as he gathered the hem of her ruined gown and tucked it by her feet.

Her arm burned, too wet for her to assume she was in the clear yet. She shifted, forced to bite back a sound of pain, of bitter anger. "Towel," she muttered.

Phin pulled one from the cabinet with the champagne. He brushed aside her hand when she would have taken it from him, then knelt at her feet and shifted his body between her legs.

Her laugh broke against her clenched teeth.

Gentle, too demanding to deny, he slid his fingertips along her jaw. Tilting her head shot sparks through her vision. His gasp when he peeled back the collar of her coat told her it was exactly as messy as she'd assumed.

"Stay with me," he said, his voice urgent. She nodded, a tiny gesture, and he pressed the towel against the bleeding, ragged furrow. Searing agony slipped her neatly into numb and black.

CHAPTER THIRTEEN

L illian was waiting in the garage. Phin pushed the car door open before it even rolled to a full stop, tires screeching. "Where's Mother?" he demanded.

Martin, white-faced but calm, hurried around the fender to prop open the hall door.

"She's prepping everything in the clinic," Lillian told him calmly. "How bad is she hurt?"

"I don't know." He didn't want to think about it. He didn't want to see the amount of blood soaked into his coat sleeves, or feel Naomi's fragility—cold and breakable as glass as he cradled her against his chest. Lillian held Naomi's head still as he maneuvered her out of the vehicle, splaying one hand over the towel wadded at her neck.

"Easy, love," Lillian said. "Hold her steady. Martin, thank you."

"Ma'am," the older man said solemnly.

Phin didn't spare him a glance. Everything he had was focused on the white edges of Naomi's slack lips. On the blood smearing her cheek, Jesus, the shortness of every breath.

She had to be okay.

"Hurry," Lillian ordered, walking awkwardly beside him as she held the towel in place. "Gemma has a bed ready."

His arms tightened. Naomi moaned, cheek turning into his chest, and Lillian braced her head with her other hand. "She'll be fine," she told him. "Phin, love, listen to me: it'll be fine. There's nothing your mother can't do, okay?"

The painful slam of his heart wanted to argue with her; *he* wanted to argue, to yell, to shake the fragile, pale—God help him, the beautiful, brave, *foolhardy* woman in his arms and demand to know everything.

To know why she did what she did.

Who was she?

Why did she protect him?

Throat tight and dry, he let Lillian trigger the brass elevator and held on to her warm, motionless body as the mechanism climbed to the clinic suite.

Who the hell was she? God damn it, *why* didn't he already know?

Swallowing the angry knot in his throat, he looked up as the elevator doors opened. He met Gemma's warm brown eyes, filled with so much worry.

He couldn't stop himself. He broke.

His shoulders sagged, grip tightening over Naomi's ribs. Her legs. "Mom." The word, the plea, broke on a note he hadn't heard from himself in too many years to recall now.

A note he didn't know how to define.

Gemma's eyes narrowed, sharp as a general in the field, and pointed to a ready bed with clean, white sheets. "There."

Phin hastened to obey, striding to the bed and laying Naomi carefully, God, so gently on the bed.

"Lily, keep that towel close. Phin, baby, get her some clothes from her suite."

"I'm not leaving her."

"Phin—"

He straightened so fast, the bed jostled. Naomi moaned again, breath catching.

Instantly contrite, face pale, he all but leaped back from the bed, hands raised. "I'm sorry," he said hoarsely.

"She's fine, she's okay," Lillian said. "Phin, calm down."

"She won't stay here," he said, shaking his head at Gemma as the woman rifled through a wide white armoire. "She'll refuse to stay in the clinic."

"Fine," Gemma replied simply. "Go get her suite ready."

"I'm *not*—"

"Phinneas Clarke." Lillian didn't have to raise her voice. She barely even had to look up, her fingers tight at the wrapped wound still seeping sluggishly from Naomi's shoulder. "Do as your mother says."

"Please," Gemma added, much softer.

Somewhere between his panic, his fear, and his fury at being sent away like an underfoot schoolboy, he saw his mothers trade knowing glances. Lillian dropped her eyes, focusing on the bloody towel, but Gemma crossed the room and took both his hands in hers. Her grip was warm, tight. Dry.

Insistent as she pulled him around, back toward the elevator doors. "She's going to be okay," she promised softly. "I will do everything in my power to ensure it."

"I just . . ." What? He just *what*?

"When she's all bandaged," she said over him, letting his hands go to cup his cheeks, "we'll put her in her own bed, and *you* need to look after her. She'll want someone she trusts. Are you hearing me?"

Phin closed his eyes. In his mind's eye, he saw blood and flashing cameras. Naomi's mouth, pinched tight with so much pain.

She didn't trust him.

He hated that he wished she would.

His mother's hands tightened on his jaw. "Phin."

"I'll go get it ready," he said, forcing his voice to sound stronger than he felt. To sound purposeful. "Bring her when she's bandaged."

"I will."

"And, Mother . . ." Gemma tilted her head as he covered her hands with his. "Be careful. I—"

"Gemma!" Lillian's voice, sharp with worry.

Phin let his mother push him back into the elevator, but his eyes remained fixed on Naomi as the doors eased shut. She was so pale around the blood smeared over her cheek. Her pins had long since scattered, leaving her dark hair pooling over the side of the narrow pillow, and all he could think was how she'd half held him as she'd shoved him into the shadows.

Stay out of the light.

Hands clenching into white-knuckled fists, he hurried to see to her room.

She slept like she fought a war in her dreams. Even in her sleep, she frowned tightly, her brow furrowed.

Phin watched her from across the darkened room, his elbows braced against his knees and too many emotions roiling through him to work out now. All he dared acknowledge was that she was safe.

The rest would sort out in the morning.

God, there had been so much blood. So much of it on his jacket, on the clinic bed. On her. Phin dropped his head into his hands, scraped rough fingers over his hair as exhaustion clawed at the back of his mind.

But he needed to see her breathe. To watch her chest rise and fall and rise again beneath the ivory sheets.

To know she was alive. With him.

Whoever she was.

The sliding door eased open behind him. He didn't have to turn to know it was one of his mothers. Lillian had checked in about an hour ago, bringing his favorite tea and admonishing him to sleep.

It didn't fail to register that they were taking shifts.

For him, not her. They'd seen to her. She was safe.

Thank God.

"Baby," Gemma murmured softly, her hands warm at his shoulders. They smelled like lavender and sage, peppermint and that indefinable something that was pure Gemma. Pure magic. His neck tingled under the brush of her fingertips, and without a word, he reached up to lace his fingers with hers.

"She's going to be just fine, you know."

He shook his head. "She just . . . took it," he said roughly. "Just got hit with a bullet and kept going."

"I know, baby." Gemma sidled around the chair, her eyes smudged by exhaustion and worry. She threaded her free hand through his tousled hair and smiled. "But she's going to be okay. By tomorrow she'll barely feel a thing. Not even a scar."

And Naomi had so many of those. Each one older than the last, some barely a blotch on her fair skin. Others still shiny and pink, like the one at her arm.

Phin tore his gaze away from Naomi's sleeping form, but he could only frown into Gemma's so-sure smile. "Who is she, Mother? How does she know how to move like that?"

"I can speculate," she murmured, "but I don't know." She bent, pressed her lips to Phin's forehead. He closed his eyes, drawing in a long, slow breath that smelled of all those ingredients and more. Like love. Familiarity.

Everything was going to be okay.

"Get some sleep," she said, pressing her cheek to the top of his head. "You'll have a busy day tomorrow."

And wouldn't he just? He pinched the bridge of his nose between his fingers. "It's the fountain, isn't it?" he asked wearily. "All of this with Alexandra and the sauna and, hell—"

"Phin," Gemma admonished gently, but she dropped a kiss into his curls. "Sleep. We'll all need you tomorrow."

She left him brooding in the dark. The bedroom door

slid shut behind him, and Phin knew she was right. In the morning he'd have to start scouring the halls, bringing in even more security, even think about closing the resort for the duration.

Two people were missing. A principal guest nearly killed. Things malfunctioning. Naomi attacked.

It had to be about the fountain. Or, and he didn't know which was worse, about the underground Timeless supported. Somehow, someone suspected witch activity, and *this* was the fucking price they'd have to pay.

Damn it.

They'd take a massive hit to the books, of course they would. But he couldn't risk the privacy of the people inside. Possibly even their lives.

But what would he tell them? What could he say that wouldn't destroy everything he and his mothers had worked so hard to build?

What the hell was going on?

He didn't know. The same questions had gone around and around in his head while he'd prepared Naomi's bed, waited for his mothers to help her. Waited for her to wake up.

Just . . . waited.

So he watched Naomi sleep instead of thinking about it. Watched her eyebrows work together into a slow knot of worry. Of anger, of something deeper. Pain.

Who the hell was she?

Shadows crept through the suite, lengthening into pitch black as the night wore on. Somewhere in the quiet, Phin lost the fight with himself. He slid into a fitful sleep shattered by images of blood and spattered brick. By corpses at his feet.

Camera flashes in his eyes.

When he jerked awake, nothing but the faint *tick*, *tick*, *tock* of his wristwatch broke the silence. He fumbled for his sleeve, squinting at the dim numbers. Three in the morning.

His back cramped as he straightened from an awkward slouch. The chair creaked, and he rubbed at his face as he stood. Quietly he stripped off his shirt.

He'd had nothing but time earlier, so he'd tidied her room while he waited. The state of her suite hadn't surprised him, not really. He'd seen worse. She wasn't kind to her clothes—as if bloodstained designer silk wasn't bad enough—so he'd hung up the articles of clothing that she'd left strewn around her empty bags.

He'd even organized her shoes.

Tomorrow he could tease her about it. When she was awake and he wasn't so. . .

Suspicious. Angry. *Terrified*.

His body aching, Phin longed for a shower. Instead he knew that he'd have to wait for daylight, and the answers he wasn't sure would be forthcoming.

Would she tell him?

Doubtful.

Smiling wryly, knowing it lacked all pretense at humor, Phin toed off his shoes and cracked open the armoire door. He hung up his shirt on a padded hangar, placed his shoes beside hers on the armoire floor, and quietly pushed the door closed again. He braced one hand on the wood for balance, rubbing at his tired, sleep-fogged head with the other.

The bedcovers rustled.

His stomach muscles clenched.

Turning slowly, so much apprehension pouring through his mind, Phin saw her framed in shadow and the faintest thread of light. Her hair fell in tousled midnight streaks, the bandage at her shoulder stark white against the shadowed outline of her pale skin. Hazy, uncertain, her eyes gleamed from the frame of a face that he instinctively knew had seen so much more than a single bullet from the night.

Why? Why did he want to soothe those shadows from her violet eyes?

She pressed the heel of her hand into her temple. "Phin?" she murmured.

Something shattered in his chest. Something coiled tight and tense low in his gut, but it was the breathless agony somewhere near his heart that broke any resolve he had. His breath eased out in a loud, shaking sigh.

"Damn it, Naomi," he said roughly, and crossed the room in short, angry strides.

She was already reaching for him. The mattress dipped under his weight as he knelt, spilling her against his chest, into his arms. With a groan, he wrapped them around her so fragile body, around the sleek muscles he knew came from doing whatever it was she did that made her so familiar with bullets and snipers.

And he didn't care.

"Kiss me," she whispered, her mouth offered like a gift, a sweet taste of heaven. Her fingers mapped his naked back. Stroked his shoulders, his biceps. "I'm fine, it doesn't hurt, Phin, just—"

He obliged. Tilting her face up, he kissed her with the warning sound of alarms wailing in his head, and he didn't care. Her mouth was soft and hungry, her lips warm, pliant.

And she deserved so much more than what she thought she wanted.

Phin gentled the kiss, eased away just enough so he could feather his lips over the curve of her bottom lip. Her cheeks. Her nose and the almost completely healed cut there. Her eyelids, her forehead.

His hands stroked over her neck, down her sides. Wordless, he scooped her into his arms. Laid her out full-length upon the mattress and stripped the simple nightshirt over her head, taking his time to look at her. Just look.

His eyes skimmed over her long, lean body, naked and so irresistible. Soft and hard, silken skin and tensile muscle. Her breasts were high and perfect, small pink nipples thrust proudly, beaded tight from wanting.

Wanting him. Phin's body clenched tightly, already achingly hard, but he didn't move. Not yet. He couldn't.

She was okay.

God, she was stunning.

Her waist was trim, her hips were, Christ, perfect for him to hold on to, to sink his fingers into, and he knew that already. Her legs were long, joined by the neat thatch of dark hair shaped and trimmed by a day at his own spa.

And the tattoo tucked just under her hipbone. A neat circle of dark ink, its detail blurred in the dark. He didn't need to see the fine lines to recognize it. To know he courted danger. That he desperately craved the undivided attention of a witch hunter.

Tomorrow. He'd ask questions tomorrow.

She moved restlessly beneath his hot gaze, one knee easing up. Hips shifting. "Phin—"

"Shh." Soft as silk, he ran his palm down the center of her chest. Across her stomach. It fluttered, physical echo of her shaking breath, and he smiled crookedly as he touched one beaded nipple with his lips. His tongue. She gasped, jerked under his hand as he threaded his fingers into that soft strip of dark hair at the vee of her legs.

He brushed against her hot, already damp cleft and made her whimper.

But he wasn't going to go too fast this time. Ignoring her urgings, her muttered curse, he split his attention between her sweet breasts and the fascinating bud of her clit. He pulled on her nipple with his lips, laved at the pink tip until she squirmed, all the while stroking her more delicate flesh with his fingers. Feeling her swell with her arousal. Grow hotter, wetter.

She writhed. Gasped. Pleaded.

Phin shifted on his knees, ran his mouth over the taut muscles of her belly. Over her abdomen, and the clench of muscle there, too. She was perfect. Fit.

Tattooed.

He ran his tongue over the faintly raised skin of the seal of St. Andrew. Tasted the sweat of her body, smelled the hot, sharp scent of her sex, and swallowed back a wild need to bury himself in her now, right now, and let it all go in the depths of her willing body.

At least for a night, they could pretend that everything was exactly what it seemed.

But that would be done too fast. Over. She deserved

better. She *needed* better. Phin was determined to give it to her.

Seizing her hips in both hands, he eased a knee between her legs. Breathed softly on the trembling flesh of her inner thigh as he whispered over her skin. Over her trimmed, damp curls. He let her know in no uncertain terms what he meant to do.

What he'd been wanting to do since he'd first seen her, trouble in curve-hugging denim.

How he meant to do it.

Naomi arched. "No, Phin, I can't— Oh, *God*."

He plunged his tongue between the soft folds of her sex, laved at the tight knot of nerves there. Gentle turned ardent as she bucked, his hands tight on her hips, holding her still when she tried to twist away. She couldn't shift out from underneath the exquisite torture he knew she suffered.

Knew she wanted desperately to avoid.

Phin didn't, couldn't stop.

Ignoring her pleading, whimpering cries, he dragged his tongue across the cleft of her body, plunged it deep inside to taste the very essence of her. Sweet and so intoxicating. He needed her to understand, to recognize that he would take his time with her tonight.

That he could press every button in her traitorous, needy body and leave her shattered and shaking at his feet. And when she was done, when *he* was done, he'd still be there to cradle her in his arms.

He would protect *her*, this time.

More, he wanted Naomi to know that he loved this. Loved the smell of her, intoxicating and seductive as no perfume ever could be. That he wanted her, *her*, stripped of masks and pretenses.

He wanted her to climax so hard, she forgot her own name in the aftermath.

Knowing it for the reckless move it was, fighting every growling urge of his own tightly wound body, he used his fingers to separate the folds of her flesh, to reveal her to the night and his scorching approval. Slowly, so slowly, he inserted one finger into her wet heat, nearly groaned aloud as her muscles clamped down on it.

His dick jerked, as demanding as she was. As unforgiving and needy.

Gritting his teeth, he rotated his wrist, crooked his finger just so, and knew he'd found that perfect erogenous zone as her back nearly bent off the bed on a sharp, wild cry. Unable to help himself, he closed his lips over her clit, sucked that bead of flesh and nerves into his mouth and quirked his finger at the same time.

She climaxed crying his name, her body shuddering, clenching hard and wet and violently around his finger and driving him to the absolute brink of sanity. In the dark, he knew she couldn't see the pure, fierce satisfaction on his face. Knowing how hard she came, how hard she fought it. And that he could make her do it again.

And would, over and over and over, before the night was out.

It was the work of a moment to strip off his slacks, leaving them discarded on the floor. She was still shaking, her hands covering her face through gasps of shock, of decadent liberation, as he crawled back up her body. She shuddered as he licked a path from navel to breast.

She stifled a groan as he closed his teeth over her left nipple, bit down gently, firmly, until her shoulders flattened against the bed and her back arched with the sweet ache.

He took his time. Gently, firmly, Phin coaxed her sweet, lushly responsive body back to attention. To slow, spiraling heat. Naomi's hands caught at his shoulders, her nails dug into his biceps, but he resisted her. Even as his cock throbbed in echo of his heartbeat, loud and heady, even as he ached from the wanting of her, he resisted her.

He wanted her mindless and twisting when he took her this time. He wanted those walls down. Just tonight.

"Easy," he breathed against her sweat-damp skin. He licked the gentle swell of her breast, braced his hands on either side of her shoulders and gave the same attentions to the other.

She twisted restlessly beneath him. "Phin," she whispered. Her eyes were closed, her full, lush mouth shaping his name the way he intuitively knew she'd shape his cock if he let her.

Which would end it all. He was wound so tight, even the muscles of his abdomen felt stretched, sensitive to every brush of her skin, every arc of heat, that wild electricity he felt whenever she so much as breathed in his vicinity.

Now he had her.

"You drive me insane," he murmured against her breast. Feathering his lips over her nipple, back again to her navel, that tattoo; Christ, she tasted so good. Sweet and salt. "Ever since you ran me down, I've watched you move, wanted you in my bed."

Her laughter trembled, twisted on a gasp as he covered her sex with one broad hand. Pushed against her flesh. "I—" She sucked in a breath, tried again. "I drive *you* insane?"

"Oh, yeah." Deftly he slid his hands under her hips. "I've dreamed about the taste of you. I've woken up with your scent haunting me."

Her sound of surprise sank into the pillow as he flipped her over, pressed one hand flat against her lower back.

"I've wanted to do this since I first saw you," he whispered, his own voice less than steady.

Naomi managed to get her elbows under her. Leveraged herself to look back over her shoulder. Her eyes smoky, dark with lust. With half the sharp awareness she usually had. "Phin," she began, and dropped her face back to the pillow as he slid his fingers along the cleft of her bottom. He lowered his mouth to the curve of her hip, ran his fingers farther, over wet skin and along the folds of her sex.

She was still so hot, still swollen from his loving, her orgasm, still tight and musky and—

She jerked when he slid two fingers deep inside her, laughed shakily as he bit the tender flesh at the curve of her bottom. She groaned, long and loud, when he dragged his fingers out of the tight sheath of her slick flesh, thrust them back inside in desperate mimicry of what his body demanded.

Her hips lifted, animal grace and reckless, frantic beckoning.

He could feel every inch of her clenching muscles, feel the sweet, sticky heat of her around his fingers.

It wasn't enough.

Her gasps, her moans; it wasn't enough.

She cried out as he pulled his fingers free of her body, arched into him as he crawled over her, nudged her legs apart with his own. The head of his cock probed at the wet entrance of her sex, teased her. Throwing her hair back, she wrenched herself to her elbows, slammed her back into his chest and rubbed. Like a cat.

Like she needed to feel him around her.

Inside her.

Groaning, Phin lost the battle with himself. With her. Braced, ready, he slid home, slid deep with her hips cradled by his and her back slick with sweat against his chest. He had no will left to fight as she pushed herself up, forced him to sit back on his heels, to catch himself, his hands spanning her waist as she rode him.

God, the pressure. The ache. The. . .

The wholeness of it all. The rightness. Of her.

Cords gathered in his neck as he held on to her waist with every ounce of strength he possessed, guided her hips to rock back against him. Over him. He thrust in long, liquid strokes, silently demanded she follow his lead as her back arched.

He watched her skin gleam with sweat in the light. Watched the play of her muscles as her back moved, sinuous, graceful. And still she milked him, rode him like nothing he'd ever had, ever dreamed of having.

Her moans tightened, her body clenched in rhythmic echo of his own heartbeat. Twining one hand in her hair, Phin held on for dear life, rode the wild, tautly coiled spring of release as it tightened in his chest. His gut.

His heart.

"Naomi," he breathed.

She threw back her head, reached behind her and seized his wrist in a grip that told him she was close. So close. Her hips slid back over his lap, her body enfolded his. Sweat made their skin slick, so smooth, and as she rose high on her knees, as he felt every sweet inch of her let him go, she used his wrist as leverage and arched her back hard. She slid back into the cradle of his hips, and the spring of his release unwound.

Detonated.

It shattered every part of him in an orgasm that had him thrusting up, thrusting hard, raking himself over that spot inside her and sending her wildly crying out her own release. Her body twanged, taut as a bowstring, shuddered as he wrapped his arms around her and held her close until the spots vanished from his eyes. Until he could feel more than raw, shuddering adrenaline and endorphins and . . .

And trouble.

Because he wasn't done. Easing his fingers into her hair, Phin blew lightly across her sweat-dampened back. Smiled slowly when she gasped and shivered.

He wasn't going to be done for a long time.

CHAPTER FOURTEEN

Sometime in the earliest hours of the morning, when the sky was still dark and the bedclothes were tangled beyond repair, they fell to exhaustion.

The suite was cozy, the mattress soft and welcoming, and Naomi woke to find her body draped over Phin's like silk, her legs tangled with his. Her cheek was warm, pillowed on the smooth planes of his muscled back.

For a long, still moment, she forgot to breathe.

Morning. And with it, a shattered illusion. She knew this game.

Slowly, carefully, she eased away from the vivid temptation of all that naked skin. As the mattress dipped beneath her weight, he shifted, turned his face into the gap between both pillows, and didn't so much as let out a sound. Naomi breathed out a silent sigh of relief.

Last night had been a lot of things. Fun. An exercise in endurance. Her body ached in places Naomi loved to feel on a morning after.

But it was daytime now, and she had work to do.

Work that included betraying Phin.

Well, not so much betraying. She'd made no promises. No guarantees. The night had been one hell of an amazing dream. Like some kind of princess, she'd been dressed and bathed and painted, and he'd stripped it all away.

Now dawn kissed the windows, and the dream was over. Bullets and blood.

She didn't have the luxury of wishing.

She surveyed the suspiciously clean floor where her clothes had been. Her bags had been emptied and folded—*folded*, for fuck's sake—and stacked neatly away. The polished door of the armoire stared at her.

Jesus bastard Christ. Had Phin shoved her clothes over a corpse in the dead of night? And didn't notice?

He couldn't have.

Only *she* could be insane enough to screw a man while a body rotted in the same damn room.

The thought didn't feel as humorous as it should have.

Although every muscle in her body *screamed* at her to get moving—and get the hell moving *right this fucking instant*—Naomi forced herself to ease from the mattress inch by nerve-bending inch. Biting her lip, she tiptoed to the closet and eased open the door. She didn't realize that she held her breath until it whooshed out of her on a soundless curse. Phin's shirt hung in the murky light, a masculine companion to the array of frothy, silky, expensive tops the Mission had stuck her with. A pair of his expensive shoes sat neatly beside her own. Her pants hung on specially designed hangers, as neat as if he'd pressed them himself.

There was no body.

Her mind whirling, she withdrew a pair of designer denim jeans and a red sweater, and grabbed the only heeled boots that wouldn't dump her flat on her ass.

Despite the mind-boggling absurdity of an ambulatory corpse, she was unable to help the faint tug of a crooked smile as she spun slowly. Or the way her eyes latched on to his sprawled, sleeping form.

He slept like he forgot he shared a bed. His face buried between the pillows, his curls wild and one foot hanging off the side of the mattress, he clung to one pillow and slept like the dead. Like a man up too long in the early hours.

She could have liked waking up to him more than a few times. Maybe if they'd been in different circumstances. Maybe if he'd just been some guy in the middle levels, or some kind of working-class stiff—

What the hell?

Wake up, Naomi, she thought grimly, and resolutely turned away. Quietly, holding her breath, she found his trousers discarded on the floor and couldn't stop the insistent rush of pride, of heat, pooling low in her belly.

She'd made him so damn eager for her. Wild for her.

He'd torn her inside out and left her wanting so much more.

Her smile faded. Hurriedly she rifled through his

pants pockets until she found his key card. Draping the charcoal gray fabric over the back of a chair, she couldn't stop herself from fingering the hem.

He'd looked good last night.

He looked utterly delicious now. The morning sun eased over one leg, trailing bars of light across his firm ass. The sheets, long since tangled in the night, gathered at his waist and did nothing to hide his gorgeously toned body from her study.

She wanted him again. The ache between her legs wasn't just the legacy of one hell of a night.

Shaking her head, she slipped out of the bedroom, eased the panel back into place, and deliberately blocked the view of his temptingly muscled butt. Backing away, she tucked the key card into the back pocket of the jeans she'd taken.

Yeah, so she was running. So what? They'd made great memories. That was it. It was all over now.

Her heart thudded in her ribs. Anxiety, she told herself. Now started the fun, the part where she got to be the hound to Joe Carson's clever fox. With the witch dead—God only knew where the hell his body was, but he was dead at least—Carson was the only damn thing that mattered now.

She wanted out.

But she pressed her palm to her chest as she searched for the pretty clutch Andy had given her. She needed her comm. She needed her gun, wherever Phin had put it.

And she needed enough time to visit Phin's office for the guest files the Mission didn't have. Possibly even a map of the place.

She found the gold purse shoved half into the cushion. In it, she found her comm, her lip gloss, and . . . no. No gun in sight.

No fucking gun.

Naomi straightened, mouthing the invectives she didn't dare say aloud. She raked the living room with a sharp, speculative gaze. The last she remembered, she'd had it in hand. Then she'd gotten shot. They'd run and. . .

Carefully she touched the shoulder that should have hurt like the very devil danced on it. All she felt was askew bandages and a dull, easily ignorable ache.

Phin had taken the weapon from her. But done what with it?

Damn it. She didn't have *time* for this.

She dressed hurriedly, laced up her boots and knew she was only delaying the inevitable as she twisted her hair up into a spiky knot.

She didn't want to go back into that room.

Where Phin Clarke slept naked. Used, muscled, gloriously naked.

Oh, God.

Silent as a ghost, she eased back into the bedroom and surveyed the too-tidy space. Resolutely avoiding the bed, she searched for his coat. It wasn't hanging on the coat rack. Not on a chair, fuck, not even on the floor.

And along with the missing corpse, she hadn't seen his coat, either.

Though it galled the hell out of her, Naomi gave up the search. There was no way she'd let Phin wander off with her gun, but she didn't have time to look now. She'd get it back.

Just as soon as she ransacked Phin's office.

She turned.

The sheets rustled. "Mmph."

Naomi froze, her heart a rapid staccato in her ears. Throat suddenly dry, she weighed her options. Run like hell?

Too awkward. And she'd be damned if she tucked her tail between her legs and made him think he had *any* sort of upper hand.

Instead she smiled, turning back. "Morning, sunshine."

Phin's back rippled as he pushed up on his elbows, rubbing both hands across his face. The motion sent muscles leaping from shoulder to ass—good God, his ass—to his strong, naked thighs, and it took everything Naomi had not to crawl back into that nice, warm bed and straddle him until they both forgot what time it was.

She gritted her teeth through her smile.

His eyes were hazy as he rolled over, one hand idly pulling the sheets across his lap. "Morning," he replied. The slow, lazy way his smile reached from his mouth to his eyes tugged on bits of her she'd thought long since too exhausted to melt now.

She was wrong.

And he was a hell of a lot sharper in the morning that she'd thought possible. Phin's smile faded as he took in her body. Her very clothed body. "Headed somewhere?"

"Breakfast," Naomi lied easily. She slid two fingers into her back pocket, securing Phin's key card as she added, "I was hoping you'd sleep long enough for me to get back." She raised a fine, dangerously eloquent eyebrow. "You know . . . bring you something sticky and sweet."

His eyes gleamed. "And then we'd eat breakfast?"

God damn it, she *really* liked this man. Naomi laughed, even as she fought not to run the hell away.

Jump his bones.

Something. *Anything* but stand here and lie.

His smile faded, warm eyes easing to something soft and melty and kind. Velvet. "Naomi—"

"Did you put away all my clothes?" she asked. Too quickly, but it was better to tear off the Band-Aid than sit and wait for him to ask.

He sat up, one hand braced over the impressive morning erection the sheet wasn't hiding very well.

God, his chest was worth staring at. Forever.

"Your what?" Muffling a yawn, he covered his mouth with his free hand and took a moment to glue her question together. He shook his head as if to clear it, but admitted, "They were all over, so I just put them away while you were . . ." He hesitated. "Getting bandaged," he finished lamely.

"And there was . . ." Jesus, was there any safe way to ask this? "There was enough room in the wardrobe?"

His lips twitched. "Plenty. You're probably the only guest in the history of Timeless to pack as light as you do."

Relief punched a hole somewhere beside growing panic.

Where. The fuck. Was the body?

But his gaze turned serious as he swung his bare feet over the side of the mattress. "Naomi, we need to talk."

Oh. *Shit*.

Before she could say anything, do anything, he smiled again, and it was as if the fight just pooled out of her. How the hell did he do that?

"It's not what you think." He chuckled. "You don't have to look so . . . braced."

She settled for a noncommittal sound, settling her hands on her hips. This, she figured, was where he pulled the white knight bullshit. Wrong time, too busy for a steady relationship, whatever.

Naomi resisted the urge to check her watch.

Even as something black and aching opened up in her chest.

Phin didn't stand. Instead, bracing his elbows on his very bare knees, he pressed his palms together and studied her over his fingers. "You're a missionary." It wasn't a question.

The floor dipped out from under her feet.

Somehow, as Naomi stared at Phin's now-serious appraisal, she locked her knees. Managed not to buckle, managed to remain upright and even casual as she tilted her head, that eyebrow raised again. "Am I?"

"I saw your tattoo."

Oh, Jesus. Of course he had. The room practically reeked of sex—as if her body needed any more reminders of the mind-blowing feel of his cock deep and hard inside her—and she was stupid enough to hope he'd missed the damn tattoo in the dark.

Fuck.

Her shoulders straightened. She knew her face closed down, could feel her expression sharpening, but it was all she could do to sound nonchalant around the sudden tightness in her throat. "And?"

He took a deep breath. "Is the Church looking for witches in Timeless?"

Shitfuck. "Let me ask you this," she said carefully. "Is there any way that you'd tell me the truth if I asked you if Timeless was harboring witches?"

Phin looked her square in the eye, his own hard. Steady. "I would," he said, so seriously that it took her a moment. Longer than it should have. When it finally made it through to her sex-addled, shell-shocked brain, she nearly fell over from relief.

Instead she sank to the chair behind her, laughter spilling from her chest. "Oh, God. Fuck, Phin."

"What?" he demanded.

"You would!" It snapped out, half a curse, half a laugh. "Jesus Christ, you would, wouldn't you? What are you going to tell me, that you're keeping a secret coven of witches out to kill your own guests?"

His eyes narrowed. "No."

"Then I think," Naomi replied, ignoring the raw ache clawing at her belly, "that it's safe to say the Church doesn't think you're harboring witches."

Which, she knew even as she refused to say it, didn't mean that witches weren't taking advantage of the Clarkes. That wasn't something she was going to mire Phin and his family down in.

The witch was dead. She'd seen no other signs. Now it was just her and Carson.

Totally different story.

"Then why are you here?" Phin asked. He linked

his fingers, watching her with such intensity that her humor faded. Eased into relief so pronounced that she thought she'd choke on it. Pressing a hand to her chest, she tried again for tact.

She was fucking bad at tact.

"I can't tell you everything," she began, and threw up a warding hand as he stood, sheet draping dangerously low on his hips. She jerked her eyes to his. "No, stop. Don't take a step, or I swear to God, I'm not going to be held responsible for what I do."

He hesitated. But his eyes—those warm velvet eyes—crinkled. "Noted."

"And hike up the sheet," she added waspishly. When he did, muscles moving like liquid steel under his tanned skin, she took a deep breath and reached for just enough truth to give credence to the lies. "The Church sent me here because I needed a break. We do that sometimes," she added dryly. "Vacations. I'm not big on . . . you know. Yoga and stuff."

"I noticed," he murmured.

She ignored that. "But I wanted time away. The Church thought I'd be more than safe up here—no one's even supposed to know I'm here." Lies, lies, and enough truth to fake the rest.

God, she hated it.

"And last night?"

Naomi touched the bandage under her hastily donned red sweater. "Someone must have recognized me. We're never really alone, you know. Even on vacation, we have partners."

Phin nodded once. "Miles."

She frowned. "You have a good memory for a hell of

a shock." Then she saw his knuckles, white with strain. Naomi hesitated.

What could she do? Comfort him?

No. She'd be gone soon. And all he'd be left with would be bullets and blood.

And lies.

"Yes," she added before he could reply. "Whoever shot at me"—*at you*, she corrected silently—"must have recognized me. I'm sure the Mission caught him."

"Him?"

"Or her," Naomi added smoothly.

Phin looked down at the floor. His jaw shifted, shoulders twitching as if he argued with himself about something. About her.

Hell, she didn't know. Naomi rose to her feet, forced herself not to get closer, then stilled as he jerked his head up, meeting her eyes directly. "So the Church isn't investigating my home?"

She blew out a deep breath. In this, at least, she didn't have to lie. "No," she said softly. *Just a shitfucker of a rogue agent who decided to sneak his way inside.*

Even she couldn't think of a better place to lie low.

Phin moved so suddenly that Naomi froze between flight and fight. He grabbed her waist in his large hands, hauling her against his chest. The sheet caught between them, dipping dangerously low, but all she felt against her palms was warm, achingly familiar skin and the slow, steady beat of his heart. "Don't ever," he said, his eyes filling her field of vision. So serious.

So heartrendingly stern.

She licked her lower lip. "What?"

His lips moved, a tic hard at his jaw. Then, as if

shaking away the words he didn't know how to say, he let go of her waist to slide his fingers through her hair. "Hell with it," he muttered, and crushed his mouth to hers.

The tender ache of her well-used body fled beneath a liquid pool of need, of wanting so tight and sharp and driven that it washed away everything else but him. His lips claimed, possessed. Took from her every fucking thing she never wanted to give—her capitulation, her craving. Her silent confession.

How badly she wanted more.

He took all that and gave her back all the things she didn't want. Couldn't force herself to name.

And still she drove her tongue into the wild heat of his mouth, rasped against his, her fingers digging into the sculpted planes of his pectorals. His heart slammed into her palm. His groan wrenched from him, his erection pulsing hard and thick against her abdomen, and she thought, *What the fuck are you doing, West?*

Dangerous. So desperately dangerous.

Wrenching away, gasping for breath, she pulled back out of his reach and held up both hands as the sheet pooled slowly to the floor at his bare feet.

Gloriously, unabashedly naked, Phin watched her with eyes that glittered as hot as the liquid heat between her legs. Hungry. Demanding.

Naomi forced a laugh. "Food," she said emphatically. "Or I swear, I'm going to die on you, and you'll seriously regret it."

She didn't have to feel his heartbeat to know how strongly that kiss affected him, too. Color rode high on his cheeks, and his cock thrust magnificent and hard from the thatch of dark hair she was trying too damn hard not to stare at.

Naomi knew full well what Phin Clarke could do for her.

And she knew *exactly* what she was going to do to him.

Betrayal.

The poor, deluded bastard.

She fled with his laughter still drifting huskily behind her.

He'd get over it, she thought as she retreated. In the sitting room, Naomi moved Phin's key card into her front pocket, shook out her hair, and knew she'd need a shower before long. The things they'd done, the things Phin had done to her . . . Her breath shuddered out. The man had some hands. Gifted, clever, fearless hands.

A good, bright memory for when she got the hell out.

She crossed the room on soundless feet and waited impatiently for the elevator to respond to the call signal. When it slid open, silent and quick, she made her escape. It was the work of moments to fix the mess Phin had once more made of her hair as the lift glided down.

She wasn't sure what time it was. The elevators opened to muted quiet, a hush so thick that it wrapped like a blanket of silence around her ears. She studied the garden with its shedding trees and slowly wilting foliage.

She needed to get to the staff floor.

The staff floors were keyed in to the staff. Ergo.

Naomi fished Phin's card from her pocket and scanned it. The elevator doors slid closed again. Too easy.

Too trusting.

When they opened, Naomi hesitated, checking the digital floor readout. It said she was in the right place, but the hallway looked like any of the others she'd seen. Nice carpet, the same pattern as everywhere else. Nice wallpaper, professional and clean.

Good lighting. Naomi frowned at the sconces lining the wall. She didn't see any cameras, but she didn't think it meant anything. Not at this point.

Phin didn't strike her as stupid. Well, not anymore.

And this late into the game, any cameras that caught her wouldn't matter. The hotel's security would be five steps behind her and answering to the Church by the time they figured out anything was wrong.

Not her problem.

The carpet dampened any noise her footfalls might have made, and she hurried down the hall with her ears straining for any signs of life. Everything was so quiet. The first door she found was narrow, marked clearly with a brass nameplate.

Maintenance. No, not there.

She passed more like it, each named for the necessary tasks. Organized to the extreme.

Finally, just as she was about to give up and try the next floor, she found it. Three doors, two on one side and a third on the other, each labeled with the same brass plates. She eyed each. All three Clarkes had their own offices.

Which was likely to hold files?

Remembering Phin's neatly hung shirt and arranged shoes, she shook her head. His office, like the others, boasted a thumb lock.

Wordlessly, she grabbed her comm unit and dialed in to Jonas's direct line. She clipped the mic to her ear and waited.

"Naomi! Man, I'm so glad to hear your voice."

"Ugh." Jonas had always been a morning person. "I need to get past a fingerprint lock," she said, deliberately ignoring his jovial greeting. "If I hook you in, can you override it?"

"Does it rain all the time in the shattered Northwest?" Jonas replied, and she heard the clattering echo of his fingers flying over computer keys. "First, though, how are you?"

Used. "Bullet crease, but that's it. I'm going to have to answer some questions today, so the sooner you hurry this up . . . ?"

"All right, all right," Jonas replied, relief clear over the line. "I'm just— You know."

She knew. Her mouth twisted.

"Now, there's a short panel in the side of your unit. Slide it off."

Naomi's fingers struggled with the tiny piece. When it cracked open, a pronged bit of metal fell into her palm. "Okay?"

"Somewhere on the lock, there should be a jack. Insert that bit and let me know when it's ready." He spoke slowly, easily, his tenor reassuringly steady.

"You sound like an info-feed line." She ran her fingers over the lock casing, bent until she could see the underside.

"And that's why you love me," Jonas said cheerfully. "Is it in yet?"

"Baby, you say all the sweetest things." Naomi

whistled softly as she found the tiny hole in the casing, ringed by bands of metal. The tiny device slid right in, clicked faintly. "It's in."

"Hold on while I do that thing I do so very well."

Biting back a smile, she waited as the lock's digital screen jerked sharply, fuzzed, and went abruptly black. She didn't touch it, barely breathing as she listened to him work over his keyboard like a performing pianist.

The screen blinked back on, flashing yellow. She heard the tumblers spin inside the door, heard them slide back and click into place. "And access granted," Jonas said in her ear.

"You're a wonder." Naomi turned the doorknob. It spun easily, opened just as easily. Phin wasn't stupid, no. But maybe a little too confident in tech that people like Jonas ate for breakfast, lunch, and dinner.

"Anything else?"

"Nope, I'll be in touch soon."

"Good. We need to get the report from last night."

Naomi frowned. "Is Miles okay?"

"Not even a scratch," Jonas reassured her. "Mighty ticked, though."

"Yeah." Naomi rolled her shoulder. The one that should have hurt. "He can join the club. Have you run the blood?"

"No match," Jonas said with a sigh. "We're looking at a relative unknown."

"Son of a bitch."

"Hopefully that was the last of the witches," Jonas said, optimism practically leaking into her ear. "Good luck. Get to it and keep in touch."

"Thanks," she muttered. She turned off the comm,

frowning at the neat stack of plastic containers arrayed against the far wall. The room boasted only a desk, a monitor, three chairs, and that overwhelming stack of boxes for furniture.

The office was clean. Way, *way* too clean. Nicely decorated in more masculine tones of dark wood and shades of burgundy and dark, damask gold, but too clean.

Pristine, even.

Did the man even use this thing?

Circling the desk, Naomi gave it a brief look-over and shook her head at the chair tucked neatly into place, the complete lack of fingerprints on the monitor, and the clean keyboard built into the polished surface of the desk.

Phin Clarke was a neat freak. Given the state of her suite this morning, this didn't surprise her. Even the leather chair lacked the kinds of nicks and scratches that the Mission office collected like blue ribbons.

Frowning, she turned toward the rows of boxes. Each boasted a label, a panel with neat, printed block letters, but they made no sense to her. A code. Some sort of personal security process.

Not stupid at all. "Damn."

"Can I help you find something?"

Naomi spun, one hand automatically reaching for the gun that wasn't tucked at her shoulder. Her fingers closed on the bandage under her sweater, her heart pounding as she met Gemma Clarke's assessing brown eyes.

The woman leaned against the doorjamb, her tailored suit sunshine gold and accented by an ivory blouse. Her hair was pinned up, so much nicer than Naomi's messy knot.

Swallowing hard, Naomi lowered her hands to her sides. "Mrs. Clarke."

Phin's mother stepped into the room, surveyed it quickly. Finding nothing out of place, that astute gaze slid back to her. Narrowed. "What are you looking for?"

She could lie. Very little could explain her presence in a locked office, but she could lie about what she intended.

But looking into Gemma's shrewd eyes, she knew it wouldn't matter. "Mrs. Clarke, I can explain."

"I expect you to," the woman said, her tone not entirely friendly. "But first, I would like to know why my son performed a rather dignified walk of shame into the family wing this morning."

Oh. "Fuck," she muttered.

Gemma's eyes narrowed. "Indeed. I would also like to know why the Church saw fit to infiltrate"—she held up a hand as Naomi opened her mouth—"yes, I mean *infiltrate* my business with spies."

Naomi fisted her hands against her hips. "What did Phin tell you?"

"I don't want you to repeat what you told my son," Gemma said, and her tone was as matter-of-fact as her regard. The woman had a bullshit meter Naomi could only envy. "I want to know what your mission is, and how it's going to interrupt our lives."

Naomi took a deep breath. "It won't," she said, and added quickly, "at least not any more than it already has. I just need a few things and then I'm out of your hair."

"Such as?"

"I need the guest lists for the past two weeks. Day-trippers and residents."

Silence greeted her candid relay. Silence, and one shaped brown eyebrow.

Naomi had slept with this woman's son. She'd spent the night screwing him until they were both blind with exhaustion. Even now, her body ached, pulsed with the memory of it.

And Gemma knew. It probably didn't make her look very good in the woman's eyes.

Not that she gave a damn what anyone else thought.

She shifted uneasily. "Look," she said, spreading her hands, "I'm here to put a stop to something that might be a problem. I don't want to cause trouble, I want to *stop* it."

Gemma's mouth thinned. "Does this problem have anything to do with the body found this morning in the laundry facility?"

"What the hell are you—" Naomi frowned. "A body?"

The woman propped a round hip at the edge of the desk. She didn't bother softening her tone. "One of my maintenance employees, Miss Ishikawa. Mark Vaughn. He was found with his skull caved in, quite dead and buried in a vat of towels."

Maintenance. Naomi thought fast. "Does maintenance have key cards to every room?"

"Of course."

Shit, shit, fucking two-timing luck. That answered *that*. The bastard witch had easy access to her room. But why? She set her jaw. "Yes," she lied. "He's one of the reasons I'm here. How long has he worked here?"

"Three weeks."

Was the timing right? Naomi took a step forward, stopped abruptly and stared at the ceiling. "Did he have any friends?"

Gemma watched her, wary. "Not many. A few of the other employees."

"Does maintenance have the run of the building?"

"They have to," Gemma replied, and her brow furrowed as Naomi's fist punched through the air.

"That's it!" she crowed. Carson bribed the witch into letting him in. It had to be as simple as that. Once the maintenance man was no longer useful—trying to kill her twice was about as *fail* as she could imagine—Carson must have just taken a copy of the man's maintenance keys and called it good.

But a hunter working with a witch?

And why remove him from the armoire?

Shit. She'd figure that out later. "Yes, Mrs. Clarke," she said in more even tones, "I can tell you it's only getting worse. I think that my target, Joe Carson, has already tried to kill one guest, and succeeded in killing your man." Lies upon lies. She was so fucking good at them anyway. "Gemma, believe me, I'm not out to hurt you."

"Aren't you?" The woman adjusted the rolled up cuff of one sleeve, smoothing the wide, flat fold. "How is your shoulder, my dear?"

Momentarily scattered, Naomi's hand flattened over the bandage. "Fine," she said. "It's only a scratch."

"Is it related?"

She nodded, once. "Given how bad the conditions

were, only a trained sniper could have made that close a shot."

Gemma's eyes narrowed. Flickered in a steely resolve that Naomi couldn't misread. "Why did you tell Phin it wasn't related to this?"

God damn it! Didn't he keep any secrets from his parents? Naomi sighed. "Because," she said, gritting her teeth, "if I had told him that I was after a trained killer, he wouldn't have let me do my job. And," she added as the woman stared at her, "you *know* he would have tried to take on Carson himself. Gemma, Carson's an assassin. What did you want me to say?"

Gemma took a slow, deep breath. Then, quietly, she met Naomi's eyes and asked, "Who was the sniper aiming for?"

This lie sprang easily to her lips. "Me."

"Fine." The woman straightened, rounded the desk, and gestured Naomi out of her way. "Then I'll get your information."

Naomi stepped aside. "Just like that?" Suspicion unfurled in her chest, her voice. "No more questions?"

Placing her hands on the top of one plastic organizer, Gemma straightened her shoulders. Without looking at Naomi, she said quietly, "I have a lot of questions, Miss Ishikawa. I want to know who you really are and what you intend with my son." Naomi flinched. "I very much want to know where one of my guests is, and whether she's in danger."

That was news. "Who?"

Gemma raised her eyebrows. "Katie Landers. She's Jordana's assistant."

Naomi flashed to an image of the mousy brunette seated alone in the breakfast nook and rapidly calculated the odds. "When was she last seen?"

"Yesterday, about mid-morning."

"What's her room?"

"Jordana's suite, seventh floor." Gemma smoothed back her curly hair and shook her head. "When this is all over, Miss Ishikawa, I really do expect answers."

"Someone will be in touch," Naomi replied by rote, knowing it for the bullshit it was. The Church didn't make apologies.

Then again, the Church didn't usually drop agents in the middle of the superrich and elite.

"The Holy Order?"

"Yes, ma'am," Naomi said. "They hold all the cards here. I'm just an agent."

Gemma's smile flipped crookedly. "I doubt that very much, Naomi. So then what you're saying, what you told Phin, was true?"

"Which part?" Naomi said flatly.

The woman's smile evened. "Touché, Miss Ishikawa. The Church doesn't suspect us of doing anything illegal? We're not under suspicion? Accused?"

Naomi shook her head. "I'm sorry. You're just the foxhole."

"Then I'll get your information," Phin's mother repeated simply. "You've had plenty of time to do worse than a little lock breaking and some white lies, and you haven't."

Worse? Naomi's smile bit hard. One corpse down and how many less-than-white lies up? She'd done worse, all right. She'd do even worse before this was done. But she said nothing as Gemma studied the labels on the boxes.

"Understand," she continued in her crisp, efficient way, "Timeless and this family are the most important things in my life. If anyone, *anyone*, tried to hurt them, there would be a reckoning like the world has never seen." She glanced over her shoulder.

Naomi stilled.

"You understand that feeling, don't you?"

Fists curling, Naomi stepped back. Retreated. "Thank you for finding those files," she said, and knew she was acting like a coward. Leashed tension tightened every word. "We'll keep them confidential."

"I'm sure you will." Gemma bent to a box on the second row. "I'll send them along. Anything else?"

"Blueprints?"

Her smile was sad. "They don't exist."

Naomi nodded, once. "I thought as much. I'll just—"

"Naomi?"

She didn't want to stop. Didn't want to hear what the woman with Phin's dark, knowing eyes had to say. But she did.

Because anything else would be unacceptable.

Coward.

She braced a hand on the door frame. "Yes?"

"Will you be staying long?"

Killer. "No," she said. "Just long enough to take care of the mess."

Gemma nodded. "Will you tell Phin before you go?"

Oh, Jesus. "He'll know," Naomi said evenly. Without her having to say a single word, he'd figure it out.

She was a killer. Not a therapist.

"All right," Gemma said. "Try not to hurt anyone."
She turned back, cracked open the sealed flaps of a box,
and Naomi fled.

Try not to hurt anyone.

That just wasn't her specialty.

CHAPTER FIFTEEN

She'd struggled only a little.

Joe didn't bother hiding her body any deeper than he had to, and the locker wouldn't afford him much time at all. Of course, he didn't need much. Either he'd get what he needed soon or he'd be dead. Naomi West was closing on his heels.

He could sense her.

It was now or never.

The rumors, the legends, were true. He knew it in his gut, and his hunches had never been wrong. That's what made him a damn good missionary. The best. Hunches and action.

Experience and raw instinct.

His gut told him that the fountain was here. That

he'd find it at last. He just needed the right key. And the right lock to fit it in.

He'd found it all right.

This time, it'd taken so much longer. The wiring, the setup, all of it had taken so much more time than he'd thought. First he'd needed the girl's key card. With that he could open the seventh floor suite. From there, it was a hop, seam, and stretch along a maze of passages that put him on the beauty floor.

From there, he could get anywhere without being seen. And no one would be the wiser.

It annoyed him that the interior halls didn't lead to any of the staff offices, but after relieving the useless bitch of her key, some clever reprogramming had granted him all the access he needed. That left him with a brief showing in the elevator camera, but he was banking on this being over before he registered as more than a blip in a uniform.

Secret halls, digital brilliance, and murder waiting to happen. *God*, he loved his job.

And though he gave the pretty boy some credit for trying to keep his office files secure, his pussy coding system hadn't deterred Joe much.

Information was a wonderful thing. He knew that the family collected all the details so meticulously for a reason—to help and soothe and comfort, and whatever the fuck all else. In his hands? It became a weapon.

Weapons were so much more entertaining.

He'd selected the next target and boy, howdy, was it going to be a winner. Abigail Montgomery was just some broad with money, far as he could tell, but it gave him the edge he needed. Her relationship to Naomi West, no matter how vague they thought it was, was going to get him the in he wanted.

Hands shaking, he'd worked for two solid hours. He'd rested only briefly when his fingers refused to cooperate any longer, then forced himself to keep working.

Keep twisting and stripping and tying.

Now it was ready. Abigail was in his sights.

When she went down, Naomi would show up, and her ties to this place would force the witches to reveal themselves. To break their silence and show their treasures.

Rich, spoiled, selfish people. They hoarded what should be his. Guarded from the world what should be shared. With him, god damn it. With people like him.

Naomi would also come, he knew, because he'd made her angry. Joe hadn't meant to hurt his fellow missionary. He'd been aiming for Clarke; to create an injury that would send them all scrambling to reveal the fountain.

Instead she'd pushed the boy out of his sights and he'd tagged her instead. She'd bled so much, and for a moment he'd been worried that he'd killed her. Death was too far out of reach, even for witchcraft, but he'd been lucky last night.

God had seen to it that his accident, his sloppiness, was met by revelation.

Healing Naomi had been the Clarkes' undoing. They had it. They had his treasure, his salvation. He hadn't returned soon enough to catch it in action, but he'd seen her walking around. Clear as day.

The fountain existed. Now he just needed to get his goddamn hands on it. Just like his contact had said.

He had found the lock. Now he just had to force the key.

CHAPTER SIXTEEN

Naomi made it halfway to the garden before she remembered that a thoroughly sexed-up Phin had taken over her bed. She drew to an abrupt halt.

Gemma had said he'd gone to his own suite, but was he waiting for her again? To bring breakfast as she'd said?

Fuck that. There was no way she'd go back to her suite now.

She ignored the small voice in her head that said she was a coward. Shower. She needed a shower first, and then she'd check in with the Mission. If she was lucky, they'd have something for her. A plan that didn't involve waiting around for her target to make another move.

If she wasn't, well, she'd come up with something.

She was good at coming up with *something*.

Going back to her residential suite to waste time screwing Phin again wasn't going to be on that list.

Not when her breath caught at the very thought of it.

She strode past the residential wing elevator, turned instead toward the double doors of the pool hall. There were showers there, complimentary soap to strip Phin's scent from her skin. Her hair.

Scrub it from her mind.

Pushing inside, she scoured the wide, echoing room. Tile flashed back at her, blues and greens complementary to the blue water of the pools and hot tubs, the lush plants saturated in the humid air. A tropical paradise at the highest reaches of New Seattle.

The sound of water filled the room to an echoing rush. Warm jets, the crystal-clear waterfall in the far corner, and under it, the steady hum of the electricity that kept it all going.

A uniformed attendant rose from the side of the pool, his attention focused on some kind of tubed thing in his hands. The smile he gave her was brief as he passed. "The pools should be fine for swimming," he assured her. "The tanning beds are awake and I'll be bringing beverages to the dressing room in just a moment."

"Thanks," she muttered, but he was gone. The door swung back and forth behind him. Efficient, anyway.

Absently Naomi scratched at the seam of the bandage, her gaze drawn to the sealed sauna. The glass had been replaced already.

They worked fast.

Her heels echoed in the vast, humid space, catching on the rosy slate tiles in sharp, staccato rhythm. Water lapped at the colorful rim of each pool, surrounded her with the echoes and ripples of what she supposed was a soothing sound.

Never mind an old woman nearly died here.

The dressing rooms split into two sections, two signs. Naomi pushed open the women's door, already pulling the sweater up over her head.

Abigail Montgomery looked up from applying her makeup in the wide, multipaneled mirror taking up the entirety of one wall. Naomi froze.

She was dressed in what Naomi assumed was the latest in resort fashion. Her white pants were pristine, crisply pressed, and her boat-neck blouse was a brilliant jewel green. She looked gorgeous, glowing, polished.

Processed for beautiful.

Her smile was perfunctory at best, a slash of glossy pink indifference. "I'll be done in a minute," she said in the same tones she'd used to dismiss Naomi just yesterday.

Cool. Cultured. Indicating clearly that anyone else should wait for her to finish before stepping into her precious air.

Naomi's fingernails scraped the door as her hands curled into fists. "Don't worry about it." The words should have choked in her throat, they were so tight. She turned back to the main hall and hesitated, jamming her elbow against the door when Abigail said, "Wait a second."

Naomi couldn't force herself to go. Couldn't say anything around the tight knot in her throat. She should have kept walking.

She didn't know why she waited.

Behind her, Abigail set down her lipstick. The metal tube clattered against the polished marble, and Naomi half turned to see the way Abigail leaned a hip against the counter, arms crossing over her chest.

Blue eyes narrowed in deep thought.

Only she wasn't considering new jewelry or the latest line of topside fashion to fill her never-ending closets with. Not this time.

"I'm sorry if this seems rude," the stranger who was her mother said, speculation lengthening each word and grating over Naomi's already exhausted nerves, "but have we met at some event or foundation before? Do we know each other?"

Naomi nearly laughed. She choked back the bitter sound, knowing that if she let it out—if it worked its way past the vicious ache in her chest—she wouldn't stop.

Instead, drawing fatigue around her like a cloak, Naomi said quietly, "No. We don't know each other."

"Are you sure? What's your name?"

Naomi closed her eyes. "Ishikawa," she said, so low the word barely reverberated in the air as sound. "Naomi Ishikawa."

The door swung closed on Abigail's sharply indrawn breath, but Naomi didn't stop to see if she'd come out. She wouldn't.

Her mother had never come for her.

Wordless with rage, with weariness, Naomi skirted

the divide and pushed into the men's room. It was empty. Clean. The shelves had been stocked with masculine fragrances and soap that smelled like wood shavings, and she grabbed whatever came to hand.

She showered under water hot enough to scald and tried to pretend that she wasn't straining to hear the sound of her mother's voice over the rush.

Tried to pretend that disappointment didn't close like a fist when it never came.

Abigail Montgomery wasn't her problem. She'd get hers, a lonely life without company or love. Every day age drew another scar on her mother's so perfect flesh. Every day she was that much closer to dying an ugly, twisted old shrew.

Naomi only regretted the fact that she'd miss the declining years. Let the woman spend her blood money on cosmetic surgery and every restorative known to man. Let her fight against age.

Nothing would help her. Nothing.

Naomi wanted to spit in her grave when she died.

But that meant outliving her. The odds of that weren't high.

Still, she thought as she rubbed herself down with a towel that smelled like warm spice and firelight, it was a nice thought. If a bullet didn't catch her first, Naomi would go to the woman's funeral and laugh.

Maybe that would fill her chest with something other than hollow rage.

And maybe, she thought as she dressed, it was the rage that kept regret at bay. Naomi gripped the edge of the bay of lockers and stared sightlessly into the neatly etched numbers, damp towel hanging limply over her shoulders. A drop of water dripped from her hair, slid down her neck. Her cheek.

Dripped into the pink stain at her feet.

She blinked at it. Opened her mouth and didn't know what to say.

Not this time.

Already knowing what she'd find—if not who—she reached for the locker latch and unhooked the metal bolt.

The body spilled out of the narrow confines like a broken doll, and Naomi stepped back in mute pity. Mousy blond hair pooled to the floor as her skull cracked against the tile, and gravity sucked the rest of her gray-tinged corpse out of the impromptu metal coffin.

Katie Landers.

Hysteria crawled up her spine, but Naomi crouched with an icy kind of calm. As if she weren't the one reaching out to roll the limp body over.

As if it weren't her hands that tipped the ashen face up to the light, revealing livid purple bruises around Katie's throat. That wouldn't have been pleasant.

But it was the stabbing that killed her.

The scent of blood had always reminded Naomi of metal; something warmer than the tang of the acid rain that pounded the city's lower streets, something meatier than anything she'd ever known before. In quantities, it filled the nose. The head.

The memory.

She didn't dream of blood anymore, but the nausea never truly went away. It splashed into her throat now as she tilted the locker door wide. Browned and thick, the dead girl's blood coated the inside. Pooled on the bottom and caught on the humidity of the pool hall to speckle the floor beneath the locker.

Another one dead. Another corpse. One in the laundry room and one here. All right, so Naomi had killed the witch and Carson had moved the body, but why was Katie dead? It had all the hallmarks of an agent kill. Quick, brutal, and thorough.

Had Carson killed her for something he wanted?

Did she happen to get in the way? See something she shouldn't?

Christ, was she one of Carson's plants?

Naomi seized the edge of the locker for balance, but her thoughts of searching the premises turned into a wordless sound of surprise as the lights flickered. Between one breath and the next, the power surged out.

For a brief four seconds, long enough to send Naomi's heart hammering hard against her ribs, the resort was deathly silent. No drone of electricity. No froth and bubble of water jets.

Impossible.

Every hair on her neck stood straight up as she forced herself to her feet in the pitch black. Failing energy gave way to a new surge of adrenaline clamping around her chest. The power guttered again, struggling to flood back through the fixtures. She crossed the room between flickers, shoved open the door and made it three sprinting strides toward the main doors when a flurry of sparks erupted to her left.

Throwing her arm up over her face, Naomi swore loudly. The crackle of open electrical currents sizzled in the air, and a feminine voice shouted something fast and startled behind her. The sparks faded, scattered to nothing on the tile, and Naomi warily circled a thick bundle of cords hanging from the ceiling.

Electricity vibrated along it, a wicked hum of warning as it coiled like a serpent, alive with a powerful electrical surge. The slack end slithered along the floor, too close to the water.

"Naomi!"

She flinched, whirling to see the redhead Phin had called Cally beckoning her away.

The cable sparked again, showered a flurry of blue and white. "Be careful, there's a fuck-ton of electricity through here," Cally shouted, her voice echoing eerily. "If it hits the water—"

"I get it!" Naomi waved her back. "Go get— Oh, my God." Her heart jumped into her throat. Tightened. "Fuck, *shit*. Call for help!"

She didn't know if the woman obeyed. She didn't know if she'd said it, or only thought it, or if the world had come to a screaming halt for only her.

She sprinted across the tiled floor in seconds, dove cleanly into the water. Half of her expected to be shocked into the next world, electrocuted into so much bubbled flesh and melted bone, but the rest of her could only thrash, struggle as her hands tangled in short blond hair.

In flowing green silk.

Gasping for breath as she resurfaced, Naomi pushed and shoved Abigail's limp body to the edge of the pool. Every nerve shuddered, violent anticipation, but Naomi forced herself to move. To seize the unresponsive woman by her hair, her clothes, her lifeless limbs, anything that put her over the edge.

It took every ounce of strength she had to do it. Her hair streamed into her eyes, the chlorine stung, but swearing, heaving, Naomi ducked under the surface, visions of charred death by voltage dancing in her mind's eye, and jammed her shoulder under Abigail's back.

The woman rolled. Threatened to topple the wrong way. Naomi's straining breath turned into a scream, and Abigail's limp body hit the tile.

She wasn't moving. Dear God, she wasn't moving, she wasn't breathing, Naomi couldn't tell if—

Out. She had to get out.

Summoning every iota of willpower, she grabbed the edge of the pool and wrenched herself out. She struggled as the water seemed to wrap around her hips, her legs, her sodden clothes. Swearing, cursing, gasping for breath, she crawled over the tile, over Abigail's inert body.

Blood ran from a gash at the woman's cheek. It painted the woman's beautiful face in a cruel mask of crimson, of running mascara.

"Ambulance," Naomi gasped. She needed, oh, God, she needed an ambulance. She needed help. She needed anyone, damn it, she needed *Phin.* "Help me!" she screamed, even as adrenaline surged through her flagging limbs. She wrenched Abigail into her arms, terror thick and acrid in her throat. Her heart.

Somehow, she didn't know how, she got to her feet. Somehow she carried her mother away from the coiling, sparking cable. Away from the water that hissed and sizzled as the cable thrashed itself into the pool. The power surged around her as the water sucked out every last current of power; the ceiling lights shattered out in an explosion of glass and sparking electricity.

Somehow Naomi made it to the double doors. Shoved out of them. Staggered.

Warm arms wrapped around hers. Caught her, caught Abigail before they buckled. Phin's voice. His orders.

His strength.

People moved around her, ants to the anthill under attack, and Naomi let Phin take Abigail from her. He carried her like the woman weighed nothing, an easy, comforting strength as he stood in the middle of chaos and calmly ordered that a gurney be brought, that emergency maintenance be called, that staff see to guests.

The ambulance was coming.

Slowly, effortlessly, Phin restored order.

And she couldn't watch. Couldn't watch him stand in the middle of everything and look so cool, so calm in his dress shirt and slacks and newly washed hair. So patient and compassionate and strong.

Cradling the woman who had abandoned her.

The woman Naomi couldn't allow herself to return the favor to.

Shaking, shivering with cold, with delayed shock, Naomi withdrew from the madness. She withdrew from the bubble of calm that beckoned her, lured her like that moth to a flame more insidious than anything she'd ever known.

Coward.

Naomi fled.

* * *

"Go." Lillian pushed Phin away from the flurry of activity around Abigail's gurney. "I know a problem when I see one, *go*."

Though it went against every executive bone in his body, Phin obeyed his mother; heard and obeyed the urgency in her voice.

He felt the same gnawing worry in his gut.

One minute Naomi had been right there. When he looked up next, she was gone. Getting into trouble, doing something stupid, chasing whatever ghost her Church had demanded she find, he didn't know.

He dialed security. "Get me Naomi Ishikawa's location," he said as the comm clicked over.

Barker cut off his own greeting with a clipped "Yes, sir." It only took a minute, but every second slammed into Phin like a dagger of apprehension.

Something was very wrong.

"She's on the athletic floor," Baker reported. "In the gym."

"Who's with her?"

"No one, it's clear."

"Good." Phin hurried across the courtyard. "Put out the word. We're closing for the duration. I want every man on your team on this."

"Yes, sir, we're already scouring the floors."

"Bring in extra help, I don't care who you have to strong-arm, but get them in here. Escort the temporaries to a safe location—*safe*, do you hear me?—and release the staff to go home as soon as everyone is out."

"Yes, sir. Mr. Clarke, about Vaughn—"

"Later." Phin let out an explosive breath as he cut the

line. He sprinted through the double doors, following the line of glass panels to the gym.

He heard her before he saw her.

Reminiscent of the first time he'd watched her, she stood in front of a heavy bag, its chains creaking as it swung wildly with every furious blow, every punch, every kick.

But it was different this time. She was different. Not nearly so controlled. She hadn't changed her clothes, and there was something wildly incongruous about a woman beating the shit out of a punching bag in jeans, soggy sweater, and high-heeled boots, but she moved as if she was used to fighting in those heels.

As if she didn't give a flying fuck what anyone else thought.

She moved like a missionary.

And he was the sucker who harbored witches.

God damn it. It didn't matter. He rounded the glass. "Naomi."

Her bare fist slammed into the bag. Too hard. It swung, but she did it again, expelling a ragged sound of thinly restrained fury with every strike. And again. A left hook, an uppercut that made him cringe. Red gleamed wetly against the vinyl casing. Her wet hair tumbled in stringy knots around her shoulders while her sodden clothes dripped onto the sealed wood floors.

"Naomi," he said again. He caught her shoulders. The ruined wool knotted and stretched beneath his fingers. "Stop, sweetheart, don't hurt—"

She rounded on him, seizing the front of his shirt in one abraded, bleeding fist. "Back off," she snarled.

Her face was so close, her eyes so haunted, that Phin couldn't, wouldn't be cowed.

Not by her. Not by the woman he had already fallen for.

He ignored her fist. Ignored her anger and slid his fingers over her cheek. "It's okay," he said softly.

The sound she made shouldn't have been possible from a human throat. Like a wounded animal, a caged beast, it ripped out of her, tore free from her chest as she wrenched away.

Phin staggered, but caught himself and took another step toward her as she faced the swinging bag, her shoulders heaving. "It's okay," he said again, as gently as if he were coaxing a wounded kitten. A scared child.

"Stop it."

He shook his head. "It's going to be okay."

"You have *no* idea," she bit out, and stiffened as he laid his palms over her shoulders.

Braced for her anger, ready in case she lashed out in whatever pain rode her now, he slid his fingers down her arms. Her body jerked, but he stepped into her space anyway. "Hey," he murmured against her cold, wet hair. "It's okay."

She sucked in a breath, and he felt it break. Some kind of leashed tension, an emotional dam crumbling in his arms. Quickly, more easily than he'd expected, he spun her around, gathered her into his embrace and only held her as she trembled.

Sometime in the near future he'd have to tell her. He'd have to explain about the people Timeless had helped, try to get her to understand that he hadn't meant to lie to her. Try to undercut the missionary he knew she was.

Someday he'd have to convince her to trust him, but for now he only held her. Braced her as she fell against him and gave him her weight. She was tall, but he didn't spend every other day in this gym for nothing. She wrapped her legs around his waist and buried her face into his shoulder, her arms tight around his neck.

Wordless, everything inside him aching with her, for her, he navigated them into the women's locker room. He cupped the back of her head and turned on the shower inside a stall. It blasted against them both, soaked through his clothes, a stream of soothing warmth and steady sound. It would muffle the tears he knew she needed to shed.

But she'd die before she did it by herself.

His fragile witch hunter.

He braced her against the wall, leaning back to thread his fingers through her hair and watch her face. Her eyes swam, vivid pools of too much emotion. Grief, fear, resentment.

Haunted.

Tipping her face up, he angled her beneath the spray. It beat over her shoulders, her chest; washed away the lingering aroma of sodden wool and chlorine and the acrid stench of ozone from the electrical current that had nearly killed her.

"Look at me," he demanded.

Because she was Naomi, she did. A hard, direct challenge. Phin's heart swelled. Overflowed. His Naomi. "I don't need—" She sucked in a breath as he flattened his palm against her breast, just over her heart.

"Listen to me," he said softly. "It's going to be okay."

"God damn it—"

"It's going to be *okay*," he said again, watching her eyes flinch. Her breath shuddered, jarred on the tears he knew were in there. She needed them out.

When was the last time she had cried?

Did the Church *let* its hunters feel? Did it care?

She struggled to get out of his arms, but he held on. He twined his hands into the back of her sweater, angling his weight to lock her against the tile. Fury etched itself into her features, twisted her mouth into a teeth-baring grimace.

It was a start.

"You risked your life— Naomi, don't," he said roughly as she lashed out. Her elbow crashed into the tile. Her fist slammed past his ear, spiked sharply into the wall over his shoulder.

Her knuckles cracked and he swore.

"*No.*" Her voice echoed in the tiled acoustics. "Don't you *dare*—"

His heart breaking with every violent denial, he shook her hard enough to snap her teeth together on the words he saw forming in the red-rimmed defiance of her eyes. "You risked your life to save a woman you don't even like," he said flatly. "Don't tell me you don't care."

"What do you know?" she hissed. Anger couldn't fill the shock-white pallor of her skin. It couldn't fill the void he saw behind her eyes, behind the twisted, bared teeth of her grimace.

"I know that she's under your skin."

"*Fuck you.*"

"I know that she hurt you," Phin continued, undeterred. He seized her wrists, pinned them over her head, and knew it was because she let him. He'd seen her fight, seen her roll with a bullet.

But she didn't shake him off.

Somewhere inside that rage, she needed him.

"I know that you—"

"She left me." It broke on a sob, a wild cry that sounded to Phin as much grief as wounded woman and, somewhere in there, a tormented little girl. She thrashed, slammed her head back into the tile. Shocked to the bone, Phin jerked her away from the wall and slipped. They hit the shower floor in a tangle of sodden limbs, but she didn't stop. She swore viciously as she tried to get away.

From him. From the memory.

He didn't know, but she wouldn't win this one.

She couldn't afford to.

He pinned her legs, dragged her back over the tile to wrap himself around her. He strained to hold her to the ground until her stream of violent, screaming curses turned into gasping silence. Beneath his shaking hands, the straining, rigid tension of her body melted into exhaustion.

The shower beating the tile around them was all the sound that filled the wrenching quiet.

Panting, Phin loosened his grip. A fraction.

She curled into the tile. Her hair pooled toward the drain, a streaming current of black, but he couldn't see her face. She'd turned away from him, toward the purple and white tile.

"Sweetheart," he whispered. It was all he could say.

Her shoulders jerked. "I was five years old." Her voice shimmered with pain, anger muffled against the floor.

Phin let her go.

She moved. Like a damn cat, liquid sleek and too fast, but she didn't try to get away this time. Twisting, scooting back into the corner, she shoved her hair from her face and the water from her eyes.

No, not water.

Oh, Christ, tears. Despite the knowledge that he'd wanted this reaction, knowing she needed it, Phin fought back the need to reach for her again, to gather her into his arms and soothe those tears away.

That wouldn't help her, either.

So he sat back on his heels. It took everything he had to strive for calm as he observed, "Young to remember."

Naomi sniffed hard, expelling the breath on a sharp, short sound of disgust. "She left the day before my fifth birthday. One day she'd been planning a party with the house staff, and the next she'd packed up her clothes and jewelry and took off."

Phin watched her. Said nothing.

He had to be so careful.

"My father worshipped her. Fuck," she snorted, a harsh sound from trembling lips. "God knows why, but he did. He wasn't the first sucker to marry her, but she never had any kids with anyone else. She used to call me her doll." Her hands trembled as she scraped them through her tangled hair. "Her little Japanese doll. She just—" Her hands splayed, slashing through the air. "She just wanted a pretty kid to show off. But she didn't like being tied down."

He couldn't imagine. The picture she painted, the matter-of-fact way she painted it couldn't hide the raw emotion beneath; it explained so much. And God, he wished it didn't.

"So about three months after she left, she served him with divorce papers." Her voice tightened, roughened. "Then he died."

"Oh, sweetheart."

She shook her head roughly. Water droplets scattered from her hair. "No one saw it coming." Her laughter bit deeply, jagged and raw. "He just . . . killed himself. His will left everything to her. Put me in an orphanage, and you know?" She couldn't muffle the sob that broke against her gritted teeth. Couldn't hide the tears that spilled over her reddened cheeks.

"You know," she tried again, "she never . . . she never once came for me."

He just couldn't bear it. Abandoned, forgotten. "I'm so sorry," he breathed, knowing it wasn't enough.

"No." Her chin came up, and it was as if she'd flipped a switch. He watched a cold kind of strength slide back into place over her eyes. Missionary eyes. "You wanted to know. Fine. My mother abandoned me to the Mission, abandoned my father and took him for everything he had. The divorce suit claimed it all, the house, the money, everything except me. Funny, isn't it?" She slammed both fists to the tile. Water splashed in a glittering arc. "A fucking goddamn comedy that she got exactly what she wanted. More money, more houses, and she never had to think about me again."

He closed his eyes, but it couldn't stop him from seeing her. Huddled in the corner, sodden, a drowned rat with her knees drawn to her chest and pain like a razored knife shimmering in her eyes.

He'd never been so out of his depth.

Or so in love.

"So, yeah," she said. Quiet, now. Cooler, as mercurial as the wind. "Yeah, I'm a missionary. I kill people for a living, Phin. I lied to you from day one because I'm here to kill someone who's out to kill other people. Does that make sense to you?" Her crack of laughter split his heart. Shattered it. "It makes perfect sense to me, but then I don't care. I just kill people. I'm here to kill a man. It's what I do, it's who I am—"

"You're Naomi Ishi—"

"Don't call me that."

Phin stilled. The wild rage, the torment that all but ripped her apart before his very eyes pinned him to the tile. She struggled to her knees, swaying, and he wanted to help her. God, to reach her. To hold her.

But she jammed her arms against the wall for balance. Straightened up without him. "My name is West." It vibrated from her lips, taut and hard. "Naomi West. I work for the Mission. I kill people. God damn it, Phin," she said on a rush, clearly frustrated as she shoved at the water sliding over her face. "Is any of this getting through to you? *I kill people*, and I don't fucking care who."

Phin crawled across the tile on his knees, caught her by the arms, and pulled her against his chest. She struggled, but he cupped her face in both hands. He met her eyes and forced himself to remain calm, not to rise to the bait she threw out like so much blood in the water.

Not to give her what she so desperately thought she wanted.

"Your name is Naomi West," he repeated softly. Seizing the advantage, he tilted her face up and brushed her lips with his, as tender as he knew how. Gentle. "You're a missionary." Again, his lower lip catching on hers. She shuddered. "You kill people in your line of work, I get that."

"I—"

"But I refuse to believe," he said over her, still as soothingly, as soft as he could, "that you don't care. I know you. Even in this small amount of time, I know you better than you think. You care. You care and it eats you alive."

Her eyes darkened.

"But you aren't alone, Naomi." Phin pressed his mouth to her chin, her cheeks. Tasted the salt of her tears and the lingering bite of chlorine. "You aren't alone, because I'm here. I love you."

She drew in a sharp breath.

"And I'm not going to leave you." He covered her lips with his, coaxed her mouth open under the gently aggressive sweep of his tongue, and tried to pour every ounce, every shred of love and need and reassurance into a single kiss.

To show her what he tried to say.

Her heartbeat shuddered in her chest, spiked in her pulse beneath his hands. It echoed the hammer of his own heart, the rush of water in his ears.

Her fingers slid over cheek. Into his hair.

Tightened.

And then she wrenched her face away. "No," she said. Rough, throaty. She pushed at his shoulders.

He eased back, giving her the space she needed, the room to breathe. His stomach in vicious knots, he watched her as she clambered to her feet, surging past him in a wild scramble of soaked denim. "You have some nerve, slick. I'll give you that."

Phin watched that so-practiced mask of hers slide firmly in place. He read it in the line of her shoulders, in the cool, faintly amused cast to her features so at odds with the ravaged color in her cheeks.

Missionary mode.

Slowly he stood. "Oh?"

"You love me?" She snorted, wildly unladylike. Pure Naomi. "Unbelievable. What kind of bullshit blackmail is that? You don't know me, Phin. You can't possibly."

Again, because he didn't know what else to say, how to frame the concern, the anxiety tightening his throat, he repeated, "Oh?"

She spun, throwing a soaking hand out toward the locker room. "Look at this," she scoffed. "Look at you! You're wearing a designer that costs more than I make in a solid year, and you just ruined it without even thinking. This fucking place is so isolated and so exclusive, you're out of touch with everything."

Phin stepped out of the shower stall. He blinked away the water that dripped into his eyes. Hard. "You think so?"

Her mouth twisted. "You have a couple of moss lickers for parents, slick." He flinched. "They haven't been murdered yet because you live nice and tidy up here where the bad shit doesn't happen."

His fists clenched by his sides.

Her jaw tightened. "The only reason you're all sweet and happy and alive is because you're *rich*. The Church wants your money, which I'll bet," she added scathingly, "you pay with a fucking smile, don't you?"

"The taxes—"

"Are bullshit hush money."

"What do you want me to say, Naomi?"

She pulled at her sweater, struggling to peel the sodden wool over her head. She threw it at his feet with a *splat*, jerking her chin up. Her dark hair clung to her lips in damp tendrils.

Phin shook his head. "What are you trying to do?"

She sliced a hand through the air. It flexed the lean, missionary muscle of her arms, bared by the black lace camisole hugging her body. She was gorgeous.

And trying hard to piss him off.

Jesus Christ, it was working.

"Fuck you," she said softly. Coolly. "Fuck you and your whole puppy love thing. That's not my problem. Jesus, fuck." She turned, stalked for the door. "I don't need your therapy, I don't need your goddamn massage, yoga, *bullshit*. You've been trying to fix me since I got here."

"You're at a spa," Phin pointed out, but his voice lashed. Growled.

Her hand jerked as she reached for the door. Her grip whitened around the handle. "You don't get it, Phin. Take your family, pack up what you need, and *get out*. As soon as I've killed everyone I need to, you can come back and live your pretty little life, and run your rich people spa, and go back to pretending like a fling means more than it does with some airheaded money-bunny who'll appreciate the lie."

"I never—"

The look she shot him over her shoulder was so contemptuous, so pitying, that anger surged hot and bright through his vision. "Don't try. I've seen what you're capable of, and, baby, this is it."

Fury pounded through his chest. His head. "Is that what you think?" he demanded softly.

Her eyes flickered. "It's what I know. Get out. I'll let you know when to collect the bodies."

She walked out without a backward glance. The door shut behind her; it didn't creak or clatter, there was no sound but the muted hum of the backup power holding steady. No sound but the echo of her voice.

Her scorn.

Phin stared at the slowly swinging door and told himself it didn't matter. That she was right. That she'd done him a favor, saved him the time and effort of falling for a woman who would *never* trust him. He didn't have to tell her about the underground now.

He wouldn't have to deal with her recriminations. Her accusations.

She'd never believe that he loved her. She'd saved him the heartache.

He was a fucking bad liar.

CHAPTER SEVENTEEN

"S orry!" Cally swung out of her way, pressing herself flat to the family wing wall as Naomi barreled past. "Hey, where are you—"

Naomi made a sound. Maybe she didn't. Her brain screamed, growled a warning, but all she knew was that she swung around, ready to fight. To hurt.

The redhead threw up her hands, fragile ward against Naomi's wild rage. "Easy," she said softly, as if talking down a rabid dog. "Hey, it's okay."

Her grunted curse raw, Naomi threw her weight against the garage door Phin had shown her earlier and slammed it hard enough behind her that it echoed like a gunshot through the parking garage. Cally's voice cut off.

Cars lined up in her pulsating vision, sleek and polished and the perfect getaway. Naomi didn't stop to weigh her options. She didn't care. Adrenaline battered her system, swirled in her chest until she was gasping for air.

She just needed out. She needed another goddamned gun, she needed—

She needed to escape. Herself. Him. Everything.

Forcing the lock on one of Phin's gorgeous sports cars was too damn easy. She tore through the echoing vault like a maniac out for blood.

Where the hell could she go?

Naomi's grip tightened on the wheel as she spun the car wildly around a corner. Drivers blared at her, vehicles swerved to avoid her as she screeched into traffic. Her chest felt too tight, but the speed, the sheer power of the engine beneath her was all that mattered now.

Crying would only make her crash.

And she'd be damned if she died for the idiocy of some asshole of a man.

He loved her. What the hell did he know? He loved an heiress. Fuck him. That's all she'd done. Sex and love; why the hell did so many people confuse the two?

That was all it was. Just lust.

Something vicious and sharp twisted in her chest.

As if by rote, she found herself on the New Seattle carousel, clouds gathering gray and dark around her. She frowned at the high-tech steering wheel, at the gadgets and buttons that filled almost every inch of the panel.

When the first fat drops of rain splattered the windshield, Naomi jerked. Swore as she nearly slammed the car into a wide, boxy luxury vehicle pacing her in the next lane. Swore again, harder, angrier as white-hot fury bubbled up from deep inside.

Her mother was dead. Killed by some madman out for blood inside Timeless, and now she was dead.

Wasn't she?

Would it matter?

There wasn't a word, a description, a feeling strong enough to fill the black, raging emptiness inside her head.

Of course it wouldn't matter.

Tears gathered, harsh and acidic. They burned, filled the ache in her throat until she thought she'd vomit from the swirl of bile. She swallowed, gritted her teeth. Adjusting her fingers around the steering wheel, she slammed the gas pedal down to the floor.

The coiling highway wrapped around the layered city like a snake, and traffic flowed like water around her. There were no security points to pass from topside to the mid-lows; they didn't care about the wealthy and bored who wanted to slum for a night.

It was coming the other way that would be a problem.

She'd gun down that issue when she got to it. For now she concentrated on making it to her small, mid-level apartment alive. She managed to do all the right things to get inside, bypass all her own Mission-verified security measures. She didn't notice. She barely cared.

She stepped around the untidy piles of clothing scattered around the floor, already pulling off the lacy camisole. She kicked off the loathed boots, the slim designer jeans, and concentrated on finding her own clothes to put on.

When she found a pair of shredded denim on the

floor, its white threads at the thighs and seat as familiar as breathing, something in her chest loosened. Relaxed.

Suddenly Naomi could breathe again.

Running her hands over the rough nap of the jeans, she focused on the cluttered mess of what had been her home for only the past several years. She didn't stay here much.

Home was where one slept.

But now it looked old. Barren. The carpet was stained and worn thin in places, the rusted water spots on the ceiling and walls looked like blood soaked into discolored plaster. She twisted her mouth into a semblance of a smile. "Honey, this is all you've got," she said aloud. The sound of her own voice anchored her somewhat.

The past few days had been only a nightmare. Not real. This was real.

Bullets and blood, *that* was real.

That shiny, glittering place towering above the mid-level poverty lines? Sure, it gleamed. Like a diamond, it glittered in the muted sunlight that only barely scraped the streets she knew, and the fuckers topside could keep it.

She had no use for diamonds.

Naomi stepped into the tiny cramped bathroom, so different from the luxurious decadence of Timeless's beautiful suites. The bolted mirror was mottled with rust and age, but Naomi forced herself to ignore the spots that marred the edges. The orange stains and cracked porcelain that made up her life.

She brushed her hair, pulled it hard into a twisted

coil, and frowned at the bandage fraying from her shoulder.

The shoulder that didn't hurt.

Leaning into the mirror, she studied the faint line that was all that remained of the slash across her nose. Her eyes narrowed.

Her breath shorted.

Tearing off the bandage, she stared at the vaguely mottled strip of flesh where a bullet crease should have been. Her fingers shook as she traced it.

"*Shitfucker*," she breathed, and felt it like a kick to the gut. Like a punch that stole her air. She braced herself on the sink, her forehead meeting the mirror with a solid *thunk*.

The small pain did nothing to ease the slow, creeping onslaught of fear.

People didn't heal like that. Medicine couldn't take away a bullet crease as if it had only been a love tap.

Magic could.

Witches could.

Witches everywhere. The whole fucking family? Just one? "Jesus bastard Christ!"

She launched herself into motion. Adrenaline spiked hard, jerked a knot in her chest so sharp, she almost doubled over from it. She couldn't afford to do that.

Couldn't take the time to think about this.

Joe Carson, first. Then. . .

Then she'd turn in the Clarkes. Them and the witches they were so obviously colluding with.

"I warned you," she whispered, kneeling to retrieve her favorite gun from beneath the mattress. "I told you what I do." The Colt was larger than Mission standard, but by God, it'd blow a hole in anyone stupid enough to get in her way.

She wiped at her cheek, scowled when her hand came away damp. Damn it, she wasn't crying. Not for witches.

Not for Phin.

"I demand to know exactly what is going on here." Michael Rook's voice rose above the others, a cacophony of discord and questions and attitude that battered at Phin's calm like a hurricane. The lobby echoed, music and fountain drowned out under the chaos of raised voices.

He spread his hands. "I'm so sorry," he said, not for the first, second, even seventeenth time. "I understand how problematic this is for you all, but we will get you to where you need to be."

"I need to be here," wailed Jordana, her hair a tumbled mass of curls around her shoulders. "What if Katie comes back looking for me?"

The gaunt man waved that away. "She's a hell of a lot smarter than you are. She'll be fine."

Jordana sucked in a breath. "You—"

"For the love of God, shut her up." One of Timeless's more reclusive guests, Grace Latterby looked frumpy and worn out. She had arrived frumpy and even more worn out, but as the forty-six-year-old owner and head of a multibillion-dollar importing company, she had that right.

She had also demanded exclusive privacy, complete seclusion, and to be left the hell alone.

Today he'd broken all of those demands.

Phin rubbed at his forehead.

"Everyone, please remain calm." Lillian stepped into the crowd, as stern as anything he'd ever seen. Her voice didn't rise, it simply pitched, carried in a way that commanded attention. Brought authority. "Ladies and gentlemen, we sincerely apologize for this inconvenience, but understand we are closing Timeless for your own safety. Until we can locate the problem—"

"The *problem* is your staff, clearly," Rook blustered. "You're too easy on them! They get the run of the place, get sloppy."

Murmurs of agreement made Phin want to climb outside his own skin for just the second it'd take to punch the man in the mouth.

"We are already aware of the cause, Mr. Rook," Lillian said firmly. "Now we just need to find it. Until then, we have no intentions of risking anyone else's safety."

It was the hardest thing he'd ever done.

As the guests filed out and staff carried their baggage with them, Phin leaned against the lobby desk and watched the world crumble to pieces at his feet.

He saw the same tired smudge of certainty around Lillian's eyes, in the line of her mouth.

Still, as she crossed the marble floor to lean against the desk beside him, she smiled. "Abigail will recover, in time. The accidents weren't fatal."

"They weren't accidents, either." A flicker in her eyes told him she'd thought the very same thing. Phin rubbed his face with both hands. It didn't help the exhaustion thick in his head. "Timeless is finished."

Lillian glanced at him, tilting her head. "Maybe. But

if so, we'll rebuild. Somewhere else, something else. We'll manage."

"Unbelievable." He rested his elbows back on the desk and let his head hang back. He closed his eyes. "Absolutely unbelievable. Timeless has been around for so long, and then one person can take it down? Just one. And it ruins so many lives."

"Phin," Lillian said softly, sympathy and reassurance shining from the single word.

"What are we going to do about the staff? We can't employ them all to do nothing." He straightened. "And the accused we send to safety? Where will they go now? How many will be caught, executed by the Church without us to keep them safe?"

"Phin, love."

"It's not fair," he snapped. Knowing it for the petulant rant it was, he knuckled his forehead, sucked in a deep breath, and repeated quietly, "It's just not fair to any of them. Or us."

Lillian slid her arms around his shoulders. "Come here, baby." Despite his taller height, he hunched, allowing himself to rest his head against her chest, her heartbeat.

His fingers twined together, arms around his mother's back, and for a single, perfect moment, everything was all right. Her pulse beat strongly in his ear, her warmth seeped into the cold fear that gripped him, strangled him.

Her nonsensical soothing sounds of love and reassurance eased the bitter sting of Naomi's wild accusations from his mind.

"Mother," he said against her shoulder.

"Mmm?"

"I want you both to go pack and get out somewhere safe. Go visit someone."

Her chuckle thrummed through his head. He straightened, frowned down at her beloved face as she shook her head. "You know we won't do that."

"This Carson guy is dangerous. Naomi wasn't making that up, Mother. You said it yourself! Two people are dead." Phin shifted, gripped her shoulders. "I don't know what I'd do if you get hurt. You have to go. Please."

Long fingers smoothed over his cheek. "We're a family, Phin. We're strongest when we're together."

"But I—"

The lobby doors swung open. Michael Rook strode back inside, his tall, gaunt figure vibrating with thinly leashed self-righteousness. Clearly the leader of his own little protest, he led Jordana back inside. She sashayed with intent, her mouth set in a purposeful pout.

"Oh, God." Phin sighed and stepped away from the desk to catch them before they crossed the lobby. "I'm sorry, but this isn't up for debate."

Behind them, Joel hurried back after them. His fingers curled, palm to palm, throttling thin air in sheer frustration.

Rook didn't stop. "No, you know what? We paid for our time and we intend to get it, one way or another. Now I suggest you contact whatever fancy-pants lawyer you've got tucked away—"

The power flickered.

Everyone paused. Frozen like a tableau of surprise,

sudden panic. The doors in the lobby slid closed, and Jordana jumped, muffling a scream.

"Delayed response," the thin man informed her irritably. "Get ahold of yourself."

She flushed, and Phin couldn't help himself from redirecting Rook's attention back to him. "Excuse me," he said firmly. "We do have the right to refuse service to anyone, and we're obligated to enforce that right when the safety of clients is in danger."

"Given the extravagant fees you charge here—"

The first slam, the first screech and slide of metal on metal seemed too surreal. Rook stopped speaking, frowning as if he wasn't sure what he heard.

Clang. Creeeaaak . . . clang.

Phin knew. He knew exactly what was happening as one by one, the vast windows of the lobby blanked out beneath a sheet of reinforced metal.

Lillian moved first. "Everyone, group together."

Phin spun around, dove for the comm on the desk. Behind him, Jordana's voice rose on a terrified wail. Rook snapped at her to shut up.

He dialed security, clenching his teeth on an angry, fearful curse as he waited. And waited.

"Get them to the lounge," he yelled over his shoulder, and sprinted for the interior double doors. As daylight turned into false night, as the power flickered around them, Phin prayed that this would end without bloodshed.

That whatever the ghost wanted, he could give.

If not, they were trapped inside the fortifications they'd had installed specifically for future disasters. They were locked down, sealed tight.

Trapped with a man who didn't mind killing to get his way. Two people dead.

His jaw clenched.

As he sprinted for the staff hallway, the intercom crackled to life. "Good afternoon. As you may have noticed, security measures have now locked you all inside this building."

The voice was pleasant enough, plain. It wasn't deep, and it wasn't shrill. Average, polite.

Phin skidded across the hallway, frantically searched for the catch that would release the hidden door. If the man was on the intercom, he wasn't in the halls. He had to move fast.

"Mr. Clarke."

Phin froze. Slowly he turned to face the security camera tucked inside one of the beveled curves of the upper wall molding.

"Yes, I see you, Mr. Clarke."

The security suite. It was the only office that had access to every monitor, every feed.

"You will do me the favor of ensuring that everyone makes their way to the pool area."

Phin's heart jumped in fear. "I don't—"

"I can't hear you, so save your breath. I shall pass the message for you. Everyone? Everyone," the voice said smoothly. Loudly. "Mr. Clarke requests that everyone still in the building—and yes, I can see you—gather at the pools. Anyone who does not comply will be made very, very sorry." A beat. "At least for as long as it takes them to die. I trust I'm clear?"

The intercom hummed, clicked off. Within moments the lobby doors swung open, and Lillian hurried out with Rook and Jordana in tow. She was pale, but she led them with that polished mask of calm she did so well.

"Phin, what's going on?" she asked.

"The bastard's in with security." Which meant his team was either somewhere else in the building, or dead. Swallowing hard, he offered his hand to his mother. "Where's everyone?"

"Your mother was in the beauty floor gathering a few things," Lillian said, twining her fingers tightly with his. "Staff is scattered, I don't know where. Most are gone already."

Behind her, Jordana looked ill, tears already tracking mascara under her eyes.

"We aren't going to huddle up like sheep, are we?" Rook slammed a bony fist into an equally bony hand. "We know where he is, why don't we just rush him?"

"Because he now has the guns," Phin said quietly. He tipped his head toward the wide hall and the pool beyond. "So in order to get out of here with as little bloodshed as possible, we're going to be good hostages."

"That's—"

Phin rounded on him. He would have stepped closer if it weren't for Lillian's restraining grasp, tight on his wrist. "You listen to me," he said, so low, so taut with menace and tension that it all but vibrated the air between them. "I will not have my family put in danger. The man has threatened to kill anyone who doesn't comply. If you have any thoughts to play hero and get my people killed, I will stuff you into the nearest maintenance closet right now and leave you until this is over, do you hear me?"

Rook took a step back. "Er . . . okay," he finally said, nodding. He smoothed down his blazer, nodded again. "Okay, I get it."

Behind them, Joel stepped into view. "Mr. Clarke, we should go."

Phin glanced at the masseuse, met his calm green eyes, and nodded. Once. "Can you handle them?"

"I always do," Joel said with a faint, crooked smile. "Come on, everyone. We'll all be okay." He slipped his arm around the wavering Jordana, and after a scowling moment, Rook followed, thin shoulders hunched.

Lillian squeezed Phin's fingers. "I love you," she murmured.

"I love you, too." He smiled at her, matched his stride to hers as they followed the others. "But that's no reason to get yourself hurt, okay?"

"I just want everyone safe."

"Me, too." Phin let go of her hand, looped an arm around her shoulders, and wondered if it would be enough. His chest tight with worry, with fear, he pushed aside the doors and met the impact of half a dozen pairs of panicked, frightened eyes.

Under his arm, Lillian straightened. "Thank you for coming," she said. "We'll do our best to make sure this goes as smoothly as possible."

Steady as she goes.

Phin echoed her posture, her ease of command. "Everyone please stay calm, and we'll get through this fine. No matter what, just do whatever he tells you. Don't try to help." A hard look at Rook. The man looked away. "And please, don't try to reason with him. You let me do the talking."

"No, I think I'll do the talking." The smooth, plain voice echoed from tiled wall to wall. Everyone turned.

Everyone froze.

The man wasn't tall, but he wasn't short, either. Average, Phin thought again, from the top of his thinning brown hair to the shape of his plain features to the tips of his workman boots. Nothing about him would have caught his eye on a good day.

The forearm pressed tight against Gemma Clarke's esophagus caught his eye now.

She looked so out of place beside him, as calm as a sunflower in the face of a storm. Phin's throat closed with fear, but she met his eyes and smiled reassuringly.

His fingers curled into fists. Lillian stiffened. Shock or anger, he didn't know, but he shifted so that she couldn't rush past him.

Stay calm. "Mr. Carson, I presume." It took effort, so much effort not to storm across the tile. To demand. "What do you want?"

The man smiled, showing crooked teeth. Averagely crooked. He pushed forward, one arm snugly around Gemma's throat as he guided her ahead of him.

To Phin, he moved in a way that seemed somehow familiar. Predatory, cautious.

Phin tensed, every muscle in his body locking as he saw the gun pressed to her back.

Lillian swallowed a sob.

"Easy," he murmured. He withdrew his arm, guided her to Joel. "Please."

Joel took her hand.

Phin continued to circle the silent crowd. Deliberately he put himself between them and him. Carson watched him with a lazy, half-amused expression and tightened his grip on Gemma's throat. "That's far enough."

Gemma gagged, her hand whitening around Carson's forearm.

Phin stopped. "Let her go. We'll give you what you want, just please don't hurt anyone."

"I wish it were that simple," Carson replied.

The words were right, but his tone suggested otherwise. The man enjoyed himself. Power, Phin thought. Control. It was clear in the avaricious glitter of his brown eyes, in the delight he took in Gemma's every rasped breath against his forearm.

"If it's money, just take me to the offices below—"

"Oh, no." The man smiled. "It's not money. You have something else I want."

"What?" Phin raised his hands slowly, spread his fingers to show he was unarmed. "Name it."

Behind him, Lillian murmured, "Phin."

"I want the fountain."

Everything inside Phin's body turned to ice. His glance flicked to his mother, back to Carson's face.

The man's smile deepened. "I know you know what I'm talking about," he said. "Don't lie to me."

"Phin," Lillian breathed again, intent. He knew what she was saying.

Knew he had no choice.

He took a step closer, holding Carson's glittering eyes. "If you mean the one in the lobby—"

The man moved like a snake. Gemma hit the tile, sprawled hard, and couldn't do anything else but protect her face from colliding with the unforgiving floor as Carson stepped in and swung the gun at Phin.

Pain exploded like wildfire behind his eyes, blood filled his mouth. He spun with the momentum, knees cracking as he buckled to the floor.

Carson seized him by the hair. "Don't lie to me, boy." Spit dripped onto Phin's burning cheek. "Don't ever lie to me, you son of a whore." He paused, and all at once, the venom eased. Dribbled out like so much oil and smoke.

Terror replaced pain as Phin stared into the suddenly laughing eyes of a madman, and he flinched as Carson chuckled. "Son of two whores, actually," he said thoughtfully. Amused. "I wonder how they managed that." He rubbed the mouth of the gun along his cheek, as if he had an itch, and glanced over Phin's head at Lillian. "Did you hire some guy to lie between you?"

Her shoulders went rigid.

Phin struggled to get to his feet. "That's enough."

So casually it seemed almost effortless, Carson twisted his fingers in Phin's collar, knocked his legs out from under him, and shoved him to the floor again. Phin grunted as his knees cracked on the slate. Choked when Carson jerked his head up.

"Or maybe," he said, lowering his mouth to Phin's ear, "they knew their unholy communion would never be sanctified by a mortal man. Maybe they got the very Devil himself to lie with them both. Shove his giant red cock inside their unclean bodies until one of them conceived, you think?"

Rage battered away pain. Across the floor, Gemma struggled to sit up, to straighten. She shook her head, touched her lips with her fingers, and traced the air in familiar encouragement.

I love you.

He swallowed hard. "I don't know what kind of fountain you need," Phin said, struggling with calm as fury licked at the black edges of his control. "But we've only got a few."

Carson went still. He breathed out a short, empty laugh and straightened. "Okay, boy. Okay." With raw, wiry strength, more than it seemed his lanky body could hold, he wrenched Phin around. His own collar choked him as Carson dragged him back to the group.

The gun pointed at Jordana, who screamed.

"Everyone stays right here," he said.

Phin turned, watching warily as Carson picked his way toward the locker room again. "I was hoping someone in this heretical blight would be reasonable, but it seems you're a stubborn bunch. You'd rather people suffer and die. Selfish, unholy bastards."

Phin wiped at his mouth with his sleeve. "You tried to kill Alexandra."

Carson smiled. Easy. "And the rich bitch. I knew you could save them both, if you wanted. Which you didn't, clearly."

"We did save them," Phin began, and then sucked in a breath as the gun shifted from Jordana, leveled at Gemma.

"Nah. A real shame, this. I had hoped that the rich bitch would be the one to make you dust off the fountain. 'Specially since Naomi West is that boy's piece of ass, and they're related, ain't they?"

Phin jerked. "You son of—"

"Glass houses, boy," Carson said flatly, tightening his grip on the gun. "Since even your girlfriend wasn't important enough to save her own family for, I'm going to give you all a little bit of time to figure things out. Maybe jar your memory."

Phin struggled to his feet. Swallowed the blood coating his tongue to say thickly, desperately, "I can't give you what you want!"

"Get to figuring it out," Carson said with a smile. "Now, you remember what I said. I'll be watching. Best be fast, though," he added, and pulled the trigger.

Thunder cracked. Once. Twice.

Screams, shouting, Jordana's terrified shriek. Someone thrashed in his peripheral vision, struggling to escape the tight knot of hostages clutching each other, but all Phin saw was crimson on sunshine yellow. Gemma's eyes widened. She touched the center of her stomach, and the shock on her face shifted to sorrow.

To regret.

She folded, slowly, crumpling into a wash of gold and red in the blue-tinged pool light, and hit the floor before Phin could coerce his shaking limbs to move.

He staggered. Sobbing, swearing, he lurched to her side, falling to his knees and ignoring the terrible lance of pain. There was so much blood everywhere. Already more blood than he knew what to do with.

Gemma's face turned sallow, her lips white as she gasped for breath.

Hands shaking, Phin gathered her in his arms. "Towels," he demanded, voice cracking. Gemma coughed. Blood spattered his shirt, soaked into his hands until he knew he'd never forget the warmth of it, the wet, liquid slide of it. "Towels!" he screamed.

Rook was at his side in an instant, his shaking hands

filled with pool towels. "My God," he said, his voice suddenly thready.

Joel sprinted across the floor. "I have some basic first aid!"

Lillian's sobs echoed as she scrambled to her wife's side, the room's acoustics bouncing back every wrenching gasp and breath.

"Baby," Gemma rasped. She looked up, a pale mask of pain. Caught Phin's shirt in her hands. "Baby, don't do it."

"I can't let you die."

"I die," Gemma whispered, her fingers tight in his shirt, "and he doesn't get anything."

His heart wrenched. Tears acidic and too hot in his eyes, he sobbed in a breath and gathered her tightly to his chest. She clutched at him. "I can't," he whispered. "I can't do it."

"Phinneas, it's bigger than you, and you know it."

Beside him, Lillian collapsed to her knees. Tendrils of golden hair tumbled around her face as she hovered trembling hands over the bleeding body of her wife. Her lover. Tears tracked silver trails through her once-perfect makeup. "Gem."

"Lily." Gemma caught her hand. Brought it to her chest, to her heart. Blood seeped sluggishly from her stomach. Through the towels Joel bunched there. "You have to tell him. Make him see."

"You can't die, love," Lillian said, her smile heart-wrenchingly bright. Encouraging. "You can't. You can't leave us, and you can't take that with you. Who knows what will happen to this world without you?"

"We can't let him have it," Gemma rasped, and she

choked, coughing. Groaning with pain, she curled into herself. Into Phin. "We can't let him."

Phin closed his eyes.

"Clarke." Beside him, Rook's voice went sharp. Odd. "Uh . . ."

"Take care of her," Phin said. He met Lillian's too-bright eyes, nodded as she touched his face. "I'm going to fix this."

"Uh . . . Clarke?" Rook said again, and this time he grabbed Phin's shoulder.

"What?" He spun, scowled at the three people who filed inside through the double doors. Each wore the uniform of Timeless. Two men, one woman. "Agatha?"

Her old chin high, the beauty floor attendant raked the room with hawk-sharp eyes. "Where is the missionary?" she demanded.

Phin growled.

One of the men leveled a bulky handgun at him. He was blue-eyed, tall with sandy blond hair, and he still wore his dishwasher's apron. Regret shaped his boyishly handsome features. "Sorry, pal," he said. "You really had a good operation here."

Temporaries. He recognized the men now, witches brought in to wait for a chance to escape the city. The Church.

Liars. Traitors.

Agatha's eyes were faded blue, icy and unyielding as they took in the knot of people, the wounded Gemma, Lillian's bloodstained hands and clothes.

His hands fisted as Agatha slashed a gnarled hand through the air. "Ward this much of the room. Begin preparations." Her tone was flat, so very different from the quiet demeanor of the woman he'd hired. "Kill the witnesses," she added coldly.

Phin surged to his feet as the third witch started toward Jordana. "What the fuck is going on here?" he roared. The man stopped, hesitated.

His gaze flicked to Agatha.

Phin pointed at her. "Don't you dare."

"Christ, she's going to bleed out," Joel gritted out behind him.

Agatha spared Phin a piteous glance. "Don't do anything stupid, boy. Right now we're the only thing keeping your mother alive."

"Bullshit—"

The second man flicked his fingers, and Gemma threw back her head on a scream of pain. Blood flecked Lillian's cheek, a fine spatter that turned her green-gold eyes to molten fury in her sallow face.

Phin's breath whooshed out on a wild rush of fear.

"Like I said," Agatha said calmly, as if murder hadn't etched itself onto Phin's features. "Marco, there's your blood. Leave them and get to it. Greg, the witnesses."

The dark-eyed man called Marco stared at him. "Out of the way," he said.

Phin fisted his hands. "Over my fucking dead body."

Behind him, Gemma wheezed. "Let them," she managed. Pain dulled her voice. Slurred her words. "Let them try. They . . . want it, too."

For the first time, a flicker of surprise touched the worn planes of Agatha's face. But she didn't deny it. "Yes," she said curtly. "And your time is running out, so you had better be quick."

Gemma's laugh raked over Phin's ears. More pain,

more anguish than humor. He turned back to her, met Lillian's warning gaze, and didn't move.

"I can't," Gemma whispered. "None of you . . . is right."

"Not right?"

"It . . . chooses."

Phin managed three steps before the blue-eyed dish-washer splayed his fingers in Phin's direction. Every muscle in Phin's body locked, tense as a bowstring. Vibrated so hard, so fast that it felt as if each tendon would tear itself from his bones. He locked his jaw on a scream, blood rushing through his ears.

Agatha narrowed her eyes at him. "Let me spell it out for you," she said evenly. "We've been waiting for the opportunity to take the fountain. We thought it was a thing." Her gaze flicked to Gemma. "Clearly we were wrong."

"Clearly," Phin bit out.

"It's not going to stop us. We can carve the damn thing out ourselves."

Phin wrenched at the magic, snarling a mangled curse as his body threatened to tear itself limb from limb.

The old woman shook her head slowly. "Stop struggling, you idiot boy. Miss Ishikawa was a problem. Then you got involved and we had to act."

It clicked. Hard, sharp as a knife. Suddenly he was seeing red. "You tried to kill her!"

"Mark tried to kill her." Her thin lips flattened into a hard, angry line. "Twice. She stuffed his body in the wardrobe, of all things, and we had to get rid of it before you saw it. We'd hoped to grab the fountain and go, but hey. No dice. This other guy'll just have to be the distraction we need." Agatha spun. "Marco, ward the room, I said. Greg!" Her voice cracked like a whip. "The *witnesses*."

The blue-eyed dishwasher dropped his hand, and suddenly Phin slammed to the floor, his head spinning. The man turned determinedly toward Jordana, stalking across the hall. The pop star cringed, desperately trying to push her way through the tiled wall.

Marco knelt to rummage in a pack, muttering in a language Phin didn't know.

Phin's muscles bunched, fingers tight as he prepared to launch himself at the witches. It was now or never.

Michael Rook beat him to it.

Greg swore as the wiry, gaunt man threw himself into his back. They hit the ground hard, skidded over the edge and into the depths of the large blue pool. Water splashed over the marble siding. Gunfire echoed in the tiled acoustics, tearing through the humid air like a trapped thunderclap. The metal bullets pinged, and Phin reeled, staggering as the pain of the sound lanced through his ears.

Agatha turned, threw out a wrinkled hand, but Phin jumped at her with a wild sound of rage. He barely even noticed the aura of fire and scorching heat. His skin seared.

The old woman's eyes clouded as she scratched at his wrists, his face. Phin barreled forward, fingers tight around her throat as he forced her back, back, farther until she hung out over the same blue water that trapped Rook and the other witch.

Phin shook the frail figure, his vision mottled with rage. "Can you heal her?" he demanded. "Can you keep her alive?"

The old woman choked. "No," she croaked around the viselike grip locked around her skinny neck.

Phin's vision flickered red. Fingers aching, he sucked in a long, hard breath.

Behind him, the secret door split open, and the flicker of motion in the corner of his vision jerked his head around. A copper-skinned teenager slipped through, his dark hair dusted with cobwebs and grime.

A slender hand curled around Phin's wrist. He jerked. Agatha thrashed weakly in his grip, and the hand tightened. "Mr. Clarke."

Phin's lip curled.

"Mr. Clarke, let her go." Liz's masseuse-conditioned grip was strong, her hands gentle as she worked her fingers under Phin's. "She's harmless now, you leave her to us. Don't murder her, Mr. Clarke."

Agatha's eyes bulged. Her tongue distended as he stared into her red face.

"Phin!" Lillian's voice. His mother's cry, desperate and scared.

Liz pried his hands apart. The old witch fell from his fingers, splashed into the water with a gasping shriek.

He whirled. Everything was chaos. He didn't know what the hell was going on. Witches betraying him. Witches helping him. His mother—Jesus, help him, his mother.

The boy Phin recognized as Hep knelt by Gemma's

side. "I'm going to have to use this," he said, frowning as he dipped his fingers in the pool of blood. "Sorry."

"He's protecting them," Liz said behind him. She touched his shoulder. "Mr. Clarke—"

"I don't understand." Phin studied them, the mishmash group of temporaries and the sodden beauty floor attendant he'd sworn had been legit. He raked his gaze over the hall, took in the ruined tangle of wires hanging from the ceiling and Jordana's too-still body sprawled on the tile. Rook was soaked and shaking, hovering over the temporary who bandaged the bullet furrow on Jordana's scalp.

All of it. Hell without the handbasket.

Phin's eyes lingered on Lillian's too-pale, too-taut face. The lines carved deeply into her brow, beside her mouth as she held fast to the bloodstained towels wrapped around Gemma's clammy body.

His jaw set. "Can you protect them?"

"For now," Liz said softly. "But we need to get out of here. Mrs. Clarke needs a doctor, and Cally went for help."

He couldn't stand it. "Keep her alive," he said roughly. "Please."

Liz shifted. But she said nothing.

"I'm going to go end this," he said, turning to pin Joel with a look that made the man flinch. "One way or another. I'll provide the distraction, you get them out. Get them *all* out."

Lillian shook her head. "Phin!"

He paused.

"Be careful. Please be careful, he's—"

"A missionary," Phin cut in. "Yeah, I know." He

hesitated. "I love you both. So much." He turned his back as her eyes softened, as tears spilled over Lillian's cheeks, and strode for the doors. He stopped only long enough to pick up a discarded gun and tuck it into the small of his back.

He knew this building. He'd grown up here, spent his life touring its maze of hidden passages and staff corridors.

All he had to do was find the bastard.

Joe Carson. A missionary. Off his rocker, but a missionary. He recognized the way Carson moved. The way he handled a gun.

The way he looked at blood and showed nothing.

It reminded him of Naomi.

CHAPTER EIGHTEEN

By the time she stepped out of the apartment, her rage had simmered to something much more caustic. Naomi could feel it, all but taste it welling up in the back of her throat. Eating at her.

Fear.

Betrayal.

He'd never leave her? Right. He'd just look her in the eye and never talk about the witchcraft in his family. Or the witches he'd been hiding.

Or the attempts to fucking kill her.

Naomi zipped the shiny peacock blue jacket up to her throat. The plastic polymer repelled the worst of the rain, its high neck protecting her from the biting wind. Under her arm the Colt felt bulky, heavy.

Comforting.

Underneath the jacket and denim, she wore a black neoprene mesh suit. Standard combat gear for a missionary on the go. It'd protect her from the cold, offer some grip if she needed it. Its Teflon weave offered a measure of protection, but mostly?

It was familiar. She desperately needed familiar right now.

The streets turned darker farther below topside. As she paused on the landing, Naomi surveyed the rough, broken pavement, the pitted sidewalk and cracked foundations of the apartment building. In a short-lived bid for beautification, they'd planted trees along the street; scraggly, stumpy things. Naked of leaves, they thrust twisted fingers toward the layered city above.

Just enough sunlight made it through the upper layers of the city to let her know it was still daylight. That the sun still struggled to shine through the drizzling gray clouds. Below these streets, she'd need a watch to know the difference.

Cars didn't come by often. Not here, this far from the carousel. The people who lived here struggled to stay living here.

Maybe that's why Naomi stayed. She both liked and loathed the odd nonquiet of a city flush with electricity and life, and the streets that didn't see either any more than they needed to.

Too fucking poor to know how to move.

Too stubborn to want to.

She rubbed the back of her neck, stepped off the landing, and picked her way across the broken path toward the sleek silver car half propped on the curb. The light darkened by increments as clouds rolled angry and fast into the layer cake that was the real heart of New Seattle.

Sliding behind the wheel, she found the wires she'd already pulled and touched them together until sparks caught, meshed. The engine turned over with a well-tuned purr of leashed power.

The rain thickened. It splattered the windshield, infected the air with the slightly acrid sting of acid.

She needed to tell the Mission. An investigation would have to be launched, they'd need to begin the proceedings.

But would it mess with her current job?

Would they pull her before she got the chance to put that bullet in Carson's skull?

Her fingers hovered over the comm unit. Curled in.

Later. When she brought in the body, she'd give a full report. She'd tell them everything.

She'd . . . do what she was good at.

Shifting the car into reverse, Naomi eased back from the curb. She frowned at the dimming light pooling through the rear windshield, at the slide of water rippling across its surface. Another storm.

Fan-fucking-tastic.

She turned, flicking on the windshield wipers as she hit the gas. The car lurched forward.

A figure loomed dark and broad out of nowhere, leaped to the side in a flash of wet denim and white. Tires screeched as Naomi swore viciously, slamming the brakes. The car swerved, spun ninety degrees, and she struggled to keep her heart from pounding right the hell out of her chest.

Her fingers cramped on the steering wheel.

Silas.

Impossible. Silas Smith had died three months ago. Her childhood training partner was nothing more than a greasy smear in the ruined underground.

The man was dead. She couldn't have just seen him standing in front of her car, the man was *dead*.

And she didn't goddamn believe in ghosts.

She threw open the door, tearing the zipper of her coat down for easy access to the Colt, but she didn't draw it. She'd feel stupid, insane, if she drew a weapon on a hysteria-induced mirage.

With her pulse still too fast in her ears, she surveyed the street. The dark alleys on either side.

She spun when footsteps crunched on the broken sidewalk behind her.

He caught her by the back of the head, blocked her fist with one forearm. Her knuckles cracked against bone. Naomi yelped as he slammed her head to the top of the car. Swore as her skull reverberated, bone to metal.

Way too familiar.

He'd always been a hands-on kind of dick.

She lashed backward, snapped out a foot that found vulnerable flesh, but he twisted, trapped her, slid in behind her. Suddenly pinned to the wet hood of the car, she struggled against a man as solid as stone, his hips to her back and one hand flattening her face to wet metal.

"Don't," he warned, and Naomi's chest tightened. She gasped for air. For sense.

For sanity to come back.

"Silas." It barely croaked out of her too-swollen throat.

Silas Smith had been a good hunter. A good friend, until he'd fallen head over dick for a witch.

That witch led him to his death.

Now, with his callused hand pressing her face to the cold metal hood and the warmth of his body pinning her flat, Naomi couldn't ignore the truth.

He wasn't dead.

Clearly he wasn't dead, and that meant he still worked for them. The other side.

He'd betrayed her.

"You're hurting me," she snapped.

His hand tightened over her head. "Like hell. If I let you go, you're not— *Fuck me*." It broke on a gasp, a thrash of mangled air as Naomi shifted, liquid quick, and rammed her elbow back into his sternum.

He staggered, opening the opportunity for her to hook a foot around one knee and jerk. Hard.

Silas hit the ground wheezing.

Naomi spun, weight on the balls of her feet, and backed away, fists clenched hard, ready. Waiting. There was no way in hell she'd roll around on the ground with a man twice her size.

His death had been good to him.

Silas had lost none of his muscle, none of his lethal grace as he sprang back to his feet, one big hand rubbing at his chest. His skin was oddly tan, healthy.

He watched her warily from gray-green eyes.

"You son of a bitch," she said tightly. "You backstabbing turncoat shitfu—"

"God damn it, Nai." It rumbled from his chest, impatience. Tension.

And . . . fear?

Good. He deserved to be afraid. To wonder if she'd put a bullet right between his fucking eyes. She circled him, watched him. "How's the witch-bitch?" A flicker of fury, of menace in his eyes made her smile flatly. "Dead, then? Like you're supposed to be?"

"Jesus." Silas put his hands out to the side. "Shut up for one second and listen—"

"You made your choice." Naomi pulled the gun from her coat, raised it fluidly, and cupped one hand under the other as he shifted hard. "Don't move. I'm not going to stand here and listen to whatever lies that bitch put you up to."

"Naomi—"

"I said no!" The words wrenched from her chest. Too hard. Too telling.

Silas froze, closing his eyes. Sympathy. Jesus Christ, she didn't need his pity.

"Save it," she said, quieter with effort. "I don't have time to put you where the Mission can get you, so I'll just have to shoot you and call it a day."

"You think you can?"

"Honey," she drawled, finger tightening on the trigger. "You're the least of my problems."

Or he should have been. She had so much more to do, so much more to be worried about, but her arms ached, shoulders too rigid as the lethal barrel centered on his chest. It shook, just enough.

Grimly she widened her stance, firmed her grip.

He'd betrayed her, betrayed the Mission. He was as much a heretic as the witch he'd decided to help.

Silas watched her.

She swallowed hard. In his eyes, in the smoky green

depths of his steady gaze, she saw the boy he'd been years ago, the stocky kid who'd pulled her nine-year-old ass out of the tree when she'd tried to run away from the orphanage.

She saw the shape of his mouth, quick enough to smile before the severity of the Mission had beaten it out of him.

Out of them both.

He eased closer. "I'm not your enemy," he said quietly. "I never have been." A pause, and then a wry slash to his mouth. "Mostly."

She raised her chin. "Don't move."

"You're not going to shoot me, Nai." Slowly he reached out a broad palm, wrapped his fingers around the barrel. "You would have if you could. I'm not here to fight with you."

If he'd tried to take it, if he'd so much as pulled a fraction of an inch, Naomi wasn't sure that she would have taken her finger off the trigger. But he didn't. He just pushed, firmly, resolutely, until the muzzle pointed down. Safely tucked toward the ground at his feet.

Her arms jerked.

"I'm not dead, Naomi."

A wash of tears all but knocked her on her ass. She buckled, righted herself, and threw her weight at him instead. He caught her, staggered.

"Oh, Christ." Pure panic. He grunted in pain as she rammed her fist into the heavy muscle at his shoulder. Into his stomach, braced for the impact. Into his chest. She dropped the gun and hammered at him, sobbed incoherent words of rage and relief and frustration. She pounded against the rock-solid wall of muscle and flesh and witch-loving heretic and it wasn't enough.

As he took the worst of it, as he turned his face away, taut with apology, with regret—with the innate inability of a man confronted by a hysterical woman—Naomi grabbed his collar and kissed him hard on the mouth.

His eyes widened.

Narrowed as she jerked her knee up into his groin. He wasn't fast enough. Soft flesh gave way to bruising bone.

Silas buckled.

She let him go. Gasping for breath, she braced herself on her knees and watched him hit the ground, hunched over the balls she knew would be too fucking sore to play with for a while. Served him right.

"Fuck," he swore, gasped it. "Why?"

"You're supposed to be dead!" She threw it at him, her accusation rough and furious, sharp as a knife. "Why couldn't you stay dead?"

He groaned. "I may as well be."

"You're fucking not, are you?"

"I thought," he gritted out between bloodless lips, "that's what the kiss was for."

"In your dreams." Naomi sniffed hard, wiping at her eyes impatiently. "What the hell are you thinking, Smith? You can't talk to me. You can't show me you're alive and then just expect to walk away. I'm still a fucking missionary, even if you aren't!"

Grunting with the effort, Silas pushed himself back to his feet. Stiffly, gingerly, he hunched over the crippling pain of his bruised groin, braced against his knees until Naomi could see his eyes begin to uncross.

He cleared his throat roughly. "That's, uh . . . Christ, Naomi."

Despite the pressure behind her eyes, too damn much emotion clawing at her, a smile caught at her mouth. "You're welcome."

"I'm here because— damn. Exactly because you're a missionary." He straightened by increments. Groaned. "Fuck me."

"Good luck with that," she bit out, but a wash of guilt slipped under the anger. The hurt. She turned away, retrieved the gun she'd dropped to the wet ground. "What do you want?"

"I want you to go back to Timeless. And you need to do it now."

She jerked straight, spun to stare at him. At the intensity of his eyes, glittering in his still-pale face. "How the fuck—"

"They're in trouble."

"Homicidal maniac stalking the joint? Yeah, I'd say." She rolled her eyes. "What's new there?"

"There's more than just the one," he replied grimly.

"What?"

"Remnants of this city's Coven of the Unbinding cell are in there, too," Silas said, his voice hoarse with the effort.

"I knew it!"

"No, Nai," he replied roughly. "They're not there because Timeless let them. They're rogue, too."

"Aren't they all?"

"I know you killed one," he said, cupping himself as

if it could take the pressure off. His mouth still pinched. "Jesus. But there's more, and your rogue agent just locked down the building."

Naomi stilled. Every nerve shimmered to sudden, complete attention. "Locked down," she repeated. If it came out hoarse, breathless with fear, Silas didn't ask.

He checked his comm. "Twenty minutes ago. He's got the family, some staff, a couple of guests. One's wounded."

She paled. "Details?"

"Not many." Gingerly Silas took a few steps. "I have someone on the inside, but contact's sporadic. Do you trust me?"

Stiff with anger, with sudden biting terror, Naomi smiled flatly. "Not ever again."

"How about for the next hour?"

"You have a plan?"

He nodded, face grim. "But you're going to have to let me drive."

Naomi glanced at the sleek, beautiful car. Back at his face, so steady. So hard. Missionary mode.

Except he wasn't a missionary anymore.

"Not on your goddamn life," Naomi said sweetly.

Silas chuckled. It strained. "Worth a shot. Get in. Time's short." He rounded the car, walking carefully. Wincing, he slid into the passenger seat.

The rain pounded the street, hammered at the car roof as Naomi pulled the door shut. She tucked the Colt back into its holster and slammed the car into drive.

"What's the deal in there?"

"A woman down"—suddenly dizzy with relief, Naomi swallowed back a roll of nausea—"and there's a handful of people all trying to save who they can. The killer's been using secret corridors."

Naomi glanced at him. "Are you fucking serious?"

"As a bullet."

"Where are they?"

Silas reached across her lap and unhooked her comm, the gesture so wordlessly familiar that she gritted her teeth around a wave of bittersweet memory. He slotted a small chip into the jack. After a moment, he held it up. "Partial blueprints. It's all she could map."

"How the fuck do you know all this?"

"I told you," Silas replied, "I have someone on the inside."

"Who, what?" She eased the car into traffic, movements stiff. Too fucking much tension. "Who just happens to know everything going on in there?"

"Something like that."

Naomi's grip ached on the wheel. "Silas."

"Yeah."

"When this is over?"

"Yeah?"

She didn't look at him, her eyes skimming the tops of the spires looming above the carousel. Smoke boiled like a blight into the sky, black on gray. "Run like hell. Don't ever let me see you again."

His laugh choked, half a snort. "Yeah."

They rode in silence until sirens overwhelmed the quiet. Emergency vehicles blitzed by them on the road. Naomi swore, slammed the pedal to the floor, and overtook them again.

"Racing them might not—"

"Fuck off, I'm trying to beat them there," Naomi

growled, deftly spinning the car between two ambu-
lances and a fire truck. Horns blared, sirens wailed, and
Silas clung to the door handle like a little girl.

She slanted him a contemptuous smile as they blitzed
through the security checks. Yellow and black road-
blocks rebounded off the hood, clattered over the windshield, and sent a security agent diving for cover.

In her rearview mirror, a sec-comp skittered higher
into the air, its programming likely set to follow any
vehicle breaking protocol. "Company," she said tightly.

"Let it." Silas hunkered down in his seat. "It'll bring
more help to the hotel."

New lights flashed on behind them, quickly left
behind as they raced up the carousel. The car ate pavement like it was nothing, tearing through the back entrance and squealing into the parking garage. Dead
silence wrapped around them like a coffin as Naomi
climbed out of the car, her heart pounding.

The smoke wasn't as thick here. Yet.

She stripped off her jacket, tossed it over the hood,
and zipped the Mission suit to her chin.

Silas checked his comm. "There's a passage here."

"I hate this place," Naomi snarled, lashing out with
a foot. The car rocked as the impact echoed through the
garage. "Hate this goddamn—"

"Naomi."

She whirled, scraping her fingers through her hair,
and didn't meet Silas's eyes. "Where's the fucking passage?"

"Down here." The feminine voice echoed from her
left. Naomi spun, gun in hand, and aimed at the floor
as a section of grating shifted. "A little help, maybe?"

Springing forward, Silas bent to the grate, yanked it hard, and shifted the whole thing away. Metal clanged against stone, ringing desperately through the garage. Red hair gleamed in the dim light as he helped Cally out of the hole.

Naomi tucked the gun back into her holster. Tawny eyes met hers. Narrowed.

Brown eyes. Not green. Naomi's fingers itched. "Shitfuck," she snarled. Before the woman could react, Naomi grabbed a handful of that shiny red hair and yanked hard enough to send Cally sprawling.

Except it came off in her hand instead.

Waves of tousled blonde hair slid to her shoulders, and Naomi stared into the rueful, impatient face of Jessie Leigh.

The witch Silas had died for.

Silas snatched her out of the air as she lunged. Shook her hard enough to rattle her teeth. "West!" he barked. His voice bounced from wall to wall.

Jessie raised her hands. "I'm sorry," she said, but Naomi flung an elbow into Silas's shoulder.

It dug into the tender muscle of his neck. He only grunted, wrestled her back from the hole, and slammed her back down on her feet. Hard.

Her ankles tweaked a warning.

"That's enough," Silas snarled.

Naomi thrust her face inches from his. "You son of a bitch. You're still—"

"Gemma Clarke is dying." Jessie's calm intensity wrapped around Naomi's brain and squeezed. Hard.

She whirled. "What?"

"Do I have your attention now?" Sympathy filled her

golden brown eyes, edged with something fiercer. Something Naomi hadn't recognized the first time they'd met.

Raw determination. *Dedication.*

Fuck. She pushed away from Silas, shrugging off his large hand in disgust. "How?"

"The missionary shot her. I can take you there."

Naomi glanced at the yawning hole at her feet. "Through there?"

"He hasn't figured out all the halls," Jessie said, nodding. "But time's running out, Miss West. He's set fire to the outlying wings and the others can only work so fast."

Naomi's smile cut. "Others."

"The witches not part of the coven," Jessie replied quietly. "We're all fighting them. It's not pretty."

Pretty. Fuck pretty. Naomi slammed her gun back into the holster. "Take me in."

Silas shifted. "I'll—"

Jessie put a hand on Silas's chest. Palm to heartbeat. Naomi flinched, turned away as something raw and emotional filled his face.

The same emotion mirrored in the witch's expression.

"You need to go find the others," she said quietly. "The accused witches and supporters Phin tried to evacuate are trapped in the basement, you need to find them and get them to safety."

Silas scowled, catching the nape of her neck as if it would make his point that much sharper. "I'm not leaving you," he said roughly.

Jessie's laugh was as smoky as the hand on his cheek was tender, and Naomi's shoulders stiffened.

He loved a goddamned witch. A *witch*.

And if it was the kind of spell the Church swore it had to be, she'd carve off her own tattoo and eat it. Goddamn him.

"I'm not alone," Jessie said softly. "Naomi will protect me."

The look Silas slanted Naomi should have gutted her where she stood. She lifted her chin, refusing to look away.

Silas let out a hard sound. Frustration. Resignation. "Be careful," he said. Pleaded, damn him. "Sunshine, you be careful. Promise me."

"It's not my fight, remember?" Jessie eased up to her toes, kissed him with all of that raw passion and something so much softer. Gentler.

Naomi couldn't watch. Not this. Not while Silas held a witch close, kissed her as thoroughly as Naomi had ever known a kiss to be.

Jessie touched his face, so sweetly, and then jerked her head at the hole. "After you, Miss West."

Silas's fists clenched. "I love you."

"I never liked you," Naomi shot back, and couldn't help a fierce surge of amusement as he made a rude gesture in her direction.

Behind her, Jessie laughed. "I love you, too," she whispered. "Go do what you have to."

"Thirty minutes," he said fiercely. "Thirty fucking minutes, not a second more or I'm coming in after you. You hear me, West?"

"I hear," she muttered, and stepped into the hole. The instant Naomi sank into the gloom beneath the parking garage, she knew it wasn't going to be as easy as that.

Smoke curled around her chest. It ghosted around her with every motion, burned her nose and throat.

Jessie landed behind her, shoes scraping against the concrete flooring. "Gemma needs you first."

"Where's Phin?"

The witch pushed past her, clicking on a flashlight that shattered the dark. Tendrils of gray curled into the beam. "Gemma first," she repeated.

"God damn it—"

Jessie turned, the flashlight beam suddenly stark in Naomi's face. She swore, her night vision shattered, and couldn't see to stop it when Jessie's hand shot out and grabbed a fistful of her collar.

"You listen to me," Jessie said tightly, her voice a lash of tightly leashed fury and pain. "Fifteen people are dead. Do you understand that? Only eight of them were caught in that fire, and we're not counting the witch you killed."

Naomi seized the thin wrist under her chin, but she didn't use it. Didn't twist her grip and send the girl flying.

Maybe it was the passion.

Maybe it was the tide of regret, of focused rage welling deep inside.

"I hear you," she said quietly. "Yeah, I get it. I'm going to kill Carson, don't you worry about that."

"That's not the part that worries me." Her fingers loosened, and Naomi let her go. "I really wish you'd been quicker on the uptake."

"Fuck you. If you know everything—"

"I don't." Jessie turned, once more following the narrow hall. "But what would you have done if I'd

come to you and said, 'Hey, if I point out a group of
people and call them witches, can you lock them up
for me?' "

Naomi opened her mouth, hesitated. Her fingers
curled into her palms as she admitted grimly, "I'd ask
all sorts of questions." She frowned. "Jesus Christ. Just
lead the way, princess."

"Funny, Miss Ishikawa." Jessie's tone flattened as the
flashlight arced through the smoky shadows. "Who's
the princess now?"

Naomi ate that one. Fucking fate.

They walked in silence, following turns and bends
that Naomi couldn't place. She didn't know where they
were. Where they'd come out of. Finally, tired to death
of staring at the faint luster of the light on Jessie's gold
hair and sage green uniform, Naomi broke the silence.
"How the hell do you know about these tunnels?"

Jessie's eyes gleamed as she glanced over her shoulder. "Spatial awareness."

"Bullshit."

The woman sighed briefly. "Didn't your last director
tell you guys anything?"

Naomi's jaw locked. "Apparently not. Peterson's
notes didn't seem out of the ordinary."

"Your new director must be having a field day,"
Jessie said wryly. "I know about this stuff because I see
the present."

"See—?"

"The present," she repeated. "Anything going on
right now, anywhere in this city, country—hell." She
sighed. "Some people see the future, right? I see anything happening right now anywhere in the world. And

without setting foot outside my door, if I wanted. It doesn't stop."

"Holy fuck." A witch with that kind of power? Naomi gritted her teeth.

For the moment, she had to trust this witch. Was she fucking surrounded by them?

"Shh." Jessie clicked off the light. "It's here somewhere . . ." Naomi waited in the dark as the other woman ran her fingers over the plain, faceless wall. Beams shifted. Dust and smoke swirled.

"Here." She paused. "Naomi, it's not good."

"Just open the fucking door."

A seam of light split the smoky darkness. Naomi surged past Jessie, threw her weight against the panel. It sprang open, slammed against the wall, and rebounded into her shoulder.

She didn't care.

All she cared about was the ring of people staring at her, eyes wide. Two held guns.

There was blood everywhere.

"Gemma." Naomi ignored the guns, ignored the gasps of fear, of surprise. Of recognition. "Jesus, Gemma!"

Two of the men held a gun, each in the Timeless uniforms. They shifted, reached out to stop her from getting past the crimson stains on the floor.

Naomi's level, murderous challenge forced one to reconsider. The other leveled a gun at her head. "Don't move," he ordered. "Please."

"Let her—"

Too fast, too reckless, Naomi palmed the gun and wrenched it, twisting his fingers. Bone grated against metal. He yelped, squawked in fear and alarm as she caught his wrist, turned, and stepped into his wide open stance as he struggled for balance. She jammed an elbow hard enough into his throat that his shout turned into a gurgle.

He collapsed to his knees, gasping for breath.

Naomi holstered the gun into the waistband of her jeans and met Liz's narrowed stare. "—come in," she finished with a muttered snort. "That wasn't necess—"

"Get the fuck out of my way," Naomi snarled.

Maybe it was the unbridled impatience. Or the sheer lethal promise Naomi didn't do anything to mitigate.

Maybe it was Jessie's wild signal in her peripheral vision.

She stepped out of the way.

Rage guttered. "Gemma."

Phin's mother was too pale, her skin gleaming with sweat. With streaks of blood. She lay on her back, her curls stuck to her forehead and cheeks. Naomi could clearly see her veins underneath her fragile, translucent skin.

Could see her lungs rising and falling in shallow, gasping breaths.

Dying in Lillian's arms.

Naomi sank to her knees beside the stiff-lipped woman, smoothed her hands over Gemma's damp cheeks. "Fuck." It was all she could say. All she could think as Phin's mother bled out around her.

Gemma's paper-thin eyelids fluttered. Her hands rose, bloody, grasping. "Naomi?"

She caught them, held tight. "I'm here," she said tightly. "I'm right here. Did Carson do this?"

"Doesn't—" Gemma coughed, cringing with the

pain that Naomi knew must fill every part of her. Burning, eating. Draining. "Doesn't matter," she managed.
"Need . . . you."

"I'm here. Where's Phin?"

Gemma's smile was weak. Her eyes glittered, fever-
ishly bright into Naomi's. "White . . . knight. N-Naomi.
You must . . . take it."

Around her, Naomi dimly registered gasps. Mutters.
Questions.

Jessie eased around the circle, a thin, fragile point
of awareness in Naomi's peripheral. She watched her,
watched Gemma, and her expression told Naomi what
she'd already known.

The woman was beyond help. Gut shot.

Tears balled in her throat. "Take what?" she asked,
her voice cracking. "What can I do?"

"The fountain." Gemma's fingers tightened. Hard
enough that Naomi's bones ground together, that pain
rippled to her elbows. "You're . . . right."

"Right?" Naomi shook her head as the first tear
trickled over her cheek. "I don't want to be right,
Gemma, I want you to get up off this floor and—"

Gemma's laugh cut her off. It wasn't the bitter,
broken laugh of a woman dying. It wasn't the angry
surge Naomi expected of anyone gunned down by a
bastard with a grudge.

It gentled. Brushed over her like a caress.

Sweet. Loving.

"I know you're right," she whispered. "Phin . . . knows
you're right." Naomi's heart twisted. "Take the power."

Her eyes widened. "The what?"

Gemma's closed. "Take it. Protect it. Pl-please."

"Naomi."

She looked up from the shiny, twisted mask of effort on Gemma's pallid face. Jessie met her eyes, her gaze vibrant gold and shimmering with regret.

"She's a witch."

Naomi's hands jerked.

Jessie grabbed her shoulder, hard enough to leave nail marks in her skin. The skin that should have been scabbed and furrowed. "Shut up, turn it off, and listen to me. The power she carries heals, but only others." The witch crouched, smoothed her hand over Gemma's forehead. "She *is* the fountain of life, Naomi."

"She's a *witch*—"

"You're the only one," Jessie said flatly, "that can keep this from dying out right now. You don't take it, something beautiful and helpful and *good* dies, and the world loses another part of its soul with it."

Naomi flinched. "This world can eat its own tail and die trying."

"It's her last wish, Miss West."

Gemma cracked open her eyes. "I can—I can do my own pitch, thank you," she said with some shadow of her former asperity. But it weakened with every word, slipped into broken lines as Naomi tightened her grip on Gemma's hands and struggled to hold it all in.

To keep her together.

Damn it, to keep herself together.

Jessie's smile flashed. Sad. "I'm sorry," she whispered. "I thought—"

"I'll do it." Naomi avoided Jessie's gaze. "Gemma, how do I help you?"

"Come down here," she whispered. "You, Cally . . .

whoever you are. You'll know when . . . we need the water. The . . . warm one. Waterfall."

"Yes, ma'am," Jessie whispered.

Around them, the loose circle stirred. Beyond the uncertain faces of the uniformed people framing the bloody circle of power drawn on the floor, Michael Rook and Jordana lay slumped together; breathing, but unconscious.

The man she'd throat-punched in her fury met her gaze, unapologetic. "They won't see anything," he rasped, fingers massaging his neck.

Her skin prickled. Magic all but thrummed in the vast, echoing hall, but her seal was dormant. Why? How?

A copper-skinned teenager laid his fingers on the man's shoulder. "Sorry, Joel," he said solemnly. "I didn't think she'd fight like a man."

Joel's lips twitched, but it did nothing to ease the shadows from his eyes.

Gemma tugged on Naomi's hands, her grip already weaker. Swallowing back the knot of tears and tension swelling in her throat, forcing herself to ignore every shrieking, Mission-trained warning in her head, Naomi bent over the dying woman.

Phin's mother.

A witch.

So the Church isn't investigating my home?

He'd known. The lying, manipulative, traitorous son of a bitch had *known*.

And he said he'd loved her.

Gemma cupped the back of her head with one crimson hand. Her eyes flared open, beautiful, chocolate brown, swimming with pain and that focused determination she'd read so often in Phin's own gaze. "I'm sorry," she breathed.

Naomi smiled crookedly. "It wouldn't be the—"

Her words died as Gemma tugged her face down, seizing her mouth in a kiss that stole the breath from her body.

She tasted the copper tang of blood and the salt of bitter sweat. She tasted peppermint, the soft warmth of Gemma's lower lip, and swallowed surprise and a sudden rush of pain that didn't feel like her own.

The world detonated around her.

For an eternity of silence, everything went white.

CHAPTER NINETEEN

The pop and crackle of the fire woke her.

Naomi drifted away from dreams she couldn't remember, away from the surreal emptiness of something she couldn't name and into snug comfort. Warmth bathed her skin. Soothed her mind, her agitated soul.

She was home.

She inhaled, smelled burning resin and the wonderful fragrance of pine as she drew it in, wrapping it around her like a blanket.

For the first time in years, nothing hurt. Nothing ached. Nothing burned or throbbed or bit sharply. Naomi was whole, peaceful.

She smiled, opening her eyes.

The mahogany mantel gleamed in the golden light,

polished to within an inch of its life and so shiny she could almost see her reflection in the beautiful sheen. The fire blazed merrily, cast a friendly warmth throughout the study.

There were no photographs framed on the mantel. No family pictures to tell her where she was, but she didn't need them to know that it was safe. Nothing could reach her here.

Around her, books lined the walls in precisely ordered reams of color. The wood matched the mantel, polished just as beautifully and all but hidden beneath row upon row of colored spines. Encyclopedias, new books printed since the earthquake, some rarer books from before.

Some had letters that gleamed gold in the light, and those were her favorite. So shiny and pretty. Others barely held up in the shadow, old and marked, their spines creased with age.

She rubbed the sleep from her eyes, the beautifully woven afghan sliding to her waist. She'd never caught her father reading any of them, but sometimes she'd take one down and leaf through its pages. Sometimes, when he wasn't looking, she'd pretend she read the mysterious books with their jumble of pictures and words she couldn't understand yet.

Naomi stretched. Froze.

Suddenly shaking, she touched her lips. Her face. The soft afghan blanket in her lap.

A core of ice slipped down her spine.

"Are you awake?"

The voice slammed into her skull, a memory plucked from the depths of her mind and transformed into a sledgehammer. Warm, serious, patient, the masculine sound of it seared every nerve she had until she shot off the couch, already knowing what she'd find and dreading it.

Hating it.

Tears welled in her eyes. "Daddy."

Katsu Ishikawa didn't look up from his neat, precise notes. The firelight flickered, gilded his slicked-back hair and thin, angled features in gold. His eyebrows moved as he spoke, a trait she'd loved.

They moved now. Furrowed. "Why are you here?"

Naomi sucked in a small, painful breath. "I don't know."

"Unacceptable." Deftly her father licked one finger. Turned the page over. Without looking up from his letter, he said, "What do you want from me?"

Too much.

No. Exactly enough. Naomi's fingers fisted. "It's too late now."

"Is it?"

"You're dead," she snarled.

"Ah." Still, he kept his eyes on the letter. Signed it, ended with the same neat signature he signed all things. He rose, straightening the tailored suit jacket that always made him look so distinguished. So handsome.

Naomi circled the settee, knew she stared. Her eyes feasted on every detail of his face, his posture. Every angle, every feature. So familiar.

The cheekbones, high and defined. Even his jaw, never overly square but perfect. And his nose, straight and strong like hers.

Half her own reflection.

"Why am I here?" she whispered.

Carefully he set the papers on his desk, just at the corner. He adjusted his cuffs, ensuring they remained precisely in place.

He'd always been so careful with everything. His study, his schedule, his evening brandy.

Her father didn't look at her as he powered down the sleek computer. "That's an excellent question. Why should I know?"

She flinched. "You're my father."

"Am I?"

Naomi sucked in a sharp breath. Anger simmered low in her belly. Bubbled. "You know you are."

"What is a father, Naomi? Is it genetic? Is it sperm count? Is that all a father is? Is it a memory?"

Still he didn't look at her. His dark eyes remained fixed on his own tasks as he moved around the desk. He crossed the carpeted floor and pulled the drapes closed.

She shook her head. "You raised me."

"For how long, pet?"

Five years. In the scheme of things, it seemed so little. She raised her chin, jaw tight. "You marked me."

His hand froze over the drapes. Now, slowly, he turned his head and met her accusing stare.

His own brimmed with regret. "For that," he said, so politely, so gently, "I am sorry. I had hoped five years would be too little time to remember me."

"Sorry?" Naomi threw out her hands, trembling with so much she couldn't define. A terrible, slashing hurt. "How could you say that?"

He looked away again, and it seemed as if his shoulders weren't as broad as she'd remembered. Not as strong. He seemed leaner, thinner than she thought. Was her memory wrong?

Was it skewed by her years spent raised among men built like brick walls?

Quietly he pulled a drapery cord from its moorings.

Naomi's anger turned to an avalanche of fear. "Daddy, no."

"Have you ever wanted something so badly," he asked as he coiled the rope around his arm in precise increments, "that you'd stop at nothing to get it?"

She shook her head as tears of fury, of terror, overwhelmed her speech.

"Then you get it." Slowly he crossed the study once more. Retraced his steps. He didn't look at her again, passed her as if she were the ghost. "And it's everything you'd hoped, everything you'd dreamed, and everything . . . you dreaded."

"No."

His voice dropped to a whisper. "And still you suffer it. Gladly. Every day a torture and a joy."

Naomi reached out to seize his shoulder. Sobbed a broken curse as her hand slid through it, flesh through smoke.

He paused, uncoiling the silken cord. "Then it's gone," he said quietly. "Just gone."

Naomi staggered backward. Her legs slammed into the settee and she sprawled. Helpless. "Daddy, don't. Don't do this."

The rope gleamed in the light as he tossed it high. It found the rafter, curled over it with ease. "What else was I supposed to do? My family's honor was ruined. My reputation tarnished. Her creditors were calling every day."

Tears crystallized, spilled over in acid grief. "You had me," Naomi said bitterly. Her hands clenched in her lap, but she couldn't look away. Couldn't do anything but watch as long, deft fingers twisted and knotted. As he coiled drapery cord into a thin noose.

"She wanted you."

Naomi's head jerked. "No, she didn't."

"She's a fickle woman. She wanted you to spite me, but I wouldn't have it. So I gave you away in secret. She got everything else."

"No." She lurched to her feet as her father stepped onto the chair he'd placed by the desk. The fire crackled, spitting sparks onto the slate floor around it.

It glittered wildly in his face. Caught the dead sheen of his eyes as he tugged the rope. Tested its hold.

Her breath shuddered in her chest. "Daddy, don't."

"I'm sorry, pet." Slowly, mechanically, Katsu Ishikawa slid the noose over his head. Tightened it behind his neck. "There is honor to consider."

"There was *me* to consider," she shouted. She lunged for his waist, his jacket, anything, and only swore viciously as he gave way like smoke. As he leaned out and sent the chair flying into her legs.

It hurt. The wood slammed into her shins and sent her staggering, hobbling. Pain ricocheted from wood and bone.

But she couldn't touch him.

Couldn't do anything but scream in bottled rage and horror as his body jerked like a twisted marionette on the edge of the rope and danced a final, twitching dance.

For a long moment, she couldn't breathe. Couldn't move.

Thump, thump. His feet hit the desk in a slow, rhythmic swing.

Naomi crumpled to the floor.

Thump, thump.

"Daddy?"

Her heart slammed into her stomach. Nausea gathered, sharp and fast.

"Daddy, Nanny says it's time for supper."

She turned, suddenly feeling as if she were made of lead. Her blood filled with it, slowing her. Freezing her in place, unable to call out, to warn the little girl who pushed open the study door.

Her hair gleamed in the firelight, as black as her father's and gathered into two pigtails, each wrapped with pink ribbon. Her skirt hung neatly pressed, her blouse frilly and so tiny. She wore saddle shoes in pink and white and cradled a small horse doll in one hand.

She'd loved that doll.

"Daddy?" Her voice wavered. Her little feet tripped over the carpet, and Naomi struggled to break the terror of memory. To wrench herself from the dream shattering her heart.

But it didn't fade.

Instead, as the little girl sat on the carpet and watched her father swing, Naomi reached out. Her fingers trembled desperately as she hovered one hand over the tiny child's glossy black hair.

The scream of the nanny threw the house into chaos.

Naomi flinched.

"This isn't your fault."

A broken sound, at least partly a laugh, tore from her chest.

"Naomi." Blue-violet eyes met hers. So wide, bright with unshed tears. Her young, childish voice resonated, matured eerily from her bow-shaped mouth. "This isn't your fault." She reached out to stroke a tiny hand over Naomi's cheek. It passed through.

Naomi shot to her feet, spun and screamed in rage, in fear, as her father's purple, bloated face swung inches from hers. Back and forth. "This isn't your fault," he wheezed, slowly spinning.

The cord creaked. *Thump, thump.*

"No." Naomi backed away. She passed through a figure wrapped in silk and expensive perfume. Trails of ghostly color clung to her face, skeins of a fragrance that haunted her dreams, her skin. Naomi staggered.

Abigail turned in a frothy sea of peach lace and cream, her smile sad. "This wasn't ever your fault."

Naomi shook her head, over and over, a high, keening wail locked behind her teeth. "No," she sobbed, the word a broken sound of understanding. "No. It's yours. All of it, it's all your fault, the both of you."

The corpse's smile turned ghastly. "There is honor to consider."

"There was still so much I had to have," Abigail said lightly.

"And you lost it all," Naomi whispered. She scrubbed at her face, furiously dashed her tears aside. "You lost honor when you abandoned your child to become a killer. When you used me like some sort of revenge."

The corpse's skin mottled.

Naomi flung a finger at Abigail, sharp accusation. "You. You lost everything. You threw it all away, hoping to find some miraculous fountain of youth, and now it's too late. Nothing of you lives on. *Nothing*."

Both specters stared at her. Watched her in brutal silence.

And five-year-old Naomi Ishikawa watched her from the floor, her eyes brimming with too much awareness.

Too much knowing.

So many untapped tears.

It'd be years until one man would break through that dam. A standstill decades long.

Naomi swallowed hard, and remembered what she'd forgotten. What she'd always known. "Your mistakes aren't my fault," she whispered. "You're right. But I can fix what *is* my fault, and fuck you, I will *not* be the twisted, lonely woman my parents made me."

"Oh, sweetie—"

"You have to go," the little girl said solemnly, cutting off Abigail's trilling laugh. "You have to go back before it's too late." Boots tromped through the halls, echoed shouts and sirens piercing the ghostly solitude. Within moments, emergency technicians poured into the study, a regulated wash of chaos.

Naomi shook her head. "How?"

Somberly the little girl with Naomi's own face moved around the adults. She pressed herself to the fringe and watched the corpse of her father hit the ground. Crumple bonelessly, bloated face jiggling. Mottled.

Dead.

"I don't know," she said.

A hot tear trickled down Naomi's cheek. The girl glanced at her. Followed the tear as it dripped from her chin and splashed over Naomi's hand.

The girl's mouth curved down. "How do you know where you belong?"

Naomi closed her eyes. She fisted her hands tightly, nails biting into the callused edge of her palms and struggled to remember.

To forget.

Warm brown eyes met hers in the dark recesses of her mind. A dimpled smile tugged at her heart.

Phin. She belonged there. At least for the moment, at least for the time it would take to say good-bye.

More than she'd ever done for anyone else.

"You just know," Naomi whispered. Shuddering, she took a deep breath.

And smelled chlorine.

Tears streamed over her cheeks as she opened her eyes. Tears of regret, bottled grief so long capped and filled to the breaking point that it raged from her now. Warm water battered at her, crimson currents swirled until the tub looked like a pool of steaming blood. Wordless, sobbing with the weight of it, with the unfairness of it all, Naomi clung to Gemma's lifeless body as anguish poured from that forgotten place deep inside.

That place Naomi had sworn didn't exist.

Steady hands bracketed her shoulders. "I know," Jessie murmured against her hair. "Let it out. It's okay. It's going to be okay."

Maybe it would be. Someday.

A high-pitched whine sliced the air into auditory

shreds. Overhead the speakers turned over into a quiet hum. "This is Phin Clarke, Carson."

His voice echoed from wall to wall. Battered at her grief. He was steady. So calm.

"I know you're in this building somewhere. You're holding innocent people hostage. Let them get out before the fire spreads, and I'll give you what you want."

Naomi sucked in a hard, shuddering breath as Lillian sobbed at the edge of the tub.

"That was unexpected," Jessie said slowly.

Gently, her heart aching with it, Naomi forced herself to let go of the woman who'd seen in her something Naomi still couldn't. She didn't know what. Maybe she'd learn, one day.

But not today.

She watched Gemma's pale body drift across the bloodied current. Watched as, shoulders shaking, Lillian wrapped her arms around the lifeless corpse of her wife.

Gemma had loved the water. Naomi didn't know how she knew that, but she did. There was solace in the water.

Solace in the fountain.

It simmered deep inside. A golden current, a whisper. *How do you know where you belong?*

"That's because," she said on a low, resigned sound of frustration, "Phin is an idiot. Put them somewhere safe, Jessie. I need my gun."

"I will. What are you going to do?"

Naomi climbed out of the tub, her skin crawling with the knowledge that she wore Gemma's blood. Like a banner. A battle standard. "Go after him before he gets killed," she said.

Another voice cracked across the hall. "No! You can't do that."

Naomi turned. Slowly. Rage dragged bleeding furrows across her heart as she met Agatha's snapping gaze from across the floor. The woman had been bound tightly, her features pale and bruised underneath a sheen of sweat. Beside her, two other witches watched in silent accusation. Hatred.

Resignation, she didn't know. She didn't care. Naomi's eyes narrowed. "Watch me."

"Don't be so stupid," Agatha hissed, struggling against the ropes. "You are the fountain, you can't—"

"I'm the only fucking one able to end this."

"You selfish—"

"By the sanctions of the Holy Order of St. Dominic," Naomi cut in grimly, checking the cartridge in her borrowed gun, "you are hereby accused and proven to be a witch."

Jessie swore behind her, a sharp crescendo in a sea of sudden mutterings. The old words didn't carry any power, but years of persecution levied a weight that reverberated.

Agatha blanched as Naomi slid the cartridge back into place. Four bullets left. "Blah, blah, blah. You know what? I just don't care anymore." With her stomach twisting into brutal knots, Naomi sighted down the barrel and squeezed the trigger. Once, twice. Again.

Screams, shouts, swearing entwined with the thunderous rapport of the gun. Jessie spat something hard and angry behind her, but Naomi threw the gun to the ground and turned her back as the three witches slumped, boneless and bloody to the floor. Silent, jaw thrust hard, she stalked across the spattered crimson tile.

"Wait—"

"Let her go." Jessie's voice cut through the chaos. Flat, exhausted. "She's going to go kill a missionary."

Naomi's smile twisted. Four witches. One missionary. Seemed fair.

CHAPTER TWENTY

"Well, well, Mr. Clarke." The intercom fuzzed as fire ate away at the systems around him. It was hot, too damn hot, but Phin knew he'd seen everything he needed to.

The bastard hadn't bothered to warn anyone. He hadn't cared.

He'd just locked the doors and set it on fire. A few matches, the right incentive. Phin could still smell the gas. Smell the rank, acrid stench of charred flesh.

The knowledge ate at Phin's soul.

He turned, flinging an arm over his face as sparks shattered over a panel that had once been covered in silk.

"Come out, you bastard," he roared, but the fire drowned it out. It leached at his breath, seared. Unable to do anything, *anything* at all, he retreated toward the tunnel door.

"I'll see you in that lovely garden," the easy voice said on the intercom. Fire licked at the edges of the metal plate, cracked the audio into broken syllables. "If—fast . . . save— Maybe . . . lucky."

Phin didn't shut the door behind him. Hatred spurred his feet, slammed his brain into automatic as he navigated the twisted, turning passages that would take him down the inclines of the secret maze. Hatred, rage.

Terror.

Kill him. Clear the way for everyone else.

Kill him, save his mother.

Just kill him.

Phin kicked the panel wide open. Carefully hidden hinges crunched, split away from the wall. Wood and plaster snapped.

Roaring his fury, Phin barreled into the smoke-filled garden. "Where are you?"

Gray, acrid fog curled around the tree limbs above him, ghostly tendrils of clinging smoke that burned his eyes. It tore strips out of his nose and throat. He spun, tried to peer into the shadows between his mother's beloved oak trees, into the smoky recess beneath the willow tree.

Wrath pounded a blood-toned staccato through his skull. "Show yourself, you coward!"

Missionaries, he should have remembered, weren't trained to play nice. Carson came at him from above, a flurry of limbs and lethal, shadowed grace.

The hair on the back of his neck prickled as he spun, only to grunt with the impact as he took Carson's full weight to the shoulders. Phin hit the dirt, rolled frantically.

Carson stayed on him, fists like hammers thudding solidly into Phin's face, his sides. Pain jarred a screeching note through his bones as he collided with a wrought-iron statue, as Carson seized his head and bounced it like a rubber ball against the raised metal.

Reeling, Phin flung a fist out. It collided with something malleable, something edged. Carson cursed, swore a vicious streak as he hit the ground beside Phin.

Blood gleamed on Carson's lip as both men clambered back to their feet.

Phin gasped for air, for breath in the smoke and fear. "You," he panted, "sorry . . . son of a bitch."

Carson straightened slowly, his shoulders lifting in a shrug as he touched dirty fingers to his mouth. They gleamed in the muted fog, crimson and wet. "Well, well," he said softly. "So the whorespawn has kitten claws."

"You aren't getting anything," Phin spat. Pain radiated from his ribs, a dull ache at his left side. Breathing jerked spots in front of his eyes, but he'd be damned before he let the man see him waver.

He'd shot his mother.

Tried to kill his guests.

Ruined everything Phin had worked so hard for. Ruined everything his mothers had spent their lives building. Ruined him.

"Then you aren't worth half as much as them ladies think, are you?" Carson shook his head, even as he hoisted the gun that had fallen out of Phin's waistband. "Oh, and your momma's going to die anyway. It's too late to help her. But maybe you can convince me to use that fountain to keep the rest from dying of smoke inhalation, what do you say?"

"Phin!" Naomi's voice pierced the fog of the garden, but the Phin made of hatred and vengeance ignored her.

Ignored the smoke, the fire, the screams that echoed in his mind, over and over and over. *Help us. Save us.*

Don't let us die.

Baby, don't let him have it.

"My mother isn't dead," he growled, so low it was practically a vibration swallowed by the smoke.

"Uh." The man smiled evenly. "Yeah. I mean, maybe not now, but nothing's going to save her. Not unless you give me that fountain." He shifted, holding out one hand. "*I'll* save her, kid. I'll save everyone you want me to."

Except Carson couldn't even do that. Tears filled his eyes as Phin laughed. Laughed until the smile faded from the man's face; laughed until he was vibrating with pent-up fury, shaking with it. "You stupid fuck," he said, hoarse. Wrecked. "You just killed the only woman who knows what the fountain *is*."

Carson's hand dropped. Slid to his waist and propped there as the man stared down at the floor, gaze speculative. Rueful.

Irritated. "Well, son of a bitch," he murmured. "Guess she's going to die for nothing after all."

Rage colored his vision, filled it, burned it redder than the fire licking at the surrounding wings. Wordless, screaming in pain and fury and soul-wrenching thunder, Phin lowered his head and bull-rushed the bastard.

Too late, Phin saw the wicked gleam of firelight on silver. Saw the casual flick of his fingers that spun the knife blade into a deadly angle.

Metal hammered. Machines pounded against the emergency reinforcements, rang like a bell through the lobby. The garden. Sharp, tinny echoes sheared off Phin's hoarse cry.

Naomi didn't waste her breath screaming as Phin's body jerked. He stared into Carson's face, his own tight with pain, with surprise, one hand fisted in the man's wrinkled, worn jacket.

She just bent low and surged through the garden, every muscle leashed into the killing machine she knew she was.

Carson pushed Phin to the floor, blood gleaming vividly on the knife he reversed in his fingers. A casual flick, a roll of his wrist, and every instinct screamed a warning. Naomi dropped to the floor, rolled to the side. The air split above her head, inches from her scalp.

Metal bent, shrieked as it tore beneath the machines the city had mustered to tear into the spa's protective layer. The echoes slammed through the garden, bounced from wall to wall until it squealed a hellish accompaniment to the steady beat of her heart.

Killer. Joe Carson was a killer, but she was *better*. The better trained, better equipped.

The better killer.

She rolled, leaped to her feet on a surge of adrenaline, determination. As smoke roiled around them, she launched herself at the man who'd ruined it all.

Her life.

Her sanity.

Her goddamn tolerance for everything else.

He backpedaled away from Phin, splayed deathly still at his feet. Away from the path that filled with choking gray. He braced himself, eyes flickering with excitement. Smile obscene, he caught her first punch in one hand, backhanded her with the other. She didn't spit out the blood bursting into her mouth.

Turning, she stepped into his space, spun her captured arm over her head as if he only guided her across a dance floor, and jammed her elbow into his cheekbone. Her forearm into his throat.

Her knee into his gut.

One, two, three.

Metal tore free of moorings. Daylight spilled through the shattered double doors. Smoke swirled as the promise of fresh oxygen sucked it through the furrows.

Carson reeled back, let her go with the sudden certainty that she was every bit as trained as he was. She could read it in his eyes, abruptly wary. No longer amused.

"Yeah. I'm here to kill you," she spat through the smoke. It parted beneath flecks of bloody red. Swirled, clung.

Choked.

He laughed. "Oh, if you only knew."

"I don't want to." Naomi pulled the Colt from its holster, aimed it with no more effort than it took to breathe. Than it took to stand, to walk, to talk. "I don't want to play with you, you turncoat son of a bitch. You're no witch." Her mouth twisted. "You're a hell of a lot *worse*."

Carson stilled. Humor drained from his face. "Never bring a knife to a gunfight," he said with a small shake of his head. "I knew that."

"Too late," she said, finger tightening on the trigger.

"Wait!" He flung out a hand as if a palm could ward off the bullet Naomi intended to put in his skull. She'd dreamed of this. Envisioned turning his brain into so much pulp and red-tinged gray matter.

Nausea blossomed in her belly. Swirled through her chest.

She hesitated.

"I didn't do this on my own," Carson said quickly. Pleadingly. "I didn't make this up. There's a thing of power here, and I'm not the only one who wants it. It's the fountain, it gives back life, it heals *anything*. It's the damn fountain of youth! And the Church wants it bad."

Naomi's heart stilled. Her blood slowed in her veins.

"Let me go, and I'll tell you all about it," he said. His voice was quiet. Hands outstretched, empty of everything but the blood that stained them. Phin's blood.

Gemma's blood.

"I can't do this," she whispered.

His eyes flickered. "I know, honey, but it'd be a shame to let this go to waste. I'm telling you, I can give you a name. I can give you the mission details."

The gun went taut in her hand.

"Shit." One hand slid behind his back, and her index finger clenched on the trigger. Smoke swirled, ghostly tendrils shuddering around a deafening burst of sound, a crack of thunder.

A small stain blossomed at his forehead, a precise round hole that widened. Tore. Split in a viscous spray of red and colored the roiling smoke around them shades of pink.

Joe Carson stared at her. Choked a single note of shattered fury, dropping the gun he'd pulled from the holster at the small of his back.

No words rose to her lips. Nothing pithy, nothing sharp or acerbic or even smart. Nothing filled the hole, the void filling her soul. Saying nothing, each breath a sob of effort, she fired twice more.

He crumpled. Slowly. Knees to waist, ass to water. Toppling, boneless and empty, he crashed into the pond beneath the willow tree. Blood blossomed like a crimson cloud.

The wall shattered behind her.

Frigid air slammed into her back, wrapped around her like a glacial blanket. Voices shouted commands, booted feet tromped on the marbled floor, the earth-packed path. The city cavalry had arrived.

Too late.

She stared down at the bloody water licking at the twisted willow roots. At the body that floated, as harmless as a shell, empty as a broken doll.

Eye for an eye.

Slowly Naomi turned. She trudged back to the path, to the emergency technicians who strapped Phin into a gurney. They padded the knife wound at his shoulder, called out things that shimmered somewhere in her mind as a distant memory.

Patch him up.

Cut him down.

Phin moved, shook his head tightly as they asked him questions, even as grief carved sharp hollows into his face. As his mouth pinched white and angry, so thin it was as if he held back the anguish she knew he must be feeling by strength of will alone.

His mother was dead. He'd professed love—oh, God, how stupid could he have been?—to a killer, and everything he'd ever known was burning to ash around him.

Blood just wasn't his color.

It never would be, the brave, fucking idiot.

And now it was over. Just like that, it was all over. Bullets and blood, exactly as she knew it would end.

Only this time there'd been too much blood. All over her. All over him.

Covering the whole goddamn cage.

Over the flurry of latex-clad hands and bloody smears of cloth, Phin's dark eyes caught hers. Held.

Her heart squeezed, vicious, pointed agony as accusation filled his eyes. Accusation and fear, pain and horror. She'd have been worried if there hadn't been revulsion.

He wouldn't be Phin if he'd been all right.

Smiling, knowing how crooked, how tight and twisted it really was, Naomi touched her lower lip with two fingers and flicked them in his direction.

His eyes narrowed.

Wordlessly she turned and walked away.

CHAPTER TWENTY-ONE

S ilas found her, just as she'd known he would.

It didn't take long. Naomi didn't have very many places to go, not without surrounding herself with crowds of people. Not without wrapping herself in synth-leather and metal and sex and throwing herself into the hungry, frenetic beat of desperate people.

She didn't want people.

So she sat on the roof of her crumbling apartment complex, buried in the heart of the city she loathed as night broke on the back of a rainstorm.

High above, where the clouds all but obscured the topside towers, a golden glow pulsed and flickered. A fiery heartbeat in the night.

Gravel crunched behind her. "The wind's down. No chance of spreading."

Naomi said nothing. What was there to say? *That's nice* seemed somehow empty, disingenuous. Suggesting the city was better off burning seemed . . . harsh.

"You got Agatha and the other two. If there were any more of the Unbinding, they're either dead or in hiding again."

Naomi stared into the black wall of towering city blocks and still said nothing.

Behind her, he sighed.

Silas was a man who took up space. Even if she hadn't heard his voice, she would have recognized him just by the pressure at her back. The awareness of his big body and the intensity that shrouded him like an electric charge.

Even after years separated, a missionary never forgot the people she trained with. She'd lived with him, learned with him night and day. Her feelings for Silas simmered into hatred, blame, and a fierce, protective friendship.

Family. He and Jonas and Eckhart had been all the family she'd known. As Mission supervisors came and went, as other missionaries died or transferred, even when Silas had left for fourteen years, that stuck.

So when his warmth filled the space behind her back, Naomi tensed.

Large hands settled at her shoulders. "Hey."

She shuddered.

"You can't go back," he rumbled, his version of quiet.

She almost laughed. "Back," she bit out. "Back where? To the place that's now on fire or to the place that should be?"

He squeezed her shoulders, as close to comfort as she'd known from him in so many years. Her throat ached with it, with the certainty that she'd lost so much.

And ruined anything else she may have found.

More her parents' child than she'd ever wanted.

"Nai, you have somewhere to go."

Her snort faded on the edge of thunder. Slowly, fat drops of rain trickled to the gritty cement she perched on. Clattered into the gravel.

Onto her head.

This was her life. Pissed on by a sky that couldn't care less in a city that tried too damn hard to pretend everything was all right.

"Nothing is all right," she said aloud, her gaze dropping to the cold, matte black gun on the ledge beside her.

Bullets and blood. That's the life she'd known.

"Phin Clarke is all right," Silas said gruffly.

"Phin Clarke is an idiot." She shrugged off his hands with sudden, violent anger. "Phin Clarke nearly got himself killed because he can't be bothered to—"

"Naomi."

She tipped her head back on her neck, closing her eyes as rain spattered over her face. "What do you want, Silas?"

There. A modicum of normal.

He shifted. When he eased to the ledge beside her, his feet planted firmly on the gravel side, she frowned at him expectantly.

His foggy green eyes didn't reflect sympathy. They edged, challenged. "I want you to give up the life of a missionary."

She laughed. It broke.

Turning her head, she struggled to swallow the rush of emotion, of pain and fear before it overwhelmed her.

She'd be lost without the Mission.

She was lost if she stayed with the Mission.

Silas bent, bracing his elbows on his knees, and continued, "I want you to join us. Help us."

"Us." A flat note.

He nodded. "Jessie and me. And Matilda." He hesitated. "She's . . . this old lady that took us in, gave us a safe place to hide. It's not a bad life, Nai."

"Really." Naomi wiped at her nose with one wet arm. Lightning eased through the dark clouds in a purple sheen, clashed with the gold heartbeat of the fire slowly devouring Timeless's beautiful walls.

Hell of a metaphor for life.

"Thing is . . ." Silas said, easing back to his feet. Gravel crunched beneath his weight. Rain splattered off his rough denim, shook off his hair as he scraped both hands through it. "I guess everyone thought this fountain of life would be a thing. Turns out it's a person." He shot her a smile that wasn't kind.

Naomi's fingers itched for the gun.

"You have a choice. You can start running now, and you'd probably do all right for a while, but between the Mission and the Coven of the Unbinding, it won't be easy."

"Are you threatening me?" And if he was, why the fuck hadn't she moved? Why didn't she step away from the ledge, where it'd be so damn easy for Silas to push her over?

End it all on a single, bloody splat.

"No, Nai. Just laying it out for you." He flattened one hand at her back. She stiffened, heart exploding into a furious pulse, but he only rested his large hand there.

Careful, manly comfort.

"Like it or not, you're a witch, now. But you don't have to go it alone. We have a place," he explained quietly. "It's safe."

She swallowed. Her eyes closed, but she said nothing.

The warmth of his hand left her back, and she heard as much as felt him sigh. "There are a lot of questions, Nai. A lot of things that aren't adding up. Like how the old Mission director could be a witch—"

Naomi's eyes snapped open. "What?"

"—and why the Church sent a missionary after another missionary," Silas continued over her shock. "Why he claimed someone else in the Church sent him."

"I didn't tell you that," Naomi said quietly.

"You didn't have to. Nai, what I'm saying is— Christ. I'm no good at this shit." He got to his feet, gravel crunching beneath his boots, and looked down at her. "Look. It's pretty simple. Jess and me, we could use a hand. If you don't want to, fine, but you better get off your ass and start running."

Again, slowly, as if afraid she'd spook beneath the weight of it, Silas laid his hand on her shoulder. "Nobody's going to let this lie," he finished, his voice a dark promise.

Naomi chewed on the inside of her lip as Silas turned away. Rain dripped off the end of her nose, and she scraped her sleeve over her face with a sudden, harsh breath. "Silas."

He hesitated. "Yeah?"

She didn't want to be lost. Closing her eyes, her fingers clamped tightly together, Naomi sat on the ledge that could end everything she hated, end the dull ache eating a terrible hole inside her chest, and knew above everything else, she was tired of being lost.

But could she fix it now?

She licked at the center of her lower lip. Took a slow, ragged breath and opened her eyes again. "I don't want to kill anymore."

"Yeah." One callused hand eased into her peripheral vision. "I figured."

Laughter battered away a twisting threat of tears. Hysteria and relief. She slid her fingers into his. "You wordy jackass. That's all you had to say."

CHAPTER TWENTY-TWO

Naomi, wait!"

The door swung hard on Silas's unhappy order, cutting off the bevy of voices that had been drilling holes into her brain for the past hour. Jumping off the porch jarred every ache and bruise she'd sustained in the last few days, but Naomi staggered only once, caught her footing, and strode the hell away from the weird green house and its weird, irritating occupants.

This was shit. Bullshit, horseshit, any kind of shit. They could take their pick.

Come join us, he'd said. *Be part of a team.*

And do *what*? Sit around for three days and talk about all the things they *couldn't* do?

Naomi crossed the rocky shore, a sharp glance taking

in her surroundings out of sheer habit. The crescent-shaped canyon inset into the Old Sea-Trench had been surprising enough. A small bay of crystal green water filled the basin, as still and smooth as glass, and the entrance to the sanctuary was so cleverly carved even she couldn't see it.

Silas had told her about the witchcraft—*wards*, he called them—that kept it hidden. It would explain why no flyovers had ever reported seeing anything but the shattered remains of rock and struggling vegetation around the city. Hell, she didn't even know how far down the fault line she was. A mile? Less?

The place was a secret hideout. Admittedly that was pretty damn astounding, all things considered.

But then he surprised her with the volcanic hot springs. *Astounding* wasn't even a word that could describe it. Heaven, maybe. Exactly what she needed to wash off the blood and dirt and soot and *memory* that clung to her skin. The first thing she'd done was soak in the vivid green water until her fingers got wrinkly.

Getting used to the persistent smell of sulfur wasn't a problem.

Getting used to an all-new team—if she could even call it that—was the issue.

Naomi pushed through a thick mass of green foliage, palm leaves and fronds bigger than anything she'd ever seen in the city. The fragrant leaves slapped back at her, smelling like wet earth and something rich and alive. And, of course, that thick, sulfurous note that filled everything.

It was alien and mysterious, as if she were in another world. Another time.

Another life.

One still without Phin.

Her chest ached; she tamped down on the thought as firmly as her boots stamped into black volcanic sand. Leaving a trail of deep footprints behind her, Naomi marched blindly toward the far cliff wall, fists tight at her sides and every muscle trembling in leashed . . . something.

Tension. Anger. Impatience.

Heartache. "Shitfuck."

"That's a new one on me."

Naomi whirled, a spray of black sand spiraling around her feet. Her hand clenched over the bulky sweater she'd borrowed from Silas, found no gun, and immediately dropped again.

But she still *did* it, damn it.

Matilda watched her from only a few yards away, her expression inscrutable. She was always inscrutable. Tall and rail-thin, with a waist-length braid gone to more gray than red, Naomi had no idea how old she was. Sixty? Seventy?

Hell if she knew. Naomi only knew that she didn't like the woman. And she suspected the feeling was mutual. "Where the hell did you come from?"

Matilda's smile was as serene as if she couldn't sense the thundercloud roiling around Naomi. Which was also bullshit. "This is my home," she said simply, and stuck her hands into the pockets of a pair of oversized overalls. Her galoshes were bright yellow, speckled with black sand, and her shirt today was something old and worn. Real cotton, rare as hell if it wasn't imported topside and sold for a fortune.

The woman collected prequake garbage like junkies collected needles.

"Yeah," Naomi said, feeling waspish. "It's yours. I get it. You want to leave me alone now?"

"Is that what you want?"

"Yes." *No.*

She wanted a do-over. She wanted to be back in her own bed, at her own office, with her own team. She wanted things to be back to normal; investigate, track down, kill.

She wanted to not be crazy anymore, to have her bed filled with a man whose smile made his eyes warm like— No. *Stop it.*

What she wanted didn't matter. Naomi turned her back, staring out over the green water. The autumn wind didn't make it into the canyon easily, so only the faintest ripples touched the shoreline. Even despite the brisk chill, the hot springs kept the air warm enough to beat the worst of the weather so far.

Footsteps crunched behind her.

Naomi stiffened.

"It's hard, isn't it?" Matilda offered quietly, coming to stand beside her.

Despite the thoughts swirling like needles and knives in her tired, aching brain, Naomi couldn't help her brief, laughing snort. "Life?"

"Choice."

"Same thing." Naomi glanced at the old woman as Matilda shook her head, her dark brown eyes searching somewhere beyond the rock face at the far end of the water.

The single, know-it-all gesture snapped Naomi's

control like a rubber band pulled too far. She could all but feel the welt as she snarled, "All right, fine. You've obviously got some sort of bullshit ulterior motive here, so can you just spit it out and go away?"

To her surprise, the witch grinned, rocking back on her heels. "What makes you say that?"

Son of a *bitch*. "Because!" Naomi exploded, and once the word rushed out of her chest, she couldn't stop the rest from following. "Ever since I've gotten here, you've done this whole *mysterious stranger* bullshit. You don't answer anything, you sit there and poke and prod and offer the occasional insight and let everyone else come to the decision you have *already made*."

The witch was silent, her grin fading to that serene curve once more.

Naomi spun, paced three steps away, came up short and paced back, fists clenched at her sides. "You keep dropping these stupid hints about who I am and what I can do and what this whole *team* thing is and isn't and it's *pissing me the fuck off*." She flung a hand toward the house. "Silas and me, we're not *used* to sitting around! We need shit to do, and the only thing we've got going is that the world's a goddamned mess and we can't do jack and shit all about it."

Matilda turned her head, tranquil eyes studying her quietly. Knowing.

Jesus God, always with the knowing.

Naomi ground her teeth so hard, her jaw popped. "Jessie," she gritted out between them, "is the biggest fucking do-gooder on this godforsaken planet, and all we can agree on is that we gotta do *something*. The Church sent a man to get a magical whatever-the-fuck, and the Mission sent *me* to stop him. A witch became a missionary—" She stopped abruptly as one faded red eyebrow lifted, and Naomi laughed bitterly. "And a missionary became a witch. Jesus bastard Christ, Matilda, what the hell are we supposed to do? *You* know everything, you tell us!"

The woman raised a gnarled hand, rubbing at her nose. For a moment, all the reply Naomi heard was her own voice, bouncing from canyon wall to wall and vanishing into the cloudy gray sky.

Naomi spat a curse and turned away.

"Naomi."

She stopped, shoulders rigid.

"How did you feel?" When she glanced over her shoulder, eyebrows snapped tightly together, Matilda had gone back to watching the water, her lined features inscrutable. "When your father killed himself?"

Naomi's mouth twisted. How did she feel? Between the bone-crushing grief and the fury that she'd been placed into an orphanage? She took a deep breath. "Relieved."

"Why?"

That was easy. "Because he didn't have to deal with the pain of his wife's rejection. That killed him way before any rope did."

"His wife." Her tone was light. "Not your mother, but his wife."

"She was never my mother," Naomi replied flatly, turning to face the old witch the same way she'd face an opponent. Chin up. Fists tight. Eyes level.

She'd be *damned* if the old biddy bested her now. She'd been through too much to eat this. "Even when she was there," she added. "*He* loved her." And so had Naomi. Once. When she was too little to understand that the polished, beautiful creature who came by now and again was every bit as shallow and merciless as a reflection.

"What about Phin?"

This voice came from behind her, feminine and younger. And with enough matter-of-fact sting to tell her without looking that Jessie had followed her. Which meant Silas wasn't far behind.

Naomi didn't turn. "What *about* Phin?"

"How did you feel when you left him?"

Empty. Hollow. Aching. "Relieved," she repeated, but even to her own ears, it lacked the same certainty. Naomi shook her head, answering the question she knew would follow. "Because it cuts him from this life. He made a mistake; I didn't hold him to it. Clarke was a good time, for the circumstances." Her voice flattened. "He was there, I was there. He's a good lay, and that's it."

Silence filled the corner edge of the bay, filled only with the faint brush of the autumn breeze. With the wind above and the odd, silent pulse of growing things.

And with the beat of Naomi's own heart, solid and strong. Even now, she could feel it underscored by something liquid smooth, golden, and warm. The fountain.

Witchcraft.

Finally Jessie sighed. "Okay, fine," she said, in a tone that said she'd let it drop . . . for now. "So we've ascertained that this isn't about you."

Naomi bit her tongue before she said something she'd regret. That Silas would regret—she owed him more than that.

"Now we have to figure out what it *is* about," Jessie continued.

"And what we can do about it." Silas's voice rumbled as it always did, always so much louder than he meant. Naomi jerked as one large hand settled on her shoulder. "Naomi, I know it's hard. We're all displaced here, and we're lacking everything we're used to having. Orders, for one," he added, and she glanced over her shoulder to find his lips quirked up.

"Jonas, for another," she admitted reluctantly. "We have limited information."

"Just what I can glean," Jessie said as she crouched by the water's edge. She trailed her fingers into the water. "And that's as much chance as it is anything else. I can't spy on your . . ." She paused. "On the Mission because I don't know where to look now. The one place I knew of was Peterson's."

"Little Miss Parker got her own pad," Naomi muttered.

Matilda watched silently, gnarled hands firmly in her pockets.

"But we're all agreed," Jessie continued, rising, her golden brown eyes serious as they touched on each of them in turn. "We have to do something. Sometimes I get lucky and a vision comes my way—"

"Which is how we learned about Timeless," Silas interjected.

Jessie nodded. "But we can't rely on that."

"There's more to consider," Matilda offered. Naomi glanced at her, shoving her own hands into the pockets of a pair of jeans the witch had loaned her. "As far as the Church is aware, you both are dead." Her head tipped toward Naomi. "But you've gone outlaw, my dear."

"Which means," Silas said, voice edged, "a bounty."

"And a sizeable one," Naomi offered. She grinned, a wide slash of teeth as Jessie tilted her head curiously. "Next to Silas, I was pretty hot shit. That means they're going to hedge their bets."

"You were better than me, Nai." Silas furrowed his brow. "It was close, but you were better."

She shrugged, but the compliment—the statement of fact—did at least a little to ease the knot in her chest. She'd been good at *something*. A damn fine missionary.

"Lousy at everything else," she said, half to herself.

Jessie blew out a hard breath. "We need an information network somewhere."

"We need a place to start," Naomi pointed out.

"We *need*," Matilda said, and somehow her quiet, easy authority cut through everything else, "to get Naomi into shape."

She bristled. "I don't—"

Understanding dawned on Jessie's face. "Right. Look," she added, turning to face Naomi fully. She wrapped her hands around Naomi's arms, just above the elbow, and leaned in until she was nearly nose to nose with her. "Listen to me closely. Okay? It's important."

Bemused, Naomi said nothing, letting the much shorter woman keep a grip on her. Partly because Silas was within easy reach, and he'd toss her on her ass if she so much as lifted a finger against his woman, and mostly because Jessie's occasional flex of steel spine amused her.

And impressed her.

"You're a witch now," Jessie said, slowly and clearly. As if talking to a child, which didn't amuse Naomi quite as much. "And you've pretty much sworn off guns, so you have to get yourself strong in the magic department."

"I can still fight—" she began, only to cut herself off as Jessie shook her head.

"We're small enough a group as is, Naomi. If one of us dies because you don't know how to use that fountain, we're screwed."

Naomi didn't have an argument for that. "So." She shrugged off Jessie's grip and bit back an edged smile as Silas stiffened, then visibly forced himself to relax. "I'm a magical healing genie, then."

"No," Matilda said, but amusement made her eyes dance. "Close. I'll help you hone your control, my dear. That I can do freely. And," she added dryly, "without motive. Every witch needs to learn control, no matter what the gift."

Slowly Naomi flicked her tongue over the divot in her lower lip, her gaze sliding from witch to ex-missionary to witch again.

What were her options?

Run, as Silas had offered. That wouldn't last long. Go back to the Mission, which would end in her inevitable discovery and subsequent execution.

Sit on her ass and do nothing?

Like hell.

"Fine," she said, but pointed a finger at Jessie. "But if I'm going to be playing doctor for you, then you're training with me."

Jessie's smile flipped crookedly. "I'm pretty good at the control stuff already, but if you want, I can sit in."

"I don't mean with witchcraft," Naomi said, and knew she sounded smug. Silas's features suddenly took on a worried glower. "I mean training, hand to hand, self-defense, cripple and run. You fight like a girl, princess."

Jessie opened her mouth. Hesitated.

Silas slid both hands down her arms and murmured, "You don't have to, but like I said, she was better than me."

Jessie's eyes narrowed as they met Naomi's. "Deal."

Success. Pounding the blond princess' face into a mat would give her something else to think about.

The empty nights were something else, but if she was lucky, between magic control and bone-rattling beat-downs, she'd be too tired to do anything but sleep. Dreamlessly.

"We still need somewhere to start." Naomi sighed, but at least her fingers uncurled. Tension leaked out of her, leaving behind a weariness—a soul-deep ache that hadn't left her since Timeless.

Silas nodded. "Give me a few weeks. You ladies work on your lessons and whatever—"

Jessie snorted. "Way to make it sound like a knitting circle."

"—and I'll see what I can rustle up," Silas said over her, but he drew her back into his arms. Rested his chin atop her blond hair with so much obvious devotion, Naomi had to look away. Her throat ached.

"Where?" Jessie asked.

"I might have a few ideas. It'll take time."

"Oh-kay," Naomi drawled. And turned back to point at Silas, her eyes narrowed. "But I want something from you, too."

"Name it," he said, so seriously that for a moment the words froze on her tongue.

Damn it. The man had a way of getting around even her. Missionaries, once. Partners for life. Slowly her lips curved into a wide, wicked smile. "Anything?"

"Fuck me," Silas muttered, and Matilda gave a crack of laughter. "Yes," he said warily. "Anything."

"Good. There's a name of a guy who owes me. I want you to collect some things from him."

"Things?" She tapped her lip with her index finger, and Silas's shoulders shook with laughter. "Oh. Why not? Sure, I'll get you your face full of metal again."

They were all smiling, she noticed. Relaxing.

Maybe, just maybe, she could get there, too. Given enough time.

Enough space from the city that had almost claimed her life.

From the man who had tried his damnedest to get his fingers into her heart.

"Great." She jerked her head back toward the house. "Let's get started on this shit, then. The sooner we get all this out of the way, the sooner we go back and kick ass, right?"

"Right," Jessie said, and took Silas's hand in hers, fingers lacing tightly. They moved almost as one, Naomi realized, watching them go. Step by step, his longer stride shortened to match hers. He tipped his head over hers as Jessie said something up at him, and his chuckles resonated like thunder.

Beside her, Matilda sighed. "Love, huh?"

"I guess."

The woman smiled. Crooked, rueful. "So."

Naomi glanced at her. Narrowed her eyes at the gleam she found reflected in Matilda's. That knowing fucking gleam again. "What?"

"I've been thinking of dismantling one of the wards I've got placed on this sanctuary," she said, as conversational as if she was talking about the clouds.

Why the fuck would she care? Naomi turned back toward the path, shaking her head. She didn't have the time, the patience, for this.

"Not the protective ones, of course," Matilda said, following behind her. "Just the one that detects falsehoods spoken in the area."

Falsehoods.

He was there, I was there. He's a good lay, and that's it.

Naomi stopped so suddenly, she half expected the woman to collide into her back. That she didn't told Naomi everything she needed to know. She spun, fists tight, murder in her voice as she warned, "You stay the hell out of my life."

The woman smiled. Sad. "I can't, my dear. You're in my home. You're part of this—" One hand swept across the foliage, the bay. Sanctuary. "And for reasons I know I'll learn someday, Silas truly admires you."

Tears clogged her throat. Burned her eyes. She swallowed hard. "Phin Clarke," she said, every word strained through a crack in her heart that she didn't dare acknowledge, "belongs topside. That's his life. It's where his grieving mother is, it's where his friends are.

It's where his money is. He can rebuild his spa and his life and mourn in peace. *That's* what matters."

Matilda nodded. Slowly. "I understand what you're saying. And," she added quietly, "what you're not. I'll respect your request, Naomi West, and leave you only with this piece of advice."

"Can I stop you?"

Matilda's smile gentled. "The ache never really goes away. But it eases, with time. I'll try to keep your mind busy."

The tears threatened to overwhelm her as Naomi nodded curtly. "Thank you," she managed.

Matilda passed her, pausing only long enough to lay a wrinkled hand over Naomi's chest. Just over her heart. "I'll give you some time to settle. We'll see you back inside when you're ready."

As the witch walked away, Naomi stared at the obsidian flagstone beneath the sole of one boot. A symbol was etched into it, something she supposed was witchy. But even if she knew how to read witch symbols, she couldn't. Her vision blurred as the tears finally slid over her lashes.

Relieved.

He'd get over her. He'd find a pretty girl to love and spoil; an adoring thing with soft hands and sweet smiles. Who liked leather seats and champagne, and didn't have a network map of scars over her silken skin.

Maybe he'd go back to Andy.

Her lips curved, but even Naomi knew how sad her smile really was. Deliberately, she drew her arm over her eyes, her mouth, and carefully rearranged her expression into one of determination.

"All right," she told the air as she strode back to the house. "A few weeks. And then ready or not, I am *so* getting out there and kicking ass."

CHAPTER TWENTY-THREE

The storm roiled overhead, twisting, coiling knots of black and gray. Lightning arced across it, lit up the mass of clouds like a flare of purple-white light smothered in a black veil.

It wouldn't rain with weather like this. This was New Seattle's winter specialty. Freezing-ass cold and wired to blow. But the charge in the air was only one part electricity.

The rest was all her.

For the first time in twenty-seven fucking days, Naomi was on a mission.

The past month had been hard. On all of them. The secret cove had been great for healing her array of bloody wounds and bruises, but a month of constant supervision and unending exercises in witchcraft left

Naomi ready to reconsider her newly found aversion to homicide.

Jessie and Silas had both struggled to find a balance with her that didn't tread on dangerous ground, and the older witch still got the hell on Naomi's nerves. She felt as much a part of them as a wolf in a herd of sheepdogs.

But it *was* getting better. Even she noticed it. Slowly, surely, she was coming to adapt to her new role as—her lips twitched—healer. Whatever the hell that meant.

Still, they didn't have much to *do*, and that was the wedge that still kept them going for each other's throats. It was hard to act when the city still crawled with missionaries and Church men; when the bounty on her head was still fresh enough that any hunter with something to prove would be keeping an eye out.

It had been Silas who saved her, and them, from a bitterly sardonic rant regarding the more murderous characteristics of knitting needles. "You're going to go get us some work," he'd said. "It's time to get off our asses, don't you think?"

Fuck, yeah.

Thunder overwhelmed the faint hum of the lower-level electricity. As she watched, gauging her next move from the shadows of an alley, the few lights in the apartment building flickered.

So did every light on the block.

Well, wasn't that just peachy? The city had more than enough generators topside, but if the lights went out here, it'd be nothing but black. And silent. Perhaps for days.

Breaking and entry in the dead quiet seemed a really bad idea.

Play nice, Jessie had warned her.

Naomi smiled as she sprinted across the road. *Nice* was all she played these days. It wasn't her fault that her *nice* and Jessie's *nice* didn't match up exactly.

Jessie's *nice* involved way, *way* more effort.

The grass crackled under her feet, already frosted into brown icicles. She left dark footprints behind her, but that was exactly why she came at the rendezvous point from the side.

Her mission was pretty simple, really. Naomi slid onto the stoop, reached up, and caught the dim side bulb in her gloved fingers. A deft twist, a jiggle, and the light guttered out.

Inside she'd find the apartment number with a contact waiting for her. She was to make sure the place was secure, get to the contact, and give him the small packet Jessie had put in her satchel.

Simple.

She felt a little like a dog getting a pat on the head, but Naomi would take it. She was sick to death of being cooped up while they waited for some kind of sign.

Even if Matilda's heated waters felt like a small slice of heaven on her faded bruises.

Keeping a wary eye on the streets, Naomi tucked her hand behind her back and tested the knob. It squeaked as it turned, but it did turn.

Did nobody believe in locked doors around here?

The lights along the street guttered again, flashed on and off as the city struggled to feed power to the impoverished levels. As thunder boomed, loud enough to rattle the slat wall, Naomi slipped inside and shut the door gently behind her.

The hall was like every other lower city hall she'd ever been in. Dingy, drab. Stained by life and time.

Grimacing, she slid her tongue along the silver ring at her lower lip and checked the door numbers as she passed. She walked quickly, soundlessly.

The appointed apartment was at the end of a short hall, its painted numbers all but peeled off the door. The outfacing window beside it had been boarded up long enough ago that the nails had eaten rust stains into the plaster. If she had to get out in a pinch, those boards would give way before she did.

"Is this guy trustworthy?" she'd asked Silas while Matilda and Jessie prepared for her departure.

He'd shot her a look that Naomi couldn't read, inscrutable as all hell. "Probably."

Naomi realized that she'd taken that at face value, and that said a hell of a lot about her new role in life. A missionary could trust her allies. She could rely on the rumors of Church justice to keep her contacts thinking twice.

A witch had a lot more to worry about. *Probably* was just another way of saying, *There's no other choice.*

Holding her breath, Naomi leaned into the door and pressed her ear tightly to the wood. Her fingertips hovered over the worn, stained panel. No sound. Not even the vibrations of footsteps. For a full five minutes, she didn't move, strained to listen.

All she heard was thunder, waves upon waves of it crashing overhead. It shook the building with every wild boom. Shattered through her bones as if the storm raged immediately overhead.

If the contact was in there, he was either asleep or had the patience of a saint.

She reached for the doorknob as the walls trembled around her. The echoes of a powerful blast of thunder shimmered into another. The door eased open—unlocked again, for God's sake—and creaked in the sudden, pitch-black silence of lost electricity.

Shit.

Naomi stilled, holding her breath as she waited to hear movement. Breathing. Footsteps, cursing, anything. Here and there, clips of activity filtered through the walls, the ceiling, but inside the black apartment, nothing so much as stirred.

If she said hello first, would it earn her a bullet for her trouble? Or a knife in the dark?

Grimly she slid through the half-open door, her eyes too wide, aching as she tried to see something, anything.

The faintest traces of light slipped through the windows between electrical flares. As it streaked through the room in shattered increments, Naomi picked out a single, open room. Furniture was sparse enough to afford her a clear path from wall to wall, only a single rickety table and one chair beside it.

Opposite, one corner boasted a mattress on the floor heaped with blankets. The kitchen was a tiny affair of peeling tiled floor and two cabinets, most of the space taken up by a small refrigerator and a two-burner stove.

She crossed the apartment in a few short strides, her grin a deep curl of memory, rueful annoyance. She'd spent more than her fair share of days in places like this.

Wordlessly she picked up the cracked mug on the table and tucked it under her nose. She grimaced when the dark, earthy fragrance of plain black tea filled her senses.

Its warmth seeped into her gloves, and she stilled.

Wood creaked behind her.

The mug fell from her fingers as she whirled. It shattered at her feet, sprayed cheap pottery and tea as she reached for the gun she no longer carried.

That she lunged away from the table, away from the figure looming out of the dark was more a credit to her reflexes than it was to her brain. That had stalled when she'd found no gun to hold on to.

Fuck.

A flashlight clicked on, ripped through the dark and her night vision. She flinched, threw up a hand as the beam caught her squarely in the face. "Jesus bastard Christ, what are you trying to do? Scare me to death?"

"I like the lip ring."

Her heart slammed in her chest.

Oh, God. Oh, no; oh, *shit*.

His voice came at her like a knife, like a whip that cracked over her skin and left her bleeding. Again. That voice. So easy, so casual, so . . . fucking *Phin*.

She closed her eyes. Took a deep breath.

And lunged at him.

The flashlight clattered to the floor.

Naomi ignored it. Ignored the cold, the thunder, the lightning that painted everything in a pearlescent tableau. All she cared about was Phin, his shirt in her hands, his lips on hers, his skin, his fingers. He caught her, his fingers wrenching at her coat as she panted for the breath she didn't have enough of.

Somehow he managed to get her coat unzipped.

Managed to tear open the laces of her fake corset, peel off the long-sleeved shirt seconds behind. Somehow she wrestled him out of his sweater, feeling as if they waltzed across the empty floor.

She fused her lips to his, kissed him with everything she'd thought she'd forgotten in a month. Everything she never could have admitted. Struggling, straining to reach the mattress, he seized her head in his large, warm hands, swept his tongue past her lips, and claimed the warm cavern of her mouth as his own. Demanded her gasps and her broken breath.

He swallowed her low, ragged sounds of fury, of need; so many emotions, she couldn't acknowledge them all.

And then they were skin to skin. Naked, straining in the sporadic staccato of lightning and rolling thunder. The hard planes of his chest flattened against her breasts as they fell to the mattress, as she wrapped her legs around his waist and helped him guide himself into her wet, welcoming body, inch by staggering, gasping inch.

He kissed her bottom lip, tongue swirling over the metal ring curved around the center of it, kissed her chin, her neck. His tongue dipped into the hollow of her throat as he thrust deep inside her body; lips, tongue, hands, and body stroking every velvet inch of her in that perfect way only he knew how.

In that perfect way that she only craved from him.

It was always him.

Naomi arched, sweat blooming over her skin as she cried out, again and again, moving in time with his thrusts, threading her fingers through his curly hair and holding his head to her breast. Urging him on. Urging him for more.

Needing everything he had.

The mattress creaked, old springs musical accompaniment to the slow, coiling tide rising in her chest. In her belly. It filled her body, welling up beneath her skin until her ears rang with it and she couldn't breathe. He slid in and out of her, long powerful strokes, filled his hands with her body and his lips with the fragrance of her skin, and she trembled on that verge.

He caught her hips, tilted her just so, and hesitated. Shaking, his voice raw, Phin whispered, "I still love you."

She sucked in a breath.

He plunged deep, held her hips, locked her to him as she shattered, wave after wave of pulsing, liquid heat roiling inside her skin. It bent everything she knew until there was only wicked, torturous pleasure, a release so wound up it caught her breath in a wild cry.

He shuddered with her, fingers tense at her waist, eyes dark and glittering in the faint glow of the forgotten flashlight. Watching her. Drinking her in.

She panted for breath as he sank to the mattress, forearms braced on either side of her shoulders. She struggled to think through the miasma of confusion, of warm, liquid aftershocks and fear.

Naomi closed her eyes as she tried to even her breathing.

It just made her that much more aware of his weight pinning her to the bed, heavy and sure. So warm. Of his heartbeat slamming against his chest.

Of his breath, a caress against her shoulder and neck.

And his finger, broad and firm against her bottom lip. "Stop it."

Despite herself, her mouth curved up. "Stop what?"

"Thinking." He traced her mouth, her nose and the completely healed skin there. Her cheek. He brushed aside her hair, tendrils of searing violet woven through the much shorter black edges. "If you keep at it, you'll talk yourself out of this."

Her smile faded. "This."

"Don't make me do it all over again. I will, you know," he warned. "If I have to take one for the team, I'm up for that challenge."

Naomi's eyes snapped open, narrowed just as fast. "What the hell." Anger snapped a live wire from the struggling part of her brain to her nerves. She shoved at his chest until he leaned away, sliding over to brace an elbow on the mattress.

She sat up, averting her eyes from his body, gloriously naked and painted in muted gold and shattered washes of white.

He was too much. Too gorgeous, too naked, too . . . sure.

Swearing under her breath, Naomi climbed from the bed and padded across the floor. She made it halfway to the flashlight before she rounded on him, fury all but spewing fire from her tongue. "You have a lot of nerve."

Propping his head up on one hand, Phin lazily trailed his gaze across her exposed flesh. Throat to breasts, which pebbled into tight buds under his hot gaze. Over her ribs, heaving with the effort of maintaining at least some semblance of cool.

To her hips, and the dark tattoo just over the dark thatch of hair between her legs.

Her fists clenched. "A lot of nerve," she repeated flatly. "Phin, what are you doing here?"

"I love you." His gaze snapped back to hers, steady and too damn certain. "And yes, I'm going to keep saying that until it gets through your thick head. I love you, Naomi."

She shook her head. "You don't know me from—"

"You look great in a dress," Phin broke in, every word a conversational dart. He shifted, eased to his knees on the mattress, as beautiful as a god kneeling on a pedestal. Naomi's throat went tight.

"That was—"

He grinned, a flash of even teeth in the dark. "You looked pretty good in the cinched-in getup you wore when you got here, but you look absolutely incredible now."

She folded her arms over her chest, knowing how ridiculous the gesture was. She was naked.

So was he.

That long, liquid pull of awareness coiled deep in her belly. Again. Still.

"You hate massages," he continued evenly, steadily. "But you love *my* massages."

She flushed. Heat swept into her cheeks, her ears, Jesus, her chest.

He braced his hands on his thighs, his smile widening. Dimples winked at his mouth, shadowed points of pure lust. Naomi swallowed hard. "You hate to be fussed over, but you love fussing with clothes. You hate tea—"

Her eyes widened. "How the hell do you know that?"

"You never drank the tea we sent up with your meals," Phin said, his eyes twinkling, "but you love coffee. Black, no cream or sugar."

Naomi threw out her hands, a wild effort to swing his words right back at him. His observations, his neat little deductions. "All right, so what? How does that—"

"Thinking." Phin sighed and held out a hand. One simple gesture. A hand, steady. Waiting, palm-up. "Come here."

Naomi stared at it.

"I'm not— No, wait," he amended. "I will probably bite. That's not a problem, is it?"

"You're naked."

Laughter washed over his features. Turned her beautiful, dimly lit god into something so very male. Approachable. So very real.

So very Phin.

"So are you," he said, and waited. Just . . . waited.

For her.

Naomi's fingers clenched, unclenched. Clenched again. Her heart pounded in her throat, roared in her ears, too loud, too crystal clear to ignore, but fear closed her throat.

Regret filled her eyes with tears.

His hand wavered. "Naomi—"

"I'm so sorry."

Every muscle in his body struggled to go to her. To climb off the bed and cross the room, pick her up, and carry her back to the bed with him. To make the decision for her.

Phin couldn't do it.

If he did, if he obeyed the impulse to make it easy for her, to remove the terrible conflict he read in her eyes, on her face, then he could never know for sure.

Never know if she really had made the choice.

Or if he'd just made it for her.

I'm so sorry.

Fear ate a terrible hole in his chest.

"For?" It took effort to keep his voice steady. To keep his hand outstretched, waiting. All she had to do was reach.

Please, God, let her reach.

She was so beautiful. Lightning painted her body with shades of white and shadow, as if the sky had dipped her in silver. Metal glittered at her lower lip, at her eyebrow. At her navel and one pebbled nipple.

Different, but Naomi through and through.

Her eyes shimmered, huge pools of regret and uncertainty. Of the same fear that ate at him.

He knew what she felt.

She shook her head. "I never—" His heart sank. "When I said the things I did," she said huskily, meeting his eyes with effort. With so much pain. "I never wanted this to happen. I never wanted to see your mother—" Her voice broke.

"Hey." He shot off the bed, ready to damn his pride and the uncertainty of the future to ease the shadows from her eyes, her memory now. But she threw out a hand, froze him in place with a single, hard look.

"Stop. Let me say this."

Phin nodded slowly. Oh, his poor Naomi.

"The things I said, I said because I wanted you to hate me. I wanted you to think you were better off." She laughed, a wan, humorless sound. "I wanted to believe what I said so that I could walk away. No strings. A pretty dream during a bad time."

Silver spilled from her eyes, a single trail of tears. Phin took a slow, deep breath, fighting every urge to go to her. Soothe her.

"I *never* wanted your family to get hurt," she said, throaty regret. "I never wanted to see you hurt, Phin, not by anyone else. Not by me."

"You broke my heart." As soon as the words left his mouth, Phin mentally kicked himself into traction. What the hell was wrong with him? He didn't mean to share that. To make it worse.

She flinched. "It was supposed to save you."

"Maybe it did." Slowly, hoping against hope, Phin offered his hand again. Palm up. "Maybe that anger got me through this past month. But it was a bandage. I need more than that."

She shoved her fingers roughly into her hair, lopsided from their lovemaking. Tangled and so perfectly Naomi, purple streaks and all.

Phin held his breath.

"I don't have any guarantees," she began, but he shook his head. She frowned. "Don't you want—?"

"All I want," he said quietly, "all I need is you."

He watched the battle rage behind her eyes. Fierce independence, fear, uncertainty; and there, slowly, like a warm spring rain, he saw it. Love.

She loved him.

Phin's heart swelled. Blossomed inside his chest like something thriving after a cold winter. He took in a slow, deep breath, threw his pride to the wind, and crossed the floor anyway.

She met him halfway.

*   *   *

Later, as the storm rolled away into silence, Phin studied the faint golden circle on the far wall and traced Naomi's spine with a feather-light touch. She shivered over him, her legs entangled with his, her head under his chin.

One finger tapped a beat against his chest in time with his heart. Her heart.

As rain trickled from the quiet night sky, the air crackled. Hummed. Lights flickered on, bathed the outside street in typical dim illumination.

The lights inside stayed off.

Naomi shifted, planted an elbow in his chest to look down into his face. He grunted. "You didn't have the lights on."

"So?" Phin winced, edged her elbow off his solar plexus. "Is that a crime, ma'am?"

"You were trying to trap me."

He grinned, wolfishly pleased, into her blue-violet eyes. So beautiful. "So?"

"You son of a—"

He raised his head, stole her words with a kiss that stole his breath in turn. Her lip ring was warm against his mouth, her breath suddenly a ragged sound.

Reluctantly he let her pull away. "You're a dirty fighter, Miss West," he said, watching as she slid from the bed. The light gleamed over her naked skin, outlined every curve, every muscle. He whistled when she bent to retrieve her clothes.

He grinned unrepentantly when she shot him a quelling look over her shoulder. "Yeah?" she shot back. "Well, you learn fast."

"That's a fact." Still, he threw back the covers, retrieved his own clothes. He dressed quickly, already shivering in the frigid winter air.

"So why you?"

"Why me, what?"

She shook her head as she eased past him to the kitchen. "Why was I supposed to meet you? Don't tell me this was some sort of elaborate booty call—"

"Whoa." Phin caught her arm, pulled her right back to frown fiercely into her surprised gaze. Her eyes flicked to his hand on her arm. Back to his face, one eyebrow raised. "Don't ever," he warned, "ever think of this, right here between us, as some sort of troll for sex."

Her lashes flared. "Easy, slick," she murmured.

"No, I'm serious." He caught her chin, held her gaze as he feathered his lips over hers. "*This* is serious."

She hummed something that sounded like capitulation, like simple enjoyment of his mouth on hers, but her mind wasn't on them. Obviously.

He let her go, unable to fight the grin that tugged at his mouth. His heart. Naomi West, the most infuriating, thorough, stubborn woman he'd ever met.

"To answer your question," he said, sitting on the mattress to pull on his socks and shoes, "I'm extending an offer to you and your group to help with a project."

"A project?" Naomi shot him a curious frown as she filled the old kettle on the stove.

"When Timeless was still operational—" Even saying it was a twist of anger, of pain in his chest. The kettle clattered to the stove.

It was a pain they both carried, he realized.

Phin stood, crossed the small room to slide his arms

around her waist as she turned on the stove. "When Timeless was still operational," he repeated, "we ran an underground railroad of sorts."

Her body stiffened. "You were a smuggler?" It wasn't surprise that raised her voice. It was anger. Self-directed, he realized as she turned in his arms. "Why the fuck didn't I know?"

He laughed, struggled to smother it as she shot him a glare, murder in her eye. "Because we've been doing it for a long time, Naomi," he managed, with somewhat of a straight face. "And we didn't smuggle things, we smuggled people. Witches, or at least those accused as such by the Church."

The conflict in her face made him tuck her hair behind her ears. Made him want to touch her, reassure her.

"We always checked, as much as we could. The people we ran through Timeless were innocent of wrongdoing. Maybe some were witches," he added, "I'm not disputing that. But they weren't like—you know, like Agatha."

Her mouth opened. Closed. Shaking her head, she sighed and draped her arms around his shoulders. "I just don't even know enough about the difference," she admitted, annoyed and rueful and so gorgeous, it hurt to look at her smile.

"They were like you," Phin explained. "Like my mother. A witch"—her eyes flinched—"but not bad. Not evil. And definitely undeserving of the Church's attentions."

"I'm only a witch because . . ." She hesitated. "Well, I guess I'm a witch now."

"She chose well." He dipped his head, kissed her forehead. "I never, ever once doubted it."

Her lips curved up into that half smile. "Says you. I wonder, though," she mused, her smile fading. "Given I wasn't born with witchcraft—hell, I don't even know how to use this damn thing. I should run some blood work on myself. If I can get the equipment— Shit." She turned as the kettle whistled shrilly.

He let her go and watched her search the cabinets for more mugs, the flex and sway of her body as she reached into the shelves.

He ran his hand over his head. "There's instant coffee on the top shelf," he admitted. "I may have . . . hoped you'd be here."

The look she shot him twisted somewhere between pleasure and stubborn pride.

He bit back a grin. "Anyway, Timeless is up in smoke and we're deflecting the Church left and right. They're looking for you, looking for excuses. We don't have the same kind of safety we used to."

"So how do we help?"

"Silas reached out a couple weeks ago. We haven't hammered out any details, but we're going to." He wrapped his hands around hers as she offered him a mug, held her close. "You, me, and the rest of your group need to meet somewhere when it's safe." Slowly he brushed his lips across hers. A whisper, a breath of warmth. "And I'm warning you now, Naomi. We're going to make this work. Whatever it takes, whatever I need to do, I'll do it."

She stared into his eyes. Searched them for whatever it was she needed to believe. Phin didn't know.

"We're going to spend a lot of time apart," she said doubtfully.

"I know," he replied. "But we'll find a way. I promise you, I'm not going to lose you, lose this, to anything. Including your own fear," he added.

She winced, but laughter eased in around it. "You're not pulling your punches."

"You wouldn't like me if I did."

"I love you."

Three words. Offhandedly said and with a *but* so obviously attached, yet he didn't care. His heart soared. "That's all I need," he said, cutting off the explanation, the excuse, whatever it was that welled in her eyes. "That's all I'll ever need, Naomi."

Frustration shaped her expression, the taut line of her body as she pulled away. Steam rolled off the mug in his hands, mingled with the steam from her own as she clattered her cup to his. "You're going to regret this."

"Never," he swore.

"You'll probably yell at me a lot."

Now he grinned, unabashedly cocky. "You'll yell at me just as much. I bet you're a dish thrower."

She sighed. "I'm not good with—"

"Naomi." She stilled. Phin caught her hand, lifted her fingers to his lips, and breathed a kiss so light, so tender over her knuckles that her hand shook in his. "Shut the *hell* up."

Her smile eased into her eyes until they shone. "I give it three months."

"Then we'll be right here again in three months," he promised. She laughed, throwing her head back with the sheer joy of it, and for the second time that night, pottery thudded to the floor. Tea and coffee splattered everywhere, hot and steaming and completely ignored as they collided.

Buttons parted, zippers hissed. Naomi hesitated, her clever fingers tunneling into the front of Phin's pants. Her skin was cold against his heated erection; shockingly exciting. He gasped.

"Oh, damn," she said suddenly, her eyes glinting. Wicked bright. "I just remembered."

"God, what?" he gasped, sweat slick on his skin. "Stove? Is something on fire? Whatever, it can wait, just—" His mind detonated in pure pleasure as she rolled her palm over him.

"No. You just never got to see the lingerie Andy let me have."

Phin screwed his eyes shut and groaned. She was sheer torture. Pure heaven. "You're going to kill me."

"Maybe," she murmured, sliding down his body like hot silk. "I'm definitely going to try." Before he could wrap his mind around her intent, she replaced her fingers with the wet heat of her mouth.

He tunneled his fingers into her hair and laughed, half amusement and half a ragged sound of soul-wrenching need as he collapsed back against the counter and prayed for patience.

Despite everything that had tried to tear them apart, despite the baggage they both carried and the memories of blood and fire, she was his.

Not a missionary. Not an heiress. Not a witch.

Naomi West. The woman he loved.

TURN THE PAGE FOR A SNEAK PEEK AT
ALL THINGS WICKED
THE NEXT BOOK FROM

KARINA
COOPER

AND AVON BOOKS
Coming Soon

There was no such thing as rest for the wicked.

Caleb Leigh opened gritty, burning eyes, giving up on the fitful doze that was all his pain-wracked body could manage for sleep. The filthy motel room came into focus as the neon lights outside the grimy, patchy curtains popped and fizzled, thrusting red and orange knives into his retinas.

How long had he managed to sleep this time? Two hours? Three? It didn't matter. Little twinges burst through his body, hellfire sparklers of pain spasming in his muscles. His skin twitched as if it wanted to crawl off his abused body and slink away for a shower.

God. He'd kill for a shower.

Muffling a groan, he reached for the shirt he'd left on the floor, caught the edge with his fingers, and froze as a whisper of a breeze ghosted across the sensitive scars on his back.

Off. The room felt off. Unbalanced.

He inhaled, smelled New Seattle's own peculiar brand of acid-tinged summer rain, acrid smog, rotting garbage, and . . . something else.

Get up!

A floorboard creaked behind him.

Caleb threw himself off the bed as a black silhouette loomed out of the dark. Rusted springs screeched, a high-pitched shriek that twanged into a crescendo as his assailant landed on the mattress. Caleb's grunt of pain as he hit the floor drowned in the raw fury clamping around his head.

He'd had no warning. Not even a *whisper* of magic.

He should have been less surprised.

The shadow pushed off the bed as Caleb leaped to his feet. Silver winked a deadly promise in the faint glow of the neon lights spilling through the single broken window; serrated steel, a knife gripped in one black-gloved hand.

It pointed at him, wicked edge gleaming. "How the hell are you not dead?"

The already cramped motel room walls slammed in tight around him. That voice. Feminine. Breathy with exertion, with fear, but so fucking familiar that it sucked out his breath on a raw sound.

Memory. Affection. Worry.

Love.

It rose like a dream, a sigh of lazy summer days and laughing secrets, and Caleb fought the slick, blissful whisper back behind gritted teeth. It wasn't *his* love. It wasn't his affection, his worry, his goddamn memory that fisted in his heart.

And Juliet Carpenter had no goddamned business being anywhere near him.

A year wasn't nearly long enough.

The neon lights snapped and crackled in rhythmic chaos outside the window. They slanted lurid color over her black hair, cut shorter than he remembered and in a fashion that suggested she was aiming for edgy and tough. The dark, choppy fringe framed her face, her faintly square jaw and the ghostly green eyes that he'd last seen half closed and luminous as he sank balls-deep inside her warm, straining body.

Promise me. His fists clenched. He'd done his part, damn it. "Get out," he said flatly.

"You son of a *bitch*." Deftly the sawlike blade in her hand rotated as Juliet jumped onto the thin mattress and launched herself at him.

Every muscle in his body locked.

Every goddamn nerve in his left side detonated as he plucked her from the air. Her legs swung to his side, knees ramming into his ribs and jarring a painful grunt from between his clenched teeth as he fisted both hands into her jacket collar and used her own momentum to slam her against the wall behind him. Plaster cracked.

The breath left her on a hard, wordless snarl.

His threatened to lodge in his chest, banded tightly under the fiery protest of unhealed wounds lancing through his weakened left side. "I said get out," he growled, glaring through the sizzling edges of his vision.

The knife glinted. He shackled her wrist with one hand and slammed it back against the wall. White dust floated to her hair in a gritty cloud.

Sweat gleamed on her face, echo of the perspiration drying across his shoulders. It wasn't all courtesy of the unusually muggy summer heat that had settled into the deepest crevasses of the city. Holding her in place shouldn't have been as hard as it was, but his body still wasn't recovered from the burns that had nearly killed him a year ago.

Every day was a lesson in pain. Pinning a witch

against a wall as her feet thrashed a foot above the floor wasn't helping.

Pinning *this* witch wasn't something he'd ever expected to do again.

She'd lost weight.

Her jacket was a little too loose, her black shirt baggy where he'd tangled his fingers into the collar of both. The warmth of her full breasts against the back of his scarred hand wasn't a reminder he needed, but he couldn't afford to let her go for his own comfort.

Breasts versus knife? He wasn't a fool. Or some teenage virgin who had never gotten a handful of a woman before. Especially *this* woman.

The dark circles under her eyes couldn't take away from the visual impact she'd always had on him. Her mouth, top-heavy and so damn expressive it made him crazy for it, twisted as she struggled in his grip. She managed to gain an inch of momentum as she jerked her hand out from under his, but Caleb locked his teeth and shoved it back. Fragile bones grated under his grip.

Pain flickered. Hers. His.

Promise me. . .

Oh, Jesus. That voice.

Caleb sucked in a breath that seemed harder than it should have to get and drowned out the words echoing through his head. "What the hell are you doing here?"

He didn't have to ask. The venom spewing at him from a look filled with revulsion was all the answer he needed.

His grip tightened on her collar. "Let me rephrase that. Where's your backup?"

Her teeth clicked together. Her gaze slid away, flicked back as she raised her chin.

She'd never been a good liar.

Caleb stared at her as fury throbbed between his temples. "You don't have backup," he said softly. Then, much less quietly, he snarled, "You came alone? You came after me *by yourself*? Jesus Christ, Jules!"

With monumental effort, Juliet raised both feet and planted them against Caleb's thigh. He braced on instinct, swore as it raised her out of his grip and threw him off balance. She reached up with her right hand, grabbed the knife out of her left, and swung it back around. Caleb swore again, jerking away, but not before the jagged teeth of the blade snagged the puckered flesh of his left arm. *Damn it!*

Raw, red static shorted his vision as he backpedaled into the mattress. His knees collided with the edge, buckled and sprawled him backward onto the springs.

Sensing her intent, he rolled, blood smearing the stained sheets, and grunted as her weight barreled into his back. Her knees rammed into the vulnerable hollow beneath his shoulder blades, dug into his scars hard enough that he threw his head back, forced to lock his teeth against a brittle surge of pain.

"Don't move!" Her fingers twisted in his too-long hair.

Caleb froze.

Her thighs clenched around his waist. They were warm, even through her pants. Warm and familiar. And the press of her soft breasts against his shoulders shouldn't have mattered more than the knife she held at his throat.

Muscles shaking, taut with the effort to stay still, Caleb waited. It hurt. God, it hurt, but it had nothing on the clash of memory, fantasy, hell, *wanting* that roiled in his blood now.

They'd never made it to a bed. He remembered that. There weren't that many beds in Old Seattle.

Behind him, on him, Juliet panted for breath. "I just," she managed, "want to know one thing."

"Then what?" His voice grated harshly. "You'll cut my throat?"

He knew it wasn't true the instant he said it, but that wasn't the point. Juliet had always been too soft. Everyone had known it.

Her sister had known it.

Promise me.

The knife at his throat jerked. A thin, slick line of fire told him how sharp the damn blade was. It'd make a bloody mess of his flesh faster than he could get it away from her.

"You could only be so lucky," she spat. "I want to know why, you bastard. Why?"

Why? She wasn't asking why he wasn't dead. He didn't have that answer, anyway. No, he knew what she asked in the single, strained syllable, and closed his eyes.

Why had he betrayed the coven?

Not precisely.

More like, why the hell had he wrapped her body around him like silk and rain? Lost himself in her, pulled her apart with anger and need and mind-scorching heat and then betrayed everything she'd ever believed in?

The fact that he'd murdered her sister was something she didn't know to ask. Fuck.

And you promised!

God, he wished he hadn't. "Why what?" he asked, and because he already knew the answer, added, "Why didn't I say no when you threw yourself at me or—"

The fingers in his hair tightened, wrenching his head back on an angle that threatened to pop his neck. She leaned over him, body pushed forward to thrust her face over his. Her eyes were wide, too wide, shimmering with tears that crawled deep inside his chest and twisted. Bloodier than the knife at his throat.

Darker than the rage that beat at the iron chains of his self-control.

"You know!" The words broke on a ragged sound. "Why did you kill them? Why? When we—"

"We," he said flatly, cutting her off with barely leashed scorn. "There never was a *we*."

She blanched. Recovered so quickly that he wasn't sure he'd seen the blood his verbal dagger had drawn. "*We*," she repeated through gritted teeth, "as in the Coven of the Unbinding. *We* as in your friends!"

"Liar." Her knee dug into the hollow beneath his left shoulder blade. Neon flashed, and only part of it was the monotonous color outside the seedy motel. The rest popped and sparkled behind his eyes, accompaniment to the ruined skin she pushed on.

"They were your family—"

"Bullshit," he rasped, all but a growl under the pressure. "They were users. Curio only kept you for your magic." And, rumor had it, for her body.

He didn't ask. Even as the words leaped to his lips, he didn't want to know.

He'd had that body, too.

One of many things he'd shared with the late coven leader.

The knife lowered, a fraction. "You killed them. All of them," she accused, a sharp whisper. "They gathered because they trusted you—"

Fuck. They'd gathered because they had intended to sacrifice Caleb and his sister for their power-hungry cause.

"—and you just . . . killed them." Her voice trembled.

"Most of them," he agreed. Some, like her, he'd managed to distract. Some he'd gotten free.

Her eyes flickered, her face upside-down but still so fragile, it stole the breath from his body. Black hair dye wouldn't make her tough. "Why?"

His jaw locked. Ticked hard. "Because I could."

He hated himself for doing it. He hated that it had to be done. But Caleb was a lot of things, and gentle wasn't one. Reversing her flimsy position of power was easy—just reaching up, seizing the back of her jacket, and hauling her bodily over his head.

His scars stretched, felt as if they split from the root to the skin, and the angry buzzing in his ears almost drowned out her howl of rage and surprise as she hit the ground on her back. The knife went flying, and Caleb rolled off the mattress seconds before it embedded itself into the wall beside them.

Plaster drifted lazily on the air as Caleb knocked her fist away, seized both hands, and pinned them above her head. The motion barked his knuckles on the rusted bed frame, and he grunted a curse as her knee found his gut. Twisting, he pinned her legs, clamped his thighs around hers, and locked her down.

She strained, but succeeded only in turning herself red with the effort. Dust puffed languidly around them. Sweat dripped from his nose as he stared down at the face he'd hoped to hell to never see again.

Love. God damn it, it had never been *his* to *feel*.

"Stop it," he ordered roughly as she twisted her hips.

"You traitorous son of—!"

"Son of a bitch. Yes, I know." He transferred her wrists to one hand, dropping his forearm to her throat. He shoved hard, forcing her head to lie still against the dirty green carpet, and met her eyes exactly because he didn't want to.

The accusation in them didn't quite hide the helplessness she struggled to bury. The grief.

Guilt had a punch like a prize fighter.

What the hell could he say? He'd done so much more to her than even she knew.

He knew, though. It was enough. His mouth thinned. "Let's get this straight, girl. Yes, I turned on your coven. Yes, I killed Curio—" He pushed hard as her back arched, fury snapping through her like a conduit. "I killed Curio," he repeated curtly, "and probably about two dozen other witches who didn't know when to get out. If I had to do it all over again, I'd make the same choices."

But he wouldn't, he thought as tears shimmered in her narrowed glare, choose to touch her again. He wouldn't commit his body and soul in a single moment of mind-blowing weakness, and he damn well wouldn't promise the impossible to Cordelia Carpenter before he killed her.

Life gave only one chance. His bed was made; he damn well was going to lie in it.

Alone.

"We can play this all day, Jules," he said, thrusting his face so close to hers that she flinched. "You're on your own, and I'm stronger than you."

Her lips twisted, teeth baring as if she would try to bite him. Under the strained pressure of his forearm, her skin flushed nearly purple. It colored her cheeks, her lips. Her eyes flashed, hatred and fear.

Protect her. Shit. Just *shit*.

Caleb relented. Loosened enough so she could breathe.

She coughed, choking. "I hate—I hate you," she managed between rough spasms. "I'm going to kill you!"

He stared at her. Then, his smile a grim slash, he reached over her head and drew the serrated knife out of the wall. She flinched as plaster crumbled around them. "Fine," he said, and put the metal hilt in her hands.

Her lashes widened, and he noticed the smudge of mascara that made them thicker. Darker.

He didn't know what color her hair was naturally, but it sure as hell had never been black.

Caleb forced her fingers to close on the knife and rolled off her, a fluid motion that belied the torturous effort it took to make it. His left side was rapidly going numb. Blood slid down his arm from the flesh wound she'd already inflicted, and he watched her eyes trace the wet gleam as she clambered to her feet.

She wouldn't have a chance.

He spread his arms. "Do it."

Juliet's full upper lip curled under her teeth, her tongue sliding along it in that way she did when she was nervous.

Just thinking it made him clench his fists. Not his to know, damn it. But the unfamiliar memories wouldn't fade. Not for as long as he lived.

Not for as long as Cordelia's lifeblood mingled with his.

"Come on," he said flatly, his voice rough. Impatient. "You want to kill me so badly, do it."

Conflict. Determination. Uncertainty. He read it all in the trembling of her hands, her white-knuckled grip around the hilt. The way she studied the bare expanse of his scarred chest.

And the flash of empathy she couldn't hide. Not from him.

Exactly the point.

He took a step forward, seizing her shoulder, relief and fury entangling together to grate across his nerves. "Then for Christ's sake," he began roughly, and she moved. Sudden. Erratic. The knife flashed once in red neon, sketched an upward arc.

Agony snagged on four inches of sawlike steel.

At Avon Books, we know your passion for romance—once you finish one of our novels, you find yourself wanting more.

May we tempt you with . . .

- **Excerpts** from our upcoming releases.

- Entertaining **extras**, including authors' personal photo albums and book lists.

- Behind-the-scenes **scoop** on your favorite characters and series.

- **Sweepstakes** for the chance to win free books, romantic getaways, and other fun prizes.

- Writing **tips** from our authors and editors.

- **Blog** with our authors and find out why they love to write romance.

- **Exclusive content** that's not contained within the pages of our novels.

Join us at
www.avonbooks.com

AVON

An Imprint of HarperCollins*Publishers*
www.avonromance.com